Dream  ...e

The Romano Family Trilogy – Book I

Debra A. Daly

iUniverse, Inc.
Bloomington

iUniverse books may be ordered through booksellers or by contacting:

iUniverse
1663 Liberty Drive
Bloomington, IN 47403
www.iuniverse.com
1-800-Authors (1-800-288-4677)

Because of the dynamic nature of the Internet, any web addresses or links contained in this book may have changed since publication and may no longer be valid. The views expressed in this work are solely those of the author and do not necessarily reflect the views of the publisher, and the publisher hereby disclaims any responsibility for them.

Any people depicted in stock imagery provided by Thinkstock are models, and such images are being used for illustrative purposes only.

Certain stock imagery © Thinkstock.

ISBN: 978-1-4620-1177-3 (sc)
ISBN: 978-1-4620-1178-0 (hc)
ISBN: 978-1-4620-1179-7 (ebook)

Library of Congress Control Number: 2011906649

Printed in the United States of America

iUniverse rev. date: 6/15/2011

This Book Is Dedicated
To All The
Hopeful Romantics
Who Never Give Up
On
The Dream

Should we believe that hidden deep within us are passions, wants, and desires waiting to be revealed?

For some, that vision of our one true perfect love is bright and alive, strong and steady, unmistakable and real. For those who believe, keep that vision clear because dreams really do come true!

Chapter One
New York
Doing what's right...

Jacqino Vincent Romano was a rather tall, dark and broad man whose mere presence commanded attention. As President and CEO of Romano Enterprises, a family-owned, fine furnishings importing company, Jack stood in his offices 32 floors above the lively hustle and bustle of 5th Avenue. He stared out over Central Park feeling deeply troubled. Instead of his eye registering the length and beauty of the park, the only image that he saw was the realization of his failing marriage that took place more than three years ago.

In his mind, Jack recalled that not long after his marriage to Victoria, she changed. The once clingy and adoring girlfriend transformed into a dark and intense wife. Even though Jack did exactly what Victoria wanted, she never seemed pleased with him. He hopelessly tried to feel this great, undying love he had only heard about, but was beginning to doubt that that was in the cards for him. It was becoming more and more obvious that icy Victoria would never warm up to him. Not even his gentlest touch or soothing tone would melt Victoria's cold façade. She absolutely refused to kiss him, always turning her head away from his lips. Making love to Victoria was probably what it was like to make love to a robot; mechanical, systematic, and detached. Once the act was complete, never, never did Victoria cling to him or want to be held.

"Maybe I need a therapist!" Jack decided aloud. *Where the hell did I acquire this "Romeo and Juliet" concept of marriage?* Jack puzzled.

Here it was three years later and little had changed between Jack and Victoria. But Jack was unlike any other man. He was determined to make his marriage work. He felt honor bound to continue a life with this standoffish, unfeeling woman.

Positioned before this incredible panoramic view from his offices high above, he didn't see that fall was at its peak. The only thing that registered with him was that he needed someone to love, and a child seemed the perfect answer. Not long after there first year of marriage, Jack began to pester Victoria about starting a family, but she always found an excuse. *We need to travel, to get to know each other, to settle down.* Despite his best efforts, Victoria seemed no closer to the idea, but Jack persisted. He needed someone. He often thought that the bond a child would create might thaw Victoria. He envisioned someone to love and teach, someone to walk with, to play silly games with, and to share secrets with, and he needed this more than air.

So Jack never let up, and Victoria grew colder with each conversation that Jack initiated about starting a family. Jack remained intractable, and Victoria, likewise, dug in her designer heels. He absolutely refused to use contraceptives, and his most recent stunt was making an appointment for both of them to be examined by a fertility specialist. Victoria flatly rejected the doctor's appointment, but Jack had insisted, in no uncertain terms, that she *would* go, even if he had to physically drag her there.

When they arrived at the fertility doctors, Jack and Victoria were led to separate examination rooms. Victoria barely looked at Jack and hadn't spoken to him since he announced their appointment with the specialist nearly three weeks earlier. After a full and complete examination, the doctor was pleased to inform Jack that he was clear for take off! "You know," the doctor smiled, "all systems go!"

Jack rose and thanked the doctor, with a blank look, and waited patiently for Victoria. When she emerged from the examination area, her face was pale, and her lips were drawn into a tight line, obviously upset. Jack crossed the waiting room in two long strides.

"What is it?" Jack asked, quietly reaching for her shoulders, but she instinctively shrugged his hands away.

"These doctors are imbeciles!" Victoria snapped, loud enough for all to hear. She pushed past him and left the doctors' offices.

Jack stared at Victoria's exiting form. He turned on his heel and burst back through the door that led to all the many examination rooms.

"I want to speak to the doctor who examined Victoria!" Jack demanded firmly.

The nurse was used to this kind of reaction. So many times, one or both patients received unpleasant news, and they wanted and needed immediate clarification. Jack's size and tone demanded instant consideration, and the nurse wasted no time getting him right in to see the doctor.

"Mr. Romano, this way please." The nurse signaled with her hand. "Doctor Kelmer is just finishing with another patient. He'll be with you shortly."

Jack followed the nurse and sat quietly in Dr. Kelmer's office. His office was subdued, with dark mahogany furniture, but the drawn shades allowed a soft light to filter through, making the room almost peaceful. Jack drew several deep breaths and tried to calm himself down. He had the most incredible urge to drive his fist through a wall.

The door opened quietly behind him. "Mr. Romano, I am Doctor Kelmer. I understand that your wife had an appointment, so I will discuss the fertility results with you." Dr. Kelmer stated in a professional manner. The doctor nodded for Jack to retake his seat then continued. "I examined your wife, and believe she is very healthy. In fact, she is equally as healthy as you are!"

"But that is not why we came here today," Jack countered. "We came here to see why we are having a problem starting a family. We have been trying for years!" Jack struggled to maintain control. This subject was becoming very difficult to discuss or even think about lately. His massive hands settled on the arms of the chair, dwarfing the large, high back.

Dr. Kelmer knew from his colleague's examination of Jack that this man was quite physically capable to bear many children. His sperm counts were off the charts. "I think you and Mrs. Romano should try to get away. Maybe a weekend away from work and just the daily grind of life itself could loosen everyone up. Perhaps that would relax you both. You and Mrs. Romano might come to a kind of understanding."

"Understanding," Jack almost choked.

"What I am saying Mr. Romano, is that I believe there is another issue."

"What issue? You say we are both good candidates to bear children, yet we have not been able to conceive."

"Excellent candidates, as a matter of fact, and I wished I had more news like this to give my other patients wanting to start a family."

Jack leaned out of his chair. His enormous chest spanned at least half the width of the doctor's massive mahogany desk.

Dr. Kelmer knew that Mr. Romano was probably the single most perfect male specimen he would ever see in his career.

Jack's black, piercing eyes bored right into Dr. Kelmer's eyes, holding his attention. "Dr. Kelmer, I think we are having trouble comprehending each other." Jack held up his hand to stop the doctor from interrupting him. "I want a child. I need a child. I want to know why we are not yet with child. Do we understand each other now?" Jack forced a smile on his face.

"Of course..." Dr. Kelmer answered confidently.

"Good." Jack relaxed, sat back and gracefully rested his foot on top of his other knee.

Silent for just a moment, then Dr. Kelmer continued. "Ahh, you see, Mr. Romano, there is no medical reason why you cannot start a family. Although it is not scientifically proven, stress can play a huge role in the conception process. That is why I gave Mrs. Romano a little homework."

Jack studied the doctor quizzically.

"I gave Mrs. Romano an ovulation kit so she can easily predict the best day and time for you to have intercourse with the highest potential to conceive."

Jack's right jaw muscle began to clench at the doctor's choice of terms. *Having intercourse,* Jack thought silently, *was exactly what sex was like with Victoria, nothing more.*

Jack quickly recovered and asked, "That is why she left here so upset, because of this kit?"

"The idea of setting a time and day for intercourse is, for some women, difficult to handle. Many women believe that when it is not natural or passionate, it is not making love."

*Passionate...*Jack didn't even know the meaning of the word. Victoria would swat at him when he tried to undress her. She had told him that she was not an invalid and was more than capable of removing her own clothing.

"Oh, I see." Jack accepted pushing the mental picture of Victoria out of his mind.

The doctor now stood and motioned for Jack to do the same. "That is why I recommended that maybe you two should get away for a few days. Talk about things; work on the kit and practice. Practice makes perfect!" Dr. Kelmer slapped Jack's shoulder with a large smile on his face. But Jack was not smiling and really did not want to practice anything with that cold-hearted woman he had married three years ago. He didn't sleep in the same bed with her anymore, and for that matter, not even in the same room with her. It was just too uncomfortable. He just wanted a child to love.

"Good-bye, Mr. Romano. Good luck!"

"Yes. Good-bye."

Jack left the doctors' offices and made his way down the elevator to the parking garage. When the elevator doors opened, he didn't even remember the ride down. As he walked to the place where he parked his silver Jag, he noticed that Victoria's black BMW was already gone. He eased his way out through the streets of Manhattan and back toward the underground parking entrance of Romano Enterprises. At the gate, a young man opened his car door, and Jack walked right past the man, heading straight for the private elevator. He looked at no one. He spoke to no one.

Now back at Romano Enterprises, Jack stood in his office and looked down at Central Park feeling lifeless. But Central Park was far from lifeless. The incredible fall spectacular, being put on by the many trees that graced the park, was poetry inspiring. People walked and mingled about. Joggers jogged and dog walkers walked amid a tangle of leashes. High above, Jack looked out and a person with a brightly red-colored cap caught his attention.

Chapter Two
That very afternoon...

In the late autumn afternoon, Francesca O'Brian, wearing her red headdress, knelt down at the edge of the Shakespeare Gardens before a nearly bare rosebush. Between her thin fingers, she held the last single yellow rose. Lowering her head, she took a deep breath of the fragrant bloom. She studied the yellow rose that refused to open or drop its petals, refused to let go of spring and summer, refused to face the long, cold winter ahead. She looked at the bloom intently and wondered why every other rosebush was already completely bare and dormant, except for this highly stubborn hybrid. Beside her insatiable passion for caring for animals as a veterinarian, she loved to study gardens. She read book after book on the rose gardens from around the world, but the ones that interested her most were the English rose gardens of the late 18th century.

Francesca, dubbed Frankie from almost birth, once again studied the color of the rose, closing her blue eyes to see if her mind remembered the color exactly. She would open her eyes and repeat the process, always studying and remembering. She did this all the time lately. Anything or anyone that was of importance to her, she studied and memorized each detail, because you just never knew. Her dog, Bruno, her constant companion, was close by her side and looked at her with his head cocked, studying her every move.

Frankie was a unique and special woman. She had a gift. She had the ability to recall her dreams, and those dreams always came true. At first, Frankie thought she was abnormal and was petrified to tell anyone about these dreams; however, she did tell her best friend, Rebecca McFarlan—Becca for short. The two were inseparable. Frankie mentioned the dreams to Becca, and Becca thought she was just going through a phase. At least that is how her mother described every mood-swing in the McFarlan household. Anyway, a few short years after Frankie told her friend, Becca soon learned that Frankie's dreams were not to be taken lightly. Frankie told Becca she had a dream that Becca was going to climb up Mrs. Critchmore's tree to save the old woman's cat.

She explained to Becca that she would break her arm by falling out of the tree while trying to rescue the cat.

At first, Becca thought that was ridiculous. "I'm not the animal lover—you are!"

A year after that dream, as Frankie had predicted, Becca found herself high up Mrs. Critchmore's tree reaching for the old woman's cat. Her footing slipped on some loose bark, and she came crashing down, breaking her arm on one of the stronger, lower tree branches, before finally hitting the ground. Becca stared up at Frankie, with a look of both pain and acknowledgement, and from that moment on, Becca accepted Frankie's dreams.

It was almost one year ago today when Frankie had her most dreaded dream. The worst nightmare ever! She had dreamed that she was diagnosed with cancer. When she woke from the terrifying nightmare, she immediately called Becca.

"Becca?" It was close to two o'clock in the morning, as Frankie whispered quietly into the phone.

"Frankie? Frankie is that you?" Becca sleepily asked.

"Yes. I'm sorry. I didn't mean to wake you but..." Frankie couldn't speak. She had a large lump in her throat blocking speech, as tears began to stream down her face, dropping to the pillow she was clutching to her chest.

"Did you have a dream?"

"Yes." Frankie barely choked the word out through the knot in her throat.

"Can you remember it?" Becca was still too sleepy to hear the fear in Frankie's voice.

There was not a sound. Then the only sound that came over the phone made Rebecca jump out of bed. It was Frankie softly crying. "Frankie! What? What happened?" Becca was fully awake, and with the cordless phone shouldered to her ear, she quickly began to dress. "I'm coming right over." Becca hung up the phone before Frankie could answer.

With stiff movements, Frankie put on her robe. Bruno, her beloved pet, woke and followed her out of the apartment. She made her way down the elevator, through the foyer and past the doorman, without as much as a "hello" to the man.

The doorman looked at her wearing her robe with raised eyebrows and at the unleashed dog. Frankie did not acknowledge him, which caused him to think that she might be sleepwalking.

He quickly jumped up from behind the desk and followed after Frankie.

"Dr. Frankie!" He tried again to get a response. "Dr. Frankie!" He was nearly shouting now. At this last call, Bruno began to growl which caused Frankie to turn and face him. He knew she was awake, and he saw a look of fear in her eyes. "Is there something I can help you with, Doc?"

"No…no thank you Mr. O'Malley, I'm just waiting for someone." Frankie answered in a dazed voice.

The doorman stood next to Frankie and Bruno just outside the building's entrance. Her long, golden hair caught the moonlight and reflected that light in an array of golden and white hues. It was a game her hair constantly played with any source of light, which never went unnoticed by anyone. Her small frame was swallowed up by the thick, terry robe of sky blue that tried, but never could match Frankie's incredible sky-blue eyes.

From around the corner, Becca came running and tripping at the same time over her untied sneakers. Frankie ran to her and they hugged each other. Frankie began to cry. Becca pulled Frankie away long enough to get her attention. "Frankie, let's go inside, I'm freezing."

Frankie nodded and Becca slowly guided her, as if she were a small child, back through the door held open by Mr. O'Malley.

Once inside her apartment, Frankie could not control her tears. "I don't want to die." Frankie revealed the terrifying dream she had about being diagnosed with cancer. "Becca, it was me. My hair was all around my feet. I had a long scar on my lower back very close to my spine. I was putting a red covering on my head to hide my baldness. I can give you the smallest of details. The details! Those are the dreams that always come true."

"Okay, Frankie. First thing in the morning, I mean today, you are going to call the best cancer doctor you know." Becca stood and began to pace in front of Frankie.

"Becca, I'm not ready to die. I don't want to leave my parents, my friends, you. I have so many patients to take care of. I haven't planted my English rose garden that I've been studying for years. And who will take care of Bruno? He drools, sheds, and snores terribly." Frankie tried to joke through a watery sob.

Both girls began to cry uncontrollably. "Listen to me, Frankie. I know that you are going to be just fine." Becca sat down on the edge of the chair opposite Frankie, took hold of her hands, and looked at her intently.

"How can you say that?" Frankie raised their clasped hands and dropped them back into her lap.

"I know because you haven't met Jacqino yet." Becca raised a knowing eyebrow to her best friend squeezing her hands.

Frankie's jaw dropped. "Jacqino…but how do you know about him? I never told anyone about…" Frankie just stared at her friend in blank shock, unable to think.

"We are best friends, right? We had sleepovers almost every weekend through most of our childhood and then shared a dorm room in college. Besides that, you talk incessantly in your sleep." Becca smiled at her dear friend as she stood up to pace the room again.

"What? I do?" Frankie blinked.

Rebecca turned to face her dear, dear friend. "You can't die, because you haven't met him, and I know that you are meant to be together. I heard you call his name and heard you plead in your sleep begging God to help you find him. I know you are going to find him. It is meant to be!"

Frankie stood and reached for her friend. They hugged each other closely; supporting one another then headed into Frankie's tiny kitchen with their heads touching, while Bruno sunk into his doggy bed and immediately began to snore.

Now close to a year later, Frankie already had the surgery that removed the tumor, which had just started to attach itself to her spine. Frankie's doctor was so pleased that the operation was quite successful; however he remained highly concerned when the tumor was determined to be malignant. He ordered eight chemotherapy treatments for Frankie, and after the second chemo treatment, her hair started to fall out. But that wasn't the worst part. The horrible nausea that followed each treatment was brutal. Frankie lost so much weight, if that was at all possible, to the shocked expressions of many. Her bones stuck out through her clothing, and the slightest thought of food made her sick to her stomach.

When Frankie's parents first learned of their only daughter's cancer, they became very parental and insisted that she come back home. But Frankie put up a strong fight, explaining she wanted and needed to work, and the doctor had spoken to Mr.

and Mrs. O'Brian at length about the necessity of keeping up their daughter's morale as well as the importance of keep up with her everyday life routine. Frankie's parents agreed to her working, but insisted on handling every other aspect of her life. Her father managed all of Frankie's financial affairs, and her mother purchased clothing and hired a maid to cook and clean for Frankie, so that Frankie's only concern would be her animal patients and herself.

It was during the course of a regular day at the Park East Animal Hospital that the significance of the red headdress from Frankie's dream was revealed. Mrs. Mastellon, who had the most vibrant-hued macaw named Max, came in for his regular check up. A most colorful macaw and in more ways than one! Max had quite the vivid vocabulary which matched his feathers.

According to the staff and other patients, this bird's lexicon was worse than any truck driver, construction worker, and oil rigger all rolled up into one, but to Frankie the bird was a perfect gentleman. This bird cursed off everyone and anyone. From inside the taxi, across the sidewalk, through the receptionist's area, even to the other patients in the waiting room, no one was spared, except for Frankie. Once Frankie entered the examination room, Max was silent and very well-behaved. Frankie would trim his nails then his beak, which could have very easily snapped off any one of her fingers. She spoke very quietly to him as she worked, and the bird remained mute and sat absolutely still. When Frankie had completed her examination and returned Max into his cage, Mrs. Mastellon handed Frankie a box wrapped in bright, red paper tied with a crisp, white bow. Frankie was shocked and told Mrs. Mastellon that it was unnecessary to bring a gift.

"This is different," Mrs. Mastellon explained.

Frankie opened the box and removed the bright, red cap... the same one from her dream.

Without a word, Mrs. Mastellon reached up and removed Frankie's scarf from her head. Mrs. Mastellon carefully placed one hand above each of Frankie's ears and tipped her head just enough so that she could place a very motherly kiss on her forehead. "It will all grow back. You will see. It will be thicker, longer, and brighter than you could have ever imagined. Your hair will once again shine brighter than a moonbeam." Mrs. Mastellon tied the headdress around Frankie's head. It fit perfectly, and it was rather cheerful. When they left the examination room, Max did not tell the receptionist "to go to hell" like he typically did. In fact, he remained very calm and unusually quiet.

Now, once again bending over the rose to take one long last look at the glorious bloom, her cell phone began to vibrate reminding her of her appointment. She stood and began to walk from the park and down the sidewalk heading toward Columbia, with her faithful companion at her side.

With Bruno keeping pace alongside her, she entered the separate cancer treatment wing door and headed to the sixth floor. Taking the stairs, Frankie used this time to encourage herself for her last treatment. "This is your last one. You can do it. It will be the last time that you get sick to your stomach." She spoke aloud trying to coax herself along. Bruno just looked up and continued to climb the stairs beside her. She tried to reflect on how lucky she was that it was almost over, but she still dreaded it. The feeling of apprehension was indescribable. The medicine that would course through her veins would make her ill for at least three days. With her hand on the doorknob at the sixth floor, Frankie almost couldn't bring herself to the point of turning it. She didn't want to put herself through it again. *I have to stop thinking like this*, she scolded herself silently. Frankie finally turned the knob and pulled the door open almost fiercely. Before she reached the nurses' station, Claire spotted her and called out.

"You're here! I thought we weren't going to see you." Claire was pleased that she was following the doctor's orders to the letter.

Claire bent down to scratch Bruno behind his ear. Frankie was fortunate there was a separate entrance into the cancer treatment unit where she was allowed to bring her dog. The medical profession was growing more agreeable to allow patients to bring with them whatever, or whoever, would help them through their treatments. In Frankie's case, her comfort had four legs instead of two.

"Are you ready?" Claire asked. "This is your last treatment. We are all going to miss you, and Bruno, too."

"I really don't feel the same way. Sorry, Claire. I'd rather see you and Patches at *my* hospital." Frankie raised her hands then just as quickly dropped them to her sides. "Hey how is your daughter's hamster, by the way?"

"Oh. Just fine. You know Samantha takes him everywhere with her."

Frankie noticed that the floor seemed awfully deserted. "Where is everybody? It seems very quiet tonight."

"Tomorrow is Thanksgiving, so only the holiday staff nurses are here, and we're understaffed for the next four days. I don't recommend your needing a hospital anytime soon," Claire wryly commented. Frankie followed Claire down the hall. "I have you all set up in room six-fifty-seven," Claire told Frankie.

"Thanks, Claire." Frankie removed her heavy sweater which covered her scrubs and settled on the bed. Bruno curled up at the foot of the bed and closed his eyes. Claire began to prepare Frankie's arm for the treatment. Even though this was her eighth treatment, Frankie could never get used to all the pricks from the needles.

Once Claire set up the monitors and began the IV, she held Frankie's hand. "Okay, Dr. Frankie, you're all set. Now are you sure you don't want to watch TV?"

"No thanks, Claire." Frankie tried to smile as she felt the liquid burn a path along her arm.

Claire didn't know how Frankie could lay there for several hours with nothing to read or watch. She shrugged and started to leave the room. "You just buzz if you need anything." Claire took note of the time on her wristwatch.

Frankie closed her eyes and settled back into the pillows. Trying not to think about the medicine burning up her arm, Frankie quickly focused on one of her most special dreams of Jacqino.

In the dream she had just two nights before, Frankie could see that her hair was growing back and reached to the very tops of her shoulders. Her hair was much brighter than she remembered. *I guess Mrs. Mastellon was right*, Frankie thought. She was standing in a very old-fashioned looking bathroom. It was quite spacious, and Frankie felt as though she had stepped back in time. The cream wallpaper was decorated with the most delicate roses in a vertical striped pattern. The green stems and leaves looked so real that Frankie reached out her hand to touch one.

There was an antique oak cabinet which supported a pair of matching cream-colored sinks topped with gleaming brass fixtures. In between the sinks were a dozen yellow roses in a clear vase, a card nestled among the blooms. Frankie could smell their fragrance filling the air as if she were standing in that room at that very moment. The bathroom had one completely mirrored wall over the sinks, and above the mirror, hung warm, polished-brass lighting fixtures, each one centered over each sink. Four etched glass globes with roses, stems, and leaves were suspended from the brass lighting fixtures.

The tub, the same color as the sinks, was rather unusual. A freestanding unit; and at least double the width of a normal tub, it stood on beautifully sculptured brass clawed feet which matched the other warm brass fixtures. A separate double-width shower stall featured etched glass doors with the same rose pattern as the glass orbs over the sinks. Lit rose-scented candles were scattered around the room filling the room with flickering light. Behind the bathroom door were two large hooks from which hung two very plush cream-colored, full-length terry cloth robes; one was monogrammed *Jack* and the other, *Frankie*.

Next to the enormous tub sat an overstuffed club chair in a soft cream, with contrasting darker cream stripes. Jacqino stood next to the tub, running the water over his hand, testing its temperature. He looked over his shoulder at her with a warm smile, which caused Frankie's heart to literally skip several beats, setting off one of the monitor's alarms.

Within seconds, Claire stepped into the room to check on Frankie, responding to the nurses' station alarm. She checked the monitors and the IV to make sure that everything was fine. Although Frankie appeared to be comfortable, Claire nevertheless reached for a blanket and covered her.

In her mind, Frankie watched the water run through Jack's fingers. Everything looked small next to him. Jack stood up straight and looked directly at her, slowly taking the few steps until he was standing before her, cradling her face gently in his hands.

"You are so beautiful, Francesca." Jack spoke softly, calling her by her proper name, just before he lowered his lips to kiss her tenderly.

When he lifted his head she looked up at him, deeply into his eyes. He was magnificent. His eyes were dark, framed by his perfectly arched eyebrows. His glossy blue-black hair was wavy and windblown, as if they had been out and had just now come home. Home...they were home. Feelings of love and tenderness were filling her heart and soul until it almost ached. He lowered his head again and kissed her mouth. At first, he placed sweet little kisses at the corners of her mouth, and after each kiss, he softly repeated the words, "I love you." Then the kisses became deeper and longer. His tongue tasted and explored, as she did the same.

He lifted his head and slowly caressed his hand along Frankie's cheek. "I have loved you forever. I just didn't know how to find you." He began to smooth the hair from Frankie's cheek and repeated the motion over and over. She watched him study her face and hair as though he hadn't seen her in years. "Your hair is softer than silk. I've wanted to touch it almost all of my life since I saw you that summer day so long ago. I remember. I remember you, Francesca. And I've never forgotten."

Frankie couldn't speak.

Slowly he reached down, pulled off his own sweater, and laid it over the back of the club chair next to the tub. He turned back and did the same to Frankie, pulling the thick Irish knit sweater over her head with care, placing it on top of his. Beneath her sweater, she wore a beautiful mauve-colored silk camisole. Taking his time, he reached out to gently stroke her breasts through the delicate fabric until the buds pressed against the silk. He ran his thumb over each bud, kissing Frankie deeply. He unfastened her jeans, slid them over her thighs to her ankles then took her hand, helping her step out of them. Her panties were the same mauve-colored silk fabric as her camisole. She watched as he stared at her for what seemed like an eternity, sensing he was drinking her in.

When he reached his hands up to her shoulders, he slowly slid the thin straps of the camisole over each shoulder, encouraging the silk down the length of her body until it pooled at her feet. Lowering his head, Frankie watched as he took her into his mouth and she felt her body tingle from his touch. She ran her fingers through his shiny, black hair as he continued to taste. The sensations were visibly causing her knees to grow weak.

Jack slowly knelt before her. She perceived the awareness of him easing off her mauve panties, replacing the discarded fabric with kisses on her stomach. He ran his hands down her thighs, gently kneading them. Frankie passed her hands over his broad shoulders and her fingertips literally tickled with the sensation of touching him. Jack held her buttocks and kissed her navel. He lowered his head, kissed each thigh and then touched her most sensitive area with his tongue. Frankie was lost, her mind filled with pleasures untold, nearly slipping into unconsciousness. Slowly, he stood up and ran his hands up and down either side of her spine until they came to rest at the small of her back. He pulled her against himself, and she could feel his ready maleness. He kissed her deeply, and Frankie felt as if the ground was caving in under her feet.

Struggling to collect herself, Frankie willed her hands up the front of his shirt, while Jack's hand still caressed her breast. Frankie shakily unbuttoned his denim shirt and slowly slid her hands underneath the fabric, over his solid chest to his broad shoulders, pushing the shirt to the floor. His skin was warm and sun-golden. He unsteadily ran his fingers through her hair. She placed a soft kiss over his heart, resting her lips there for a moment. Standing on tiptoe, she pulled down his head to place a kiss at the base of his throat.

Grasping a handful of hair, he suddenly angled her head back, pressing his mouth over hers placing his tongue into her warm, welcoming mouth over and over again. "Francesca, how I love you!" He groaned the words into her mouth, and her body trembled from the power emanating from those spoken words.

Frankie watched as Jack studied her expression as she started to unbutton his pants. An emotion raced across his handsome features when he swept her hands aside, and in one motion, released the waist button and zipper allowing the pants to join the denim shirt at his feet. His arousal and intentions were clear, unlike the mirrors and glass shower doors which were fogged from the warm water filling the bath. Frankie didn't know how much more of this she could endure. Simply standing was a challenge to her.

Jack sat back onto the club chair, reached for Frankie, lifted her by her waist, and slid her onto his shaft. Frankie gratefully began to move as Jack's fingers knitted together at the small of her back. In her dream she watched herself close her eyes and cry out his name.

"Jacqino. Jacqino."

"I am here, my love, my beautiful angel. We will always be together." Jack's hands slid up the sides of her breasts and kneaded them and caressed them with hardened palms. He took one nipple into his warm, wet mouth and then the other. The ancient pace grew faster and faster until each one was reaching for the other, skin against skin, with an effort to please one another—they exploded as one.

Jack buried his head into Frankie's shoulder as she ran her fingers through his dark soft hair at the very nape of his neck, before depositing tiny kisses there. He was strong and soft. He was muscular and gentle. He was all to her. Still intimately connected, Jack stood up and kissed Frankie with her legs wrapped around his hips, his hands cradling her buttocks. He placed his tongue into her mouth, and she greeted him so sweetly and gently.

"Francesca," his voice choked. Looking into her eyes he slowly lifted her from his loving embrace, set her feet to the floor then guided her toward the bathtub. He poured some salts into the water gushing from the spigot and swept his hand back and forth to stir the salts. He climbed into the tub first, then held her hand and settled into the bath.

Frankie rested her back against his chest, sensing the warm water permeating her body. Slowly, Jack began to slide his hands up and down her arms and shoulders, over her breasts and neck, massaging and kneading her. After some time, he reached for a bottle from the side of the tub and lovingly shampooed her hair. Tilting her head back with the tip of his finger, he picked up the sprayer and rinsed her tresses clean, stopping to kiss her throat. .

After a short time, Frankie returned his caresses. She knelt in the water before him and lathered his scalp with shampoo, while he played with her breasts. He leaned forward and kissed one breast, then nipped the other. He smiled a little devilishly as Frankie's right hand sprang to her left breast.

Claire watched as Frankie covered her left breast, as she continued to check the monitors and IV.

Frankie took the sprayer and rinsed Jack's hair clean. Jack reached for one of the large, soft washcloths and rubbed a pink bar of soap into the cloth until it began to lather. He washed Frankie's arms and neck, shoulders and back, breasts and waist. He soaped the cloth again and ran the cloth beneath the water; up and down her legs and to the very tops of her inner thighs. She let her head fall back, resting it against the rim of the tub as she let his touch relax her. Some moments later, he pulled her face up toward him and kissed her.

"My turn," he whispered.

Frankie took the washcloth from him and smoothed the pink soap over the cloth. She slid the cloth up his long muscular arms as he continued to caress her breasts. He could not stay still. He kept touching her and moving about.

"I can't concentrate on washing you if you keep touching me like that," Frankie gently scolded.

Jack's sexy, husky laughter filled the room. "Good," he said with his eyes closed and smiling. "Then you will have to start all over again, from the beginning."

As he held out his arm for her to wash yet again, Frankie was happy to oblige and marveled at the size of bunched muscles along his arms. Each time she slid the cloth over him, he reacted differently. Sometimes his muscles would leap at her touch, and other times he shot hot, wanting eyes at her. After she washed him thoroughly, Jack took the cloth from her hand, stood, and helped her to her feet. They were both soapy and rose-scented. He reached for the sprayer and first rinsed Frankie down from head to toe, then did the same to himself. He stepped out of the tub and held out his hand to her. She placed her hand into his and stepped from the tub. He reached for one of the oversized, plush, cream-colored towels hanging over a brass bar near the tub.

"I want to look at you." Jack's tone was still husky as he held the towel away from her. When she felt her cheeks warm from blushing, he laughed a throaty laugh and began to pat her skin dry. Turning her around he dried her back, where he stopped and lowered his head to kiss the line on her back that marked her surgery. Her mind went blank, unable to comprehend this tenderness. He straightened and slid his hands around her waist, pulling her into him. He felt warm to the touch, warm beyond belief and safe. And at that moment, Frankie never felt so secure in her life. He wrapped Frankie in the towel and then wrapped the other matching towel around his waist. He walked over to the large brass hooks and took down a terry-clothed robe for her and one for him.

Jack helped Frankie into her robe, then closed the front and tied the sash. He started to dry himself, and Frankie reached for the towel and dried every beautiful inch of him. She kissed his strong chest, covered with dark hair and pressed kisses on his flat stomach. When she walked behind him to dry his shoulders, she had to stand on tiptoe and still didn't reach. She pressed kisses all the way down his spine and when she reached the small of his back she stopped and stood up straight, slid her hands around his waist, pressing her cheek against his back. He reached his hands behind her pulling her in closer to his body. Then in one quick movement, he turned around in her arms and scooped her up, her dainty legs draping over his arm.

"Francesca, I think you are trying to drive me mad with wanting you," Jack moaned. Naked, he held her close as she ran her hand over anything she could reach: his cheek, neck, chest, and shoulder. Frankie reached out and pulled the bathroom's hand-painted porcelain doorknob. Jack carried her into the huge master bedroom where an enormous white iron bed was dressed in white linen sheets, and a crisp, white duvet covered a plump down comforter. He lowered her onto the comforter and loosened the belt on her robe...

"BEEP, BEEP, BEEP!" The monitors began to sound and Frankie stirred from the noise.

"Okay, Dr. Frankie, you're all done."

Frankie sat up, blinked several times, and watched as Claire started to remove the equipment that was attached to her. She always used this time to re-familiarize herself with her surroundings. When Claire was done, she helped Frankie from the bed. Together they walked from the room and down the hall, with Bruno following behind.

"You have a Happy Thanksgiving!" Claire announced cheerfully to Frankie, as she pulled her in for a quick hug.

"You, too, Claire. Thanks again!" Frankie answered as she stepped into the elevator with Bruno. She pressed the "L" to go to the lower level. She felt a little drowsy so she thought she would leave through the emergency room area, cut through a couple of alleys, and save some time getting home. She pressed her back against the elevator wall and tried to regain her concentration. Mentally, she was still in Jack's arms and almost hated to step back into reality.

Chapter Three
That very night...

Jack stepped into his apartment on Madison Avenue and still, after all these years, could not get used to the place. It was done exactly the way Victoria wanted it, all marble and metal, glass and steel. It was cold, he thought, just like Victoria. He had called Victoria from his office just an hour before and told her that they needed to go to dinner to discuss what happened at the fertility doctor's office. At first, Victoria had refused and complained of a headache, but Jack wasn't taking "No" for an answer.

Victoria heard the front door open as she made her way from the master bedroom. "Do you want to change before we go?" Victoria called out to him. She wore all black and her black hair was slicked back and tightly rolled into a coil at the base of her neck. She had been wearing her hair that exact same way since Jack first met her. In fact, he could not even remember a time when he ever saw her wear it any other way.

"Yes, I would like to put on a fresh shirt before we leave," Jack replied politely while leafing through the mail that lay on a metal and glass table in the center of the foyer. His heels echoed on the cold, highly polished, black marble floor. The marble turned a stormy, gray color through the living room, and at that moment, Jack was struck by how depressing the colors were in the entire apartment. Cold and dark, with no warmth whatsoever, so much like Victoria, both clad in black and full of depressive gray shadows. He shook his head to clear it, because he knew he needed to stop thinking like this. He was going to make every attempt to come to some sort of reconciliation with Victoria. He did not want a divorce, and he was not one to give up at anything without a fight. But his mind was playing tricks on him as the words kept repeating over and over in his mind. *Fight for what?* He questioned himself silently. *Why do I want to fight to continue to live a life with a cold, unfeeling wife? To live the rest of my life alone, empty, and possibly without children! To live only to run Romano Enterprises!* He began to rub his head, the dull throbbing unabated since he had left the fertility doctors' parking lot.

"Jack," Victoria called quietly. But there was no response from him. "Jack!" She called louder and this time Jack turned to look at her. "Maybe we should just stay home. I could have Lilly prepare..." but before she could finish her sentence Jack interrupted.

"No!" Jack raised his voice, and Victoria took a step back from him. "I mean, I would really like for us to go out for a quiet dinner just the two of us. I'll just be a minute." He turned away from her and made his way through the apartment. The damn place reminded him of a crypt. He never realized how much he hated it until this moment. He shook his head and tried to concentrate on his goal. Once inside the master bedroom he stopped in front of Victoria's walk-in closet. Every piece of clothing was black or varying shades of dark gray. *Why hadn't I noticed this before?* He entered his closet, removing his jacket, tie, and shirt. He pulled a fresh shirt from the wardrobe and walked into the master bathroom. The sinks were black marble with light silver flecks veining through the stone. He reached for the polished chrome faucet and began to run the water, letting the water run through his fingers, waiting for it to warm up, but it never seemed to get hot enough as he splashed it onto his face.

Looking at his reflection in the mirror, water dripping off his face, he noticed how dark the circles were under his eyes. His eyes were sunken and almost lifeless. He couldn't remember the last time he'd slept for more than just a few hours, instead pacing until the early morning hours, trying to find answers to impossible questions. He looked down at the sink and noticed that his hands were trembling, shaking nearly uncontrollably. "Get a grip," Jack scolded his reflection in the mirror. "You love her." He kept repeating as if trying to convince himself. "You have to make it work." He dried his face with a black monogrammed towel and buttoned up a fresh shirt. He walked back into his closet, grabbed a tie, and swung it about his neck, knotting it hurriedly. He shrugged into his jacket as he made his way from the closet through the bedroom and into the living room adjusting his tie.

Victoria stood looking out the enormous wall of windows which stretched the full length of the living room from floor to ceiling. He could see her grim reflection in the glass. She was miserable and...frightened. They both just stared at the other's reflection. She wasn't happy; he could see that and neither was he. *What does she want with me?* Jack wondered silently.

"I'm ready. Shall we go?"

Victoria nodded.

Paul, their chauffeur, entered the room waiting for their destination plans for the evening. "Where to Mr. R?"

"I think I'm going to drive tonight, Paul. The traffic in the city is pretty snarled up, because of the Thanksgiving holiday. I think it might be easier to maneuver through traffic if I take the Jag," Jack almost suggested. "Besides, if you took the limo for a spin, that might confuse some of our persistent, uninvited guests." Jack just rolled his eyes referring to the press which seemed to be everywhere and anywhere. He wanted as much uninterrupted time with Victoria as possible. He wanted to tell her what the doctors had explained to him. *And maybe, just maybe,* Jack thought quietly, *I'll ask her if she still wants to be married to me.*

Paul just shrugged. It didn't matter to him. He was more than happy to play hide-n-go-seek with the press. "No problem, Mr. R. I'll park the limo out front and bring the Jag 'round back."

"Thanks, Paul." Jack called back.

Silence once again fell upon Victoria and Jack. Jack reached for Victoria's full-length, black mink coat that lay over the back of the muted-gray contemporary sofa and held it up for her. She slowly walked over to him, sliding her thin black-clad arms into the coat. He rested his hands on her shoulders and gently squeezed them, but he could feel her body stiffen from his touch. "Let's go to Megu in Tribecca and relax." Jack wanted to sound reassuring and comforting. He thought her favorite Asian restaurant might please her. Very mechanically, she walked to the foyer. Jack held the door open for her as she walked past him without as much as a sidewise glance. Even though much was obviously wrong with their relationship, Jack kept up his morale. *I'll order her favorite sake; we can talk about what happened at the doctors today and maybe plan a short vacation. I have to make this work,* he kept coaxing himself, but in the back of his mind something or someone kept asking, *why?*

At the rear of the high-rise, Paul held the car door for Victoria. "Enjoy yourselves now!" Paul called to them as he shut the door after Victoria slid into the passenger seat.

Jack eased the sports car into traffic, even though most of the bulk of the holiday rush was over. He slowly glided down several back streets, eventually making it across town. Jack reached for Victoria's hand and squeezed it trying to again make some kind of connection with her. Accelerating through one green light, Jack managed to hit a string of several green lights. As he approached the green light at Park and East 59th Street, he easily coasted through that intersection as well, until he noticed from the corner of his eye two headlights coming directly at Victoria's side of the car. Before Jack could react, the Jag smashed and crumpled all around him.

The impact was devastating with metal grinding and crunching, glass bits flying, and tires screeching. When Jack opened his eyes, he was covered in glass. The car was pushed across the intersection until Jack's side slammed into a telephone pole. Airbags deployed and Jack and Victoria were tossed around the Jag like rag dolls. The accident seemed to take place in slow motion, but in reality, it was but a few seconds.

As airbags began to deflate, Jack tried to absorb his surroundings. He felt the weight of the car crushing down on his shoulder and hip. Most of the windows were smashed as the car alarm rang out. Jack shut off the engine and, for a moment, just looked around. He could see the front of the truck's grill above the top half of Victoria's passenger side window, glass littered all over her body and hair. No one came near the car, even though there were people standing on the sidewalk staring at the scene. Jack blinked several times trying to clear his head. Slowly, he reached for Victoria and gently pulled her back against the seat. Her head, limp, rolled from side to side. He winced and slowly laid her head against the back of the seat. He reached for the cell phone and quickly dialed 911.

The police were already called and were the first to arrive at the scene. Firemen appeared next and told Jack that they were going to have him out in minutes. Jack protested that he wanted Victoria removed first, knowing she urgently needed help more than he did. A fireman, in full gear, climbed over the hood of the truck and reached through the smashed window opening. He placed two fingers at the base of Victoria's throat, just beneath her jaw line, feeling for her pulse. The fireman spoke quietly to the EMTs who had just arrived. Within seconds, an EMT carefully placed a neck brace around Victoria's neck. Now that her neck was stabilized, the fireman appeared again and cut her seatbelt with a knife. Together, the fireman and EMT angled a body board through the passenger side window opening and carefully slid Victoria's limp body directly onto the body board. Glass cascaded from her mink coat and tinkled from her hair, as Jack watched and listened in disbelief. Jack turned just in time to see the same fireman reach in through Victoria's side and place a canvas over his head for protection. The jaws-of-life separated the metal around his side of the car, its noise deafening and eerie all at the same time. Within a few minutes, he was freed. The canvas shield was removed from his head and a neck brace was wrapped underneath his jaw. Just like Victoria, his body was maneuvered onto a body board, to a waiting gurney then wheeled to the ambulance. Serious faces in matching uniform shirts began to prod and poke at him. At one point during the confusion, Jack caught a glimpse of Victoria. Through blurry eyes he watched as the EMTs appeared to be working frantically on her. One straddled her and pounded her chest while another injected something into her.

"Victoria," Jack whispered.

The fireman who pulled Jack from the car reached out and touched Jack's arm. "We're taking you both to Columbia. Your girlfriend is going right now, and we'll follow. Do you understand?"

"She's my wife," Jack muttered, but no one heard him.

The fireman slammed the ambulance doors shut and smacked the glass twice. Jack lay perfectly still. He still couldn't believe this was happening! Victoria's words kept playing over and over in his mind. "Maybe we should just stay home. Maybe we should just stay home."

The attending medic settled in next to Jack. "We think the truck driver had a massive coronary while driving. Unfortunately, your car and the telephone pole you slammed into stopped him."

Jack only nodded, but his head hurt even to do that. Jack knew that the truck driver was dead. No one helped the driver who was draped with a large sheet. Before he knew it, they were at the hospital backing into the emergency entrance parking, while loud beeping confirmed the reverse motion of the ambulance. Three men kept working on Victoria while she was being whirled in through the swinging glass doors. One continued to squeeze a bag over her mouth; another man held an IV line above his head and guided the front of the gurney, while the remaining EMT steered from the back. They moved rapidly, and doctors had already taken over for the man with the breathing device.

"Let's go home, boy." Frankie bent down to pet her beloved boxer's large, furry head. Taking the elevator to the lower level, Frankie would cut through the ER which would shave several minutes off their walk home. When the doors opened soundlessly, she heard a man shouting, his voice growing more loudly as he came closer. Still not quite in focus from her treatment, Frankie stopped for just a moment and witnessed a tall, dark man quickly eating up the distance between them. Frankie backed against the wall. She dropped her sweater just before pulling Bruno into a sitting position beside her, so that the agitated man could pass.

"Where is she?" The man kept shouting and made a beeline for Frankie, stopping directly in front of her, his wall of chest blocking her exit.

The stranger placed his enormous hands on her upper arms and began to shake her.

"Where is Victoria?" The man demanded.

Bruno stood and growled at the stranger protectively, moving his body between Frankie and the man.

"Cease!" The man bellowed and the dog surprisingly lowered himself to the floor. "Aren't you a doctor?" The stranger demanded in a deep, resounding tone. "I want some answers!" He continued to shake her and shout.

"I'm not a..." Frankie's voice trailed off as her own eyes grew wide with déjà vu recognition. For a split second she thought her mind was playing tricks on her. Then she realized that it was the man from her dreams! The man she held and kissed and made love to only in her dreams was standing before her now! As she stared at him in wonder, those precious dreams began to jumble together in an array of imagining. Suddenly, her surroundings swam before her eyes, her legs gave way, and slowly she crumpled to the floor slipping into unconsciousness.

Jack held onto her and in one effortless movement swept her up into his arms. He looked into her face and something deep within his chest began to tighten painfully. Bruno stood up and plastered himself to Jack's leg.

Dr. John Brenelli walked back through the swinging doors just as Frankie collapsed into the man's arms. "Mr. Romano, please bring her in here." John knew Frankie very well since she was his vet who had cared for his stallion which he kept at Manhattan

Racing Stable near Central Park. He rapidly guessed that Frankie must have been in the hospital for a chemo treatment. John's staff had informed him who Jack Romano was before his wife's surgery, but there was no time to speak to him then.

Jack turned toward John and slowly followed him into a nearby room still holding Frankie very close against his chest. She felt so cold that Jack pulled her even closer trying to warm her. John motioned for Jack to place her on the bed, but Jack just held her close. John cocked his head, glaring up at Jack, compelling him to lower Frankie onto the hospital bed. Jack couldn't believe how thin and weightless she was. He slowly removed his jacket and placed it over her blue scrubs. The red cap slipped off her head and Jack stared at this woman before him. Not the baldness or the emaciated skeleton, but how beautiful she was. Without warning, Jack felt a large hand come down hard onto his shoulder. Jack did not move. Instead, he watched as John began to lift Frankie's lids to flash a light into her eyes.

"What's your problem, Romano? Can't you follow the rules like everybody else? You were supposed to go to X-ray, not harass the living crap out of the doctors!" Jack recognized the fireman's voice from the accident scene. He kept shouting at the back of his head making him wince with pain.

Scott knew Frankie. It seemed everyone who had a pet knew the Doc. She had been taking care of his Dalmatian since she was a puppy. Scott was forever pursuing Frankie, asking her to dinner or a movie, but she always made excuses.

"Quiet, Scott, I'm trying to listen for her heartbeat." John glowered at Scott. Everyone quieted, as Bruno lowered himself under the bed.

In the absence of any sound, Jack began to get this horrible overwhelming feeling. Everything seemed to be spiraling downward. The pain that shot into his head was making him nauseous. Scott could see that Jack was wavering and growing paler by the minute. He guided him out into the hall and toward a chair against the wall. Jack sat and placed his elbows on his knees, his face in his hands with Scott taking the adjacent chair.

Staring ahead into space, Jack raised his head, his clasped hands supporting his chin, and asked softly, "Do you know what has happened to Victoria?"

Scott knew the truth, but he wasn't the one to tell Jack. "I just got here myself." Scott lied, sitting exactly like Jack, with his elbows on his knees and his head in his hands. Scott and Jack were so similar in size, but completely opposite in coloring.

From the corner of his eye, Jack could see someone quickly approaching. He turned his face in his hands and saw his brother, Anthony, sprinting toward him. Wearing his black tuxedo, Anthony looked totally out of place, weaving around doctors, nurses, and patients. Jack sat back in his chair and looked up at his brother, who towered over him from his seated position.

"Jack, are you all right? Was Victoria with you?" Anthony was obviously upset.

Jack nodded. Then reality hit Jack like another blow to the side of his skull. *Why would they call my brother to the hospital?*

"Who is the doctor in charge?" Anthony asked.

Scott looked from one to the other. *This guy must be a Romano, too*, Scott thought. *These guys went straight to the top.*

"He's in there," Jack pointed. "He's looking after the woman who just fainted in my arms," Jack told his brother matter-of-factly.

"What? What are you talking about?" Anthony thought his brother must have suffered quite a blow to the head, because he made absolutely no sense whatsoever.

John walked out into the hallway looking for the recent widower. "Mr. Romano." John called.

Both Jack and Anthony answered in unison. "Yes."

"Please, let's go into my office. It is right this way."

"What has happened? Where is Victoria?" Jack asked again, turning John around to face him. Their eyes met, and Jack knew something was terribly wrong.

"Mr. Romano, please, right this way, and I'll answer all of your questions."

Jack and Anthony glanced at each other before they quickly followed John down the hall and through another set of wooden swinging doors. They all entered a small, windowless office containing only a small, utilitarian steel desk and four chairs. John motioned for Jack and Anthony to take a seat.

John began very softly. "I'm very sorry, Mr. Romano."

Jack just stared at him, unblinking, and thought that Victoria's injuries must be worse than he thought. *Was she was paralyzed or in a coma?*

"Your wife died during surgery," John began. "We tried our best, but her injuries were too numerous and extremely substantial. I'm very sorry."

Jack said nothing. He felt nothing—neither sorrow nor pain. He just stared straight ahead.

Anthony was on his feet, unbuttoned his tuxedo jacket, placed his hands on his waist, and began to pace the small office; his spotless tuxedo jacket waving black before Jack's eyes.

"We would like your permission to harvest her organs," John spoke with extreme respect, continuing solemnly. "Many people could live from your wife's passing. Many could have a second chance at life."

Jack could not believe what he was hearing. *We were just going to dinner,* he thought. Now he had to give permission to donate Victoria's organs! His mind was still stuck on trying to talk her into starting a family with him. Jack began to rub his face with his hands. *This can't be happening!* In a blink of an eye, his life changed.

Anthony could tell that Jack was struggling to process all of this at once. He gently placed his hand on his brother's broad shoulder and spoke softly. "I think you should let them use whatever organs they need." Anthony spoke to Jack as though they were in church and watched as his brother could only nod.

"You are going to have to sign some paperwork, Mr. Romano," John instructed.

"I'll take care of that." Anthony interjected, and John wasn't about to argue. "I'd like to get him out of here." Dr. Brenelli nodded in agreement.

Turning to Jack, Anthony bent his head low and spoke very softly to his brother once again. "Paul is waiting for you by the emergency room entrance. Why don't you go home, and I'll take care of everything here? I'll come right over when this is done." Again, the most Jack could do was nod. John picked up the telephone and asked the nurse at the head station to move the press to the front entrance for a formal press conference. With the press gathering to one spot to catch the morning paper's scoop, Jack would be able to leave the hospital with little or no interference.

Jack rose from his chair and almost as though he was outside his body watching from a distance, he walked down the hall and through the swinging wooden doors. But instead of following the signs toward the emergency room, something tugged at him to walk the other direction and down the hallway to the room where he had deposited the thin woman. Jack stood in the doorway and watched the woman breathing very slowly. Her dog was lying down with his head on her red cap. Bruno picked up his head, got up and walked slowly over to Jack moving his huge head under Jack's hand. Jack stroked the large, soft head for many minutes, just watching the thin woman on the bed. She didn't look like a woman but more like a child...so small, so helpless and frail. He noticed her shivering, and he quickly moved into the room adjusting his jacket up over her while he studied her face. He stroked the back of his hand gently along her cheek and, again, his chest tightened.

Frankie turned her head towards his touch, but her eyes remained closed. He didn't want to abandon this woman, because he knew what it felt like to be completely alone. Hadn't he been alone for the last three years? After lifting and tucking his jacket under her small frame, Jack forced himself to leave. Bruno waited for him by the doorway.

"She'll be fine, boy," Jack spoke softly to Bruno, while rubbing his soft head. Standing up straight, he shot one last glance at her then turned, and walked down the hall with his hands deep in his pockets, his head lowered. He could still feel the softness of her cheek against the back of his hand. He headed out the emergency room exit to the waiting limo. Paul opened the limo door, and Jack fell into the back seat. Paul shut the door, raced around to the driver's side and slid in behind the wheel.

"I'm gonna bring you right home, Mr. R," Paul sounded frightened. "Don't you worry 'bout nothin'."

Jack stared out the side of the limo. "I don't want to go back to the apartment." Jack spoke in a deep tone, barely above a whisper. "Take me to The Rose."

Paul nodded, and eased the limo out of the hospital parking area and into traffic. Paul picked up the cell phone to let the captain know that Mr. R would be arriving shortly. The 35-foot yacht was docked at Jack's private dock. He purchased it when he began to design and build The Rose along with a select, few handpicked superior boat builders. A sturdy ship, she could tolerate many types of seas and serious weather conditions, but the sight of her was simply breathtaking.

In the hospital, Anthony had just finished the gruesome task of discussing what organs they hoped to retrieve from Victoria. He did not argue with Dr. Brenelli and told him to take anything they wanted. He could not believe that any good could come out of that cold, unfeeling witch. He felt no loss or sadness about his sister-in-law's death. In his opinion, she had, and God only knows why, made his brother's life empty and cold. He felt no guilt for feeling this way and resolved to make damn sure that his brother would not grieve for that bitch for any length of time, if at all.

He was looking down as he placed the paperwork into his tuxedo breast pocket that Dr. Brenelli gave him when he smacked right into a small woman dressed in a cranberry-colored turtleneck and jeans. Her short, shiny, brown curls sprang back and forth as Anthony reached quickly for her arm so that she didn't fall backwards. "I beg your pardon," Anthony stated sincerely, still holding onto her upper arm for just a split second longer. Her curvaceous body filled out the sweater in all the right places, catching Anthony's attention.

"Oh, I wasn't paying attention to where I was going, either." Becca apologized as she removed her hands from Anthony's chest. Studying people was what she did for a living as she quickly gathered information. This man was young, fair in complexion, tall and solid, and very well dressed, not to mention, extremely handsome with stunning gray-blue eyes.

Anthony stepped to the side, waving his hand as he bowed, gesturing for Rebecca to pass. She turned back and smiled, then quickly headed down the hall to Frankie's room. Anthony started to walk away, then turned back to watch the adorable woman bounce down the hall. As she disappeared around a corner, Anthony headed back through the emergency room. It was chaotic, and he couldn't wait to get the hell out of the place. Hospitals just unnerved him. He reached into his breast pocket and withdrew a long cigar and paused a moment to light it. He drew on the end of the cigar, its tip burning bright red with the first drag he took. Exhaling, smoke billowed about him. He watched for

Paul's return, but when another darker, silver Romano limo glided up to the curb, he climbed in without looking back.

Becca met up with John as he led her to Frankie's room. Frankie was sitting up in bed, with Jack's jacket over her shoulders, swinging her legs that dangled over the side of the bed to and fro. She looked miniscule under the large jacket draped over her shoulders.

"And where do you think you're going?" John asked Frankie.

"Home," Frankie stated defiantly with a smile.

"I don't think so," Becca chimed in.

"Come on John...Becca. I was just a little more tired than usual." She whimpered uncharacteristically.

Becca stared at her in disbelief. *Was Frankie about to cry?* "What is it?" Becca asked Frankie, sensing something must be wrong because Frankie never argued or complained and very rarely cried.

"I saw him, Becca. He's real!" Frankie whispered just for Becca to hear. Clutching the jacket until each lapel overlapped, Frankie again spoke in no more than a whisper. "I can still smell him. This is his jacket! You were right, Becca. You were right!"

"No way!" Becca nearly shouted as her brown eyes grew wide, while her hand flew to stem the words flying from her open mouth. She turned on John and spoke authoritatively. "You have to discharge her immediately." Becca stared John down until he reached up to rub his now-throbbing temple.

John looked from one woman to the other and then the dog, which was a clear violation of hospital policy. "Look Frankie, you fainted and hospital procedure requires that I..." John stopped speaking because Frankie and Becca were completely ignoring him, and Frankie was climbing down from the bed.

"Are you sure it was him?" Becca whispered into Frankie's ear and Frankie quickly nodded her bright blue eyes wide and alive. "I can't believe this. Finally!" Becca declared.

Just then Scott walked into the room. "You can't believe what?" Scott asked, but no one even noticed him. "How are you feeling Frankie?" Scott asked this question an octave louder, since his first question was completely ignored.

"Why are you always shouting?" John whirled to face Scott.

Scott wondered what the hell John was pissed off about.

"Frankie, I insist that you stay for observation while we run some tests." John recited his usual dialogue sounding very much like the doctor he was.

"Observation?!" Frankie, Becca, and Scott replied in near unison.

John threw up his hands in defeat. He had had enough of this night and grabbed the clipboard, signing off under the discharge section.

Frankie and Becca were still whispering when Scott returned with a wheelchair. "Hospital rules," Scott winked. "Your carriage ride, madam," Scott dramatically waved his hand over the wheelchair.

Frankie wasn't about to argue. She snatched up her red cap just before she plopped into the wheelchair. Scott eased the wheelchair down the hall and backwards through the wooden swinging doors, then through the still-insane emergency waiting room, filled with patients not yet seen.

Once outside the hospital doors, Frankie looked back over her shoulder. "Scott, you can stop right here."

"I don't think so. I think I'll wheel you home myself." Scott spoke to Frankie in an affectionate, almost loving tone, but Becca knew he was wasting his time. She knew that Frankie would never let anyone near her, especially now that the man that she had dreamed about for years just appeared before her eyes. *The man from Frankie's dreams was real,* Becca thought, trying to absorb the magnitude of Frankie's dreaming capabilities. It was amazing and mind-boggling all at once.

Chapter Four
Very early the next morning...

Jack opened the limo door before Paul could run to his side. With his hands deep in his pockets, his head bowed and his tie flipping about in the breeze, Jack walked the length of dock up to The Rose. He looked up at The Rose, the ship he had built from his own designs four years ago, and was relieved that he did not have to go back to the apartment.

All of the appointments on the boat were done in highly polished rosewood and the main salon entrance had double doors that were full-length stained glass of roses set in rosewood frames; hence, the yacht's name. Anthony had bought the stunning stained-glass doors for him in Spain while Jack's yacht was being built. He called it a yacht-building present, and Jack immediately incorporated them into his design. Anthony was always doing things like that, he thought quietly.

Jack stopped before the doors and ran his hand over the glass. He studied the masterpiece of jeweled-colored glass before him, as though he was seeing it for the first time. A retired captain came to the boat daily to run the motors, effect minor repairs, clean and polish the fixtures, and keep it in good repair. The yacht had three levels and was quite lavish. All the draperies, rugs, and upholstered furniture were in varying hues of green, from deep, forest green to light, sage green, which complimented the rosewood. And almost two-thirds of the rooms on the boat had large windows.

Once in the salon, Jack made his way to the rosewood-paneled wall. The wood panel slid to the right and revealed a bar with sparkling crystal glasses for any and every drink imaginable, another one of Anthony's gifts. It had taken Jack weeks to design the special wooden racks that held the crystal glasses in place to prevent breakage when the ship was underway or encountered rough seas. He poured himself a Macallan Estate Reserve and downed it in just one gulp instead of sipping the fine whiskey. The liquid burned the back of his throat, and Jack stood still waiting for the liquor to stop his racing thoughts and the pounding in his head.

Anthony walked into the salon and removed his tuxedo jacket, throwing it over the back of the u-shaped, sage green sofa. Jack removed another crystal glass and poured his brother the same drink. Anthony took the glass from his brother's outstretched hand and studied the crystal. *Beautiful,* he thought soundlessly. Anthony sat down on the couch with his elbows on his knees and stared at Jack's back.

"I will take care of all the funeral arrangements. I already called Mom and Dad and Victoria's parents, as well." Anthony spoke carefully, as he wasn't quite sure of Jack's frame of mind. Their parents were shocked and wanted to speak with their son, but Anthony insisted that what Jack needed was rest. The doctor made it quite clear to Anthony that Jack should be x-rayed and left before he was properly examined, but Anthony reassured the doctor that if his brother wasn't feeling well he would bring him right back to the hospital. Anthony was certain Jack just needed rest.

The call made to Victoria's family was in a word—strange. He would have thought that they would have openly wailed for their only daughter, but silence is what Anthony encountered on the other end of the phone and nothing more. It was eerie and unsettling.

Jack moved slowly as he took a seat on the opposite couch, being very grateful to have such a brother. Jack was always the strong one. He always watched after Anthony in such a way that no one ever dared to lay a hand on him his whole life. Whatever scrapes or battles Anthony got into, Jack got him out. Now Anthony was being the strong one, and Jack was thankful.

"Paul is going to bring over some of your things." Anthony spoke to the crystal glass he turned in his hands.

Jack did not respond; instead, he downed a second glass of whiskey in one gulp. Both men sat in silence until Paul appeared with a suitcase and garment bag. Jack took the cases from Paul, turned, and left the salon without a word, making his way to his stateroom. He tossed the cases onto a green couch with a tiny rose print. Two matching club chairs covered in complementary deep, forest-green velvet filled out the room. He couldn't wait to remove his soiled, blood-stained clothes and left them in a heap on the bathroom floor. The dark green marble under Jack's feet was contrasted with the ceiling's lighter shade of the same veined marble, and the walls were covered in striped wallpaper of green and taupe. He turned on the water in the large shower stall and water shot out from four different spouts: one spout came from each of three walls, and the fourth spout released water like a rainstorm from overhead. Jack stepped into the steamy shower and let the hot water soak into his body. He leaned with his hands against the marble shower walls, and let the water pelt his large muscular form.

Chapter Five
Still that very same morning…

Frankie, Scott, Becca, and Bruno all made their way down the street to Frankie's apartment building, with Frankie still in the hospital wheelchair.

"Why don't you take Bruno for a walk?" Scott suggested to Becca. What he really meant was for Becca to get lost for a few minutes. Becca took the hint and grabbed Bruno's collar.

"I'll be right back, Frankie." Becca turned, stopped at a trash can for some newspaper then ducked down an alley with Bruno. Frankie shivered, and as she reached to snuggle deeper into Jack's jacket, Scott knelt down in front of her and began to rub her arms.

"You must be freezing."

"I'm fine." Frankie looked at Scott. He was very strong and handsome, but he wasn't Jack. Jack was the man she wanted. The one she wanted to make love to and not just in her dreams. She buried her face into Jack's jacket and breathed in the spicy scent. The fragrance released a flutter of butterflies inside her and caused her skin to tingle.

"Frankie, let me take care of you," Scott said as he lifted her chin and looked deeply into her eyes.

Frankie stared back, expressionless. *Is he going to kiss me?* She feared in disbelief. Frankie lifted her hand and pushed it against Scott's chest, but that was useless. *Close friends*, Scott thought, *she always holds me at arm's length, but not tonight.* He raised his hand and touched her cheek. He had never been this intimate to her before, and the feel of her skin was making his heart hammer.

Just as he started to push against Frankie's hand, Becca jogged up behind them with Bruno barking and leaping, breaking the spell. Scott stood and scowled at Becca. "Great timing, Becca."

"You're welcome," Becca answered with a giggle in her voice, reaching for Frankie's hand and helping her out of the wheelchair. Frankie and Becca watched Scott leave, pushing the empty wheelchair back to the hospital.

Upstairs in her apartment, Frankie collapsed on the couch.

Becca took Bruno to the kitchen and fed him. When she returned she plopped herself into the adjacent club chair, toed off her shoes and swung her feet up over the chair's large, round arm.

"Now, tell me. Tell me everything. Don't leave out the slightest detail!" Becca demanded excitedly.

Frankie looked at her best friend and began to tell her what had led up to her running into Jack. "When I stepped out of the elevator, Jack was headed right for me. He was shouting, 'Where is she?' At first I felt like I was in one of my dreams, but then Bruno nearly took his head off when he started to shake me."

Becca's eyes grew wide as saucers. "Oh my."

"His voice bellowed 'Cease' or something like that, and the next thing I knew I felt my legs give out from under me. I don't remember a thing until I woke up."

"My goodness," Becca managed to whisper.

"When he grabbed my arms," Frankie spoke, unconsciously rubbing her upper arms still clad with Jack's jacket, "he looked into my eyes, and it was as though he looked right into my soul. For a split second, I could swear that he recognized me. Like he knew about me—about us! Is that possible? Becca, I have kissed this man thousands of times. I've made love to him, beautiful, sweet love, and I have never had sex in my life!" Frankie's chin sank, shaking it from side to side, finding it so hard to believe.

Becca raised her hand to cover her mouth. She was never quite sure about Frankie's sex life, and now the truth was told. Becca spoke quietly. "Did you have this dream about what happened in the hospital today?"

Frankie shook her head. "No. When I think about it, I really had no idea that this man even existed." Frankie stared at Becca, and both remained silent trying to absorb the events that unfolded that day.

Frankie kicked off her shoes, swung her legs onto the couch, and pulled the afghan that draped the back of the couch over her body. Frankie pulled Jack's jacket up to just under her nose, keeping his scent close. Becca settled back, too, and reached for the throw that hung over the back of the club chair. Bruno came into the living room, circled around in his bed then plopped down, falling fast asleep.

Later that night, Frankie began to shiver uncontrollably. She was too cold to move and not quite fully awake.

Back on the yacht, Jack woke with a start. He had gone to bed right after his shower and was now shivering from head to toe. With an unsteady hand, he reached for the down comforter that graced the foot of the enormous bed and pulled it up over his broad shoulders. He reached for the pillow next to him and nestled it close to his chest. At that precise moment, Frankie turned on her side pressing her back into the cushions of the sofa. She instantly felt warmer as she drifted back to sleep.

Chapter Six
Thanksgiving Day...

Jack was completely unaware of what day it was or even what time, for that matter. He walked into the galley and thought he heard the captain cursing as he tried to prepare breakfast. Jack poured himself a large mug of steaming hot coffee and took the newspaper from the table. He walked the stairs to the main salon and put the paper down on the coffee table; when it flopped open, exposing the front page headline: "Jack Romano and Wife in Fatal Car Accident!" with a picture of Jack and his wife at a recent charity fundraiser. Jack didn't notice the headline. He didn't notice anything really. He stood at the large window and looked out at the Hudson River watching without observing. A barge was slowly passing, and The Rose swayed slightly in its wake. He never noticed Anthony, either, who had been there for quite some time sipping his coffee.

"It feels like we might get snow," Anthony announced to his brother's back, trying to get Jack's attention.

When Jack turned toward the sound of his brother's voice, Anthony was taken aback by the dark circles under his brother's eyes and the purpling bruise on the left side of his forehead. Anthony cleared his throat and tried to sound reassuring. "I have made all of the arrangements, and Paul will be picking you up here tomorrow morning. I've arranged for a mass service at St. Stephen's then a light meal to follow the cemetery service."

Jack turned back to the window, quietly thanking his brother. Anthony finished his coffee and left a short time later, tucking the newspaper under his arm. He couldn't stand to watch his brother mourn for that evil woman! She didn't deserve it. "I should have taken care of her myself before their wedding," Anthony muttered to himself, making his way down the dock toward the waiting limo.

Frankie and Becca were heading towards Frankie's parents' brownstone for Thanksgiving. For years, the O'Brians and McFarlans had been sharing holidays together—Thanksgiving at the O'Brian's and Christmas at the McFarlan's. Becca wisely insisted on driving, and Frankie didn't have the strength to protest.

They left at noon, and Becca deftly maneuvered Frankie's Suburban through the building traffic. Frankie's mind began to wander as they sat in unmoving traffic for some unknown reason. She rested her head against the passenger door, and could hear Bruno growling, in between snoring, at something while he slept. Frankie closed her eyes and began to replay the dream she had just last night.

Jack was standing on a large boat; its color reminded her of a pearl, both creamy and luminous. He was holding out his hand to her calling her name so sweetly. "Francesca." She heard the timbre of his voice in her mind, and it made her senses spark alive, her skin tingle, just like when she wrapped herself in his jacket. She placed her hand into his oversized palm and watched his leg muscles tighten under his khakis as he easily assisted her aboard. She looked up and was lost in his eyes. He was so warm and real. He spoke barely above a whisper, his hand reaching up to cup her cheek.

"I want to make love to you, Francesca," he said, as he guided her along the deck of the yacht toward a set of stained glass doors, with...*yellow roses*; Frankie recalled the detail. The doors led into a sort of living room. The wood was highly polished almost to a mirror finish and she watched herself reach her hand out to touch the smooth wood, so warm, so beautiful, and Jack smiled at her over his shoulder. They walked together into a corridor with many doors. He opened a second set of double doors into a sitting room, then closed the doors behind her and through a third set of French doors that led into a large master bedroom suite. The enormous bed was built right into the same, highly polished wood paneling.

As in the rest of the yacht, this room was appointed in shades of dark, rich green, earthy tones, which complimented the woodwork. The coverlet on the bed was dark green and the pillows were ivory, sage, and deep forest-green velvet. There was a huge, down comforter rolled up at the foot of the bed, clad in an ivory-colored duvet. On either side of the bed were glass windows that peered out into darkness. An open door led into the master bath. Frankie could see the dark, green marble on the floor. Jack turned to Frankie and spoke to her softly as she stood frozen at the French doors.

"You are so beautiful." Her hair was just to her ears, and Jack ran his hand through her golden tresses, over and over again, trying to tuck one, short strand behind her ear.

Soon, Frankie thought silently, stopping her dream for just a moment to touch her head. *This is going to happen soon.* Now that she had her last treatment, her hair would start to grow back again.

Frankie turned her head to the left as the dream continued to play. He stroked her cheek as he looked lovingly into her eyes. She turned her face slightly and gently kissed the palm of his enormous hand and, for some reason, his expression changed. Frankie stood quietly at first, almost too shy to move, not sure what she had done or what she was supposed to do.

An observer now, Frankie noticed that she wore a short-sleeved red, silk blouse and billowing, white linen slacks. Jack began to unbutton her blouse. Frankie watched as her trembling hands could only manage to unbutton a few buttons of his crisp, white oxford. She moved her hands under his shirt and caressed his skin, marveling at the feel of his hard chest roughed with dark, curly hair. She passed her hands over his chest and the sensation she felt was sparks shooting through her fingertips.

Without any warning, Jack tore off his shirt, sending buttons soaring through the air and before Frankie could react, Jack tugged the last two buttons off her blouse, hearing the sound of tearing material. He kissed her hungrily, and Frankie leaned into him trying to meet the intensity of his rising passion. He swept her up into his arms and lowered her onto the bed, never taking his eyes from her. He unbuttoned her linen slacks and eased them off her legs, running his hands up and down her thighs. He removed his pants and slid next to Frankie. Lying together they started kissing, touching, and caressing each other for a dizzying amount of time. His breathing was coming faster, and Frankie could hear her own short, steady gasps. In an unfamiliar husky tone, Jack looked into her eyes and tried to speak in between his labored breathing. "I want you. I want you, Francesca. Do you hear me?" He asked, almost unsure of himself.

"Yes," was all Frankie could manage because he had rolled onto his back and pulled Frankie on top of him, surprising her. She sat up straight as he slid his hands over her waist and between her breasts. She could see that her ribs were no longer sticking out as his hands traced along her skin. He unclasped her bra from the front, sliding his hands under the lace fabric, brushing it away from her breasts and down her arms. First he looked at her then stretched up to kiss her neck and breast. He took the bud of her right breast, closing his mouth over it, paying no attention to the other. She watched herself begin to plead with him to take the other into his mouth, sensing a need. She could hear herself speak in a whispered tone with an urgency she never expressed before this moment.

"Please, Jacqino, please," she begged. She could see the silver color in his eyes lighten when he raised his head smiling. His voice was deep and asked her, "Do you want me Francesca? Do you?" Still kissing her but refusing to give into her pleas.

"Yes, I want you, Jacqino." With that, he closed onto the forgotten, sensitive, pink bud. New discovered sensations crashed over her like waves. Within minutes, they were both skin against skin under the sumptuous coverlet, resting their heads on the cool, sage-green down pillows. He pulled her close, as Frankie pressed a kiss to his chest directly over his heart. Her lips rested there on his warm, golden skin roughened with dark, curly hair for a long while. She could feel the beating of his heart against her lips. Jack groaned so deeply before pressing her onto her back. His tongue slid down the center of her breasts, placing kisses under each breast then traveled to her stomach, where he left wet circles all the way down her body. When he reached the triangle just above Frankie's legs, he caressed her slowly. Spreading her legs gently apart, he slid his long fingers into her, one at a time. He knew just what to do and was sending her right out of her mind as her vision began to blur.

"I want you inside of me," Frankie heard herself say to him as she reached for his face, pulling his mouth to hers. He closed his mouth over hers for a long, deep kiss, with their tongues twisted around each other. Jack eased himself between her legs, seeming to understand the need for gentleness and slowness when he stopped abruptly, frozen in his movements, studying her expression. His eyes were dark except for the silver flecks that glistened and sparkled.

"Francesca..." he spoke so quietly, gently caressing her cheek, as an array of emotions danced across his flushed face.

The dream felt so real, as if she could feel his weight on her at that exact moment. Suddenly, a loud horn blared from behind her and jolted Frankie from her daydream. Her eyes flew open, and she noticed that Becca was staring right at her. With the traffic moving again, Becca hit the accelerator and continued the drive to Thanksgiving dinner.

Once inside the O'Brian's home, Frankie and Becca settled into a comfortable family reunion of sorts. Becca's Mom and Dad, and Becca's older brother, Stephen, were there. Stephen, of course, had another girl with him. Who could keep up? He changed girlfriends like people changed their socks, making it impossible to take anyone of them seriously. At 30, it didn't seem odd to Frankie that Stephen hadn't settled down yet. She just supposed he hadn't found the woman of his dreams, at least not yet. Everyone hugged each other, and Stephen kissed his sister and Frankie happily. Frankie's father, Thomas, held Becca first then Frankie for a long time, while kissing the very top of her covered head.

"How are you, beautiful?" he whispered, holding her face between his hands so close to his, studying her eyes, which were the exact color of his mother's.

"I'm a little tired." Frankie was always honest with her father and mother. Frankie's mother, Corrine, was a little more stubborn than her father, but Frankie blamed that on her mother's Sicilian background. Frankie loved her parents dearly, but Frankie's father's peacemaking, gentle Irish ways just called to her a little more deeply than her mother's tough, Sicilian, often-obstinate ways.

Since Frankie's illness, her father was handling all of her finances. An accountant, he had little trouble turning Frankie's money into a small fortune practically overnight. He could not believe the sum of money she had in her checking account after she had signed the power-of-attorney to have him address all of her finances while she recuperated. She had her paychecks directly deposited into her account, and because Frankie spent relatively little, the money accumulated making the actual dollar amount staggering.

"Let's take a walk for a bit of air," Thomas urged after they had eaten.

"Sure Dad, a little walk sounds great after all that delicious food." Frankie stood up and walked to the door grabbing her coat. Her father helped her into it—he was so courteous, almost chivalrous, a true gentleman. Frankie glanced over at Bruno passed out under the dining room table and shrugged.

Once outside, Frankie placed her hand under her father's arm, covering it with his large hand. He was really quite a beautiful man, tall and very blond, like Frankie. Most of his blond hair was mixed with the whitest gray, and many tiny, laugh lines crinkled the corners of his pale, blue eyes. He was broad and still physically very strong. Even though he spent his days behind a desk, he remained active. He had an enormous sailboat, and he and Frankie's mother spent many weeks traveling up and down the Eastern Seaboard. Frankie secretly believed that her father liked sailing so much because it was his only opportunity to boss her mother about. He ran a tight ship, and Corrine obeyed his every bidding when they were under sail.

"I have a bit of a surprise for you. I've made a little investment with all the money you have accumulated in your account since the day you started working for the animal hospital," speaking softly to her.

Frankie looked curiously, not really understanding him. "What money?"

"Francesca, love, you had a quarter of a million dollars in your checking account. After I made a few stock purchases I have tripled it!" Her father spoke rather professionally.

"Oh, Dad, that couldn't be!" Frankie was shocked.

"No, really, it's true. I don't think you've spent more than the bare minimum on living expenses since you started working. Your overhead is next to nothing. The biggest expense is your apartment and that monster truck you drive. Since you barely drive it, you don't even have much of a gas expense. I'm not going to watch you give most of it back to the government, so I thought it was time you invested in something that could be both a tax benefit and maybe get you out of the city. You know, slow your pace down a bit."

"Oh, Dad, that's silly. My pace is fine. In fact I've really slowed down after my internship…"

But before Frankie could finish, Thomas waved his hand in a most unfamiliar manner and said, "Well, it really doesn't matter, because since you gave me power-of-attorney, I already made a significant purchase on your behalf." Stopping and gazing directly into his daughter's eyes, he continued. "I bought you a farm," he declared, still smiling down at his daughter's beautiful upturned face.

"A what?"

"A farm!"

"A farm! Dad—you can't be serious." But Frankie watched in disbelief as he nodded. "It's a good thing Becca's here, because I think you need to speak to a shrink. How am I going to take care of a farm? You just told me that I need to slow down, and you buy me a farm? What were you thinking?" Frankie started to raise her voice. She couldn't believe what he had done.

Thomas just waved his hand at nothing in particular. "Oh, you can't live there. Not yet, anyway. The house is just about ready to fall down," he explained nonchalantly.

"Fall down?" Frankie blinked.

"Oh, yes, the farmhouse is in great disrepair."

"I don't even want to know what you paid for it. What *I* paid for it!" Frankie clarified.

"I got it for a steal." Thomas waved his hand again. "Do you remember my client, Mr. O'Mara? He retired permanently and has left the area. He used to keep his children's horses up at this farm, but he hasn't used the place in almost twenty years."

"Twenty years, oh no...can we sell it before it's too late?" Frankie's mind raced.

"No...no, we aren't going to sell it. You see, he is very well off and really needed a loss for tax purposes this year, so the timing was perfect."

Frankie's head was beginning to hurt. She hated discussing tax mumbo-jumbo. "Dad, please. I don't want to hear the newest laws on tax relief."

"Well, nevertheless, he sold the property at an enormous loss, which will greatly benefit him. And since none of his children wanted the place, he was more than happy to unload it."

"Unload?" Frankie's eyes were wide.

"The money you have in your account, minus the initial cost of the farm, will certainly cover most of the expenses."

"Most?" Frankie asked, almost afraid to hear the answer.

"Well, we will need an architect and a general contractor who will hire a crew. So with a little creative financing, I think we can pull it off."

"Architect? General contractor? Crew? Pull it off? Oh, I think I need to sit down." Frankie looked around for a seat.

"The land is perfect, the view of the Hudson is breathtaking, and it has water rights and a dock slip along the river's bank. There's a small cottage and a barn on the property. I thought you could board Reflections there."

"Dad, you bought me a farm with my money so that I could board my horse on it?"

Waving his hand again in that peculiar new way, Thomas continued. "No, no, Francesca." He never called her Frankie because he thought her name was as beautiful as she was. "I bought the farm, because I was hoping that you could open a small veterinarian office there and slow down."

"How do you expect me to support myself?" Frankie asked, completely stunned as her father's hand continued to wave.

"Francesca, since I started managing your money, it was so easy to increase your rate of return. I took a portion of the profit on the original amount and put it into the hands of my able-bodied broker, who invested the money in some high-risk funds. Of course, I don't like to put *my* money in those funds, but you're still young."

"High risk!" Frankie gulped.

Thomas gently replaced his daughter's hand on his arm and slowly started walking back home. "Since my broker has been handling that portion of your money, it has...well, let's just say, it has catapulted you into a new tax bracket. In fact, your retirement plan is better than mine at the moment! At this point, you really don't have to earn very much at all once the farm is completed. You could take on other horse boarders, run a small practice in the barn, and Nelson and his wife, Henrietta, will practically jump to assist you with the barn and the house. Retta can cook and clean, and Nelson is very gentle with the animals. In fact, my client never made Nelson or his wife leave the property. They still live there today. He said that Nelson took care of his children's horses, dogs, and the property in general, while his wife used to watch his kids, cook, and clean. He said they are very honorable and trustworthy people."

"Wait. Wait. Let me guess. Because of the work they do, they receive a salary and pay no rent for this cottage they live in?" Frankie was trying to calculate numbers in her mind, yet they weren't adding up.

"Exactly! Nelson and Retta live there, so they will be there when the contractors begin. They will be able to supervise the progress when you or I cannot be there." Thomas was happy to see his daughter was catching on.

"But who is going to pay for the architect and contractors, Nelson and his wife?"

"Why, you are!" Thomas replied with raised eyebrows. Obviously, she wasn't grasping the whole concept.

Stopping on the sidewalk, Frankie looked up at her father. "Okay, so let me see if I have this straight," Frankie began. "Not only did you buy me a farm that is completely unlivable, with my money, but I also need to support myself, my apartment, Norman and his wife, Harriet, and their cottage, and I'll need to pay for complete renovations to a farmhouse and convert a barn into an animal hospital!" Frankie stopped to draw in a deep breath.

"Nelson and Henrietta, dear. Oh, and their place could use some sprucing up as well." Thomas corrected smiling. He turned his daughter around again and slowly led her back to the house. "Come now, daughter. You will see. I will take care of everything. You will love the farm, and you will never want to go back to the city again. You will be thanking me profusely in a few short months from now," Thomas stated confidently, as he watched Frankie shake her head in disbelief.

Thanksgiving meant absolutely nothing to Jack. His parents had called him from Italy very early that morning expressing their sorrow for his loss and said they were headed home. Jack's mother silently thanked God that her son was spared and couldn't wait to embrace him again.

Anthony stopped by The Rose and begged Jack to come out with him to get a bite to eat, but Jack just stood still and shook his head. He didn't want to be around anyone or anything. He stayed on the yacht that day, just staring into oblivion.

Chapter Seven
The funeral...

The day after Thanksgiving was Victoria's funeral. Jack stood perfectly still on the deck of The Rose as he waited for the limo to pick him up. As Paul drove into the parking area near the dock, Jack made his way from the yacht. The wind was howling, the sky a gloomy gray. Jack did not feel the wind, but quickened his pace unconsciously. He spoke not a word as he sat in the back seat beside his brother.

Inside the chapel of St. Stephen's, many of Jack's family started to arrive. His cousins traveled from Staten Island and Long Island, as well as the Romano cousins from New Jersey, and this was just the immediate family. Each cousin kissed Jack on each cheek and, under their breath, cursed his dead wife who lay in the closed casket.

Uncle Tony pulled Anthony to the side and in an almost muffled tone spoke quietly and succinctly. "We thank the good Lord that he took her and not our Jackie," Uncle Tony started.

"Please, Uncle Ton, she's dead, it's over." Anthony raised his hands then let them drop.

"Over!" Uncle Tony almost shouted then quickly lowered his voice. Trying to calm himself in the house of God, he reached into his breast pocket and removed a long cigar and twirled the cigar between his lips. In a deep throaty voice, his godfather continued. "Over! Anthony that...family of hers should all drop dead!" Uncle Tony hissed. "Do you know that her mother called our family's attorneys the day she died—*the day she died*—just before midnight, and wanted to know what kind of settlement they were going to receive for the loss of their daughter? The grieving family—like hell!" Uncle Tony turned his face to the side to view the black, lacquered casket with brushed chrome handles, and Victoria's parents sitting in the front pew next to Jack. When he looked back at Anthony, what Anthony saw scared him; his uncle had a look on his face that could frighten someone to death. Murder was in his eyes. Anthony stood still and tried to comprehend what his uncle was saying. *Victoria's family was well off, right? Why the hell were they even talking about a lump sum?* Everything was starting to get to him as chills ran down his spine.

"I've already taken care of it," Uncle Tony stated curtly, making sure that Anthony understood.

"Uncle Tony, I would have settled it quickly."

"There was nothing to settle, *capisce?*"

Anthony kissed his uncle's cheeks, reached into his jacket, and took one of his uncle's fine cigars from his breast pocket then walked back over to sit on the other side of Jack.

And still Jack remained silent. He sat absolutely stone still in the pew, next to his brother and parents and Victoria's parents. Anthony could tell he was on autopilot, moving about, and speaking only when spoken to. The vocalist sang *Ave Maria*, but no one shed a tear for this loss, even though the song itself beseeched tears.

At the cemetery, everyone was shivering from the biting wind, but Jack did not even place his hands in his pockets; his unbuttoned coat blew open and closed. He stood as though cut from the same marble as the statutes around him. When the cemetery service was over, Anthony rested his hand gently on his brother's shoulder, which broke Jack's trance. They walked back to the limo, as the frigid wind whipped viciously at their uncovered faces and fingers. The caravan of luxurious limos made their way out of the cemetery to Mario's Restaurant.

Once inside Mario's, Jack felt restless. He did not want to speak to anyone—he just wanted to take a walk. Perhaps that would clear his head. How could he explain that he was feeling nothing for the loss of his wife? She was dead and the only thing he could think about, the one thing that kept playing over in his mind, was that he was never going to have a child to love, that he was going to be alone for the rest of his life. At that moment, he felt that he was never going to be able to find a special woman who was in love with him, *for him* and not his fortune. Someone whose love he could return. When Jack saw an opening, he quietly left through the back kitchen door and began to walk in no particular direction.

Night drew its dark curtain around him, yet Jack felt solace for the first time in days. The wind and frigid temperatures were making others wrap their coats closer to themselves, but Jack felt warmth from something intangible. As he turned the corner,

Jack walked right past Engine Company No. 2 as they were stringing Christmas lights onto the firehouse, and Scott spotted him instantaneously. Jack was not noticing much of anything and was startled when a big hand came down hard on his shoulder. With a start, he turned.

"What?!" Jack wheeled in order to face the form behind him.

"Hey, Romano." Scott could see that Jack didn't remember him; Jack's black, piercing eyes looked at him with rage, with the intention to strike. Scott motioned to the huge rig in the parking garage of the firehouse. Jack tried to make his mind work. "I'm the fireman who was on duty the night of your accident. How are you doin'?" Scott asked genuinely.

"Her funeral was today," Jack stated without any sign of emotion.

"I'm sorry," Scott spoke softly. He always wondered why this guy never referred to *her* as his *wife*. He had heard all the talk at the hospital about Romano being probably the richest man in the country, but that kind of thing never impressed Scott. What impressed Scott was a man's will.

Jack started to walk away, but Scott caught his arm. "Hey listen, I just got off duty. You wanna get a beer? We could go to Brady's. It's just down the street."

Jack shrugged, and Scott accepted that as a "yes."

Together, the two huge men, one blond and fair, the other dark and brooding, strode down the street purposefully. Each man resembled the other in build, but Scott was just a little wider and Jack just an inch taller. Scott had measured up Jack on the night of the accident, which was just something he always did. He believed that Jack could probably match him stride for stride in any of his fireman's duties. Scott could sense a deep, inner strength in Jack simply because the man exuded confidence and a force of will. Jack's stature and wealth immediately commanded respect, but he seemed to be a gentleman through and through. Scott couldn't help but notice how Jack unconsciously let women by first or stood off to one side or the other to let a mother pass with her stroller. He even picked up an old woman's dropped glove and caught up with her to return it. Scott could see he was doing these things as if they were second nature to him.

As they rounded the corner, Frankie ran right into Jack's chest.

Frankie falling backwards looked up as Jack's hands rested on her upper arms, trying to steady her from their accidental collision. She was out jogging with Bruno and turned to look back at him for just an instant, because he was starting to fall behind, and that is precisely when she collided into Jack. She could feel the heat from his hands penetrating right through her university sweatshirt. Frankie and Jack just stared into each others' eyes.

"I'm sorry, excuse me," they both whispered, only to each other.

"Hey, Frankie, you look better." Scott broke the spell and grabbed her from Jack, giving her a hug. "Happy Thanksgiving."

"Happy Thanksgiving." Frankie replied and glanced at Jack quickly still trying to absorb that the man from her dreams existed and was standing before her once again.

Bruno ran back toward Frankie, but started to lick Jack's hand as if it were his most favorite toy. Scott bent down on one knee and whistled for Bruno. "Come here, boy," but Bruno sat next to Jack's well-dressed clad leg and would not move.

"Hey, Romano, you attract dogs!" Scott teased as he stood up, slapping Jack's back. Bruno gave a low, rumbled growl, but when Jack began to stroke the dog's enormous soft-furred head, Bruno quieted and sat at attention.

"Frankie, this is Jack," Scott started the introductions.

"Hello," Frankie said very quietly, as she removed one mitten and extended her hand. She had to drop her eyes because she could no longer look into his dark ones. Those were the same eyes she looked into night after night and daydreamed about, day after day, which would turn the color of quicksilver whenever they made love.

"Jack, this is Doctor Frankie," Scott continued. "And we know you already know Bruno." He laughed again at his own joke.

"Hello." Jack responded softly then asked, "Frankie??" He reached for her tiny hand and held it as she lifted her gaze to meet his eyes. His other hand continued to stroke the dog's broad head. Jack was amazed when he saw Frankie's eyes start to change color right before his. His surprised expression made Frankie suddenly divert her attention back to their clasped hands.

"Francesca" was about all Frankie could manage to say in reply because her heart was racing wildly. His hand still held hers, and she could feel the warmth of his palm despite his lack of gloves. Her mind sprang to how many times she had kissed that very same hand in her dreams. How she would press her lips into the center of his palm. How that very same hand stroked her breasts. *Oh no, don't faint again,* she scolded herself.

"Francesca. That is a beautiful name, and it suits you."

"Thank you," Frankie barely whispered. Her head bowed again looking at their hands touching.

"About the other night, I should apologize for my..." Jack gently squeezed her hand.

Frankie quickly stopped him. "No, please. I'm sorry for your loss." Doctor Brenelli had called her the day after the incident in the hospital to see how she was feeling. He explained to her that the man who was shouting at her had just lost his wife.

"Thank you," Jack murmured as he stared into her deep pools of blue. *Sorry for your loss,* it was a phrase repeated to him since the accident, yet it brought no comfort because he felt no loss. Victoria was gone, and sick as it may sound, was going to be forgotten, because Jack finally accepted that he didn't love her. He never did. In fact, he didn't even like her. *God forgive me* he silently prayed, as he felt a wave of relief sweep over him. No longer would he have to work at a relationship that was never one to begin with. In that instant, as Jack looked into the clear blue pools before him, something felt oddly familiar.

"Jack and I were just heading over to Brady's. Do you want to join us?" Scott interjected.

Frankie retrieved her hand and quickly reached up to pull her knit cap tighter down over her ears, shaking her head from side to side. "We're trying to work off Thanksgiving." Frankie eyed Bruno who had over indulged himself with begging at the Thanksgiving table. So much so, that she and Becca had to practically haul his butt up into her truck when it was time to leave. "Another time," Frankie suggested, as she tried to avoid eye contact with Jack, whom she felt watching her. She turned back and looked deeply into his eyes.

Jack stared into the now familiar, blue pools almost wanting to dive in. He drew in a quick breath as he watched her blue eyes deepen in color. His chest began to tighten, and he placed his hand over his heart unconsciously.

Frankie looked back at Scott then back at Jack. She had no idea that Jack was this big. In fact he was even a bit taller than

Scott. Frankie clapped her hands together and started around them. "Let's go Bruno!" she called, as she started to jog away from the two men. Her knees felt like liquid, because her head began to swim with images of Jack's strong nude body.

As she jogged off, she glanced back and saw that Bruno was unmoving from Jack's side. Jack watched her eyes, quickly following their path to the dog at his feet. In a deep tone that commanded obedience, he ordered, "Bruno, go to Francesca." Jack pointed, and with that, Bruno leapt up and quickly caught up with Frankie.

"'Bye Scott! Nice to meet you, Jack," Frankie called out, and then half-whispered to herself, "Jacqino." Frankie watched Jack's expression of disbelief.

Did she just call me Jacqino? No one called him by his birth name. His father was the only person who used his given name, and that was usually when he wanted Jack's undivided attention, which was most of the time.

"'Bye," Scott called out to her. Jack watched her receding form and waved his hand in a goodbye. Bruno barked his goodbye twice then caught up with Frankie. Jack's eyes were shining.

"Frankie's beautiful, isn't she?" Scott asked, but already knew Jack's answer.

"Very. What's wrong with her?" Jack questioned sincerely.

"She's been battling cancer, but my friend, who works at the hospital, says she's just about got it beat. The worst part is over for her now. Come on, let's get that beer!" Scott flung his arm around Jack's shoulders, and the two unlikely friends set off down the street in the direction of Brady's.

When they entered the bar, Jack felt as though he had stepped into a pub in Ireland; its décor and walls covered with Irish paraphernalia. As they drank their dark beers, Scott spoke openly about his Irish family, and about his life as a fireman. He went into grueling detail about how intensive the training was to become a New York City fireman. Many hours later when they left the pub, Paul was waiting outside with the limo running, which was no surprise to Jack. He knew he would be there. That's just the way it was when you were a Romano. Jack turned to Scott and shook hands with him, their hands clasped in their new friendship. Quickly, Jack climbed into the back of the limo, and Scott watched the glow of the "Romano1" license plate fade into the distance.

Chapter Eight
Several months later…

Frankie's next few months were more of a blur than anything else. The holidays came and went in a never-ending mixture of gray skies, tiny white blinking Christmas lights, discarded wrapping paper, a burst of snow flurries that quickly turned black when they hit the city streets, and unlimited work. Work at Park East seemed to double overnight. In fact the partners of the hospital were so pleased that new referrals were always asking to see Dr. Frankie, they wasted no time in making certain she remained on staff. Frankie blinked many times when they substantially increased her salary. *I better not let my father know about this,* Frankie thought to herself. *He just might go out and buy me a castle which would need a new moat and a staff of a hundred!* She giggled under her breath and plunged ahead through her appointments.

Every night she would jog with Bruno the same way in the hopes of bumping into Jack again, yet she didn't see him. But because she was just feeling generally better, her morale was on the rise regardless. Her energy level and appetite steadily increased with the completion of her chemo treatments, and everyone commented on the bit of weight she gained. Her hair start to grow back—fine, blonde, peach fuzz graced her head like a golden halo and seemed so much brighter than before. *I guess Mrs. Mastellon was right,* Frankie thought.

One day she took a ride up to see the farmhouse for herself. She stood next to her father, and her mouth hung open in shock. The place was in appalling condition. The barn's roof sagged in the middle with a visible gaping hole in it, and the cottage, although kept clean, was severely outdated and in need of some major repairs the caretakers couldn't possibly afford. Nelson and Retta weren't there when they stopped up, but her father explained how Retta sold her home-baked goods in town to earn some extra money and to keep busy, since there was no one to take care of anymore. But as she looked around, she could see why her father bought the place. The land and view of the Hudson River below were incredible even in the cold, winter months with the trees bare and the wind whistling through their tangled limbs. She stood in the open field in front of the farmhouse and something seemed oddly familiar. She turned around—the farmhouse at her back—and for a split second Frankie could not breathe. She felt as though an unseen force had struck her.

"This is the place. This is the place in my dreams with Jacqino," she whispered to herself, covering her mouth with a trembling hand, sharply drawing in a long breath.

Her father stared at her thinking she was overwhelmed by the amount of work that needed to be done to the place. He wrapped his arm around her shoulder, propelling her back into her truck, and insisted she head back to the city.

Chapter Nine
Early spring…

After Jack's chance meeting with Scott, he started to view things a little differently. He wanted to change his life, and Romano Enterprises was preventing him from making the change. Scott spoke incessantly about how he wouldn't be anything else but a fireman, and Jack knew he didn't want to be anything else but an architect. He thought about this long and hard and finally after many months of planning, he called a board of directors meeting. Everyone was shocked with this impromptu meeting, but no one was more shocked than Anthony. He knew his brother well, and he knew that when Jack called a non-scheduled meeting, it would have colossal ramifications.

"Did we pick up a new account?" Anthony asked Jack's personal secretary.

"No, nothing like that, just a lot of updating and making sure that everything is in perfect order," Anna clarified and then elaborated further. "Mr. Romano, to be frank, your brother is driving the staff to the brink of exhaustion. He has us working around the clock throwing old files out, cleaning up current files. The officers are almost afraid to bump into him in the halls, because he grills them on this account or that. It's like he's a machine, and no matter how much work we all do, no one knows how to shut him off." Anna sighed.

Anthony scanned the office. Everyone seemed to be rushing about nervously. He even noticed dark circles around Anna's eyes. "Oh, I see." Anthony caught a passing manager whose eyes were likewise rimmed with visible circles and bags complementing the dark rings.

Jack was planning something, and Anthony could sense that it was big. The elevator doors slid open and out walked an older version of Jack. It was their father, Nicholas Romano, and to many, they were clones of each other. Same height and breadth—even those deep, black eyes were identical. The only differences were the fine lines around his eyes and a few silvery gray strands streaking through his father's gleaming blue-black hair. He was in excellent shape compared to his uncles who were just as old. His uncles were much shorter and lost their hard bodies long ago with too much red wine, too much fine Italian cuisine, and not enough exercise.

"Anthony. Why has Jacqino called this meeting?" Nicholas spoke in a deep, low tone, which Jack also inherited.

"He didn't say." Anthony raised his hands up slightly then dropped them back down. They both walked into the boardroom, Nicholas tall and dark, and Anthony tall and light.

The meeting was called to order once Uncle Tony took a seat. Uncle Tony always deliberately ran late in an effort to ruffle feathers. It was a gift he had. He just loved to agitate anyone. After all he was a Scarpelli. The well-dressed directors, most of them relatives, settled back into their deep, burgundy leather chairs which surrounded a huge, carved mahogany table with enormous, lion-clawed feet at each corner and a cluster of large clawed feet centered directly under the center of the table.

Romano Enterprises kept everyone wealthy beyond anyone's original imagination. With a quick scan of the room, Jack absorbed just how much wealth exuded from each and every director and the power that came with such monetary standing. Jack noticed everyone seemed anxious to start the meeting, except for Uncle Tony.

Uncle Tony, who was Nicholas' brother-in-law and Anthony's godfather, lit a long, thick cigar and began to puff at it repeatedly. Uncle Vinny, who was Nicholas' brother and Jack's godfather, waved at the smoke.

"Jack!" Uncle Vinny coughed. "I thought Romano Enterprises issued a 'no smoking' policy?" Uncle Vinny curled his lip at the smoke, prompting Uncle Tony to purposely blow more smoke in his direction.

"Please, Uncle Ton, *Padrino* Vinny," Jack pleaded.

"*Che*?!" They both answered him in unison as if there was nothing wrong with their constant back-and-forth.

"I would like to begin." Jack stood up and walked over to the windows, looking down at Central Park, something he never paid attention to before—how grand it was, so green, and bustling with life. Not until today. It was the first week in April, and the flowering trees were ripe with blooms. Jack thought, perhaps, he would take a walk in the grand old park after the meeting, something he never considered before. He had just let life pass him by. But that was all about to change, he prayed silently.

Turning to face his board members and the secretaries who took notes during the meeting, Jack spoke in a clear, confident voice. "Ladies, Father, uncles, gentlemen, I will get directly to the point. I am resigning as President of Romano Enterprises, effective June first." Complete silence fell over the room. All mouths hung open—and only Anthony seemed to be prepared for this speech as he leaned back to study his pen.

"You knew!" Uncle Tony accused, watching Anthony's expressionless face.

"Nope, not a clue!" Anthony quickly responded to his godfather.

"Uncle Ton," Jack continued, "no one knew anything about this, not even the staff. I just made this decision recently. I have already met with the legal department and specifically directed them not to speak about it to anyone. I will waive any severance, but will hold my stocks of Romano Enterprises. I will also waive the balance of my annual salary, even though my employment contract states otherwise. You all know that Romano Enterprises is having an incredible run, and first quarter profits were the best in the history of the company. The business portfolio is in the black and will continue to be profitable for many, many years to come."

Nicholas began to shake his head from side to side. He could not believe that his eldest son would make such an immense decision without first discussing it with him. He felt his heart rate increase, certain that it was going to explode. He rose up slowly from his chair, to his full six-foot-two inches, and spoke in a deep, direct tone of voice. "Leave me and my son." Nicholas glowered only at Jack.

Anthony watched his father and brother with a raised eyebrow, as the identical pairs of black eyes pierced back and forth in a duel of wills. Anthony recognized that look, and so did Nicholas. They had both seen that same look of determination and defiance in Jack's eyes before, and its resolve was unmistakable. Jack was determined, Nicholas knew, but he would try to change his son's mind, nonetheless. Everyone made their way out of the boardroom as quickly as they could, with the exception of Uncle Tony and Uncle Vinny, who were elbowing each other. Uncle Vinny continued to cough and complain about the stench Uncle Tony's oversized cigar was causing, announcing that he could finally get a breath of fresh air.

Anthony stood up and took the cigar from his godfather. "I'll take that outside for you, *Padrino*," Anthony suggested, bringing the cigar to his lips and taking a deep drag.

"But Anthony!" Uncle Tony protested.

Jack quickly shot out, "Anthony—stay!"

Anthony turned, cigar between his teeth, meeting his father's eyes imploring him for an answer. He hated when these two went at it. It was like watching two planets collide, explosive and powerful. Anthony would rather stand out in the hall between Uncle Tony and Uncle Vinny or even in oncoming traffic. Either choice was safer than staying, he mused.

"Leave us." Nicholas bellowed to Anthony's unspoken question.

"Stay, damn it." Jack defied their father.

Anthony kicked the door closed and flung himself back into his chair, shaking his head not knowing which direction to go.

"How dare you? How could you be so ungrateful?" Nicholas hissed slamming his hand flat onto the dark, mahogany table, making pens, glasses, even eyeglasses leap. "This is a disgrace to me and our family! How could you?" Nicholas scowled, shooting the same black, piercing eyes right back into Jack's eyes.

"*Padre*," Jack spoke softly to his father in Italian, "please don't turn this into something it doesn't have to be…please." Jack pleaded softly.

Anthony could not believe the quiet reserve Jack was showing. Jack never backed down from his father. Never! And he certainly never begged. It was at that moment Anthony started to understand the full impact of this meeting. Jack was going to leave Romano Enterprises, and if that meant never speaking to his family again, so be it.

In that same instant, Nicholas absorbed Jack's tone and meaning as well. Never had Nicholas heard his son speak in such a defeated voice. The three of them looked from one to the other. Strong, beautiful Italian men filled with passion.

Jack turned toward the windows and spoke just barely above a whisper. "I have to start to live my life. This is the first day I have felt happy in years," Jack explained quietly as he stared out the window.

Nicholas felt something deep within his gut twist. His son was sad, unhappy. "Does this have anything to do with Victoria?"

Nicholas spoke softly while walking over to stand next to Jack at the large windows.

"I'm not sure," Jack managed and lowered his head.

Nicholas faced his son, reached up and rested his hand on Jack's shoulder. Jack turned towards his father, and Nicholas embraced Jack as he if were a small boy all over again. Pressing a kiss against his son's cheek, he tried to lessen the pain he could see through his son's eyes.

"I love you, my son," Nicholas' voice choked with tenderness.

Anthony joined his father and brother, swinging his arms around the two men who meant everything to him.

"Thank you," Jack said to both his father and brother, fighting back deep emotions. "I love you both."

The board members were asked to return to the boardroom, and Jack continued his meeting. "Please know that I mean no disrespect. It has been a great honor for me to be President of RE." Jack's eyes scanned the room's occupants, trying to gauge the reaction of the board members.

"At this time, I would like to suggest a replacement. I highly recommend that the board appoint Anthony, my brother, to succeed me as President of Romano Enterprises." Jack spoke clearly from the head of the long, hand-carved table.

Anthony looked from his brother, to his father, then to his uncles and the other board members. He held the cigar he was finishing for his uncle just before his lips.

"But, Jacqino, you have a head for all the numbers. Anthony is good at the traveling and buying for RE," Uncle Vinny stated flatly.

"No, *Padrino*," Jack answered his godfather respectfully. "Anthony is knowledgeable in every aspect of Romano Enterprises. In fact, I could never do Anthony's job, but he could quite easily do mine." There was great silence, and Jack turned to look out the windows down to the green park below, which somehow beckoned him. He could taste his freedom, and was not about to let it go for anything. "I will leave you to your decision. Thank you, ladies, Father, Uncles, *Padrino*, brother, and loyal friends." Jack left the boardroom and walked the length of hall to the elevators. The secretarial staff watched his retreating figure, grateful he wasn't piling more work on them, as the news of his recent resignation was spreading like wildfire.

Once inside the elevators, he let out a long-held breath he didn't realize he was holding, and a wave of calm descended on him. He walked out of the elevator, surprising security, who was always informed as to Mr. Romano's appointments.

"Mr. Romano, can I...ahh...call your chauffeur?" The security guard stood up quickly from behind a counter near the entrance of Romano Enterprises.

"No..." Jack paused to read the nametag. He passed this man for many years, even before he became president and didn't know his name. He never wanted to know his name. *That's going to change, too*, he thought with a smile. "...Sam. I'm going for a walk. In fact, you should, too. It is such a beautiful, spring day."

The guard stared at Jack as if Jack had just grown two heads right before his eyes. Jack flashed him a white, bright smile as he left the building, trotting across the street, eating up the distance to the entrance of the park which had called to him all day. Jack stood at the park's entrance for a moment, studying the day, the noises, and the emerald-green colors of the newly formed leaves and grass. The air was crisp and clean, and the sun shone strongly amid a clear robin's-egg blue sky, warming life up again.

With his hands deep in his pockets, Jack walked for quite awhile. He headed around the lake that he saw from his office windows high above and took a trail off to the right instead of continuing around the lake. He wound his way along the path and started to think about his future. He had all the degrees to be an architect, but no job. "I guess I'm going to have to get a job!" Jack laughed at himself quietly. "A multimillionaire seeking employment!" Jack started to laugh a little louder, his laughter continued to grow.

People were passing by him, trying not to stare at him strangely. They just figured it was another corporate exec apparently losing his mind from all the pressures of working in the city.

Within seconds of Jack's outburst of laughter, an enormous dog came bounding straight towards him. Just behind the dog was a blond woman wearing scrubs, chasing after him, and shouting an exasperated *'Heel'* at the top of her lungs. Jack recognized the dog immediately. He bent down on one knee as Bruno practically knocked him over. The big dog licked his face and hands. Bruno began to box with Jack, lifting first one paw and knocking it against Jack's hand and then the other.

Frankie stopped a distance from the scene. Her body knew who it was long before her mind could assimilate. She felt as though her entire being was being pulled in, as she held her breath.

"Cease! Cease you beast!" Jack half-laughed, half-commanded and Bruno immediately sat erect next to Jack's leg. Jack looked up from his crouched position, staring straight into Frankie's eyes. He noticed that her hair was just about to her ears, still very short, and that her face was flushed from her chase.

Jack slowly stood to his full height and began to close the distance between them to stand just in front of her. He looked down at her and had to fight the urge to reach out and touch her hair. It was blowing about her in a halo of gold.

Frankie unconsciously raised a hand trying to tuck a piece of hair behind her ear that would not reach. Her hand held there for a moment before she dropped it to her side.

"Francesca, you look well," Jack spoke gently, looking into her blue eyes that were starting to darken.

"Thank you, Jacqino. So do you." This was the first time she had ever spoken his name directly to him.

"You...called me Jacqino?" Jack appeared shocked.

"It is your name, isn't it?" Frankie asked.

"Yes, but not too many people call me..."

Before Jack could finish, Frankie quickly changed the subject. "Bruno, I have a good mind to leave you in the apartment all day tomorrow," she scolded him. Bruno lied down next to Jack's right highly polished, black leather shoe, looking up at Frankie with that *What did I do* look upon his face. She supposed her dog was really *man's* best friend.

"Beautiful," Jack spoke softly.

"Excuse me?" Frankie asked turning her attention back to Jack as a great gust of wind started blowing her hair about again.

Jack couldn't resist the impulse to smooth away her hair that just reached her eyes. His hand stroked her incredibly soft golden hair away from her eyes. The fragrance of roses was filling his senses. The feel of her hair against his fingertips, *just like silk*, he thought, was causing his heart hammer in his chest.

Frankie could barely breathe. His hand was large and warm,

and his actual touch was like nothing Frankie could've ever imagined or recalled from her dreams. It was magical, almost spellbinding.

Jack began to notice that her blue eyes were deepening further. "Beautiful day." Jack clarified, letting his hand drop to his side so as not to frighten this golden beauty away. "Let's walk, Francesca," Jack suggested with a nod of his head.

Bruno rose and began to walk beside Jack, ignoring Frankie completely. Frankie bowed her head feeling the warmth of his body intensifying just inches from her, causing the hairs on her exposed arm closest to him to rise in anticipation of his touch. She began to rub her bare arm and before Frankie could protest, Jack slipped off his jacket, draping it over Frankie's shoulders. It was enormous on her, but the warmth inside of it and his scent that emanated from it was making her mind dance with images of him from the many dreams she'd had of him. As his fragrance surrounded her, she could feel him close his jacket around her, drawing her in close to him, just before he kissed her forehead.

Frankie's dreams could never have prepared her for the first touch of his lips. Her senses startled to life. She closed her eyes trying to calm her reaction as he pressed his lips onto her skin.

"Better?" he asked, lifting her chin so that she looked directly into his eyes.

"Yes," Frankie barely answered.

He took her hand into his, lacing his large fingers through her small ones as they started to walk together. Neither spoke a word to the other.

Jack could not believe he just kissed her. *What are you thinking, man?* He scolded himself silently. *You are going to scare her off!*

Frankie struggled to walk on legs that felt wobbly and unsteady. Her heart was pounding in her chest. Being so near him, feeling her hand cradled in his, was wreaking havoc inside her because of all of the intimate things they had done with each other in her dreams. She tried to push those thoughts out of her mind, but it was impossible. She was always trying to remember every detail of any dream she ever had of him at every waking moment, and now she was forcing her mind to do the complete opposite.

BEEP, BEEP, BEEP! Frankie's beeper sounded off. Then the cell phone started in, followed by that stupid vibrating device that she still couldn't figure out and was contemplating tossing into the lake. She stopped and looked up at Jack. *He's all man*, she studied, *projecting a quiet strength and virility*. She slowly unlaced her fingers from his. She pulled open his jacket and lifted the side of her scrub to read the number flashing on the pager.

"It's an emergency," she stated depressingly. "I have to go." She started to remove his jacket, but his hands reached up and pulled it back onto her shoulders, resting his hands there.

"When will I see you again?" Jack spoke softly. He wasn't about to let this chance meeting slip by without making an attempt to see her again or finding out a way to contact her.

Frankie was completely unable to answer him. His nearness was making it impossible for her to think, let alone speak coherently. *I'm in love with you. I want to make love to you, Jacqino*, her mind kept screaming inside the walls of her head.

"I have to go," Frankie choked out softly.

"I have a boat at Pier 32. Her name is The Rose," Jack almost pleaded.

"I have to..." Frankie stopped speaking because Jack's hand began to smooth her away her hair. With his other hand, he lifted her chin while lowering his head. Gently he placed a soft kiss on her lips. It was their first real kiss, and his touch was magical. She felt her body begin to rise with longing for him. She placed her hands on his chest to steady herself feeling his heart drumming under her right hand.

When Jack lifted his dark head, he waited for her eyes to open. When they did, he was amazed to see that her dark blue pools deepened to a shade of midnight blue. Jack felt that mysterious pull in his chest again as he tugged his jacket even tighter around her shoulders. "Return it to me," Jack suggested.

Frankie turned away, speechless, and quickened her pace out of the park, with Bruno right at her side.

Jack could still smell her scent long after she disappeared out of sight. Roses, he could still smell roses.

Chapter Ten
When will my dream come true…

After her chance meeting with Jack, Frankie was valiantly trying to gather up enough courage to return both of his jackets she now had. Standing at the head of Pier 32, Frankie clutched the jackets close to her, pressing her face into them to inhale once again his spicy sandalwood scent. She was in love with what that fragrance did to her senses, how it entwined her insides into knots, how it turned her knees to liquid. She stared at The Rose the only craft moored to the pier, and recognized it from her dreams. It was a rather large boat and appeared much larger in person than from her dreams, though its color stood true and reminded Frankie of a pearl.

From her dreams, she knew what some of the ship looked like on the inside and conjured up those pictures in her mind. The cool, late-spring breeze tossed her hair about. She tried to will her legs to move forward, but they seemed to have a mind of their own. It was as if something or someone was telling her that now was not the right time. Clutching the jackets to her breasts, she quickly turned on her heel and ran from the pier, racing home. With tears streaming down her face she passed a newsstand. The headlines read "Romano Enterprises President Resigns," with a full-blown picture of Jack across the front page. The article inside went into great detail about this family's great fortune and recent misfortune with the loss of Jack's wife, but Frankie didn't notice. She was too caught up in the waiting and the wondering of what was going to happen next. It was driving her to the edge of insanity. When were they going to be together? Where? What time? The unknown was causing her sensibilities to falter. She needed to get away from the city.

That afternoon, she drove up to her farm and still could not believe how decrepit the place looked. Pulling up the drive, she noticed that her father looked very annoyed and somewhat distressed. Frankie stopped her truck and held the door open as Bruno bounded out of the truck in one leap, making tracks at a feverish pace towards the water's edge.

"Dad, this place looks even more frightening than the last time I was here." Frankie was being blunt.

"I know..." Thomas trailed off because Bruno caught his eye. The dog was speeding at a maddening pace towards the dilapidated dock. "This place is a nightmare, I have to admit."

They both laughed as Thomas quickly kissed his daughter's rosy cheek, happy to see how healthy and beautiful she was looking these last few weeks, as he wrapped her in his arms. Thomas watched Bruno over his daughter's golden head, as the dog tried to stand on the dock which hung rather precariously into the river, barking downriver at nothing or maybe something in particular.

"I just fired the architect." Thomas explained the latest dilemma as he pulled back to watch her expression. "He was an idiot. He wanted me to agree to tear down the farmhouse, to start from the foundation up, but I just can't see doing that." Thomas seemed to be asking his daughter for approval.

"I have to agree, the place is starting to grow on me. I'm sure you'll find the right person soon. Give it a little time," Frankie suggested as she lifted her hand over her father's handsome cheek. She left it all up to him, because she just did not have the time to devote to such an enormous project.

"Come daughter, I want you to meet Nelson and Retta. You are going to love them." Thomas smiled down at her as he led her towards the cottage, glancing over his shoulder for just a moment to watch Bruno still barking incessantly at nothing downriver. "Is there something wrong with him?" Thomas asked.

"Nothing medically," Frankie shrugged and laughed.

Frankie's father was right about Nelson and Retta. She did fall in love with them, so warm and friendly they both were. Nelson was a dark, gentle giant. He kept calling Frankie, "Doc," and Retta, with her large brown hands, kept putting home-baked foods in front of her. It was the beginning of June, and the farm was alive with colors and sounds. The trees were filled with green leaves, and the fields around the farm and cottage sprung tall with new sweet grass and wildflowers all the way to the river's bank.

"I was hoping that I could spend the weekend up here, but I guess the house isn't ready for that yet?" Frankie asked her father.

"There is no reason why you can't," Thomas replied.

"Really!" Frankie sounded almost relieved. She couldn't go

back to the city so close to Jack. She needed time to think. She needed to accept whatever the future held for her.

"Sure, the bedroom and bath on the south side of the house are actually livable and in working order," Thomas explained.

Frankie and her father left Nelson and Retta and strolled from the cottage along the rear of the farmhouse. Quite suddenly, Frankie got the most indescribable feeling as something flashed through her mind. The farm seemed to be familiar in her dreams of Jack, she knew. But, just at that moment, her mind unconsciously began to replay a beautiful day she and Jack spent together, kissing and holding each other tightly, right at this very spot where she now stood. It wasn't a remembered dream; it was a prediction, a premonition. Without any warning, Bruno came charging up toward them, breaking Frankie's concentration. Frankie turned to her father, whose expression appeared perplexed, as she realized that she had not been answering him for some time.

Thomas knew he needed to get this place squared away so his daughter could have some peace. From the way she acting, Thomas knew she was not at peace and was convinced that her job and the pressures associated with it were making her ill.

From the front steps of the old farmhouse, Frankie waved goodbye to her father. She closed the large door and began to walk through the old house and, in an odd way, everything felt familiar to her—it felt like home. She made her way up the large formal staircase to the only bedroom not demolished from the contractors, whom the original architect had hired. She washed and undressed for bed. She reached into her overnight bag, drew out a short, pale-blue, cotton nightgown, and pulled the gown over her head. Digging through her overnight bag, she found her thick hairbrush. It felt wonderful to have hair again and the rhythmic pull of the brush through her hair began to relax her. She returned her brush to her bag and climbed into the bed, thinking about the wonderful day she spent with her father, Nelson, and Retta. It was a relief to get away from the city for even just a day. She enjoyed sharing Retta's wonderfully delicious dinner and how they laughed and teased each other as if they had all known each other for years.

As Bruno settled down for the night at the foot of the bed, Frankie looked around the bedroom and was happy with the peace the old farm brought to her. She tried to relax, but her thoughts of Jack continued to persist. Most everything here at the farm reminded Frankie of her dreams of him. Pulling the sheet up her body, she listened to a large tanker drift down the Hudson sounding its low bullhorn in the late spring night. The windows in the bedroom were open just a little. The sounds from the passing ships and barges, together with the gentle summer breeze and the sound of water lapping along the bank lulled Frankie into a deep sleep.

Jack tossed and turned on The Rose. He got out of bed and winced at the pain in his upper thighs and throbbing biceps. Recently, Scott had convinced him to start working out with him, but Jack soon realized that the man had no limitation. In fact, Scott was a borderline lunatic when it came to exercise. He ran Jack for miles, made him lift enormous amounts of weights, and now every muscle in his body was screaming with pain at the slightest movement.

Stiffly, Jack eased himself out of bed, hobbling to the window overlooking the lights that outlined the passing ships and barges. He rubbed his bicep, but that only made the ache worse. His mind was working in overdrive.

So many things had happened since that day he announced his resignation from Romano Enterprises. He had worked long, hard hours to ready the company for his brother's presidency. And on June 1st, the changing of the guard took place. The press and photographers had a feeding frenzy with the latest transfer of power at Romano Enterprises. Jack closed his eyes and, in just that moment, he called to mind the non-stop flash of camera bulbs and the mountains of questions shot at Anthony. His brother, smiling smugly from behind the desk Jack once occupied, handled the press like no president of Romano Enterprises ever had. He teased and joked with them and kept the atmosphere light and playful. *Guaranteed,* Jack grinned, *that smug will be a frown before the end of the week.*

After the press conference, Anthony needled Jack incessantly that if he couldn't find work, Anthony could always find something for him to do in an entry-level position at Romano's. But Jack had no monetary problems whatsoever. His portfolio was vast and consistently profitable, allowing Jack his freedom.

When Jack was in college, he loved his architectural studies and thought that maybe, someday he could design for a living. The architecture studies were like second-nature to Jack, but the business studies were another story. He thought he would never get past quantitative analysis, but he did it. He never did want the presidency of Romano Enterprises and was only chosen because of his business studies that would benefit Romano Enterprises. His brother, Anthony, was the one who should have been made president; since it was in Anthony's blood to travel the world buying goods and predicting the future, knowing what people wanted and needed, before they wanted and needed it. Anthony would stare in great wonder when he discovered a 17th-century armoire with original hand-painting on it from France or just gape at a 16th-century silver candelabrum envisioning a dozen glowing, tall, tapered candles that once graced a Duke's 30-foot long banquet table.

But for Jack, there was no thrill in such findings and purchases. Instead he used any overseas trip to study any architectural wonder. Now it was Jack's turn to follow his creative heart and pursue architecture and design. He took some time to set up a room on The Rose just for drafting. He purchased a drafting table with a built-in diffuser panel—Anthony probably could've done a much better job with Jack's other purchases: an ergonomic high chair, swing-arm lamp, mechanical pencils, straight edges, plotter pens, vellum, drafting film, and blueprint sheets to transfer copies. He also purchased a new computer with the latest version of AutoCad and a specialty printer and began to draw anything and everything that popped into his head. It felt so good to draw again, to channel those creative juices.

Just today, Jack and the skipper of The Rose decided to stretch her sea legs a bit. They navigated her upriver, and Jack remembered just how much he enjoyed boating and just how much he missed it. It was great to take The Rose out for a jaunt, and Jack was grateful to escape from Scott and his relentless workouts. Jack peered through his quintessential set of binoculars and scrutinized all the architectural wonders along the river's banks. One large, white building, in great disrepair, stood out in particular. Jack noticed a dilapidated farmhouse, an old barn with a sagging roofline, and a cottage just to the side of the barn. There was a dog barking from a dilapidated dock which leaned precariously to one side. He noticed some people walking around the property and wondered how anyone could live there. He asked his skipper to mark the location of the area so he could research the property's owner.

Once they were docked back at the pier, Jack input the information into his computer and within seconds a Thomas O'Brian, with his phone number, appeared on the screen. Jack called Mr. O'Brian, and to Jack's great surprise, the man actually agreed to meet with him the following day at noon, to view the property. Jack explained that he had recently made a career change and if they could come to an agreement, the farmhouse would be his first architectural project. This O'Brian didn't seem put-off and Jack couldn't be more pleased. *Wouldn't Anthony get a kick out of that?* Jack smiled at the thought.

Jack shifted his weight to his other leg and silently cursed the day he agreed to work out with Scott. *Even my hands hurt*, Jack inwardly groaned, as he studied his bruised hands in horror. Scott made him climb a rope at the gym with weights strapped to his ankles and wrists. *I must have been out of my mind to have ever agreed to that stunt*; Jack again scolded himself while examining his growing blisters and calluses.

Hobbling back toward the bed Jack recalled yesterday's phone call with his brother Anthony. Anthony made it quite clear to Jack that the presidents of Romano Enterprises had been grossly underpaid, most likely, since the inception of the company. Jack smiled as he replayed the recent conversation. Anthony spoke about business matters with ease, and Jack knew he already had a handle on the position. He also asked, rather cautiously, if Jack needed any help cleaning out the apartment that he and Victoria shared, but Jack declined his brother's help, and when Anthony pressed him again, Jack insisted that he would do it himself.

The only thing that seemed to keep him calm in all of this turmoil in his life was this golden angel named Francesca. The mere thought of her gave him such an instant feeling of peacefulness. He kept hoping that she would come by The Rose, but she didn't. He was just beginning to realize how innocent and shy she must be, and that it was highly unlikely she was ever going to make a move like that. Jack wanted to see her again, so much so, that he made a point of walking through Central Park everyday and to even pass by the emergency room entrance at the hospital where she worked. But he hadn't seen her—it was like she vanished into thin air. He thought about asking Scott how he could get in touch with her, but he just didn't find the right time to ask, and wasn't sure if there was any history there. *Timing was*, he thought, *without a doubt, everything.* He watched the ships and barges pass, listening to the sounds of their deep bullhorns, their wakes gently swaying the yacht. But Jack's mind kept drifting back to Francesca. He thought about how silky her hair felt between his fingertips. How incredibly soft her skin was when he pressed his lips to her forehead and how her mouth opened slightly for a tender kiss. How tiny her hand was in his when he held it. How his hand smelled of roses long after she left.

"Scott!" Jack hissed as he struggled to settle himself back in the bed. Tears nearly sprang to his eyes. He cursed Scott as he lifted the sheet up over his taut nude body. His arms and legs were throbbing. Earlier that evening, Scott had them run through all five boroughs. Okay, maybe that was an exaggeration, but it sure felt like it.

Jack slowly closed his eyes, feeling the boat subtly sway, as a vision of Francesca danced in his mind. Jack summoned up her kind smile and the way her eyes turned to sapphires whenever he looked into them. The mere thought of her relaxed his mind, his muscles gradually began to ease, and he began to drift off to sleep.

Jack could see Francesca smile and pictured her wearing worn jeans and a white T-shirt. She was walking with him across an open, green field. In his mind, he stopped to look at her, unconsciously lifting his hand, smoothing a strand of golden hair behind her ear. Her hair was a little longer since he'd last seen her. A gentle breeze blew as she looked up at him—he leaned his head down to kiss her lips gently at first, then much more deeply. He watched as she traced her hands over his chest and up around his neck. His hands slid up and down the sides of her breasts. Jack could feel her hands move to his shoulders, clinging to him as he continued to caress her. He lowered her down into the tall grass, enveloping them both in a sea of sweet-smelling green. He ran his hand onto her flat stomach under her T-shirt, her skin felt warm and soft. The scent of roses filled the air. His hand continued up under her T-shirt until her lace bra tickled his fingertips. Slowly she unbuttoned several buttons on his shirt, slipped her small hand inside his shirt and caressed his chest. She stopped and rested her hand over his heart; they looked deeply into each other's eyes. Jack could feel her warm hand against his chest, and the sensation of her touch made everything serene. He could see himself taking her lips once more. She parted her lips slightly, and he wasted no time dipping his tongue deep inside her warm, inviting mouth, tasting her as she tasted him. He could feel his heart hammering against her tiny hand and the feeling in his chest was almost painful, yet somehow comforting. Jack slipped into a very deep sleep with his hand resting over his heart.

The next morning, Jack woke, began to stretch, and then let out a bark of pain. His muscles almost snapped, as his teeth clenched together. Silently, cursing the day Scott was born, he vowed to avoid that man like the plague! He sat up in bed and started to bring to mind his dream. He dreamed of his Francesca, beautiful, open, and willing. *But it was only a dream, right? His Francesca*, he thought, with a smile crossing his lips. He was going to find some way to see her again, even if that meant that he had to whistle for that dog of hers all over the damn city. With that, he threw off the covers and stiffly walked into the bathroom to get ready for his meeting with Mr. O'Brian.

Jack eased his car onto the highway towards the farmhouse, about an hour's drive from the city. His muscles in his right leg still throbbed as he stepped down on the gas.

Jack brought his vintage red Corvette to a steady cruising speed and simply enjoyed the ride. The sky was clear blue, and the air was warm with a hint of humidity. Jack felt relief that he was no longer under the massive responsibilities of Romano Enterprises. Today he was free to think about the rough plans he drafted for the farmhouse, rolled up in a long canister in the trunk. The ride went by quickly with the view of the Hudson River never really leaving his sight for long. The directions got a little haphazard after he left the main highway, because there were no street signs and most of the roads were dirt. After driving a while on one dirt road, Jack made a right past the old stump that looked like a frog, and then a left at Thompson's Dairy Farm.

Three miles past the dairy farm, Jack caught his first view of the old farmhouse.

This project was perfect for him. His mind quickly scanned the current architecture, and he knew from the overall height of the building that the ceilings had to be at least 12 feet, if not more, in some places. He could hardly contain himself. He stepped on the accelerator as the Corvette made a trail of dust behind him, kicking up pebbles and dirt as he pulled onto a gravel driveway.

Thomas O'Brian came back to the farm early that morning hoping to convince his daughter to stay to meet the potential new architect, but she had already left for the city. Retta told him that Frankie had some tea and a slice of freshly baked cinnamon toast and said she would call her father during the week. As a red sports car pulled into the drive, Thomas walked the length of the porch to the steps.

Jack watched as the tall, casually dressed man bounded down the few steps and walked right over to Jack's car. He stopped the Corvette and climbed out, wincing from his still-aching muscles, stiff from the past hour's drive in the car's tight quarters. He closed the car door and reached for Mr. O'Brian's outstretched hand.

"Hi. I'm Jack Romano."

"Yes, Jack, good to meet you. I'm Thomas O'Brian."

"Mr. O'Brian." Jack shook the older gentleman's hand.

"Please, just Thomas."

"Alright, Thomas," Jack agreed, looking directly at Thomas.

Thomas felt instinctively that this was the man for the job. He could tell by Jack's expression he was impressed with the farm. Thomas also took note in the way he carried himself. It spoke of a quiet confidence and integrity.

"This place is great!" Jack lifted his hands heavenward. "I'm sure you have lots of ideas and I want to hear all of them. Why don't we get started? Here are my credentials, Mister...ahh... Thomas. I just want to remind you that this is my first architectural assignment."

Thomas looked at Jack and took the papers he held out to him. Something was familiar about this young man, but Thomas just couldn't put his finger on it. "Son, if you put as much enthusiasm in this place as I see in your eyes, I don't think I need to see these," Thomas stated firmly, returning to Jack his credentials.

"Please, I insist." Jack pushed them back into Thomas' hand.

Thomas wasted no time telling Jack exactly what he wanted. He wanted the farmhouse brought back to its original glory, but with modern modifications. He explained to Jack that he needed the barn to be expanded to accommodate a veterinary hospital, and Jack was both impressed with the idea and thrilled with the challenge. He was going to have to do some research on the types of equipment that would be housed in a facility like that.

Thomas explained there was a brick patio buried under the back of the farmhouse that connected all the buildings and how this patio swelled out at the rear and side of the farmhouse in a circular pattern, offering the best view of the river. He wanted it uncovered and extended to accommodate a new driveway, hoping that Jack could find salvaged brick to complete the look. He also discussed his plan to tier the steps to the dock and that he wanted the dock rebuilt. He also wanted the cottage refurbished. They walked through each building, with Jack taking constant notes and sketching tiny pictures here and there. During the discussion of the dock, the subject of boating and sailing kept the conversation flowing for many hours as both men were very experienced boat owners.

"Well, I do have some rough, preliminary drawings that I would like to go over with you." Jack removed the canister from the trunk of his car and spread the drawings onto the hood.

Thomas' eyes bulged. The drawings only showed the outside of each building, but he could see that each architectural detail was restored. He was surprised that Jack had done this much work to prepare for this first meeting in such a short period of time, as he told him he only spotted the property from the river yesterday. *Thank God he's not like the last architect*, Thomas glanced heavenward. "This is exactly what I had in mind." Thomas looked at the drawings in disbelief.

"I'm glad to hear that. So many times, it is more cost effective to level the buildings and start all over again. I was afraid you were going to suggest that at first."

"No, but I have been down that road already." Thomas shook his head in disgust.

"I need to snap some pictures, inside and out, take lots of measurements, and then I'll call you in a week to set up another appointment to review the plans. The barn conversion will be, by far, the most challenging aspect to the project, and I am sure that will take several drafts. Then the fun really begins," Jack looked back at the old farmhouse, "because that is when we roll up our sleeves and turn this great, old place around."

Thomas was so pleased with Jack he was speechless and almost wanted to hug the boy. Instead, he silently thanked God again for delivering this young man to him, because for the last few days, he was seriously considering selling the place. But Jack had eased his fears with his apparent knowledge and confidence. He demonstrated all the signs of being professional and businesslike. Funny, Thomas thought he knew Jack from somewhere. Thomas could tell that Jack was a fine young man, and he was glad that Jack was eager to begin. Thomas liked the sound of that. He knew this man was going to do a great job and get the job done quickly, which meant his daughter could leave the city and start her practice here sooner.

"Since both of us have boats, why don't we make that dock our first priority? That way you could dock here if you like and keep a close eye on the progress, and if you wouldn't mind, I could dock my boat here as well," Jack suggested. "That would certainly save me the time driving up here each day to make sure all the contractors are doing things exactly the way we want them to be done. Also, if anything comes up, I'll be right here to address each situation as it arises."

This was music to Thomas' ears. Finally, he was going to get his daughter off that treadmill of a job. Thomas agreed immediately with Jack's suggestion, and Jack thought he saw tears glisten in Thomas' eyes. Allergies, Jack mused.

Jack had the plans and budget for the project ready in three days. The hospital was, of course, the biggest expense. After their meeting to review Jack's plans, Thomas was impressed and thrilled with everything Jack had incorporated into his plans from the many ideas Thomas suggested from their original meeting. The price was a little more than the previous architect had quoted, but Thomas didn't care if it was double.

Once Jack took hold of the project, Thomas knew he couldn't have picked a better man for the job. It seemed that progress was Jack's middle name. In just the first week, Jack already had the old dock torn down and hauled away. A new apron had been secured along the shoreline, and a new floating dock was being shipped upriver by barge to be permanently installed onto the apron. Incorporated into the dock design were motors to run during the winter months to prevent freezing. The new dock would be ready for the Fourth of July weekend, and Jack prepared to take The Rose up to the new dock on Friday. The Rose would remain docked at the site for the next six months, which was the estimated time to complete all of the renovations.

"To think, in six months my daughter will finally leave that city."

"Your daughter?!" Jack asked surprised, as they watched the crane remove the dock from the barge.

"You see, son, my daughter is a vet at Park East Animal Hospital, and she works non-stop. I purchased the farm on her behalf, originally unbeknownst to her, so that she could leave that hectic pace and open her own practice. She has a great reputation, and people come from all over just to have her take care of their pets."

"Shouldn't I meet with her to go over these plans, especially the hospital?" Jack looked worried. "After all she is going to be living here and will be doctoring the animals in this hospital. I'd like to include any special features she might want."

"She won't take the time to do that." Thomas dismissed the thought. "I'm telling you, Jack, that daughter of mine has been driving me and my wife to a state of indescribable worry. She has no life but those animals. She is constantly being paged and is forever flying off on this emergency or that. I should have insisted she study accounting and made her work for me. Her mother and I are concerned about her health, and we just want her to enjoy her life."

Jack knew the feeling. "I can certainly relate to that," Jack nodded understandingly.

Jack and the skipper took The Rose to the newly constructed dock at the farmhouse. The skipper and two hands made arrangements to get rides back with some of the construction workers. The dock was built with new synthetic materials as hard as concrete, but stronger and more lightweight. It went into place quickly and efficiently. Jack already drove the head contractor crazy with demands, but he didn't mind because he knew Jack would make him rich. He knew that once word got out about the kind of architect Jack Romano was, referrals would start pouring in, high-end referrals, and he wanted to be aboard for the ride.

Once The Rose was moored in place, Jack, the skipper, and crew immediately began to clean the yacht down after her trip up the Hudson. The physical exercise was just what Jack needed. Now his muscles ached from non-use, and Jack silently cursed Scott again. *The guy is a pain even when he isn't around*, Jack thought, a smile crossing his lips.

It was about eleven on Friday morning, and Jack was to meet Thomas' daughter later in the day to review the plans for the house, hospital-barn, and cottage. Thomas said he had to twist her arm, but that she was coming.

Jack quickly showered and changed into a pair of clean, crisp khakis and a white, button-down oxford shirt that he kept open at the throat, his shirt sleeves rolled up to his forearms. He combed his dark, wet hair back and rolled the plans back inside the tube canister under his arm. He walked the length of the new dock and observed that the contractor missed a cover on one of the massive screw heads. As he stepped off the dock, he noticed the treacherous stairs that led up toward the farmhouse. *These steps are next.* Jack made a mental note to himself, since he wouldn't be the only one to use them. Thomas would be sailing up and docking here as well.

He walked across the large, green field buzzing with bees and chirping with birds that seemed to dance with the breeze from the river. It was just noon, and Thomas told Jack to come to the cottage for lunch. There was a large, red truck parked in the driveway and from the corner of his eye he spotted something headed straight for him at a startling pace. It was BRUNO! *What the hell is this dog doing here?* Jack quickly stepped aside as the dog lunged directly at his clean khakis. Bruno flew past Jack, narrowly missing his slacks as Jack turned and commanded, "CEASE!" The dog skidded to a halt, kicking up a trail of dust all around him. Jack smiled and scratched the dog's meaty head. "Are you following me, boy?" Jack spoke softly to the upturned face, the dog's tongue hanging out of his mouth, caked with dirt and bits of grass. His paws were filthy and green from the grass he was obviously digging up. Jack froze with an instant realization. This was Francesca's dog! When Jack looked up, Thomas was walking toward him with a small, blonde woman, her hand neatly tucked under his arm.

"Jack, this is my daughter, Francesca." Thomas spoke proudly as Jack stood up, straight and tall.

"Good to see you again, Francesca." Jack's tone was deep, and as he stared at her in disbelief, a smile swept across his face. It baffled him how this woman just seemed to reappear.

"You know each other?!" Thomas asked, staring from one to the other.

"We have a mutual friend," Jack answered, never taking his eyes off Francesca's and watching those beautiful eyes change color, as he knew they would.

"Wonderful!" Thomas declared. "That is just wonderful!"

"A vet," Jack asked. His eyebrows were raised from not really understanding, because he'd seen her at Columbia, and he presumed she was a medical doctor, not a vet. *Assumed wrong, Romano*, Jack silently scolded himself.

"Yes." Frankie could barely choke out the single word. She could hardly believe her eyes, or blink them for that matter. *JACK was her ARCHITECT!* Her mind was screaming. Things were going to start to happen, and the thought made her knees weak and her head light. She already recognized several places in and around the farm from her many dreams of him. She just wasn't sure when Jack was going to enter the picture. But here he was and, now she knew her life was about to change forever.

Thomas suggested they all go to the cottage, bringing Jack and Francesca back to the present. "Retta has prepared lunch for us." Thomas spoke to the sides of each of their faces slowly drawing Francesca and Jack's attention away from one another.

Retta served a delicious lunch of thick chicken salad sandwiches on fresh-baked, whole grain bread. While they ate, Jack unrolled the plans and began to explain his designs for the hospital. He researched the subject in depth and finally decided how to attack the design challenge of converting the barn into a hospital, with room left to board six horses. Frankie was impressed. She detected that Jack incorporated many skylights and windows into his design. He wanted the hospital to have as much natural light and sun on the inside, and Frankie absolutely fell in love with his ideas. She changed a few minor details, and Jack quickly re-sketched some of her changes right onto his beautiful blueprints. He told her that he had the plans for the house and cottage on his boat, which was currently moored on her new dock.

"I would really like for you to see them," Jack insisted. "That way if you have changes, we could make them now before the contractors start on Tuesday. Of course, the plans can always be tweaked as the project moves along, but it's always more expensive to make changes once work has started." Jack wanted to see her reaction to his plans and, besides, this was an opportunity to see her for a little longer.

"Jack is right," Thomas agreed. "You should review the plans with him. On Tuesday, after the Fourth of July weekend, there will be quite a crew of contractors here, so now is the best time to see the rest of the plans."

Frankie studied her watch. She had to go back to the city and check on a few patients that were being hospitalized. "I have appointments late this afternoon, but I could come back up first thing in the morning…that is, if you don't mind working on Saturday?" Frankie asked, not sure if he had plans for the weekend.

"First thing in the morning—it would be my pleasure." Jack flashed her one of his quick bright, white smiles.

"You can review the plans over breakfast!" Thomas suggested.

"Does that include Retta's cooking? I think I would work every Saturday for that deal!" Jack winked at Retta and she couldn't help but blush, waving a large dishtowel at him.

On the drive back to the city, Frankie could barely focus. Her thoughts were on Jack completely. She found it next to impossible to keep her truck on the road. Bruno absolutely refused to go back with her, so Jack volunteered that he and Nelson could easily take care of him until she came back up tomorrow.

Frankie called Becca from her cell phone and told her what had happened. "Becca, I'm so nervous, I can barely see straight. I don't know if I can even drive back without running off the road." Frankie blinked her eyes to re-focus on the highway before her.

"Frankie, just let nature take its course. Don't think about the dreams you've had of him, just let your mind relax when you are near him," Becca coached. "Just stay in the moment, don't think ahead."

"Easier said than done! I can't stop imagining his nude body when he is near me. Tomorrow morning, we are going over the farmhouse plans. You think I should tell him about my dreams?" Frankie tentatively asked.

"NO! I mean...ahh...I don't know if that is such a good idea just yet." Becca actually thought the idea was a *REALLY BAD* idea! It had taken her a long time to understand Frankie's predicting dream capabilities. "Maybe you should wait and see what happens first. He might think you're some kind of freak. No offense, Frankie, but do you remember the first time I found out? I was scared to death of you."

"I certainly don't want that reaction from him! You're right—I'll just let everything unfold naturally and force my mind to think of something else when he is around."

"Good. Call me if you need me. I have to go; my next appointment is here early."

"Try to have a good weekend, Bec."

"I have a feeling you will!" Becca giggled as she disengaged the call.

In the early evening, Jack was having a hell of a time rounding up Bruno to take him in for the night. The dog just wanted to run free. He promised Frankie that he would take care of him for her, and he wasn't about to let anything happen to that beast.

"Bruno, come!" Jack commanded as he stood on the dock. Bruno had one front paw on the dock still looking back to the open fields and woods.

"If you don't get your hairy butt over here, seriously...you're not getting dinner! YOU GOT IT?"

Bruno's ears twitched at the inflection in Jack's voice and slowly paced the distance between the two of them. Once he was near, Jack bent down, scooped up the dog, and carried him onto The Rose.

"You stink! Jeez, what the heck were you rolling in?" Jack easily managed to haul the heavy dog onto the boat. He closed the gate on The Rose's railing and made his way to the galley.

"Come on, boy, you gotta be hungry!"

Bruno barked and Jack laughed as they made their way to the galley for a meal of steak and potatoes. After Bruno gobbled his very own steak, he gnawed on a bone, while Jack cleaned up.

Jack made his way to the master stateroom, Bruno padding behind him. Jack removed his clothes and stepped into the bathroom to wash up before bed. When he walked back into the bedroom, he found Bruno smack in the middle of his bed snoring, rather loudly, with a tiny piece of bone next to his front paw.

"Get down, before I make a throw rug out of you," Jack corrected the situation immediately. He pulled down the comforter and climbed into bed. Bruno curled up on the floor next to Jack and let out a long sigh. "Get used to it, boy." Jack glanced down at the dog for a moment.

Jack tried to relax, folding his arms behind his head, lying very still. He couldn't stop thinking about Francesca, and it made him smile. She made his pulse race and his temperature rise. Just standing near her made his brow sweat. "A vet! I would never have guessed that!" Now that she was his client, he was going to have to keep their relationship on a business level. *Great*, he thought, *just great*. He tried to still his thoughts, but Francesca's lovely face danced before his eyes, mentally noting that her hair was getting longer. *I wonder how long she will let it grow*, he wondered. He was thinking about the way her eyes turned a deep sapphire whenever she looked into his, and just thinking about those eyes made his skin grow so warm, that he kicked off the covers. *I have to slow down*, he kept saying to himself as he drifted off to sleep. *I have to slow down.*

Chapter Eleven
A new beginning...

The next morning Jack woke up bright and early, but for no other reason than because Bruno wanted out. Jack's body felt stiff, and he still cursed Scott repeatedly, because now his body hurt from not working out.

"I'm going to wring Scott's neck," Jack spoke to Bruno through clenched teeth.

He decided a jog might loosen up his muscles and maybe tire Bruno out. But the dog increased the pace as they ran down a dirt road that led into the center of town. Jack's legs actually began to feel better as he eased into a steady, fast stride. He was jogging along when a large truck pulled alongside of him. The tinted window glided down, and Francesca poked her head out.

"Want a ride back?"

Jack couldn't help but smile at her as he jogged alongside her truck, her scent started to fill his senses.

"I'm trying to tire out your dog, but I think he is trying to tire me out instead. Did you know he snores?" Jack smiled while he kept up the pace.

Frankie laughed. Many nights Bruno had wakened her from a sound sleep.

"How about I design a dog house with a dog run for your beast...ahh...I mean wonderful pet. No extra charge. Just think of all the peaceful nights you will get without this beast...ahh... charming animal, snoring the wallpaper off the walls."

Frankie laughed again, and called to her pet. Bruno instantly barked, jumping all around Jack. Frankie eased the truck alongside them, as they slowly made their way back to the farm.

"I have to shower and get my plans. I'll be back before you know I'm gone." And with that, Jack bolted across the field with Bruno on his heels, ran straight down the hill completely avoiding the dilapidated stairs, raced along the dock, and vaulted over the boat's railing, leaving Bruno barking madly at the disappearing figure.

Frankie pulled the truck into the driveway of the farmhouse and headed over to the cottage. She called to Nelson, who was feeding the small pen of chickens they kept on the side of the cottage.

"Good morning, Nelson!" Frankie waved hello.

"Mornin', Doc! Hope you're hungry? Retta's scrambled and fried every egg we had this morning. Had to be close to two dozen," Nelson called back.

Frankie smiled as she made her way to the back of the cottage. She was sure that Jack could easily eat a dozen eggs all by himself.

"Retta, it smells wonderful in here." Frankie poked her head through the top open half of the Dutch kitchen door.

"Mornin', Doc," Retta called back waving her in.

Frankie wasn't even remotely prepared for the quantity of food Retta cooked, now covering nearly every surface of the kitchen counters and table.

"You must have started cooking yesterday when I left. You've cooked enough for an army!" Frankie stared in disbelief. There were hot apple turnovers, a dozen each of corn and blueberry muffins, and a mountain of bacon, and Retta was still fixing something at the stove.

"That boy's gonna need his strength fixin' this old place."

Frankie grinned and knew Retta was already beguiled by Jack's charming smile and irresistible ways.

Jack knocked on the front door of the small cottage door and Retta called out, "Come on in!"

"Good morning!" Jack called from the front door.

Frankie's body froze with the sound of his voice. She could already smell his wonderful spicy scent that did strange things to all of her senses.

Retta watched Frankie for a moment before calling back, "We're in the kitchen."

"Retta, it smells like heaven in here." Jack came up behind her to see what she was cooking at the stove. "I'm starved." When he turned and looked at Frankie, his breath caught for a moment as he remembered those jeans and crisp white T-shirt from his dream of her. Quickly he averted his eyes, as Retta watched him approach the table. He reached around Frankie and grabbed a hot apple turnover and spoke while chewing, "My favorite."

Nelson walked in and started laughing.

While they shared Retta's delicious breakfast, Jack and

Frankie listened to the stories Retta and Nelson told about some of the old folks who lived in the area. The atmosphere on the farm was like stepping back in time and magically created a bond among the people who came there.

The budding friendship in the kitchen was blooming just like the countryside outside the cottage's door. The smell that was summer danced in through the open top half of the old, Dutch door, filling the kitchen with summer sounds and floral fragrances.

After breakfast, Frankie and Jack walked around the back of the cottage and into the farmhouse. Jack explained how he was going to convert the eight-bedroom farmhouse into six, turning several bedrooms into one large, master bedroom suite.

Frankie was finding it very difficult to concentrate in Jack's presence. They were standing at the top of the stairs, and Frankie was staring at his hands and his still-wet hair. She wanted to reach up and touch that shiny, black hair that curled just along his collar.

Jack seemed to sense Frankie's nearness and turned to face her. She smelled wonderfully of roses, as they both looked at each other. The air around them was warm and electrified. He reached up and smoothed a strand of her golden hair behind her ear, as Frankie raised her hand to touch the dark shiny lock just reaching his collar. They were so lost in the moment, gazing at one another, that they didn't notice Thomas and Corrine standing in the foyer entrance below. Frankie's parents looked up at the scene above them, and Thomas reached for Corrine's hand, smiling at one other.

"Top of the mornin' to you both," Thomas bellowed from the front hall, and both Frankie and Jack jumped at the intrusion of sound.

Jack's hand quickly caught Frankie's arm, as she was much too close to the top of the stairs.

Frankie stared down at her father below. "I swear the man is trying to kill me," she said just loudly enough for Jack to hear. "First he buys this scary farm which needs the funds it takes to run a small country to fix, and then he shouts when you least expect it."

Jack smiled and called down to Thomas and Corrine below. "Mornin', we were just checking out the plans!"

"Yes, we can see that, son." Thomas called back, and Corrine squeezed his hand. "This is my wife, Corrine."

"Nice to meet you Mrs. O'Brian," Jack nodded.

"Please, just Corrine."

"Why don't you both come up and we can let Mrs.—ahh, I mean, Corrine, in on the plans," Jack suggested as he released Frankie's arm.

"Frankie," Corrine called to her daughter as she climbed the stairs. "Honestly, I can't imagine what your father was thinking when he bought this place with your money. It's an awful mess." Corrine shot her husband a look of horror.

Jack looked on as Frankie's mother smiled and kissed her daughter's cheek. "Once the place is restored, this estate will be worth so much more." Jack spoke confidently, backing up Thomas' foresight, as Thomas shot him a winning grin.

Jack continued the tour holding the plans against the wall in this room and that. Frankie was finding it nearly impossible to keep her train of thought, even in front of her parents! When he turned to hold a drawing up on the wall, Frankie's eyes would watch his back and how his muscles played under his shirt. Then her eyes would drift up to his dark hair and several times, she shook her head to clear it.

Thomas noticed it each time.

When they were reviewing the plans for the kitchen, Retta was asked for her opinion, and although everyone spoke openly and freely, Retta remained silent. She didn't want to suggest anything at first, but Frankie coaxed her.

"Retta, I already have to neuter every dog and cat from here to Jersey and back to pay for the other renovations, so please don't hold back." Everyone laughed and Retta slowly began to suggest things that no one would have thought might be important. She explained the need for warmers—equipment that would hold both plates and food, so that the whole meal would stay warm until served. Jack immediately brainstormed these new ideas with Retta.

"Yes, that would be fine right next to the stove, dear. And if it's not too much trouble, could you put an extra sink in the island that would help some when preparing vegetables? And one of those under-the-counter refrigerators in the island might be just the thing to store those items? And wouldn't a garbage disposal in the main sink be a big help with the cleanin' up and all?" She spoke to Jack as if he were her son. After the plans had been discussed, then discussed again, everyone sat down at the old table in the farmhouse. Retta brought in a pot of strong, black coffee and poured the hot brew for everyone to enjoy.

"Tonight are the fireworks down the Hudson," Jack spoke into his cup of steamy coffee feeling, most unusually shy. "I thought about taking The Rose down river to watch the fireworks, but I'm going to need some help, because my skipper is off for the weekend."

"Sounds like a fine idea," Thomas chimed in.

"I'll prepare a feast for the trip," Retta spoke up.

Frankie just listened as everyone would do this or bring that, watching Jack watching her.

"Frankie," Corrine spoke. "Your father and I have to stop at the window treatment designers in Barley, just the next town over. We are taking Jack's window measurements and ordering the window treatments. We could be back by six."

"Is that all right?" Frankie asked Jack.

"Perfect," Jack mentally calculated.

"I need to get started with the cookin'. Excuse me, folks." Retta gathered up the cups and saucers onto a tray and left the farmhouse, reading aloud her mental list of what she needed to get from the market for their little river trip.

"Yes, we need to be on our way, too. Thomas?" Corrine called then pulled Thomas along.

"I really don't have to go with you, Corrine. Why don't you take Francesca?" Thomas whined.

"No. Francesca needs to relax. Anyway she has already seen the fabrics the designer suggested. Isn't that right dear? Move it, Thomas," Corrine playfully threatened in a very low voice, then in her softest, sweetest voice ever, "Let's leave them alone... hmm?"

"Good thinking, Cory." Thomas pinched her buttocks. Corrine's eyes flashed at him as she giggled, quickly leaving Frankie and Jack alone.

"Must be something in the air up here, it makes everyone act overly friendly," Frankie observed as she watched her parents leave.

Jack was studying Francesca's face, and his heart was

pounding in his chest. He wanted to touch her from the moment he saw her this morning, and now his body craved her. He pulled her slim shoulder back so that she was facing him.

"Let's take a walk. It's such a beautiful day." Jack reached down and laced his fingers with Frankie's as they left the farmhouse kitchen and walked toward the river. Bruno raced off ahead of them, barking at nothing.

In the early afternoon, the sun shone strongly, but the constant breeze from the Hudson River made the day very comfortable. The sun felt wonderful. Frankie closed her eyes and raised her face so that the sun could shine directly on it. Jack stood still and looked at this fair angel before his eyes. His chest ached, and he realized that she was taking his breath away, as he drew in an unsteady breath.

Frankie opened her eyes and Jack watched them turn that incredible shade of blue sapphires, which always brought a smile to his face. He guided her along a trail that wound through the back of the property towards the river. He led her over some fallen logs and two small creeks, pointing to how far her property extended.

A huge tree had fallen over, blocking the path, and Jack swept her up into his arms and lifted her over the log. Jack continued to carry Frankie holding her close to his chest. She smelled wonderfully of roses and he inhaled her scent filling his senses to capacity. He felt her place one hand around his neck and the other over his heart. To Jack, it felt as though her tiny hand was burning a hole right through his shirt, scorching his skin.

"I think we're over the log," Frankie spoke to his chin. Frankie could feel his heart hammering in his chest, and she quickly removed her hand from his shirtfront.

"I recently started working out with Scott. So this is a good way for me to keep up with my weight training while I'm away from the city for a few months," Jack explained.

"Glad to be of assistance." Frankie laughed as she crossed her ankles, swinging them just a bit from her heightened position. "What are you training for?"

"Nothing really, Scott just asked me if I wanted to workout with him, but that was before I found out that he is an exercise junkie. His regime of training is like something out of the Navy Seals. He makes me run, until there is no land left to run on, and lift enormous amounts of weight. In fact, you're a breeze to carry compared to the weights he has tied to my wrists and ankles. He even makes me climb ropes at the gym with those same weights tied to my ankles and wrists. This is the first time in weeks I've been able to stand up without crying in pain!"

Frankie felt a giggle rising up within her. She knew Scott was in the utmost physical shape because his job demanded it. "You poor thing," Frankie stifled a chuckle.

"You think it is funny, do you?" Jack began to tickle her side, and Frankie unconsciously placed her hand back over Jack's heart.

They had reached a beautiful, green field where the grass was tall. Bruno was running all around them in maddening circles. Jack looked down at Frankie and placed his lips on hers. Frankie's mind took a mental snapshot of that moment, from his scent, to the feel of his lips against hers, back to his scent. She could hear the rustling of the breeze in the bird-filled trees off to her left and Bruno's distant bark encouraging them to follow.

Jack deepened their kiss touching his tongue to hers. Their tongues began to dance with each other, but Jack pulled away for just a moment, to make sure he wasn't dreaming. He watched Frankie's eyes fly open. He couldn't believe that this angel was in his arms, and she was opening up to him. *So willing*, he thought. He lowered her slowly to her feet then gently tugged her hand. Sinking into the tall grass, Jack captured her face between his hands and kissed her again. He kissed her neck and nibbled on her ear, and she smiled and softly hummed. He never felt like this in his whole life. He felt free and alive and wanted. His kisses and touches were accepted and greeted with openness and returned.

"Francesca, my angel, I feel like I have been waiting for you my whole life." He spoke quietly.

"Jacqino," Frankie could only manage to whisper his name, because the sound of his voice turning husky made her remember deeply passionate moments in her dreams.

His hand was resting on her tiny waist, and his fingers splayed out over her ribs. "I think I have dreamed of this," Jack spoke softly into her ear and Frankie looked at him startled.

Did he dream of us, too? She wondered silently. She was afraid to speak for fear he might stop.

"Does that surprise you?" he asked her quietly, leaning back just a little.

"No," Frankie whispered just as quietly.

Jack's hand slid under her shirt watching her eyelids flutter shut. He caressed her breast still covered by her bra, the lace tickling his palm, until he felt her hardened nipple brush against his palm. He kissed her lips, and his tongue was deep in her mouth as he drank from her endless supply of tenderness.

Frankie tried to pull herself back. She began to unbutton his shirt and touched his strong chest covered with dark hair. She splayed her fingers across his chest, as his muscles sprang to life under her touch.

"Your touch, Francesca, makes me feel alive," Jack huskily whispered.

Frankie could feel him speak the words against her lips. "Jacqino, I have dreamed of you, too."

Jack groaned and again kissed Francesca deeply. He slipped her T-shirt off and looked down at the beauty adorned in white lace before him. "You are my beautiful, golden angel." He placed his lips on her neck and began to kiss her to the spot just between her breasts, his tongue making little circles on her sun-warmed flesh. When he unsnapped her bra, it was at that precise moment that Bruno came diving over the tops of their heads in a flash of flying fur. Being his usual playful, energetic self, he took off with Frankie's T-shirt in his mouth, as they both shot up straight and watched in shock and disbelief as the dog ran away like a thief.

"Oh, no," Frankie gasped, quickly covering one hand over her lips, the other clasping her bra in place.

Jack watched in horror. "What are the chances of us getting that back?!"

Frankie's mouth hung open with nothing much coming out. "Ahh...slim to none," Frankie answered, her mouth turning into a grin.

They both laughed hysterically and fell back onto the sweet grass. They rolled in each other's arms still laughing, hugging and holding each other, looking up at the glorious, blue sky above. Jack pulled Frankie close to him for a moment, caressing her bare shoulder and arm, looking deeply into her eyes, studying her face, her expression. Then in one quick movement, he pulled her up from the ground, re-clasped her bra, and removed his shirt.

He made Frankie slide her arms into his warm shirtsleeves and slowly buttoned it closed.

Frankie reached up placing each hand on his enormous chest, as he rolled up the cuffs. *He is truly magnificent*, she thought. She watched as he lowered his head and kissed the top of her golden head.

The dog raced back with the now filthy, once-white T-shirt, flying from one side of his mouth. And they couldn't help but laugh while they made their way back to the farmhouse.

Retta looked out the cottage's enormous bay window over the kitchen sink. The young couple was walking towards the back of the farmhouse. To Retta's surprise, Jack was shirtless. Frankie was close to his side with her arms wrapped around his waist. Jack's arm was wrapped around her shoulders, obviously pulling her in closely. Her cheek was resting against his upper rib cage and she was wearing his shirt, which hung down past her knees. They looked as though they had been together their whole lives, and Retta was pleased to see the tall, dark, handsome man and small, fair beauty together.

"Now you have two of my jackets and one of my shirts," Jack teased when they reached the back door of the house. Holding his own shirtfront, he asked "Do you plan on taking my wardrobe piece by piece and selling them so that you can pay for the renovations to the farm?" He kidded.

Frankie smiled and placed her forehead against his strong chest, inhaling his scent. She never wanted this moment to end. "Yup, that's the plan! And, yeah, the dog—he's my accomplice," Frankie razzed, motioning her head back towards the careening dog.

Jack reached down and placed a large hand under her chin, turning her head so that he could look into her breathtaking eyes.

"I'm going to get The Rose ready," he glanced at his watch. "We'll be casting off in less than two hours. I'll see you later, right?" He carefully asked, afraid that she might disappear again. He watched her nod her head. Slowly he dipped his head to kiss her, but hesitated just before he reached her lips and added firmly, "…and no dogs allowed!"

Frankie laughed, as he placed a gentle kiss on her smiling lips. Then in a flash, Jack turned and jogged down toward the dock, with Bruno tagging along behind at the same pace, the T-shirt dragging from his mouth. Jack glanced over his shoulder and waved. He could feel her eyes on him, and he knew that she wanted him as much as he wanted her. He needed to remind himself again to slow down. Something deep inside him told him to go slow.

Frankie's parents arrived back at the farm about an hour before it was time to leave. Bruno was still bounding around with Frankie's dirty T-shirt, and her mother looked at the excited dog with one eyebrow raised. They entered the farmhouse and Frankie came down the stairs wearing a clean T-shirt.

"How did it go?" Frankie asked her mother.

"Oh, just fine, the window treatments will be ready in about six months."

"I am positively bored to death," Thomas proclaimed, still quite annoyed at the whole window treatment shopping process. "I think I'll head down to the dock and see if Jack needs some help."

"We'll be down in a bit, dear," Corrine told her husband. She reached out, grabbed Frankie's hand, her other hand holding a shopping bag, and led her daughter up the stairs to the sole usable bedroom in the house.

"What's up, Mom?" Frankie asked just outside the bedroom.

"I bought you a few things, dear. You know you have so little time to shop. Well, you just take a look at them and if you like what I got—great, if not...no big deal, I'll bring them back next week. Why don't you try them on and see if you want to wear anything for tonight?"

Frankie always loved the things her mother bought for her. She took the bag and headed into the bedroom. When she peered into the bag her breath caught as she removed a red silk blouse. Carefully, she set it on the bed. When she reached back into the bag she pulled out a pair of crisp, white, linen slacks. These were the same clothes she wore in her dream, the dream where she made love to Jack. Because she had many dreams of Jack, she was unsure of the sequence. With these clothes came the meaning that this would be her first time with a man. Her hands began to tremble concerning her mother enough to quickly come to her side.

"Francesca, what is it?"

"Nothing, Mom," Frankie's voice quivered. "I'm fine, really. The clothes are perfect. I don't know what I would do without you and Dad." She turned and hugged her mother tightly.

Corrine noticed the tears welling up in her daughter's eyes. "Francesca, we love you. Come on now. Let's get ready so that we don't keep the men waiting down at the dock. The fresh air and the river ride will do us all good."

With that, Frankie headed into the bathroom. She showered with her favorite rose-scented soaps. When she toweled off, she began to smooth rose-scented cream on her legs and arms. It was such a treat because she rarely had any time for this kind of pampering, and she was enjoying it. She slipped on a fresh, lace bra and matching panties. She reached for the silk blouse with hands that trembled again. But this time, she silently spoke to herself, in an effort to be calm. *Francesca, you have dreamed of this man almost your whole life and now the moment is here. Embrace it,* she kept saying to herself. She slipped her arms into the red silk blouse then stepped into the wide-leg, linen slacks. As soon as she walked out of the bathroom, her mother appeared with another shopping bag and revealed a pair of white boat sneakers. They dressed down the whole outfit, which made it perfect for this Fourth of July trip down the Hudson. She slipped her feet into the new sneakers and looked up at her mother.

"How do I look?" Frankie twirled.

"I don't think anyone would recognize you without those drab, green scrubs you wear," Frankie's mother teased. Corrine held up some newly purchased makeup—not much, just some mascara, lipstick, and pale-pink blush. Frankie's mother applied the makeup, ever so lightly, to her daughter's already flawless face and stood back to scrutinize her work.

"Perfect, Francesca. You are going to make Jack's heart stop."

"Mother," Frankie looked shocked.

"Don't 'Mother' me, Francesca Catherine O'Brian. I wasn't born yesterday," Corrine scolded her daughter while closing the tube of mascara. "I like Jack. Your father says he is very respectful." Corrine placed the tube back into the bag taking a moment to formulate her words. "Francesca, your whole life your father and I kept reinforcing that you should wait to be ahh...with a man...that it should only be your husband."

"Oh my God," Frankie raised a hand to her forehead. "Don't tell me you are going to give me the 'birds and bees' lecture now? I'm twenty-six years old!"

"I know how old you are, dear. I just don't want you to wait anymore."

Frankie stared at her mother. Her mouth dropped practically to the floor. "Wait," Frankie choked.

"Dear, I'm your mother. You know, that whole 'eyes in the back of my head' and stuff. It comes with the territory. Anyway," Corrine began again with a wave of her hand, "your father and I want you to know love. We don't want you to live a life of work without loving a man, without knowing what it is like to be wanted and touched." Corrine could not contain her own emotions a moment longer. She could only think about the time her daughter was diagnosed with cancer. She wanted so many things for her only daughter. She wanted her to be healthy. She wanted her to be loved by a man who was good and kind to her. She wanted her to have her own family and love them the way she loved hers.

Frankie hugged her mother tightly. Pulling back to study her mother's watery expression, Frankie spoke softly. "Mom you must understand that I know so many kinds of love. Love from good and caring parents, good friends and colleagues. Love from the animals I care for. Mother, the love from a good man will come and, when it does, I will not hold back." Frankie held her mother close, and when they pulled apart, Corrine quickly wiped her eyes dry.

"Francesca," Corrine said, "let's head down to the dock. I'm sure the men are waiting for us."

Frankie and her mother made their way down the rickety steps to the new dock. Frankie wasn't shocked to see the yacht, but her mother was.

"Welcome aboard," Thomas yelled from the deck of The Rose, as Nelson and Retta stood next to him.

Jack was standing just behind them, studying Francesca. His chest tightened, as he watched her approach holding her mother's hand. The breeze blew at her silk blouse and wide-legged slacks. It played with her hair, and he watched as she reached up to tuck a piece of golden hair behind her ear.

Frankie looked up at Jack, her hand still looping her hair behind her ear. Her dreams didn't do Jack's looks justice. He was the most beautiful man she had ever seen in her entire life. He was all alpha-male and strength. He was confidence and pride. He walked behind her father to the railing never taking his eyes from her. That kind of direct attention was spellbinding. He slowly opened the railing and took her hand in his.

The touch of his skin was making Francesca blush, and she was sure her face matched her blouse.

Jack was not unaffected, either. Once she was aboard, Jack was lost in her scent. *Roses*, he thought, *always roses*. Then he fell into her darkening pools.

Francesca's mother threw him a verbal life line, breaking Francesca's spell over him. "Hello! Jack, dear, did you forget me?" Corrine called to Jack and Frankie.

"Oh...Corrine, here, let me help you aboard." Jack reached down and easily helped Corrine up. "Let's get underway," Jack commanded Thomas and Nelson, sending them off in different directions. Jack paused for a moment looking right into Francesca's incredible eyes, placing his hands on her silk-clad shoulders. "I'm going to have my hands full at the helm with this monster, so don't think I've forgotten about you."

"I won't," Frankie whispered softly, smiling.

Frankie, Corrine, and Retta sat on the upper deck on beautiful, wood chaises covered in yellow-and-white striped canvas. The ride down the Hudson was refreshing. The night was unseasonably cool with a clean breeze that felt wonderful. Jack, Thomas, and Nelson were quite busy manning the yacht, which normally took five men to man, but since Jack and Thomas were so experienced, they managed with relative ease.

Jack occasionally glanced down to the deck below to look at Francesca. The river breeze was tousling her hair, and her blouse was blowing about, showing glimpses of her white lace bra beneath. He quickly drew his attention back to steering the large yacht downriver, avoiding any possible mishaps. They anchored once they reached a cove not far from the fireworks, but far enough away from the mingling of smaller crafts that sped about in the river.

Retta, Corrine, and Frankie started readying the meal, while the men anchored The Rose. The women brought the food into the dining area just off the main salon which was completely glassed in. Retta made smoked salmon on a bed of wild rice with fresh vegetables. Jack opened the wine as everyone gathered around the glossy, rosewood table. He could feel Francesca's eyes on him, but he didn't turn to let her know he could sense her eyes upon him. She was too innocent to realize that, and Jack didn't want to scare her.

They all sat in couples, with Jack next to Frankie, Corrine next to Thomas, and Nelson next to Retta, at the round dining table. Everyone helped serve the meal, and Jack kept the fine, blush wine flowing. They spoke of how delicious the meal was that Retta prepared for their trip and just enjoyed each other's company. Jack and Frankie looked on as the married couples joshed each other good-naturedly.

"I like the way Jack commands and you jump, Thomas," Corrine said with the snap of her fingers.

"Well he is the captain and I the mate tonight."

"Maybe I could have Jack tape a few commands for me, like 'take out the trash' or 'pick up your socks' and maybe 'stop switching the channels on the TV' and then I could play them and watch you jump," Corrine continued to tease.

Jack and Frankie watched and laughed. He reached for her hand which was resting on her napkin in her lap, and they both looked at each other, unaware of the others watching.

Frankie studied his hand which was strong and warm and so much larger than hers. Jack's shirt cuffs were rolled up to his forearms allowing Frankie to run her free hand over the dark hair of his forearm. *Hmm, I love the way he smells of spice and wood*, Frankie inhaled.

"It was the funniest thing today," Nelson began, "that crazy dog of yours—you do know that dog is crazy, right, Doc?" Nelson asked and apologized all at once with a shrug. "Well, he had somebody's shirt in his mouth. He was chewing it and pawing it and when I tried to take it from him, he took off, most likely even buried it by now."

"Nelson, hush now about Doc Frankie's dog. He's a fine animal," Retta scolded, recalling the scene earlier that day.

Jack raised an eyebrow, and Frankie began to laugh.

"I'll tell you something else," Nelson continued "I had a heck of a time locking him in the barn before we left. I thought he was gonna take my head off, but I slammed the barn doors shut just before he lunged at me. That animal sure has a lot of energy."

Frankie and Jack, still holding the other's gaze, started to smile. Frankie lowered her eyes, and Jack squeezed her hand before he released it. She could still feel his touch and was trying hard not to think of the night she knew they would soon share.

"Francesca and I will do the dishes," Jack announced to everyone at the table. With that, Jack stood and began placing the dishes on a large tray as Frankie gathered some plates in her hands. They went through the dining area and down a few steps to the galley. Jack placed the tray of dirty plates on the counter and took the remaining plates from Frankie' hands. When he turned back, he pulled her into a tight embrace in order to kiss her deeply. When Jack lifted his head he spoke in a husky, male tone, "I've wanted to do that since you came aboard."

"I've wanted you to do that, too," she confessed while her bones turned elastic.

But Jack barely let her finish. He held her face in his hands and kissed her again desperately. His tongue touched the outside of her lips, and his hopes were to make her feel the same things he was feeling. He slowly moved his hand to smooth away a strand of golden blonde hair that tickled his cheek. He tucked the strand behind her ear and kissed her cheek. He needed to touch her. He needed to kiss her. Jack was stunned with the overwhelming need he had for this woman.

Lifting his face and pulling himself back to the present, he spoke just above a whisper. "I'll load the dishwasher, and you can get the rest of the plates and dry," Jack softly suggested.

"Aye, aye, Captain," Frankie saluted playfully, then turned to retrieve the rest of the plates when she felt a sting on her butt. Jack had taken a dishtowel and swatted at her. "Oww," Frankie shouted and started to rub the spot he hit.

"I could rub that for you..." Jack started to advance on her, but Frankie quickly took off up the few steps that led back to the dining area. She gathered the rest of the plates and forks onto the serving tray and cleared the entire table. She replaced the centerpiece that anchored in a groove in the middle of the wooden table then carried the tray back to the galley. Jack had most of the dishes in the dishwasher and was washing the large platters by hand. Frankie took the dishtowel and began to dry. He told her where everything went, and she finally began to absorb the details of the magnificent yacht. "I designed and built The Rose," Jack explained.

"You did? It's magnificent!"

"I don't know about magnificent, but it is efficient," Jack stated humbly.

"This ship is a work of art. The details, of what little I have seen, are very handsome."

"Thank you milady," Jack bowed. "Let's head up to the deck. The fireworks should be starting soon."

"Okay."

Jack held Frankie's hand and kissed her palm softly. He pulled her along behind him as they made their way to Frankie's parents and Nelson and Retta.

The fireworks had just begun, and Frankie stood by the railing; her mother was next to her, and Retta next to Corrine. The men came up behind them and, one by one, held their wives around the waist. Jack followed suit. He reached around Frankie's waist and pulled her back against his chest. She rested her head against him and watched the spectacular display. The tiny vessels before them bobbed in the water as the fireworks drifted along the sky, falling to the water while lighting a path during their descent.

Oohs and aahs could be heard from the surrounding vessels and Frankie closed her eyes, trying to memorize the feeling of her back resting against Jack's chest. He was warm and steady, as he began to nuzzle her neck.

Jack was intoxicated with her scent and with everything about her. He could feel his pulse quicken and tried to quiet himself, but it was nearly impossible. He almost couldn't stand to be this near her and not have her. He lifted his head from her neck and kissed the top of her soft, blonde hair. The texture of the silken strands beneath his lips was not helping matters. Everything about her was calling to his most masculine senses. He lowered his left arm, wrapped his arm around her waist, and rested his right hand on her ribcage, while his thumb secretly grazed just under her left breast.

Frankie was beyond comprehension. Her head was reeling with the sensation and nearness of him. His hands and lips were wreaking havoc with her ability to keep her mind firmly on the deck of The Rose. The ship swayed softly and the feeling of being held so closely against Jack's bold frame made her feel sheltered and protected. The fireworks paled in comparison to the excitement Frankie felt within herself. In fact, all three couples were nuzzling, quietly embracing each other, embracing love.

Long after the fireworks stopped, most of the small crafts left, and slowly each couple began to move about. The men began the task of bringing The Rose back up the Hudson. This time Frankie stayed with Jack at the helm as he navigated the ship with one hand and draped the other over Frankie's collarbone, as she rested her back against his side. His arm slung around her just barely resting on her breast with his hand closing over her upper arm. She leaned her head back into his side.

As Jack maneuvered The Rose back up the Hudson with grace and ease, he quietly absorbed the woman who wanted to be held by him. Jack knew at that moment that he needed her, probably more than she knew or needed him.

When they reached the dock, the women waited alongside the railing as Nelson and Thomas hopped off The Rose to begin the task of knotting her hawsers to the dock. The large yacht eased into its slip as Jack reversed the engines. Once Jack cut the engines, he quickly bounded down from the bridge to assist Thomas and Nelson. The three men were more than capable of fastening The Rose with ease. Retta and Corrine were the first ones off The Rose, walking down the dock, followed by Nelson and Thomas.

Jack grabbed Frankie's hand and pulled her back. "Please don't leave. Not yet," Jack pleaded quietly.

"My parents?" Frankie looked uncomfortable.

"Please," Jack whispered to Frankie, as his other hand smoothed away that stray strand of golden hair, tucking it behind her ear.

Retta called over her shoulder up to Frankie still on The Rose. "I'll have Nelson take care of Bruno, Doc." Retta looked back over her shoulder to Frankie and Jack, watching for just a moment the two beautiful, young people so full of life, hope and love. Retta started to think of Frankie as the daughter she wished she could have had.

"Goodnight," Jack called.

"Goodnight! Great trip Jack!" Thomas called. "Francesca, your mother and I are heading home, and we won't be back up until Tuesday. We'll talk to you then." He spoke in a voice that carried back to the yacht, as he swung his arm around Nelson's shoulders.

"Alright Dad. Goodnight," Frankie called back as she watched their retreating forms wind up the steps.

Jack was studying Frankie's profile. He reached his hand up and gently tucked that same strand of soft golden hair behind her ear. And when she turned and looked up into his dark eyes, his heart wrenched with her innocent beauty. "I'm afraid if I move, you will disappear," Jack confessed.

"I won't," Frankie promised. She lowered her head blushing from the closeness and the realization they were now very much alone.

Jack began to speak the words she had only dreamed about. Lifting her face he spoke softly as his hand cradled her cheek, "I want to make love to you, Francesca." His intentions clearly presented, he waited for her response. When she held out her hand, he took the surrender in his, and gently guided her along the highly polished deck of The Rose through the stained glass doors accented with intricate yellow roses. He led her through the living room and through a dark, paneled door. Frankie reached out to touch the wood, marveling at the graining as Jack smiled at her. *Just like in my dream*, she thought. He opened the double doors that led through the sitting room and into the beautifully appointed master stateroom, softly lit with small brass lamps, topped with sage green shades, on each side of the bed. Everything was stunning, just as it was in her dream. Jack turned Frankie to face him and took her face in his hands.

"You are so beautiful," he spoke in a husky voice and ran his hand through her hair. *Maybe it is too soon*, Jack silently questioned, *too soon to be this intimate*, as he searched her expression for a sign. But something deep inside of him told him this was the right time to make love to her, and he listened to his inner heart.

The sensation of being kissed with such love in his touch was already clouding Frankie's ability to think clearly. Jack was larger than life. *He is the one who is beautiful*, Frankie thought silently, so *beautiful*. Frankie rested her hands on the front of his crisp, white oxford. Slowly she began to unbutton his shirt at the same time Jack unbuttoned hers. Frankie slipped her hands under the nearly unbuttoned shirt, sliding her hands over his strong, powerful chest covered with dark hair. Then in one fast, fluid movement, Jack tore off his shirt and gently tugged at Frankie's blouse until the buttons silently sailed to the sage-green carpet below followed by the silk blouse.

Jack kissed Francesca with a passion he never knew existed within him, as she pressed up against him, open, warm and willing. He took a deep breath to catch up with his racing heart. She was soft and welcoming, and he was going to make her his and his alone. He scooped her into his arms and walked to the bed, studying the amazing, ever-changing color in her eyes. Lowering her and himself onto the bed, he released the breath he hadn't even realized he held, as she smiled at him and rested her cheek against his chest. She could feel his thundering heart. Her petite hand lingered just below his jaw and the beat in his neck matched the rhythm of his heart.

Jack slowly removed her linen slacks and pulled his off as well. She was so tiny next to him, and he felt this uncontrollable need to shelter her. He pulled her close to him, kissing her, his passion rising quickly, and Francesca met it. He tried to slow the pace, but that was becoming impossible as she revealed a vulnerable, loving expression, he beheld.

Francesca closed her eyes knowing what was to happen next.

"I want you," Jack stated firmly with that deep, hoarse timbre. "Do you hear me, Francesca?"

"Yes," Francesca answered, feeling her body react to his husky tone before opening her eyes to see the silver flecks in his eyes begin to sparkle.

Jack smiled at her, as he pulled her on top of him. He slowly ran his hands up her waist to the front of Francesca's white lace bra. He easily undid the clasp and slid the fabric away. *She is perfect*, he thought. Her breasts were perfectly formed mounds and firm as he placed a hand over her breast. He was captivated with her reaction as her eyelids fluttered shut and her head fell back. She was exhilarating and enticing, and he couldn't resist the urge to kiss her neck and breast. Jack's touch caused Frankie's eyes to fly open, as she watched him suckle her right breast but gave no attention to the other. She had no idea how wonderful it would feel until this moment, as her desire climbed, building and building. She could feel the words leave her mouth before she had time to recall them from her dream. "Please, Jacqino, please," Francesca begged as she grabbed his hair trying to pull him to her neglected breast. When he looked into her pleading eyes, she could see that they had turned to pure silver. She barely whispered his name, so lost was she in a sea of tenderness. "Jacqino."

"Do you want me, Francesca? Do you?" Still kissing her breast tenderly, but refusing to give into her pleas in a voice thick with passion and desire.

"Yes. Yes, I want you." Once she whispered the words he wanted to hear, he took her other breast into his wet, warm mouth. His first touch on that excluded skin stole her breath away.

Jack gently pulled her down and removed the rest of their clothing. When he pulled her close she pressed her lips over his heart. He released a groan he thought only he could hear, but when he looked into her eyes she was smiling at him. He pushed her onto her back, tracing little circles with his tongue down her flat stomach. Jack caressed her thighs slowly and gently nudged her legs open for his touch. He sensed a slight hesitation from her, but in an instant he felt her submit. One by one he slid his fingers into the warm moist opening that he was longing to enter.

"I want *you* inside of me, Jacqino," she whispered onto his lips.

Her declaration caused Jack to kiss her passionately, their tongues tasting and dipping. He raised himself over her placing his knees between her legs and slowly lifted her hips as he pressed himself into her. He didn't want to crush her, moving ever so slowly, as her moist opening began to encase him. Jack's slow movements were only making his consciousness scream to move faster, but he did not. As he entered her more fully he felt a distinctive tug and heard her gasp. Jack knew instantly from her reaction, she was still a virgin!

"Francesca…why…you could have told me," Jack whispered in between a breath labored with desire for her.

But Frankie could not speak.

Jack looked deeply into her eyes, holding her face to study her reaction. "Am I hurting you?" Jack barely managed to whisper.

Frankie still could not speak, he was deep within her, and she could not get the words out. She shook her head, not wanting him to stop. He smoothed the hair away from her eyes as he held still, cupping her flawless, flushed cheek. He watched as she turned her head pressing her lips to the center of his palm. Then without warning he felt her lift her hips. Jack let her movements take center stage, constantly searching her expression for signs of regret, but all he saw was love.

At first, Frankie moved awkwardly, wanting to please, then her responses became more fluid and smooth when Jack joined her. Their passion rose as her whole body pulsated. She found it hard to keep her senses about her. She felt as though she were drifting off in a wave of bliss. Then their lovemaking became more urgent, and Frankie reached for something unknowingly.

"Francesca, my innocent angel...I will give you everything you need," Jack whispered.

Frankie and Jack exploded together, both spinning into a blur of spent desire.

Jack lifted onto his forearms sparing her his full weight, while still intimately joined together for a few more moments, gazing lovingly into her incredible eyes.

Frankie could not explain this feeling, but at that moment she knew what it felt like to be complete. This man, who was once only a dream, was now holding and touching her, his hand smoothing her hair away from her eyes, his weight pressing down on her. He gave her a pleasure she had only, until this moment, dreamed about.

"Am I crushing you?" Jack whispered to Frankie as he kissed her neck, cheek, eyes, and lips.

"No," Frankie just about got out.

"Come here." Jack laughed in a low deep tone, as he rolled off her and pulled her close. He did not want to let her go, not yet. He ran his hand over her shoulder and down her arm, and over her waist and hip. He slid his hand to her back gliding it up and down.

"Why didn't you tell me?" Jack spoke softly into Francesca's hair on the top of her head. He reached for her chin and lifted it until she looked into his eyes. Her eyes were that incredible shade of sapphire, which caused his heart to skip a beat.

Frankie found it hard to speak. "It's not an easy subject to talk about." Frankie found it hard to look into his eyes as well, for they made her muscles dissolve until she felt nearly liquefied.

Jack took Frankie's hand, helped her out of bed and into the master bathroom. She felt embarrassed standing naked next to his nude body while he pulled open the etched, glass shower doors to turn on the water. He was incredibly handsome and strong, studying the blood stain along the front of his thighs. He took her hand and brought her into the shower with him. Francesca was actually more nervous now than she had been before, because her dreams never revealed this detail. She had no idea what to expect.

Water seemed to shoot out in every direction as he guided her under the hot water. The bathroom and the soap smelled like Jack—rich, spicy sandalwood. He reached for the shampoo bottle and placed a small amount into the palm of his enormous hand. He rubbed his hands together and slowly shampooed her hair. His large hands gently rubbed her scalp, and the sensation of his touch in her hair, on her scalp, was making her whole body tingle and sway.

"Close those amazing eyes, angel." He positioned her back under the water to rinse the soap from her hair. He couldn't take his eyes from her throat as she leaned her head back under the water. He wondered if he could wait until they showered before he took her again. He reached for the conditioner and placed a small amount into the center of his palm. Jack rubbed the conditioner between his hands then into her hair, running his fingers through it before he rinsed her tresses under the spray of water.

Frankie was almost unable to breathe. His nearness, the way he gently washed her hair was so sensual, it was as if she were being tossed about in open seas unable to take hold of anything steady. Gathering herself, Frankie reached for the shampoo, placing a small amount in the center of her hand. He lowered his head so that she could reach it. His hands were about her waist and his thumbs traced tiny circles just below her breasts. She found it difficult to concentrate on what she was doing. His mouth closed over her left breast causing her to pause and get swept away by his touch momentarily.

Slowly he lifted his head, placing it under the water, as she lifted herself up on tiptoe to run her fingers through his hair to rinse out the soap. His breathing changed, coming in shorter and faster breaths. She placed some conditioner onto her hand, but before she could reach up to rub it into his hair, his mouth covered hers and they kissed each other with unabated longing. When he angled his face to continue the kiss, Frankie slowly ran her fingers through his hair. He kissed her deeply, as her hands massaged his scalp. He pressed a kiss just to the right of her mouth, her cheek, her eyes, and her forehead. He moved his mouth back to her lips and his tongue touched hers in a slow circular motion, as Frankie followed his lead.

Lifting his head, Jack quickly rinsed his hair off before he reached for the soap. Frankie watched as he worked the soap into lather between his enormous hands. He ran his hands along her shoulders, up her neck, down her arms, and up along the sides of her breasts. Then he soaped her breasts, his thumbs moving in circular patterns over her nipples causing her to become overcome with passion. She placed her hands on his chest in an effort to steady herself. He slid his soapy hands over her buttocks as he pulled her close to him, and she could feel his intensity.

"Open your eyes, Francesca." Jack just barely spoke the words, so infused with passion. He studied her eyes, trying to remember everything about them. "Do you know that they turn to sapphires when you are near me?"

Frankie blinked. She wanted to tell him that was because she loved him. That she waited for him her whole life and that she did nothing but dream of him. She reached up and touched his cheek feeling the stubble just forming along his jaw. He flashed that quick, white smile at her as he lathered his hands again. On bended knee he started to soap her legs. Up and down his hands slid over her legs kneading and massaging. He ran his hands just to the top of her inner thighs, and Frankie placed her hands on his shoulders for support, finding it more and more difficult to stand. He stood up, and turned Frankie around to wash her back. When he pressed his lips softly to the scar at her lower back, her eyes squeezed shut almost unable to comprehend such tenderness. They moved together under the water, and he ran his hands over every part of her body while the water rinsed off the soap.

Frankie stepped away from the water and reached for the soap. She twirled the soap between her hands gathering lather between them and began to wash Jack. He was all muscles and dark hair. She soaped his chest and his arms, and he laughed that throaty laugh when she tickled him. He kept his eyes closed while she ran her small, soapy hands over his flat, rippled stomach. She traced his skin over his inner thighs where her blood still stained. His maleness increased with his obvious pleasure of her touch.

Jack seemed frozen. His eyes were still closed, but his expression changed. Frankie could hear his breathing coming faster and faster again as she lathered below his waist. She stood behind him soaping his broad back and his buttocks.

Jack turned to her and grabbed her to him almost violently. He opened his eyes, and they flashed like polished steel. He lifted her until her legs were around his waist pushing her back against the steamy green marble walls warmed from the hot water. He lowered her slowly onto him, placing his hands on her buttocks, as he began to lift her up and down. He was so strong and impressive.

Frankie clung to his strong broad shoulders, her nails biting into his skin. Her head fell back and rested against the warm marble.

The image at the white of her throat was just stunning. "Beautiful," Jack managed to squeeze the words through his labored breathing, just before he lowered his lips to her throat.

Water rained down between them as their lovemaking intensified. Frankie could not believe how he effortlessly supported her while making passionate love to her. She felt as if she was in a tropical rainforest, so green, so hot with steam everywhere. She reached up and smoothed his hair away from his face, and his eyes flashed to honed steel.

"Francesca, Francesca." His breath was coming faster and faster, and Frankie was finding it harder to breathe as well. She clung to him as his restraint snapped. Out of control, Jack could not stop himself from thrusting deeply into her again and again, pressing her back against the hot marble.

Frankie could feel her need as well as his, as he moved faster and deeper. She called out his name as a release washed over her. "Jacqino," she sighed.

In one final mind blurring thrust, Jack exploded into her. He began to shudder, and Frankie could hear his groan. It filled the shower and danced around them. She finally released a long, withheld breath, and kissed Jack's neck, feeling his pulse still racing. He released her from his manhood and set her back under the water with him. He held her so close, while they swayed back and forth in a soothing motion under the warm water. His hands rubbed her back up and down.

Frankie spoke quietly in the steamy air cupping his strong jaw in her small hand, "Your eyes lighten when you are near me." Shy after her observation, she bowed her head.

Jack had never experienced such tenderness and love. Love is what this shy, tender woman was showing him. "Francesca?"

Frankie pulled her head back to look into Jack's questioning eyes. She loved him. She knew it from the very first dream she had of him, but she couldn't tell him. *It was impossible to mention love this soon, right?* Her eyes answered him as he spoke softly caressing her cheek, as the water cascaded over them.

Jack exhaled and spoke so softly. "I feel like I have been waiting for you my whole life."

Frankie just closed her eyes and rested her forehead against his chest. His pounding heart slowed, and she could feel his muscles relax. He reached behind her and turned off the water. He opened the glass door and helped Frankie out onto the plush, ivory throw rug. He reached for an ivory-colored bath sheet and wrapped it around her, but not before cupping her breast, tantalizing her nipple with his thumb several times. He grabbed a towel for himself, folded it in half then secured it around his waist. Jack then took another smaller sage-green towel and began to towel her hair dry. Taking her by the hand, he led her back to the bedroom.

Jack pulled back the covers and removed Frankie's towel drying off her shoulders, arms, and legs. He lifted her in his arms and placed his lips over hers for a long, deep kiss. He gracefully lowered her to the bed. *Roses, she still smells like roses*, he thought. He studied her and she grew very hot from his stare, blushing from head to toe. "You are so beautiful, Francesca."

Frankie slid over in the bed, as Jack dropped his towel. She lowered her gaze and could not take her eyes off of him, either.

Jack smiled, happy that he pleased her. With her arms extended toward him, he slid into the bed holding her for a moment. With one large arm, he turned her back against his chest, so very close to him, and threw one large leg over both of her legs, bringing the sheet up to cover them. One arm rested under her pillow, as he reached around her neck covering her breast with his hand. He placed his other arm around her waist pulling her against him.

Frankie could not move and oddly enough the feeling was wonderful. She was completely wrapped up in this strong man's embrace, and it was better than any dream she had ever had as she placed her hands over his large, strong hands. *I can't believe this is real!* Frankie said to herself.

Just then Jack pinched the flattest part of her stomach.

"Ouch!" Frankie looked back over her shoulder to see Jack's eyes closed and a wicked smile upon his face.

"Shh, you're going to need your rest when I wake you from a sound sleep to make love to you again."

Jack flashed that bright, white smile, *my special smile*, she thought. He pulled her closer, if that was at all possible, and slowly they began to relax, the boat lulling them to sleep, a warm breeze wafting through the open windows from the river.

They woke just as the sun rose. Jack still held Frankie in his embrace, and the feeling of being in each other's arms meant something different to each of them.

Frankie wasn't sure if it was just another dream. But when she turned in Jack's arms and faced him, she knew for certain her life had changed forever.

Jack woke and could not believe that this warm, willing angel had slept in his arms all night. He smoothed Frankie's hair and tucked that stubborn, golden strand behind her ear.

"Good morning, angel," he whispered before he placed a soft kiss on her forehead. He woke in the middle of the night and watched her sleep. His need grew for her, but he held back worried that she might be tender from her first experience. That amazed and stunned him all at once. He lost his virginity when he was thirteen, and it wasn't pretty and it certainly wasn't special. It was just two hormonal teens who went too far one night, but not Francesca; she was pure until last night.

"Good mor…" but before Frankie could finish they both heard the unmistakable sound of Bruno barking at the top of his lungs from the dock.

"I think I just might shoot that dog of yours, but you would inevitably remove the bullet, right? Save him."

"Right, that pesky code of ethics gets me every time," she confirmed.

Jack held her close for a moment and then got out of bed, pulling her with him as he held her close again. "Come on, let's see what Retta's cooked up for breakfast, otherwise I might be tempted to eat your dog." Jack quipped and Frankie giggled.

They freshened up quickly; then Jack helped Frankie get dressed, kissing her skin before each layer of clothing covered her. Jack pulled her blouse closed because that was the best he could do with most of the buttons missing. Smiling shyly, he asked, "Did I do that?" His killer smile flashed white and bright at her as she nodded her head with a positive reply. Jack dressed in jeans and a T-shirt and quickly pulled on his sneakers. He reached for Frankie's hand, leading her through the yacht as she jogged behind him, trying to keep pace with his elongated strides. When they reached the deck, Bruno spotted them and began to bark in a high pitched "glad to see ya" bark while spinning in circles.

"Did you ever take that beast, ahh...I mean...precious animal to obedience school?"

"It wouldn't have helped. He's a boxer!" Frankie shrugged. When they reached the end of the dock, Bruno practically bowled them over, licking, yelping, and nipping until Jack had to physically control him by his collar. Jack released Bruno, as they walked up the bank to the farmhouse holding each other close. Bruno charged about them, running off then tearing back, just narrowly missing them, causing them to laugh.

"You're a vet—can't you prescribe something for him?" Jack stared at the circling dog with a grin upon his face.

"That's funny, because my father just asked me the same thing." Frankie giggled and kept walking. She went into the farmhouse, ran up the stairs two at a time and changed quickly into a pair of light tan shorts and a pale pink T-shirt. She brushed her teeth and ran her fingers through her hair. She looked at her reflection in the mirror. It was different—she looked relaxed and happy, really happy. Her reflection revealed what she looked like in love, and she liked what she saw in the mirror. Running back down the stairs, Jack scooped her up and swung her around in the foyer, kissing her soundly on the mouth making her laugh and throw her head back.

Hand in hand, Jack and Frankie walked over to the cottage and knocked on the bottom half of the back Dutch door; the upper half was already opened. Retta appeared, hugging Frankie for a long time, throwing Jack a wink and a wicked grin over Frankie's shoulder.

"You both must be starved," Retta said, keeping any further comments to herself.

"Starved doesn't begin to describe it," Jack replied.

"It smells delicious in here. It *always* smells delicious in here," Frankie declared.

They both sat down to towering stacks of pancakes, bacon, home fries, and a never-ending pot of coffee. Nelson joined them, and the four of them ate and talked about so many things, but especially about the barn renovations.

After breakfast, Frankie helped Retta with the dishes, while Jack and Nelson went over to the barn to check on a few, final details where the horses were to be boarded. Once the men were gone, Retta held Frankie close for a moment. "If I had a daughter..." she started to wave her hand in that familiar gesture her father, mother, and Jack had all been doing. "If I could've had a daughter, I would've wanted her to be just like you."

Frankie didn't know what to say, so she pulled Retta into her arms and hugged her until Retta started waving her hands about again.

The weekend flew by with colors, fragrances, and tall, sweet grasses. Frankie and Jack spent every minute together, laughing, playing, kissing, and making love. It was the most wonderful experience in Frankie's life, and she never wanted it to end.

Chapter Twelve
Sweet summer...

As the summer drew to an end, the barn and hospital were completed, and the contractors started working full tilt on the farmhouse. Frankie could hardly wait. Reflections was moved up to the farm, and Frankie could see the transformation in her horse almost immediately. He galloped, bucked, and neighed loudly with his new surroundings. It was clear to Frankie that the river's breeze breathed new life into everything it touched.

Even Bruno stayed at the farm permanently. He would chase Frankie's truck whenever she left, but once she hit the street, Bruno sat still and watched her drive off. She couldn't blame him. The place was wonderful. The air was clean, the grass was green and with all those wide-open spaces, Bruno would run after nothing, or something, depending on his mood.

Frankie came up only on weekends and stayed on The Rose with Jack. With the demands of work and her patient load practically doubling, she was finding it impossible to go to the farmhouse on Friday nights. Most Saturdays she worked until noon; then she would drive straight up to the farmhouse without even stopping at her apartment to change. And Jack was always waiting for her with open arms. He would twirl her around and kiss her in front of anyone and everyone. It was no secret. They loved each other, but still hadn't said the words to one another. Not yet.

During the week, there were so many men working at the farmhouse that Frankie found it more relaxing to actually go back to work. She couldn't stand the mess and confusion, not to mention the noise from saws and hammers amid men shouting, and Jack flaying his arms when the merest instruction wasn't followed to the letter.

But on the weekends, none of that confusion existed. All the workmen, and even the skipper of The Rose, went home to their families, and probably also to get away from Jack. He was a perfectionist, yet he was always open to any suggestion.

These precious weekends during the summer never even compared to Frankie's dreams. So many wonderful nights of love making, as Jack held her close making her body soar with fulfillment and her heart sing with joy.

All was quiet and peaceful, as Frankie and Jack lay together in each other's arms on The Rose. She could hear his racing heartbeat slow down from their lovemaking.

"I missed you so much all week," Jack spoke breathlessly to the top of her golden crown. He was so in love with her that it actually scared him. He was afraid for himself. Afraid if she didn't feel the same things for him, as he felt for her. It was such a deep and profound love. *This is the girl of my dreams*, he thought silently. The girl he should have waited for. The girl he wanted to marry. His stomach was in knots with fear. He was afraid to tell her how much he loved her, for it would expose his heart to the unknown and the what-ifs. But tonight, he promised his heart and himself that he would tell her. Holding her close, breathing in her fragrance, he gently pressed his lips to the very top of her silky golden hair. Frankie lifted her chin to look up at him, as he looked deeply into her eyes. *She knows*, Jack thought. *She already knows that I am madly in love with her.*

"I'm in love with you, Francesca." True to his promise, Jack spoke the words to her, as he knew he would. He had said these words to Victoria, but now he realized that he never loved her and never meant those words once spoken, because he never really loved anyone until Francesca. He watched the expression of her face soften and the color of her blue pools, still darkened from their passionate lovemaking, darken further to an almost midnight blue. "I'm in love with you and to the very core of my soul," Jack confessed.

"Oh Jacqino I love you. I've loved you forever. I was so afraid to tell you," Frankie whispered back, as she reached up to touch his lips with her fingertips. He gently kissed each small pad, still searching her eyes.

"Stay with me here on The Rose. Now that the hospital is done, you could start your own practice at the barn and be close to me," Jack suggested, as he held Francesca in the circle of his arms. He found it hard to concentrate when she wasn't around, because all he thought about was her, and then he found it next to impossible to concentrate when she was around, because all he wanted to do was make love to her.

"I don't think that would sit very well with my parents.

Contrary to the way they act around you, they are really quite old-fashioned," Frankie answered before pressing her forehead against his chest.

"Marry me." Jack spoke genuinely as he tilted her chin up so that he could witness her expression. "How do you think that will sit with your parents?"

"Jacqino?!" Frankie asked.

"Francesca, I've wanted to ask you since the time your dog chased me down in Central Park. I just didn't want to scare you off. Please, say you'll be my wife," Jack pleaded while caressing her cheek. *She won't say no, please God*, Jack prayed silently. *Please let her say "Yes."*

Frankie couldn't believe her ears—he told her that he loved her and now he was proposing to her all in one night. She felt her whole body melt. She was going to marry the man of her dreams. The man she waited for and loved her whole life. "Yes, yes, I'll marry you! I love you, I love you." Francesca threw her arms around Jack's neck, nuzzling her lips against his throat.

"I love you," Jack spoke while pulling back to look into her eyes. "Now I don't suppose you'd want to elope or maybe just have a small wedding, like say...oh I don't know...by the end of next week, would you?" Jack teased as he caressed her cheek with the back of his hand over her soft-scented skin. He always wanted to touch her, so soft and beautiful. He always wanted to breathe her in. Roses, always roses.

Francesca just shook her head.

"So you're going to make me wait, hmm?" Jack questioned, while nuzzling her neck as she barely nodded her head in answer.

Chapter Thirteen
Just a week later...

The following Saturday at about noon, a black, stretch limo pulled into the gravel driveway of the farmhouse. An enormous box, slightly protruded from the trunk of the limo, held down with rope. Anthony had warned Paul that if *anything* happened to that box, it would cost him his job, but Paul told him to relax, that it would be safe for the trip.

Jack looked up from his plans with eyes widened. He rolled up the plans and began to eat up the distance between the limo and himself.

Anthony stepped out of the car before Paul had a chance to even stop the vehicle, flinging the door open, and immediately turning all of his attention to the box in the trunk.

"One scratch, Paul, and your head will roll!" Anthony threatened in that quasi-diplomatic tone that only Anthony could pull off.

"I guarantee, Mr. Romano, not one scratch!" Paul countered.

"Anthony?" Jack asked.

"Jack, yeah, just give us a minute please," Anthony spoke as he began to untie the ropes that held the enormous box in place. "Hey, come over here and help us lower this damn thing before it falls out, and then I will still have to fire Paul," Anthony continued.

Jack waved for Nelson to give them a hand. After a brief introduction, the four men struggled to lift the box from the trunk and rest it on the ground. Paul pulled a knife from his pocket and expertly began to cut the ropes that held the box closed. The sides of the box fell open to reveal a huge tub with brass, clawed feet. It was made of fine porcelain and the brass fixtures were in an open box in the bottom of the tub. Anthony ran his hand along the rim of the tub to check for chips, scrutinizing every detail.

"See Mr. Romano, just like I said, not a scratch," Paul declared with that smug 'I told you so' look all over his face.

Anthony looked up at Paul raising one eyebrow menacingly. He didn't understand how Jack had put up with Paul all these years. Paul was absolutely driving him nuts. Literally! Always telling him when to come and when to go instead of being told when and where he was to pick up and when and where he was to drop off. Between Paul and the reporters who seemed to be everywhere, Anthony mentally recalled how he and Paul had a hell of a time losing the press after they started dogging him early that morning. They had to switch limos once they reached the warehouse and then left through the "Truck Entry Only." Anthony could not believe the constant press attention in his everyday daily life, including weekends, and the process was starting to grate on his nerves. How did Jack ever tolerate it, he wondered, and for all those years, without a single complaint? Anthony shrugged off the feeling and turned all smiles to his beloved brother.

"What do you think, Jack?" Anthony asked, gesturing his hand over the tub. "When you said you were renovating an old farmhouse, I remembered this tub I had picked up in England."

"We had a hell of a time finding it in the warehouse," Paul added.

Anthony again turned to Paul and once again, raised his eyebrow threateningly.

"Well?" Anthony asked Jack, waiting for his brother's response.

"It's perfect. Vintage...and timeless, I think Francesca will love it," Jack answered while he kneeled down to inspect the sides of the tub. It was huge and could easily seat two people comfortably, if not more. "Let's bring her inside and see how she looks," Jack suggested.

Francesca, Anthony thought silently. *Who is Francesca?*

Paul couldn't resist verbally guiding Anthony and Jack as they walked backwards, all struggling under the weight of the enormous tub.

"To your right, Mr. Romano," Paul instructed.

"We are both Mr. Romano. For the love of Pete, man, which one of us do you mean?" Anthony cursed under his breath mumbling something about Paul constantly bossing him around, as they continued struggling to haul the tub to the second floor. The tub had to be tipped on its side in order to slip it through the doorway of the master bathroom. Once inside the bathroom, Jack took note that some minor plumbing would need to be reworked to accommodate the tub.

"Perfect," Anthony exclaimed, while Jack, Nelson, and Paul were still trying to straighten their backs. "I'm sure we have two matching sinks and the commode. I think I even bought the light fixtures. Hmm, I'll look for that when we go back to the city," Anthony continued while surveying the room.

Nelson offered Paul a cold drink, but Paul asked for a rain check explaining that he had cousins in the area that he wanted to visit before they went back to the city.

Anthony was happy to spend some time alone with his brother. He hadn't seen Jack in months and missed him. Anthony quickly pulled his brother to him and held him tight. Jack hugged him back realizing just how much he missed Anthony, too.

"How about giving me the tour? I need a break from RE and Paul," Anthony admitted. He wanted to catch up with Jack and didn't want Paul pestering him about traffic or anything else for that matter.

"Sure. I hope you can stay until Francesca comes," Jack answered. "I want you to meet her."

"Francesca. Really! Someone new," Anthony asked.

But Jack didn't answer. Instead he just had this stupid look on his face. Like a kid who just got his first two-wheeler.

As they walked around inside the house, Jack explained the remodeling plans to Anthony, who was impressed with Jack's vision. His brother looked great. No dark circles under his eyes. Trim, but not too lean, and relaxed...very relaxed and happy. The two brothers walked over to see the barn and the new animal hospital. Anthony was even more impressed. The place was gleaming and obviously ready to do business at a moment's notice, but Anthony couldn't figure out why Jack would set up an animal hospital in his barn.

As they made their way out of the barn and walked around the farmhouse, Frankie's truck was parked in the driveway. Bruno, knowing the difference in the noise of each vehicle, came tearing up from the river's edge to see her. She knew he was going to do this. It became his routine lately. She had waited in her truck, then slowly emerged, watching as Bruno charged past the truck, skidding to a halt, kicking up dirt, leaves, and clumps of grass. He spun around and charged the short distance back to Frankie, kicking up more dirt and grass. Then he planted his paws perfectly still in front of her so she could rub the spot just between his ears. Soft, so soft. She just loved that spot on him.

When she looked up she saw Jack and another man beside

him. As they neared her, she could see that Jack's eyes were smiling even from that distance. The other man was the same size as Jack, but blonde, very blonde.

"Francesca," Jack called, smiling as he reached for her shoulders and kissed her cheek sweetly. Frankie smiled up at Jack; it was so good to see him. Being welcomed home by this beautiful man was priceless.

"Anthony, this is Dr. Francesca O'Brian." Jack looked from his brother back to Frankie. "Francesca, let me introduce my brother, Anthony."

"Hello, it's nice to meet you," Frankie said, putting her hand out to shake Anthony's.

"Hello," Anthony replied in a deep tone, very similar to Jack's, but different somehow, more proper. Anthony stared at Jack and then the dog. He couldn't help but wonder what was going on here. Who was this girl? Why does Jack look so happy? And then it clicked.

Francesca looked at him as he registered some kind of understanding. He quickly recovered by taking Francesca's hand and pressing a kiss on the back of it speaking softly in a foreign tongue, making Jack grunt.

"The pleasure is mine," Anthony stated rather formerly. Jack eased Frankie's hand away from Anthony and spoke into his brother's face.

"Francesca is the owner of this wonderful farmhouse and has agreed to let me design the renovations," Jack explained. "Francesca, Anthony has just solved the master bathroom dilemma."

"Oh?" Frankie asked.

"I hope you do not think it forward of me, ahh...may I call you Francesca?" Anthony continued after Frankie nodded. "Yes, well, I heard that Jack was renovating this old farmhouse, but I had no idea that it was not his." Anthony shot his brother a look of imminent death then in the most diplomatic way continued. "Well, anyway, I remembered that I had the most wonderful period tub that would work in an old farmhouse. So I brought it up. I think you should have a look at it, and let Jack know if you like it or not." Anthony almost felt uncomfortable. He had no idea that his brother was working for someone else. He was under the impression that his brother had bought the farm to renovate it and sell after the renovations were completed. Kind of like a rehab project just to get his feet wet.

Frankie spoke very softly. "Is it cream-colored and quite large with gleaming brass-clawed feet?" Frankie blinked innocently.

Jack and Anthony both stared at each other in disbelief, then back to look at Frankie.

"How did you know?" Jack questioned with his mouth gaping in shock.

"I saw all of you struggling with it through the upstairs window as I drove up the drive," Frankie teasingly pointed to the second floor windows open wide.

"Oh," Anthony said as he reached for his heart. He was finding it hard to think clearly around her.

"Of course I know I will just love it. Anyway, I wouldn't dream of making you take that enormous tub back down that flight of stairs," Frankie joked. *Especially since I know that tub, only too well, from my dreams,* she thought silently.

"My back thanks you." Anthony bowed slightly and turned to show Frankie his hand rubbing his sore, lower back.

Jack threw back his head speaking directly to heaven. "Thank you." He laughed and slapped his brother on the shoulder. "I think it's time for you to get out from behind that big desk of yours, little brother."

They all started to make their way into the farmhouse. Bruno shot away from them and started to speed around the open fields again at that maddening pace of his. Anthony stopped and stared, one eyebrow raised in question.

"Francesca is a vet," Jack answered Anthony's unspoken questions.

"Okay, but the dog?" Anthony pointed.

"Hers and completely insane," Jack whispered.

"I see." Anthony watched the dog hunker down and increase his pace towards the river's bank.

After a tour of the much-teased-about tub, and a continued tour of the house, dock, and grounds, Anthony found that he had to physically close his mouth several times as he caught it hanging open. He never knew his brother was so talented and creative. He was impressed by Jack's architectural complements to the very old building. Not to mention the incredible design challenges to the barn/hospital conversion.

Frankie, Jack, and Anthony stopped by the cottage to introduce Anthony to Retta. Retta always prepared extra food on the weekends for Frankie's visits. Jack, Anthony, Frankie, Retta and Nelson all sat, ate and enjoyed each other's company. Anthony couldn't help but notice the way Jack kept holding Francesca's hand and the way they couldn't seem to take their eyes off each other. It was obvious these two were very serious about each other.

Anthony's cell phone rang near the end of their meal. He excused himself politely and stepped outside the cottage to take the call. Once he hung up, he called Paul and told him they had to leave. He had just received a disturbing phone call and needed to get back to the city immediately. Of course, Paul argued that the timing couldn't have been worse with traffic, but Anthony hung up on him. When he reentered the cottage, he was mumbling something about firing that good-for-nothing driver and that Paul gave him more lip than any employee, probably ever, in the history of Romano Enterprises.

When Paul started blowing the horn in a most annoying way about ten minutes after Anthony called him, Anthony stood up rigidly, excused himself again, with all the grace of a dignitary, and walked from the cottage. From inside the cottage, everyone could hear Anthony bellowing at the top of his lungs at the limo driver. "Remove your blasted hand from the car horn, Paul, before I remove your hand from your limb!" Anthony turned and walked back into the cottage as if he never shouted a word to anyone and graciously thanked Retta and Nelson for the delicious lunch. He shook Jack's hand, pulling him close to hug him. He reached for Frankie, leaning in close to kiss her cheek. Anthony whispered quite softly into her ear, "Please be gentle with my brother's heart."

Frankie could hear the concern in his voice and quickly whispered back so softly that he had to struggle to hear her. "Jacqino's heart will always be safe with me."

Anthony looked at her for a moment and could hear the love in her voice. *She called him Jacqino.*

Frankie and Jack walked Anthony down the drive and waved as Anthony left mumbling something about Paul having the manners of a baboon.

The two lovers started to walk around the back of the

farmhouse and Jack pulled Frankie quickly into his arms. He was holding her so tightly she could barely breathe. Then his mouth crushed down on hers with hunger and wanting. His tongue tasted and danced, and long after he drank from her he lifted his head and pulled her close, continuing their walk around the property. Jack stopped every few steps to pull Frankie into his arms and kiss her again. "I miss you so much when you're not here. I can't even think straight," he whispered above her lips, just before he kissed her again deeply.

Frankie couldn't think straight either, especially when he kissed her like that. "I think about you constantly too, Jacqino." Frankie admitted, whispering back to his softened lips.

Chapter Fourteen
A bump in the road...

"Scarpelli!" Anthony hissed the name through clenched teeth. The whole situation stunk to high heaven of him. When he was visiting with his brother, he received the call that the warehouse on Fuller Street had been trashed very early Saturday morning. The Scarpelli and Romano families had bad blood between them, but the Scarpellis had been quiet for so many years. *For the love of...*Anthony's thoughts trailed off. *My own mother is a Scarpelli and even my godfather. Why would he do this?*

Since the time of the arranged marriage between Anthony's father and mother more than 30 years ago, normally heightened tensions between these two families increased to a near volcanic eruption. Then when Nicholas Romano made Tony Scarpelli, John's brother, a member of the board of Romano Enterprises, John Scarpelli seemed to just snap. He purposely exiled himself from the family, vowing vengeance.

But why now? Anthony questioned. He crossed the large office suite to the wall of windows. He looked at his reflection in the window and hated his features. So blonde with blue eyes—it screamed of Scarpelli. Anthony bore his mother's and godfather's Scarpelli likenesses, and he hated that about himself. He looked past his reflection out at the grand park below. But his mind didn't register the lush green lawns, the clear, blue lake and matching sky, or that the trees were crowned with bright, waxy-green leaves. Instead, his mind focused on smashed crystal and glassware, slashed upholstery, and carved gouges in priceless furnishings. "Damn it," Anthony cursed loudly. He called his father directly so that they could discuss the recent Scarpelli situation. A gentle knock and a slight squeak of his office door hinge announced Nicholas Romano's appearance.

Nicholas Romano entered the office, so large, so strong, so dark, Anthony thought. His father's presence filled even the largest of rooms. Nicholas was clad in a charcoal gray suit, impeccably tailored to fit him like a glove—an impressive glove. The door closed quietly.

"What has happened?" Nicholas turned, asking softly.

Anthony could never understand how such a strong, broad man spoke so temperately.

"Scarpelli!" Anthony sneered.

"What? How?" Nicholas sat gracefully onto the sofa near the coffee table.

"Very early this morning. The warehouse down on Fuller Street was broken into. Two security guards were tossed around like a house salad and thrown in a separate storage area. They trashed the place Dad. Broken crystal, slashed upholstery, carved-up furniture. But nothing, NOTHING, was taken—just destroyed." Anthony started shouting then caught himself. "The place is a godforsaken mess. It will take us months to clean it up, probably a year or better to process the insurance claims on the goods, and, oh, one more thing, they knew the alarm code. It was an inside job. Security said their faces were covered with ski masks, punched the alarm code, waltzed right into the warehouse, kicked the crap out of them, and then went to town on Romano Enterprises' goods."

"How are the security guards?" Nicholas questioned softly, forcing Anthony to struggle to hear him.

"Mike has a concussion, and Pete has a few loose teeth," Anthony sighed, raking his fingers through his white-blonde hair.

"Are you certain it was Scarpelli? I mean Scarpelli hasn't really made any waves in years. After I made your godfather a member of the board, John did seem despondent, but I had every intention of finding a position for him as well." Nicholas sat up and propped his elbows on his knees, his chin resting on his fists. Marrying a Scarpelli was accepted, because it was arranged by two very powerful men, Nicholas' grandfather and Angelina's grandfather, but putting a Scarpelli on the board made a lot of Romanos angry and nervous. Nicholas couldn't help but think about his wife. The arranged marriage was done so in an effort to join two feuding families. The marriage was a great success, but some of the bad blood between the families persevered.

"Dad, please. They took nothing! Typical Scarpelli! Uncle Tony always told me stories about how his grandfather and great uncles never took—only destroyed." Anthony looked at his father sadly. He didn't want him to think he wasn't capable of being a good president. Nothing like this happened when Jack was here. In fact, nothing like this had happened in over 20 years.

"I need to call a board meeting." Anthony reached for the phone.

Nicholas was up faster than Anthony could comprehend, took the phone from his son, and replaced the receiver back into the cradle.

"Anthony, please, we need to discuss this. If you call a board meeting, Uncle Tony is going to be uncontrollable. We would have to chain him to his chair just to have him sit still through the meeting."

Anthony half smiled. Uncle Tony, his godfather, would be a maniac when he heard about this. The man either passionately loved or passionately hated. There was no in-between for him.

"Dad, you know the procedures. Any kind of damage or robbery over a million dollars has to be signed off by the board of directors. This Scarpelli stunt will probably run into the millions. What do you want me to do?" Anthony raised his hands in defeat.

"I want you to give me some time, twenty-four hours, to make some calls." Nicholas spoke confidently and in that deep, rich tone that Jack inherited, along with the dark, strong looks.

"Dad, ahh…while you're making those phone calls I think you better put a guy on a Francesca O'Brian." Anthony looked down at the burgundy, leather desktop tracing the engraved gilt border with his index finger.

"Why? Who is she?" Nicholas sat down from across the desk already knowing of the new woman in Jack's life.

"I think Jack intends to marry her, that is, if he has not already asked."

"Write down everything you know about her. I'll see that it is taken care of." Nicholas stood up while Anthony scrawled down some basic information.

Anthony handed the piece of paper to his father and watched him fold it in two, then place it inside his breast pocket. As Nicholas turned and started for the door, Anthony called out to him.

"Dad, one more thing…"

Nicholas turned around and looked at Anthony. *Was Anthony blushing?* Nicholas kept his face expressionless. Anthony had already made a call from the limo on the ride back to the city to have his investigator check out Francesca O'Brian. The investigator came back within the hour. He didn't tell Anthony that Mr. Romano senior had already called for a background check on Francesca O'Brian. However, what he did do was dutifully inform Anthony that she was clean, clean as a whistle, in fact. She even saved the Mayor's dog not that long ago, except that she hung around with a Rebecca McFarlan. And that girl seemed to lead two lives. She worked and had a good job as a social worker in Manhattan during the day, but at night she followed a completely opposite set of rules. She apparently liked men and a lot of them. From the investigator's description, Anthony had recognized her as the girl he bumped into in the hospital the night of Jack's accident. It was odd the way he had only seen her for a split second and couldn't seem to get her out of his mind.

"There is one more person." Anthony reported while starting to write down another name and basic information.

Nicholas walked over and reached for the paper with the additional name scrawled on it. "Who is Rebecca McFarlan?" Nicholas asked, truly not hearing this name before.

Anthony didn't answer his father. He kept his face stone still.

"*Marone*, Anthony, it's supposed to get easier to be a parent when their children get older, but with you and Jacqino...ahh, never mind. I'll call you when I know something." Nicholas turned and left soundlessly.

Chapter Fifteen
Autumn is such a lovely time of year...

Now that Jack and Francesca planned to make the farm their home, Jack designed a three-car garage that resembled a carriage house. Above the garage, over one bay, would be his office, and over the remaining two would be a guest suite that would be equipped with two bedrooms, two full baths, a living room, and small eat-in kitchen.

The second floor of the farmhouse was just about finished. The master bedroom and bath were fully completed, and the other five bedrooms and two baths were also just about done, except the heat wasn't fully functional. Frankie was slowly moving her things up to the farmhouse, and even though it was hard to think about leaving Park East Animal Hospital, inside she really couldn't wait to open her very own animal clinic.

It was fall and the leaves were starting to change all those wonderful colors of crimson and gold. With the window rolled down, Frankie could hear the tires on her truck crunch the leaves as she drove up the dirt road to the farm.

Since the time Anthony brought the tub up to the farm, he seemed to be obsessed with bringing more items that Frankie would never have time to buy, but definitely needed, to complete the farmhouse. Anthony had delivered lighting fixtures, sinks, and, at one point, an enormous stained glass window that, although covered up in the middle, looked quite colorful from its exposed edges. The place was really starting to shape up and didn't look so forlorn anymore.

This weekend, her parents, Jack's parents, Anthony, Scott, Robin, her assistant from Park East Animal Hospital, and Becca were coming up on Saturday for dinner. They were invited to see the farm and the improvements that had been made all summer long, but it was for another reason entirely.

Jack and Frankie intended to announce to everyone their intention to marry next spring. Frankie had already given her job notice that, right after the New Year, she would no longer be working for Park East Animal Hospital. But since her patient load was so heavy, Frankie was starting to doubt whether that date would materialize.

Frankie already asked Robin, her assistant at Park East Animal Hospital, if she would consider working for her at the barn clinic, although she knew it meant that Robin would probably have to relocate. She asked Robin to think on it for a while before deciding. Frankie had some suitcases in her truck and planned on moving the rest of her belongings, little by little, to the farmhouse. Scott offered to move some of her furnishings she intended on keeping. She was actually starting to enjoy planning out the rooms and decided that her couch would be perfect in the master bedroom suite opposite the fireplace. The rest of her apartment was just stuff borrowed and found, so Frankie planned on returning and giving the rest of her things away. Her apartment was nothing more than a place to sleep, shower, and occasionally eat. She usually worked so many hours, that she never spent any real time there. And it felt so good to be moving up to the farmhouse, even if it was slowly, because she knew she belonged there.

Each time Frankie went to the farmhouse, she was amazed with the glorious furnishings and paintings Anthony kept bringing up with him. Beautiful and so tasteful. Frankie, at one point, wondered if she could afford such fine things. When she asked Anthony about it, he just waved his hand and said he was cleaning out his warehouses to make room for new inventory. That hand waving thing that Retta did was apparently very catchy, and it took Anthony no time at all to pick up on it.

Frankie really knew very little about the Romano Enterprises' empire, and she was unaware that Jack had already told Anthony that he proposed to her. Anthony was relieved and could tell that his brother was the happiest he had ever seen him. So once Anthony got the news of their intended engagement, the furnishings from Romano Enterprises tripled in delivery. He knew that both Jack and Frankie were far too busy to furnish the place themselves, and Anthony confessed he just loved doing that sort of thing anyway.

Frankie stopped her truck before she reached the farm, because she wanted to check her reflection in her mirror. She purposely went back to her apartment after work, showered, and changed into tweed slacks, with a jeweled-neckline, cream-colored sweater and matching cream blazer. She dabbed a little lipstick on her lips and ran her fingers through her shiny, blonde hair that just touched her shoulders. She snapped the mirror closed and hoped that Jack's parents would like her. She drove the last mile to the farm feeling very nervous.

Originally, Frankie's plan of working only until noon on Saturdays quickly changed to having hours until four in the afternoon. This afternoon she felt a little tired when she left the animal hospital, because one of her appointments lingered. She had a visit from Mr. Scarpelli. He lived next to her parents since Frankie's family moved into that old brownstone neighborhood more than two decades ago. He brought in his bulldog, Nick, about every two weeks to have his nails trimmed and to ask general questions. He could have easily taken the dog to any groomer in the city, but he insisted on seeing Dr. Frankie. He was such a sweet, old man, but he was a bit strange. He always asked her to pick a horse in the upcoming horse races or pick some numbers for the upcoming lottery. *Silly stuff,* she thought, but she would clip Nick's nails and dispense four digits that Mr. Scarpelli would quickly scratch down on a little piece of paper and stuff into his coat pocket. She had already told Mr. Scarpelli that she would be leaving the animal hospital and opening her own place upstate.

"When are you officially leaving the animal hospital?" Mr. Scarpelli asked, studying his own nails, while Frankie clipped his bulldog's trying to appear unruffled by this news.

"Probably the first of the year," Frankie replied without looking up from her task.

"I want you to write down the directions, so that I can bring Nick to your new hospital." Mr. Scarpelli insisted, looking down at his shoes.

"Mr. Scarpelli, the drive is at least an hour on a clear day in one direction. You could easily keep bringing Nick here or to any groomer in the city. Nick only really needs to come to the animal hospital once a year for his usual check-up and vaccinations." Frankie tried to be diplomatic.

"NO!" Mr. Scarpelli raised his voice then caught himself, clearing his throat. "I mean…no. Nick is very good with you, and I wouldn't want him to snap at someone because I was too lazy to take him on, what I am sure, is a pleasant drive every couple of weeks."

Frankie noticed that his face looked like it was glistening, as though he were perspiring. She certainly didn't want to upset him further.

"Mr. Scarpelli, I'm not a fool. I'm not going to turn away your business. I'll be more than happy to take care of Nick. I'll write down very clear directions, and you and Nick can take a road trip. It is really quite lovely up there."

"Good," Mr. Scarpelli affirmed, closing the subject for any further discussion.

That conversation and directions to the farm kept Frankie longer than usual. Once she got home and readied herself for tonight, she couldn't seem to catch her second wind.

As she entered the farmhouse and heard the voices of the many people she loved so dearly, her energy level naturally increased. Her heels clicked on the striking black-and-white marble floor in the foyer, which was exposed once the old carpeting from the floor was torn up. It looked brand new, once it had been cleaned and polished, and Frankie loved those little hidden treasures the farmhouse revealed. She walked to the foot of the staircase, turned left, then stopped at the double-pocket door entryway into the dining room. Frankie peeked in and saw her family and friends talking to each other. Anthony seemed to be glued to Becca and Scott couldn't take his eyes off Robin. Her parents, Retta and Nelson, and obviously Jack's parents from the resemblance of the distinguished gentleman standing next to Jack, were all chatting amiably with each other. Jack looked almost nervous, not really speaking to anyone in particular. He wore dark slacks and a crisp, white, button-down shirt. His tie captured the colors of early November, with deep browns, grays, and a little wisp of orange to match the spectacular autumn foliage outside.

Jack lifted his gaze and saw Frankie smiling at him. Returning her smile, Jack wove through the crowd, never taking his dark eyes from her. An inviting blaze burned in the fireplace, and Jack patted Nelson's shoulder as he passed behind him. The large worktable now doubled as a dining room table, covered with fine Irish linen, exquisite bone china—obviously another of Anthony's purchases—and light-catching crystal goblets. Numerous candles flickered from the silver candlestick holders to the sconces holding tall tapers on either side of the mantel. No one seemed to notice the plaster was torn down, exposing wood lathe and wires in several places. The people in the room filled

Frankie's soul with happiness. When Jack finally reached her, he embraced her as if he hadn't held her in years, softly pressing a tender kiss on her cheek. "I missed you, my love," Jack whispered raising his hand to smooth her hair away from her face, that so-familiar gesture that Frankie adored. She looked back into Jack's eyes and couldn't be happier.

"Jack, step aside and let me say hello properly," Anthony instructed over Jack's shoulder in a brotherly fashion, while reaching his hand around to pull Frankie away from him. Anthony bent down and whispered softly into Frankie's ear. "Welcome to the family." Anthony planted a kiss on each of her cheeks, even though the announcement hadn't been made yet.

Another deep, male voice bellowed from beside Anthony's shoulder. "Come on, Romano, quit hogging her, she's not engaged yet. I don't see any claim on her hand, so she's still available as far as I can tell," Scott announced for everyone to hear.

Anthony just glared at Scott and his obvious lack of manners.

Scott reached around Anthony, fearless as usual, muttering something about the Romanos always getting whatever they wanted, whenever they wanted, and hugged Frankie to him whispering to her softly, "You look great, but Jack looks a little soft. Don't worry, I'm gonna have him workout with me tomorrow."

Frankie giggled remembering Jack's complaints.

Jack reached for her hand, pulling her away from Scott and leading her around the dining room. She kissed Retta and Nelson, Robin and Becca, and then her parents. Jack guided her toward his parents, and Frankie could not believe how Jack was a near-clone of his father, except for the few strands of silver that streaked the older gentleman's hair, bringing out the silver in his eyes, just like Jack's. The crinkles around his eyes were from smiling, and Frankie wanted to reach up and touch them.

Nicholas was as tall as Jack and just as broad. He even appeared to be, quite possibly, as fit as Jack. Jack's mother was in complete contrast to Nicholas. She was fair and beautiful, petite and trim, but very shapely. Angelina's blonde-white hair, so much like Anthony's, had shiny, silver strands running through it, but they were hard to find. She wore her hair in a classic chignon, which seemed familiar to Frankie.

"Mother, Father, may I present Francesca Catherine O'Brian,"

Jack introduced her formerly. "Francesca, this is my mother, Angelina Marie Romano, and my father, Nicholas Romano."

"Lovely, just lovely." Angelina spoke first. "It's a pleasure to meet you," she said, while pressing a kiss on both of Frankie's cheeks.

Nicholas took Francesca's hand, pressing a soft kiss delicately to it while speaking serenely to her in Italian. *"Angela, da dove viene?"*

Frankie had no idea what he said, but it sounded very personal.

Jack quickly pulled her hand away from his father and shook his head. Angelina giggled and reached for her husband's arm. Frankie's mother understood every word and moved her hand over her mouth to stifle her giggle. Frankie heard Scott muttering something about Jack learning to be smooth from his father and heard Scott grunt, as Anthony slammed his elbow into his ribs, never once breaking his smile.

They all sat around the enormous worktable, candles flickering and dancing all around them, making the room appear romantic and cozy. No one seemed to notice the assorted unmatched chairs found in the attic and around the farm. They oddly seemed to reflect the varying personalities of the guests. Frankie realized that Retta, somehow, had everyone paired off, including Anthony and Becca, and Scott with Robin, except for Frankie, at one end of the table and Jack at the other. Jack started to protest when Retta led Frankie away from him, but went along with her seating arrangements, with a "yes ma'am."

The women carried out large platters of roast beef and chicken, potatoes, a wide variety of vegetables, and gravy. Nicholas put himself in charge of the wine and circled the table, red in his right hand and white in his left, alternately filling the glasses and speaking in that melodic, soothing tone reminiscent of Jack's.

Before anyone started to eat, Jack stood with his glass raised and lightly tapped the side of his crystal goblet to get everyone's attention. With an air of pride and strength he announced their engagement. "I have asked Francesca to marry me, and she has graciously accepted my proposal. Please raise your glasses and toast our engagement. We will be wed in the spring, here at the farm."

"Wait just one damn minute Romano! I don't see an

engagement ring on her finger." Scott was not going to make this easy. After all he had been pursuing Frankie for years.

"Farrell!" Anthony immediately jumped to Jack's defense.

Jack, a true gentleman, shrugged off Scott's outburst. "I got that covered, Scott. I just thought I would present Francesca with a small token of our engagement in front of our families and friends so that there would be no mistake as to who was smart enough to ask for her hand first," Jack grinned like the proverbial cat, leaving Scott alone in his embarrassment and wincing from the subtle verbal blow.

Jack slowly walked to the other end of the table, where Frankie sat. He knelt down beside her, and she felt the blood rush to her cheeks and her heart begin to race. He reached for her hand and in a serious voice that could be heard by all, he looked at the woman who had stolen his heart. "Francesca, for as long as any Romano man can remember in the history of my father's family, a Romano always asked for the hand of the woman he loves before family and friends, and I want to continue that tradition."

Jack paused as he smiled at his bride-to-be. With no embarrassment at the romantic nature of his proposal in front of so many witnesses, he continued. "Francesca, it would be my great honor if you would be my wife and bear my name for all eternity."

It makes him almost more than a man, Frankie thought. *Here this beautiful man, kneeling before me, and humbling himself before our families and friends.*

Remaining on one knee before Francesca, he opened the black, velvet box, removed the ring, and slid an enormous emerald-cut diamond ring onto her finger. It was magnificent, but Jack's humility outshone the stone's brilliance.

Robin oohed, and Becca gasped.

Francesca, with just as much love in her sweet, clear voice looked up and responded, "Jacqino, I would be honored to be your wife."

Jack blinked, caught off guard that she would accept his formal proposal with such emotion, because she was so timid. He stood and took her hand to stand with him, kissing her passionately before everyone.

Angelina tugged an embroidered handkerchief from her tiny purse and pressed it against the corner of each eye.

Nicholas rested his hand on Jack's shoulder, revealing his love and happiness in his son's joy. Nicholas had proposed to Angelina in exactly the same way, in front of a very large, teasing family and many close friends, not to mention the entire adversarial Scarpelli family, so many years ago. Their marriage was arranged, yet Nicholas had carried on the traditions as his father before him. Nicholas thought back to the time when each one told anyone who cared to listen that they were not in love with each other. What they didn't realize was that they would fall very much in love with each other. At that time, even though Nicholas knew Angelina didn't want him, he still treated Angelina to all the simple Romano traditions by showing that he was proud to make her his wife.

Angelina continued to dab the corners of her eyes and remembered that time as well. She thought she could never hate anyone as much as she despised Nicholas Romano, especially at the time of his announcement of proposal of their impending marriage. Now she knew she could never live without her gentle *Niko*.

Nicholas sensed her melancholy and reached for her hand under the table. Leaning toward her, he whispered to her the familiar words he always spoke to her. "*Mi amore*."

Angelina, Corrine, Retta, and Robin, all in tears, rushed over to hug Frankie. Becca stood off to the side, refusing to be sucked into the romantic moment. Anthony studied her reaction over the rim of his wine glass, while she sulked.

A short while later, Nicholas stood, raising his glass. "Umm, umm…" he cleared his throat, "*Salute!*"

"Let's eat, before everything gets cold," Retta spoke through tears and hand waving as she reached for the huge platter of roast beef.

"Amen to that," Nelson declared.

Nicholas didn't sit still for a moment, keeping everyone's glass filled with the delicious wines. Eventually everyone moved down a seat so that Frankie and Jack could sit together, with Scott muttering under his breath, *they're gonna spend their whole lives together, so what's one meal?*

Jack held her hand while they ate, refusing to let go of it so that she had to cut her food with her fork, but she didn't mind. She felt protected and loved. She took in the conversations taking place around the room and the connections going on between them. The bantering between Anthony and Scott, the Italian exchange between Corrine and Angelina, and the sweet looks Nelson gave Retta, as he tended the fire. The way her father laughed at something Nick had just softly said to him, as he refilled his glass, yet again. The way Anthony stole glances at Becca in between bouts with Scott, and the way Scott looked at Robin, in between threatening to take all these weak, romantically sickening men away on a three-day training sabbatical.

Frankie turned back to look at Jack. "I love you," he whispered softly, tucking that perpetually errant strand of golden hair behind her ear.

Frankie answered, "So much."

Everyone was extremely intoxicated thanks to Nicholas' refusal to accept "no, thank you" as an answer, so everyone slept wherever they could find a place. Jack's parents headed for The Rose, and Frankie's parents slept on their sailboat, Tax Relief, which was moored next to The Rose. Retta and Nelson went back to their cottage, after bringing all the sleeping bags and blankets they could find. Jack made a fire in one of the bedrooms Becca and Robin would share. Then Jack informed Scott and Anthony that if they wanted to keep warm they better make their own damn fires or get another blanket.

Anthony stepped outside onto the front porch to enjoy a cigar and Jack followed him for a breath of fresh air. The nights were growing colder, as the autumn winds propelled the promise of winter. *So much like Uncle Tony*, Jack thought, watching Anthony light the cigar.

"I'm happy for you, Jack," Anthony spoke between dragging the pungent cigar smoke in deeply only to release it creating a smoke screen around his golden face.

"Thank you," Jack answered placing his hand on his brother's shoulder. "Is everything alright at Romano Enterprises? I feel rather replaceable since you have only called me once since you took office," Jack joked.

"Believe me, Jack, I have dialed your cell at least a thousand times, but hung up when I thought I would be bothering you. Everything is just peachy at Romano Enterprises," Anthony lied, lifting his cigar to take another drag, as he stared out at the river.

Jack took the cigar from his brother for a deep draw. "Why don't you sleep on The Rose? There is plenty of room."

"Are you kidding me?" Anthony looked horrified while snatching back his cigar. "Don't tell me you didn't see the way Mom and Dad were looking at each other tonight?"

"Stop! Don't go there!" Jack quickly raised his hands in warning, releasing the held cigar smoke.

"Too late. That is precisely the reason why I am sleeping on the floor upstairs." Anthony would rather do that than call Paul and listen to him complain about the distance.

Jack started to leave Anthony on the front porch to finish his cigar. Anthony was mumbling under his breath again that, *if I had a real chauffeur, instead of a pretend one, I could go home. And because our parents still are not able to keep their hands off each other and in public no less, and at their age, too, how could I possibly sleep on The Rose? I am probably going to wake up stiff, sore, and in need of a psychiatrist with the way our parents are acting.*

Jack laughed at his brother's comments pulling him in for a quick bear hug, before making his way upstairs, unable to stop smiling. In fact, his face actually hurt from all the smiling he did tonight. When he entered the master bedroom, he closed the door by clicking the doorknob closed before turning around. Frankie was standing by the bed before her open suitcase. She stood still and gazed at Jack contentedly from across the room. She opened her arms inviting him to hold her close. When she slipped her arms around his waist, he cradled her face in his hands and kissed her deeply, lifting her up on her toes. She tasted the pungent, rich smoke as she dipped her tongue into his warm, welcoming mouth. He kissed her face, her eyes, and the tip of her nose as she giggled at his whimsicalness.

"Let me start a fire so we will be warm...hmm..." Jack kissed her forehead. Jack started working on placing the kindling into the hearth and looked over his shoulder to the beautiful girl who would soon be his wife. *Not soon enough*, he thought, *not nearly soon enough.*

Frankie slipped into the bathroom to get herself ready. She slipped the ring off to study it for a moment and knew Jack's family was wealthy, but wondered how he could afford such a ring or to build such a ship as The Rose. Maybe his father lent or gave him the money, Frankie rationalized. She brushed her teeth and washed her face and hands. After she dried off, she rubbed some rose-scented cream into her hands and put the ring back on. It was sparkling and shining so brightly. *Dear Lord*, Frankie prayed, *please don't ever let me lose this or my mother will surely kill me!*

She looked at herself in the mirror. *Still too thin*, she thought, *but my hair is growing.* Slowly she slipped on the sheer, pale-pink baby-doll nightgown which stopped high up on her thighs— another one of her mother's purchases. She put her things away, hung up the towel, and laid her clothes over the club chair in the bathroom. She would take care of them tomorrow. She wanted Jack now.

Frankie walked out of the bathroom toward Jack who was standing before the fireplace. The fire filled the room with glowing light, warmth, and crackling sounds. Frankie's bare feet crushed into the deep, plush Persian rug under the seating arrangement near the fireplace. She slowly reached her hands around Jack's flat, trim waist and pressed her cheek into his back. Frankie stood still just holding him tightly, pressing her face even deeper into his spine.

Roses, Jack thought, *she smells wonderfully of roses.* "Francesca," Jack whispered softly over his shoulder.

"Jacqino, the way...the way you proposed to me. The way you humbled yourself before my family, your family, and our friends, I will never forget it." Frankie spoke softly from behind him.

Jack looked down to see the engagement ring he purchased with his brother's help just last week grace her slender finger. It suited her as he caressed her hand which pressed against his ribs. He turned around to face her and lowered his head to kiss her. He kissed her mouth at the corners, her cheeks, eyes, and forehead. He kissed her again, tasting just the opening before plunging his tongue into her mouth deeply, while gathering her into a tight embrace.

Frankie felt weak and wound her arms around his neck to help support herself. He began to study the lace nightgown, "You are so beautiful. I can't believe I found you and that you and I will be together forever," Jack whispered softly. "Let's get under the covers," Jack passionately suggested.

Chapter Sixteen
In the early light of dawn…

At first light, the men gathered deciding to go for a run. Bruno was bouncing around like a kangaroo, knowing that when Jack tied his sneakers on the porch like that, it meant he was going to take him running.

Frankie kissed Jack, and Scott started teasing him about getting soft with all that female pampering he was getting lately. He was secretly pissed off to see Frankie kiss him, anyway. He felt that Jack had stolen Frankie from him.

The men all stood together, in the front yard, each one eyeing the other wondering which one would cave first. Nelson stayed behind, muttering that he had *real work to do and this male bonding stuff, or whatever you called it, was like male birds preening themselves.*

When they started to run, to Scott's shock and amazement, Anthony, Nick, and Thomas seemed to have little trouble keeping pace with Scott and Jack, who had been running seriously for months now.

Thomas and Nicholas sprang out ahead of the others and Scott, Jack and Anthony watched as their backs grew dim in the distance. Since Thomas retired, he had started a physical routine at his local fitness center where he swam and ran almost every day. He was always active with sailing, fishing, and hunting—things he had enjoyed as a child with his father and never stopped enjoying as he grew older.

Nicholas, too, was no exception. Although he worked in business and traveled extensively, he always made time for exercise. He, too, had a sailboat and found the physical activity of sailing to be relaxing, yet physically demanding.

As the group of men jogged, Nick and Thomas picked up the pace, leaving more distance between them and the younger men.

"Tom, let's show these boys what men are really made of!" Nicholas conspired.

"You got it, Nick," Thomas shot back and the pair left the three younger men literally in the dust.

"What's up with them?" Scott asked Jack.

"Just letting us know who the real men are," Jack joked.

The three younger men never caught up with Nicholas or Thomas. When they finally made it back to the farm, they could not believe how rested Thomas and Nicholas looked. In fact, Nicholas and Thomas had already shared a cup of coffee with the ladies in the dining room.

"Dad," Anthony asked.

"*Che*," Nicholas looked up from his plate of eggs.

"A friendly jog," Anthony asked his father a bit more pointedly.

"Jog, son? I was under the impression that everyone wanted to run. If I wished to go for a walk, I would have taken your mother for a stroll around the grounds."

Angelina swatted Nicholas with her napkin. "Careful what you wish for Nicholas," Angelina joked, implying that she could very easily leave him behind as well.

Jack came in last and went right to Frankie. He was sweaty, but he pulled her into his arms and kissed her soundly on the mouth in front of all.

"Jacqino, you are soaked!" Frankie tried to pull away, but he held her close and rubbed his sweaty head into her neck, making her giggle.

"Alright, I'm trying to eat here, Romano." Scott was feeling rather left out with all the demonstrative love he had to endure this weekend, and none of it coming his way. Robin glanced up at him and Scott smiled back, forgetting momentarily about Jack and Frankie.

Becca looked over at Anthony, but quickly averted her eyes so as to not make direct eye contact. She did not want him to notice that she was looking at him.

"Rebecca, would you like me to fill your plate?" Anthony asked with his usual display of fine manners.

"No thank you. I never eat breakfast." Becca stated firmly, with a coffee cup held in both her hands just before her lips.

"But surely you know that it is the most important meal of the day, and everything is so delicious. Perhaps I can interest you in one of Retta's apple turnovers or a warm corn muffin?" Anthony tried to entice her with a warm smile on his handsome face.

"That jog must have jiggled something loose. No thank you." Rebecca stated more firmly.

But Anthony refused to take no for an answer and figured she was a muffin eater, so he placed a steamy hot muffin on her plate anyway.

"Frankie!" Becca declared. "You're a vet. Maybe you should check Anthony out." Becca stood up and left the dining room in a huff.

Anthony quickly finished his breakfast and excused himself, thanking Retta with a sweet kiss on her plump cheek. He saw Becca down by the river and started to walk toward her.

"Oh, damn," Becca cursed quietly to herself. "That idiot is making his way towards me." Becca braced herself, as she saw him wind his way toward her.

"Rebecca, would you like to go for a walk?" Anthony asked.

"No, I have to get back to the city," Becca replied.

Anthony stood directly in front of her. His clothes were not quite wide enough to accommodate his body, and between that and his sweat making them cling to his skin, Becca could make out each muscle on his chest and stomach. She didn't dare look lower. But, on second thought, why not? Nothing ever stopped her from doing that before. When she looked back up and into Anthony's eyes, his expression had changed.

"Why are you looking at me so strangely?" Becca asked.

"Marry me." Anthony stated with utmost sincerity.

"Whaaaat? I really think you need to sit down. Apparently that run took more out of you than you realize." Becca reached her hand up to touch his forehead, but Anthony intercepted its course, turned her hand over a pressed a kiss to the underside of her wrist, feeling her pulse quicken.

Anthony lowered her hand. "I feel wonderful and believe me, I meant what I said. I aim to make you my wife," Anthony spoke softly, but clearly.

Becca studied him for a moment. His blonde hair shone in the bright, crisp morning sunlight and his gentle blue-gray eyes reminded her so much of Frankie's except that Anthony's had silver flecks which made his eyes twinkle and dance. He was very handsome and Becca felt her palm start to sweat, even though it was a cool autumn morning.

"Do you normally just go up to any woman in this day and age and tell her you aim to make her your wife?!" Becca was astounded. "I don't even know you! I think you could have some deep psychological imbalances. That could take years of therapy and, quite possibly, medication."

"Then it is a good thing my future wife is a therapist." Anthony spoke softly and began to lean toward her. He pressed his lips to hers and when she parted her lips he dipped his tongue in just slightly for his first taste of her. When he lifted his head to look into her eyes, she was looking right back at him. He studied her soft brown hair, itching to touch a curl. Her large, gentle, brown eyes were wide and golden. He lowered his head again, but this time Becca turned her face away and started to sprint back to the farmhouse. Anthony raked his hand through his hair, and started to scold himself. *What the hell are you doing Romano? You fool! Why didn't you just ask her to dinner or the theater? Aim to make you my wife? Where did that come from?* Anthony just shook his head.

Becca ran past the farmhouse and down the drive to her car. She jumped behind the wheel, started it up and gunned the engine, kicking up gravel and dust.

Frankie and Jack watched the scene from the front porch, and Frankie shrugged her shoulders at Jack. Together they started to walk back into the house, arm in arm. She was still trying to keep his damp, smelly body away from hers. "Jacqino, really, you reek!" He laughed at her and picked her up, swinging her around in a circle before they walked into the house leaning closely together.

Frankie had showered while Jack was running and was now tidying up as Jack took his shower. When he came out of the bathroom he was wearing just a towel, as Frankie looked over her shoulder while pulling up the sheet on the bed. He came up behind her, leaning over to kiss her flawless cheek, while she continued to make the bed.

"You definitely smell much better now." She dropped the sheet and held his arms that hugged her waist. She never wanted to miss an opportunity to touch him.

"Retta will be very upset if you make the bed. You know she wants to do the housekeeping." Jack spoke softly into her ear.

Frankie felt his clean-shaven face rub along her neck, causing goose bumps to start to rise on her arms. He smelled soapy and spicy and she inhaled, filling her senses with his scent. "I want to make our bed, because it reminds me of the night we shared together and makes me wonder what tonight will bring." Frankie spoke to his strong arms holding her. She never wanted him to let her go. She leaned against him when she heard him groan.

"Francesca," Jack whispered turning her around. He kissed her deeply and pulled back to look at his beautiful bride-to-be. "Maybe we better get out of this room, before we have to remake the bed. Let's take a walk, or better yet, why don't we take Tax Relief out for a sail up the Hudson," Jack suggested.

"That sounds like fun. I haven't been sailing in years," Frankie answered. "I just want to finish here."

"On second thought..." Jack shot the bed a hot look and swept Frankie up into his arms so quickly that she didn't even see it coming.

"Jacqino! You have to put me down! What will Retta and Nelson think?" Frankie asked.

"They will think that we cannot get our fill of each other."

"Then they will have thought right," Frankie confessed while placing a gentle kiss on his chest. "I would really enjoy going sailing with you though, and it will certainly keep our hands otherwise busy. It is such a pretty autumn day for it. You can have your way with me later."

Jack laughed and reluctantly released her from his embrace. He tucked that golden strand behind her ear, brushing it off her cheek, now bared for his gentle kiss.

Chapter Seventeen
A fine day for sailing…

The day couldn't be more beautiful. The sky was clear and bright blue with not a cloud in sight. Frankie and Jack made their way to the sailboat with a basket packed by Retta, filled with roast beef sandwiches from last night's dinner's leftovers, some cold potato salad, and an assortment of fruit. Jack included chilled club soda, because he was still nursing a slight hangover.

They walked together to the dock holding hands and leaning on each other, stopping several times along the way to kiss. Bruno trotted behind them to the dock.

"Do we have to bring him?" Jack groaned, nodding his head toward the dog.

"Of course! I hardly even see my dog anymore!" Frankie whimpered back.

"Believe me, you're not missing much. Let me fill you in on what you have been missing. He drools, smells, and then drools some more, and snores, extra loudly. Besides, I know that if he falls overboard, you're going to make me go in after him and haul his wet, hairy butt back onto that boat."

"Probably," Frankie crossed her arms over her chest.

But Bruno wanted nothing to do with the boat. He kept backing away every time they called to him.

"Good dog," Jack called from the deck of Tax Relief. "You just stay right where you are, and we'll see you when we get back."

"Come, Bruno, come," Frankie called. "I wonder why he doesn't want to come. He is usually game for any kind of activity. Maybe I should check him out before we leave." Frankie frowned at Jack.

"He's fine. Once we're gone, he will probably chase the chickens, and then Nelson will chase him, and then Retta will chase Nelson, hollering in that unique melodious voice of hers." Jack started to imitate her, "Nelson, if you harm one hair on Doc Frankie's dog, I'll…I'll…well, only the good Lord knows what I'll do!"

Frankie giggled. Retta did sound just like that. She would threaten Nelson, or anyone else for that matter, without stating any true repercussion.

Frankie untied Tax Relief, and Jack started the motor. Frankie hopped on, as Jack slowly guided the boat away from the dock. Bruno was barking at them in that "hurry up and come back soon" bark. Frankie waved and called for him to be a good boy and to leave Retta's chickens alone. She ran to Jack's side, as he held her close while guiding the boat away from the river's edge, heading upstream.

It was colder out on the water, and their thick, cable-knit sweaters were definitely needed. But once the sails were set, and the activity that goes with trimming them was underway, Jack and Frankie warmed up quickly. Frankie steered and Jack trimmed the sails and then traded places with each other. They were both impressed with each other's sailing abilities.

Jack watched while Frankie worked, thinking *I have asked this girl to marry me, and I didn't even know she could sail and that she loves boating as much as I do. I want to know everything about her. I know I will love everything and anything about her. She is so gentle and loving and I am lucky enough to have a lifetime to get to know her every secret.*

Frankie felt Jack's eyes on her, and she smiled back at him. It was a new experience for her to be wanted this way—the sensation of knowing that someone loved you so much that they studied you. As they passed West Point, the view from the Hudson up toward the old fortress was spectacular. The colors of autumn were all around them; bright gold, crisp crimsons, and vibrant oranges. Frankie took it all in.

"Francesca," Jack called. He waved for her to come and join him at the helm. She got up and ran right at him playfully knocking into him. "You knock me off my feet," Jack teased, as he caught his balance easily and pulled her close.

"That's the plan."

"I like that plan." Jack pulled her in close.

Frankie buried her face into Jack's thick sweater, breathing in his scent. She was enjoying everything about the day and how the sun shone in an endless blue sky. She listened to the sounds of the birds and watched the gulls soar high overhead. She listened to the quick snap of the sail, as the bright, white canvas caught the wind. She looked at Jack's large, strong hand on the helm, the same hand that touched her so gently. The feel of his arm around her shoulders, the weight of it, the warmth of him, she was mentally banking memories. All of them!

They pulled over into a little cove not far past West Point and dropped anchor. Jack laid a blanket on the deck as Frankie opened up the picnic basket. She placed the food on the blanket, and Jack poured the club soda into two glasses he found in the galley. Frankie sat while Jack reclined on his side on the blanket, eating and joking about the night before.

"What a day!" Frankie looked at Jack.

"Just perfect!" Jack agreed with a wave of his hand.

"Uh oh."

"What?" Jack asked looking around. He thought the press had found out their location.

"That hand-waving thing you just did." Frankie rolled her eyes.

"What hand-waving thing?" Jack asked.

"The thing you just did with your hand. Everyone is picking that up from Retta. It's highly contagious."

"I do not do anything with my hand," Jack defended.

"Oh yes you do. And so does my father, my mother, your father, your brother and now you." Frankie was still listing names. "Anthony's chauffeur, the head carpenter…"

"No! Really? Do I? I have to stop that right now. Come here so that I can keep my hands busy." Jack grinned with his eyes.

"Oh, no, you don't." Frankie started to back off the blanket.

"Don't make me chase you! I will only catch you and then probably take more than what I originally wanted." Jack started to ease up slowly off the blanket from his half-reclined position, a playful grin dancing across his face.

"Jacqino…" warned Frankie, her hand raised, as she started to back up.

"I love it when you call me that. Have I ever told you how it excites me when you simply call my name?" Jack stepped forward.

"No, I don't believe you have." Frankie kept walking backward, smiling uncontrollably.

"There is nowhere to go." Jack established by waving his hand to encompass the boat. But Frankie kept backing away from him. "Did I ever tell you the story about my parents?" Jack tried to distract her while creeping forward.

Frankie shook her head no, but continued to step backwards.

"Their marriage was arranged," Jack stated.

"Really, and they agreed willingly?" Frankie paused in her retreat to absorb this newly disclosed fact.

"Well, no, not at first. Anyway in order to keep my mother, or maybe it would be better to describe her as the not-so-willing-bride, from taking flight after the wedding ceremony, my father took my mother on his sailboat for their honeymoon; more or less bride-napped her."

"I can't see your father doing anything like that. He is so gentle, so like you." Frankie stopped to listen to the story. "I'm not so sure I believe you, because they didn't act to me like an arranged married couple last night."

"They don't have any problems now." Jack started to wave his hands and then looked down at them as if his hands had a mind of their own and wondered how the heck he ever picked up this ridiculous habit. Quickly he dug his hands into his pockets. "So, the Romano family added this new tradition. We always take our new brides out-to-sea."

"I'm not your bride yet," Frankie countered, raising her eyebrows and continued to back up again at Jack's advancing form.

"If we did it my way we would be here on our honeymoon, probably right now at this moment. Soooo…" But before Jack finished his sentence, he was holding Frankie before she could blink, caressing her cheek with the back of his hand, running his other hand through her hair, and looping it behind her ear sweeping it off her shoulder. He was kissing her eyes, her cheeks, her chin, and her smiling mouth, as she giggled. He walked her back to the blanket and together they lay down, wrapped in each other's arms, looking up at the sky.

"Tell me what you were like as a child." Jack kissed the very top of her head.

"I had the best childhood and adolescence ever. Come to think of it, young adulthood isn't so bad either." Frankie tilted her chin to look up at Jack who smiled at her quip. "Rebecca and I were inseparable. She is the sister I never had."

"Anthony is a brother anyone would love to have. I just happened to be lucky enough that he is mine." Jack spoke softly into her hair.

"That's sweet." Frankie gently kissed his square chin. "So basically, Rebecca and I were in every grade together, and when we weren't, we made such a scene about it, crying and carrying on, that the teachers finally gave up and switched one of us so that we could always be together."

Jack just rolled his eyes. "Sounds like you two were troublemakers."

"No," Frankie defended, "more like partners-in-crime. We just wanted to be together. It is hard to be an only child. Anyway, when we were about ten, we absolutely refused to go to summer camp. We badgered our parents until we were certain their ears would fall off. My father shouted, 'Enough. Enough! I don't want to hear another word about summer camp. You don't have to go! You don't have to go! Just stop whining'."

"Problem child," Jack rolled his eyes again.

"No, I wasn't! We just thought we were so mature. We went to Coney Island. We would take the train and that felt so grown up. We would go to the Bronx Zoo—always my favorite trip."

"Because of the animals," Jack nodded knowingly, wondering if she was at the zoo the same time he was when he was growing up.

"Umm, that summer was so much fun. At the end of each day, we walked to Mr. Luigi's Candy Store for an Italian Ice."

"Mr. Luigi's," Jack asked sitting up and looking down at Francesca.

"Yes," Frankie nodded. Her eyes were closed as her face pointed up in the direction of the sun.

"You're talking about THE Mr. Luigi's on the corner of Central Park West and Main?" Jack asked.

"Yes." Frankie opened her eyes.

"Anthony and I went to Mr. Luigi's whenever we visited my Aunt Rose."

"I know."

"You know? How do you know?" Jack asked pulling her chin back.

"My parents live just two doors down from your aunt and uncle. Every once in a while, we would see you and your brother at Mr. Luigi's."

"Aunt Rose and Uncle John live right next door to each other. My aunt is my mother's sister and Uncle John is my mother's brother."

"Yes, your aunt never married. Her name is Rose Scarpelli. John Scarpelli is your uncle, and his wife died before I left for college. They have been my parents' neighbors for over twenty years. His bulldog is one of my patients."

"Really? But how do you know it was me and my brother you saw?" Jack was shocked.

"I didn't know then, but now I do. Every once in a while, Becca and I would see the limousine with the "R" scrawled on the doors drive past. We waited to see who got out. It was always two boys and a woman. You, your brother, and your mother, right?"

"Yes. I can't believe this!" Jack looked at her in wonder.

"Whenever we saw you come into Mr. Luigi's, Becca made me leave with her out the back door. You two were very cute, and she was very shy and still is, especially around strangers."

Jack was stunned. This is the girl, the one he spied on the sidewalk those warm summer days so long ago. It was hard to believe she was now this young, beautiful woman before him. "I think I remember seeing you by my Aunt's brownstone. Your hair. I will never forget it. Your golden hair was so long. It was blowing around and around."

Frankie looked deeply into his dark eyes where the silver flecks danced.

He touched her hair, brushing it off her shoulder and began to kiss her as if she might disappear again. He captured her face, as he deepened the kiss dipping his tongue in and out then twining his with hers. As Jack settled back down on the blanket, he pulled her close trying to understand fate. This was the girl from that summer day so long ago. Destiny was an incredible force, because he finally found her, and she was going to be his forever.

Jack just held her close and told her over and over that he loved her. He touched her face and kissed her so tenderly. The sailboat rocked them gently into a late afternoon nap. Sometime later, they slowly untangled themselves, and Frankie thought that this afternoon had been the most romantic time she had ever spent with him.

Now, as they gathered up the picnic lunch and started to head back to the farm, the sun hung lower in the sky, but was still strong. The warm, autumn day was rapidly growing cooler as the wind kicked up making the return trip a thrill. Jack handled the sailboat with ease.

"Who taught you to sail?" Frankie asked, tucked under Jack's arm, as he controlled the craft with the other.

"My father. He learned from my grandfather in Sicily. My great, great-grandfather was a fisherman before he came to America," Jack answered her in that deep, rich voice she adored. "My father makes sailing look like child's play."

"So do you."

When they got back to the farm, Bruno was waiting for them on the dock. It looked like he stayed in the same spot the whole day, just waiting.

"Did you chase the chickens?" Frankie called out, as Bruno cocked his head from side to side wagging his short tail. Then, without warning, he took off toward the farm.

They tied down the sailboat, folded the sails, wiped down the deck, and gathered up the picnic basket. They made their way back to the farmhouse holding hands, enjoying the last of the beautiful, autumn day. Retta watched the young lovers hold each other close, and she called to Nelson to look. It was so sweet. That wonderful kind of affection just seemed to rub off on everyone. Nelson held Retta close in his strong arms, nuzzling his head into her neck. Nelson was so happy to see this young couple bringing back so much life to the old farmhouse. It just did his heart good.

"Did you enjoy your sail?" Retta asked, dispensing huge mugs of coffee with a slice of hot apple pie.

"Wonderful," Jack replied. "Francesca is an excellent first mate."

"Thank you, Captain." Frankie saluted Jack playfully. "The Hudson is such a beautiful place. You don't realize how beautiful it is when you are stuck on River Drive in bumper-to-bumper traffic. It's a completely different point of view when you're seeing it from the river. You should come with us next time."

"Oh that would be nice," Retta responded for both herself and Nelson.

"It looks like a lot of work, not like The Rose," Nelson mused aloud.

"You're right. But the work is different. It never really seems like work to me, though," Jack answered. "The Rose is larger and a little more cumbersome to maneuver, but she gives you a different experience than a sailboat. Steady, very steady. Tax Relief, on the other hand, well...she makes you feel like you're flying above the water."

When they finished their coffee, Jack and Frankie thanked Retta for the picnic lunch, coffee, and pie. As they walked back to the farmhouse hand in hand along the brick walkway from the cottage to the farmhouse, Frankie stopped to look up at the beautiful, dusky sky and watched as some of the stars started emerging in the late sunset skies. It was just breathtaking.

"Let's try out our new tub," Jack suggested with a wiggle of his dark eyebrows.

And then the dream flashed before her eyes filled with images, scents, and touches. Frankie just nodded. It was at that moment that she realized what she was wearing, and the details started to dance before her mind.

Jack led her through the farmhouse, up the stairs, and into the master bedroom. He started to rebuild the fire in the fireplace. Once the kindling caught the log, he replaced the fireplace screen. Jack joined Frankie standing at the window, looking out at the river. He lifted her hand and gently placed a kiss in the center of her palm, then guided her toward the bathroom. The sheer deliberateness of his movements began to stir her senses.

He closed the bathroom door behind them then kissed her gently. Jack moved them toward the tub and turned on the water, running his hand under the faucet. The water did indeed look small next to his large hand, which Frankie recalled from her dream. Frankie lit the tiny, tea lights then walked over to the two dozen yellow roses. She read the card that was tucked in between the buds; "To my beautiful yellow rose, my future wife, my love forever, Jacqino."

Frankie looked back at Jack who was watching her. He stood up very straight and tall, looked directly at her, and now she matched his look with her own. It spoke of her own desire and more. Much more. Without speaking, her expression said thank you for the roses, thank you for asking me to be your wife and thank you for your love forever.

Looking directly into her eyes, Jacqino closed the short distance between them and cradled her face gently in his hands. "You are so beautiful, Francesca." Jack spoke just above a whisper. It was so difficult to be with her all day and not have her. Now he would take and give. He would make her his again, as he lowered his lips onto hers for a long, deep kiss.

When he lifted his head, Frankie started to register everything; his dark eyes with the silver flecks dancing, his height, breadth, his glossy-black, windblown hair, and his sun-kissed cheeks. *Tenderness,* she thought. *This man is going to be tender with me my whole life.*

Jack kissed her mouth again. He placed those sweet little kisses on each corner of her mouth and after each kiss he whispered, "I love you."

Their kisses became deeper, longer, and more urgent. His tongue tasted and explored, and she responded to his desire.

"I have loved you forever," Jack almost forced the words out of his throat so instantly choked with emotions, as he smoothed his hand over her cheek. He began to run his hand through her hair, brushing it off her face. "Your hair is softer than silk. I wanted to touch it when I saw you that summer day so long ago. I remember. I remember you, Francesca."

"I remember you too, Jacqino." Frankie could barely speak.

Jack reached down and pulled off his sweater, laying it over the back of the club chair before slipping Frankie's sweater off next to join his on the same chair. She hadn't even realized that she was wearing the soft, mauve-colored silk camisole from her dream as Jack began to rub his thumbs over each bud, stroking them gently until they swelled against the silk of the camisole.

Kissing Frankie gently, Jack slowly unfastened her jeans, sliding them down her thighs to her ankles, and drank in the beauty before him—golden hair, perfectly formed mounds rising and falling in anticipation of his next touch, and a tiny waist. He took hold of her hand and helped her from the puddle of jeans on the floor, studying her long, lovely legs. And her scent was always of sweet roses. He slid the thin straps of the camisole down each arm, and watched as the fabric slipped just enough to give Jack what he wanted. He lowered his head taking her into his mouth, tenderly, so gently.

Frankie's knees grew weak and she felt the ground giving way. When Jack knelt before her, she was sure she was going to collapse. His sweet kisses advanced down her stomach to her inner thighs, teasing her panties to the floor. He began tasting her very center, making her forget when and how to breathe. Frankie ran her fingers through his dark, glossy hair and traced them along his strong shoulders. Her line between fantasy and reality blurred. Jack stood and pulled her close, tracing his hands up and down her back and Frankie could feel his readiness, as he kissed her deeply.

Frankie ran her palms up his denim shirtfront trying to concentrate on unfastening each button while Jack caressed her. With shaky fingers she slowly slid her hands under the denim and up over his shoulders making the shirt drop to the floor. He was warm and tawny. His hand left her breast but for a moment as he ran his fingers through her hair. Frankie placed a kiss over his heart, breathing deeply his scent. It was so hard to speak, so difficult to breathe, to swallow. Simple movements became concerted efforts.

"God, how I love you," Jack spoke the words into her mouth, and she could feel her body tremble with the truth and force of them. Jack watched Francesca's eyes darken. It amazed him as he watched the effect of his touch through her gentle eyes.

Frankie began to unbutton his pants, but Jack swept her hands aside dropping his pants swiftly.

Mirrors and shower doors fogged over and Frankie wasn't sure how much longer she could actually stand, because her knees felt like liquid. Jack sat down on the club chair and in one fluid motion pulled Frankie onto his stiffness. She began to move, as Jack held her waist, guiding her and caressing her.

"Jacqino, Jacqino?" Frankie asked, blind with desire.

"I am here, my love, my beautiful angel," Jack whispered, sliding his hands up to the sides of her breasts, covering them, caressing them, placing his warm mouth onto each raised bud that ached for his touch. The pace intensified, hot from the steam, hot from their need to please each other, and they both exploded.

Jack found it difficult to breathe, to think, as he buried his head into her shoulder.

Frankie ran her hands through his hair and pressed her lips gently against his neck. He passed his strong hands up and down her back. Without warning, almost effortlessly, he stood with Frankie still intimately joined to him, cradling her buttocks, as he curved his tongue into her mouth, as she meet him.

"Francesca," Jack whispered, looking deeply into her ever-changing blue pools. Slowly he released her and guided her to the bath. He poured salts into the water and swept his hand back and forth. He held her hand as she stepped into the hot, steamy, scented water. Jack climbed in behind her and lowered himself into the old tub, resting his head back against the rim, gathering Frankie so that her back rested against his chest.

Frankie could still feel the thunder of his heartbeat.

Jack never thought he would ever experience this kind of passion. It was so surprising to him, as he tried to absorb this intense emotion. He had so much love to give her, and he intended to make sure she knew it in every way that his love for her was true and right. His need for her added another level to their relationship that Jack couldn't comprehend, either. He still needed her again and could not resist sliding his hands up and down her arms, across her shoulders, massaging her neck, collarbone and breasts. He reached for the shampoo bottle, placed some of the liquid into his palm, and gently began to shampoo her hair, massaging with his fingertips behind her ears, along her nape, never pausing in his gentle kneading. He reached for the sprayer, stopping to kiss her throat that was calling for a taste. He ran his hands through her silky strands, rinsing out the lather.

Frankie's head tingled from his touch, but she forced herself to focus. She placed a small amount of shampoo in her hand and kneeled to reach his wonderfully dark, glossy hair. When she started to massage his scalp, he felt his neck relax from her touch. Even though his eyes were closed, he reached his hands out to touch her. He caressed her, leaning forward every so often to kiss a hardened pink bud. Without warning he nipped her left breast, causing Frankie to protect it, his devilish grin on his face, his eyes still closed. She rinsed his head clean and lowered herself back into the warm water facing him.

Jack lathered up a large soft washcloth. He reached out and started to slide the cloth up her arms, over her shoulders, along her collarbone, around her breasts, down to her waist. He soaped the cloth again and ran it beneath the water washing her flat stomach, long lean legs and inner thighs. She rested her head against the antique tub, her hands holding onto the rim, her finger sparkled with the engagement diamond he gave her the night before, that she refused to take off to go sailing or even now as they bathed. Jack pulled her up from her reclined position, kissed her and whispered softly, "My turn."

Frankie's deep, sapphire eyes opened as she retrieved the cloth. She soaped it well and began to wash his large hands, sliding the cloth up his long muscular arms. He held her breast again, running his thumb over the pink bud now soapy from his hand.

"I can't concentrate if you keep touching me like that," Frankie softly scolded as Jack laughed in a deep tone that swirled around them filling the room.

"Good," Jack stated without opening his eyes, his hand still caressing her breast. "Then you will have to start all over again from the beginning." Jack held out his arm to be washed again.

Frankie was more than happy to oblige. He was so beautiful, magnificent, so strong and muscular. Frankie remembered vividly from her dream that if she touched him on his chest, right *there*, his muscles seemed to leap toward her, and when she ran the cloth over his strong muscular legs, his eyes shot open diving into hers—just like that!

They were both soapy and scented and stood to rinse each other off. Stepping out of the tub first, Jack couldn't help but drink her in as he helped her step out of the tub.

"I want to look at you."

He drank in her long legs, flat stomach, and ribs just barely visible now, breasts rising and falling with each breath she took, her long neck, her silky hair slicked back off her forehead, and eyes of deep, deep blue. Her cheeks flushed. Laughing in a low, deep tone he patted her skin with a fluffy towel. Turning her around he dried her back, stopping to kiss the scar on her lower back. He straightened, circled his hands around her narrow waist, and pulled her firmly against his body.

Frankie could feel his strength and that strength made her feel secure and warm, reaching straight to her very heart, her very soul. Jack wrapped her up in her towel then grabbed one for himself, wrapping it around his waist. He took down a terry-clothed robe from the large brass hooks behind the door and held it for her. Frankie let her towel fall to the floor, turned her back toward him, and slid her arms into the sleeves. When she turned around to face him, he tied the oversized robe closed in the front.

Jack pulled the towel loose from around his waist and quickly began to dry himself off, but Frankie reached for the towel and didn't stop until she dried every incredible inch of him. She dried his long muscular arms. She marveled at his chest covered in dark, curly hair, stole a sweet kiss over his heart, dried his flat, rippled stomach then stopped to kiss each defined muscle. Jack remained motionless. She walked around behind him and could barely reach his shoulders. Frankie dried off his back and placed small kisses down his spine, and when she reached the small of his back she stopped and slid her hands around his waist and pressed her cheek to his back. He reached around behind him to pull her closer against his back then turned quickly in her embrace, sweeping her up into his arms, just like her dream.

"Francesca, I think you are trying to drive me mad with wanting you," Jack throatily groaned.

Frankie just wanted to touch him. She reached for his cheek, which was beginning to form that handsome stubble, and his throat and shoulders, so clearly defined as he carried her. Never taking his eyes from her, he bent down so that she could reach the doorknob, opening it wide to enter the master bedroom. The fire was burning happily in the fireplace, snapping, crackling, sizzling.

Jack lowered her down onto the comforter, untied the belt of her robe, parting it. She was pink and naked, warm and blushing. She was his, now and always.

Chapter Eighteen
It's a wonder...

As Jack and Frankie relaxed on the couch in the library of the farmhouse with a fire burning brightly, Jack replayed the holidays, impossible to stop the smile that played across his face. Holding Frankie close, Jack mentally replayed Thanksgiving Day. He recalled how he played chauffeur, driving Francesca's truck filled to capacity and, yes, even the damn dog. He couldn't help but compare this Thanksgiving with every Thanksgiving he spent with Victoria and one word summed it up-empty.

This Thanksgiving all the Romanos and McFarlans were invited to the O'Brians, along with Retta, Nelson and Aunt Rose, too. In Jack's estimation, the women easily cooked enough food to feed the First Battalion of the United States Army. Jack remembered listening to Anthony and Becca exchanging verbal jabs. She was complaining that he was in her way with Anthony countering that 'he wasn't anywhere near her.' Then he took Bruno for a walk just to get away from his Aunt Rose who insisted he hadn't eaten nearly enough. He watched the football game with the men, stole kisses with Francesca in the kitchen, and topped it all off with a sampling of many kinds of desserts. He remembered taking inventory of his precious occupants on the drive that day. Frankie had been stretched out in the front seat softly napping against his side with his arm draped around her. He recalled that from the rearview mirror he saw Retta and Nelson quietly dozing in the back seat with Retta resting her head on Nelson's strong shoulder. And in the far rear of the vehicle, Bruno was attempting to snore the tint right off the windows.

Jack shook his head in disbelief. *Who would have thought that my life would have totally changed and all because of the dream resting quietly by my side? Certainly not me,* he admitted silently.

He couldn't believe how his life had changed. What a difference from last year, at least from what he could remember, since he had spent most of the time between Thanksgiving through New Year's close to legally intoxicated every waking moment. At night, while he was still President of Romano Enterprises, he tried to mask his hollow loneliness, trying to forget those feelings of guilt about the love he never felt for Victoria and how every aspect of his life felt meaningless. It was Scott's constant badgering to workout that helped pull him out of what could have become an irreversible problem. Thank God, Scott didn't take 'No' for an answer. The man definitely missed his calling as a drill sergeant, but hadn't missed his calling for being such a good friend to Jack.

Holding fast to family traditions, they spent Christmas Eve at Uncle Tony's and Christmas Day at the McFarlans. Jack couldn't understand why Victoria kept him away from his family and these happy gatherings for all those years. He remembered how she made him either attend just at end or not at all. That was something he would never understand.

Frankie and Jack had exchanged Christmas gifts first thing that morning by the little Christmas tree they set up in the library. But, in the quiet glow of Christmas evening, while they sat together in front of the fireplace within the library's massive hearth that shimmered with flames and filled the room with the scent of cherry wood, Jack reached into his pocket to pull out a small box.

"I almost forgot this." Jack placed the crushed blue velvet box into her hand as she rested against him, her legs tucked beneath an afghan, stretched out on the dark, brown, leather sofa.

"Jacqino, what is this? You have already given me far too much."

"Never angel, never enough," Jack spoke softly.

"Please don't think that. You are enough for me in every way." Frankie spoke softly and cuddled up closer to Jack.

"The gifts are my backup plan in case you get tired of looking at my face."

"That isn't going to happen," Frankie assured him.

"Please, open it. When I saw the color, it reminded me of you."

Frankie pulled the lid back and a large sapphire necklace, in the shape of a teardrop encircled with diamonds, winked at her. "Oh my...Jacqino, it's beautiful!"

Jack spoke so softly that Frankie had to lean toward him to hear. "The color matches your eyes when I am deep inside of you." The intimacy of his confessed admission was emotionally touching, while he swept his hand along her soft cheek, warmed by the fire's glow.

Frankie turned her face to kiss the center of his large hand.

"You'll need this as well." Jack pulled another blue velvet box from the same pocket and carefully opened the lid to reveal matching earrings. "And of course, what would the set be without this?" Jack pulled yet another velvet box, opening it again, because he was far too eager to wait for her to open it herself, and revealed a ring in the same shape and stones. The set was quite stunning and looked monumentally expensive.

"Jacqino, these are incredible, but the cost must have been..."

"Didn't I ever tell you that I am independently wealthy?" Jack half joked, waiting for her to bring up his family's name and fortune that went with it. But she said nothing about his family or his wealth and he was a bit thankful, as she pulled his face close to hers and started to nibble on his jaw.

"Didn't you have enough at dinner?"

"Apparently not," Frankie immersed herself completely into Jack's embrace as he laughed and nuzzled her neck. "Make love to me," Frankie whispered into his ear before she gently nibbled on that as well.

"Francesca..." Jack groaned pulling her down in front of the fire, kissing her, before falling into her deep, dark blue pools.

Chapter Nineteen
Back to reality...

Monday meant back to reality, back to the animal hospital, and it was absolutely insane and packed. Slowly it leaked out that Dr. Frankie would not be there after the first of the year, a few days away, and her patients were in a panic. The partners of the firm were less than pleased that the information of her leaving was spreading like wildfire.

"Dr. Frankie, you have a phone call on line one," Betty called over the intercom.

"Okay, just ask them to hang on—I'll be right there," Frankie answered while examining the ear of a large Doberman. "Mr. Ferrara, it looks like Samson's ear infection is much better, but I am still going to give you another prescription for two more weeks. You are to use it exactly the way you used the last one. After the two weeks, just swing Samson by anytime to have one of the vets' just take a quick peek at his ear. Alright?"

"*Si*, Dr. Frankie. But I would...ahh...like to make appointment with you in two weeks, if that's okay." Mr. Ferrara spoke in broken English, rolling his r's in a deep, rich Hispanic voice.

"Oh, I won't be here in two weeks." Frankie looked up from her task.

"But we want to see you."

"Umm..." Frankie thought out loud. This was the seventh patient this morning who wanted her new address, and it was making her feel very uncomfortable. "I haven't opened for business yet. How about I call you in a few weeks and see if you want to make the trip?"

"Okay, Dr. Frankie. That sounds good to me," Mr. Ferrara agreed.

"Alright. But you still need to bring Samson in two weeks for a re-check." Frankie wanted to make herself clear.

"Okay."

"Alright, I'll call you when I'm open for business. Bye, Mr. Ferrara—bye, Samson," Frankie said, popping a doggie cookie into Samson's mouth.

Frankie reached for the phone, pressing the blinking green light. "Dr. Frankie." Frankie answered in a business-like voice.

"Frankie? It's Becca."

"Oh, Becca, sorry I kept you holding. It's a zoo here today. No pun intended. It's like everyone woke up today and had to bring their pets in for overdue injections and ear infection rechecks. I'm telling you—its nuts!"

"No, I have the nuts, remember? Anyway, how about we have dinner tonight at your place, say seven o'clock?"

"I don't even know if I am going to be done by seven."

"I'll just let myself in and wait for you. You feel like Chinese or Italian?"

"Italian," Frankie smiled.

"Ugh, I forgot, Romano. You're always going to want Italian."

Frankie giggled. "Got to go, see you tonight. I should smell like the elephant exhibit by the time I get out of here tonight."

"Great, that should increase my appetite. See ya later."

The day, even into the late afternoon and early evening hours, was a buzz of animals, appointments, and emergencies. When someone brought in a stray cat whose paw was badly cut, Frankie was almost too wiped out to deal with the claws and teeth. The poor kitty was in such pain and wasn't about to let anyone even remotely near her. In fact, the poor animal's paw was so badly infected that after they wrestled the feline down and anesthetized her, Frankie seriously contemplated whether they would be able to save her leg. Frankie managed to remove a glass shard embedded deeply within the wound by looking through a huge, magnifying glass. *What next?* Frankie thought, as she painstakingly removed the glass, flushed the wound and stitched up the very deep gouges. When Robin suggested naming the feline Crystal, everyone agreed.

"Dr. Frankie, you have a call on line three." Betty announced over the intercom in the operating room.

"Robin, can you please finish wrapping her paw? And let's start the steroid drip."

"You got it, Frankie."

"What line did Betty say I had a call on?" Frankie asked Robin, but Robin just shrugged as she finished padding the kitty's paw.

"Dr. Frankie?" Frankie asked, tentatively.

"Are you sure?" Jack teased.

"Jacqino! I wasn't sure what line to pick up." Frankie whispered placing her free hand over her other ear so that all she could hear was him—just him.

"You sound busy."

"Nuts, absolutely nuts today."

"I love you, I miss you, come home tonight, or I'll come down to the city," Jack begged.

"I love you, and I miss you, too." Frankie smiled. "I already made plans to see Becca for dinner, but I could cancel. I could be at the farm at about nine."

"No, don't cancel with Becca. I'm sure she misses you, too. Where are you going to eat?"

"Take home, Italian, my place."

"Italian? I guess I'm starting to rub off on you, hmm?"

"You have no idea. I can still feel your hands in my hair," Frankie confessed quietly, tilting her face down pretending to study her shoes.

"Is that the only place?" Jack asked closing his eyes envisioning her before him. He could picture her golden head bent forward, blonde hair forming a golden curtain concealing her usual blushing.

"No..." Frankie answered after clearing her throat, "... everywhere."

"I can feel you, too." Jack opened his dark eyes looking out the window of the farmhouse's library, which rewarded him with a spectacular view of the river. He was missing her terribly and everything he saw and did made him fall in love with her all over again. It was an amazing feeling. "Have a good time tonight. Bruno and I are going to watch a western I rented from that video store in town. The store is so antiquated that they haven't even started renting DVDs. I think this thing's got to be twenty years old, maybe more. I have to ask Nelson if he has a VHS player." Jack looked down at the video in his hand.

Frankie giggled, picturing Bruno all comfortable and snoring so loudly that Jack would never even be able to hear a word of the movie.

"I love you, angel," Jack whispered gently listening to her quiet laughter.

"I love you," Frankie whispered back.

"I'll call you in the morning. Bye, my love."

"Bye."

"Dr. Frankie." Betty's intercom announcement brought Frankie right back to reality. "Your six o'clock is waiting in room two."

"Thanks, Betty."

Frankie walked into the examination room and was greeted by Mr. Scarpelli and Little Nick, his bulldog.

"Hello, Mr. Scarpelli." Frankie was looking down at his chart. *Wasn't he just here last week?* "Hello, Nick." Frankie scratched the dog gently behind his ear, as his eyes began to close from being touched in his most favorite spot.

"Hello, Dr. Frankie."

"How are we doing today?" Frankie was still looking down at Nick's record, filling in today's date and searching for what Nick needed during this examination.

"I think Nick's hair is falling out." Mr. Scarpelli sounded very worried.

"Oh, Mr. Scarpelli, that is normal. Remember, when the seasons change, some animals lose some of their coat to grow in their winter coat, and the same thing happens in the spring to thin their coat."

"Right, winter. Everywhere I looked I saw white fur. I forgot." Mr. Scarpelli tapped his temple.

"It should stop soon." Frankie skimmed her fingers in the opposite direction of Nick's plush white coat; her diamond ring sparkled under the fluorescent lights. "He is a very healthy bulldog, just normal."

"Is that an engagement ring? Did you get engaged? Your parents never said anything about that!" Mr. Scarpelli frowned, but still managed to plaster a fake smile when Frankie looked up at him.

"Yes—yes, I did, just before Thanksgiving."

"I never noticed the ring before. That is quite a diamond!"

"Thank you."

"Who is the lucky man?"

"Actually, I just recently found out that you are related to my fiancé." Frankie suddenly felt awkward.

"Really! How wonderful! Then you will be part of the family now." *Even though I'm not,* thought John silently. He pasted an artificial smile on his face and asked with great enthusiasm, "Who is he? Which nephew, which cousin? Stop keeping an old man in suspense!" Mr. Scarpelli scolded, wagging his finger, already knowing of his nephew's engagement to Francesca.

"Jack Romano." Frankie spoke while she was examining Nick's ears and the folds around his snout. Frankie thought it odd that no one in Jack's family ever spoke about John Scarpelli. She just assumed that he was a bit of a black sheep, or maybe when his wife passed, he became sort of a recluse. It was none of her business.

Jack Romano, John Scarpelli thought, silently filling himself with the hate he felt for that name, that family. His fists began to clench just as Frankie looked up and noticed his lips looked a little pale.

"Are you alright, Mr. Scarpelli? You know I could have made a house call if you weren't feeling well. I would have been more than happy to stop in to check on Nick for you if you didn't feel up to making the trip down here." Frankie offered.

"Oh, I'm fine. Just worried about Nick, that's all. Well isn't that something! Just wait until I get a hold of my sister, Angelina. I'm very angry she didn't tell me. Welcome to the family, Dr. Frankie." Mr. Scarpelli reached over and kissed Frankie on each cheek, promising silently, that he would do whatever it takes to prevent the Romanos from taking away his goose that lays the golden eggs. Francesca was something he felt he owned exclusively—at least for the past 20 years, he did. *Why did they always have to take away something that belonged to him?*

Just before John Scarpelli left the animal hospital, he requested the usual from Frankie; a few numbers to play. As she finished with Nick, she rattled off a few numbers, as John silently swore to himself that he would stop this wedding. He hated the Romanos, all of them, and he was not going to let them take her like they took his sister away from him. Dr. Frankie belonged to him. She could predict things—he wasn't sure how—but she could, and she belonged to him, a Scarpelli, not a Romano! The Romanos took his sister away from him but they would never take Frankie.

Chapter Twenty
There should be no secrets…

Frankie turned the key to her apartment and pushed the door open as Becca pulled it from the inside.

"Hey." Becca reached out to pull Frankie in for a hug. "I was beginning to think I was going to have to eat both dinners myself."

"I would have killed you. I have had appointments starting since eight this morning, and I didn't even get a lunch break today. What did you get me? I'm starved." Frankie squeezed Becca quickly.

"Pasta primavera," Becca closed the apartment door.

"Hmm, I can't wait to dig in." Frankie shrugged out of her coat and reached for the coat tree she kept by the door of her apartment, but realized she gave it back to her mother. Creatures of habit, she thought.

"Park East Animal Hospital is going to be in for a rude awakening when you leave. Gosh, they are going to have to hire three people just to replace you. You never know what you got until it's gone."

"Thanks, but I feel sorry for my patients. They're confused. They want to be loyal to me, but the trip to the farm, I know, will stop many of them from making the switch." Frankie walked into her bedroom removing her filthy, pet hair-covered scrubs, replacing them with a comfortable pair of sweats and sweatshirt. She walked into her bathroom and scrubbed her hands and arms and then thoroughly washed her face. As she entered the kitchen, she eyed her dinner with the appetite of a person ten times her size.

"I got a feeling it won't take long for you to be very busy at the farm. You're good, Frankie, really good."

"Thanks. Wow dinner smells great! Come on, let's eat." Frankie pulled the lid back on her aluminum tray. She twirled some of her pasta on her fork, using a large spoon to cradle the pasta then popped the whole thing into her mouth.

"Good?" Becca asked.

"The best," Frankie twirled her fork into her tray again.

"You know, this pasta is going to do a real number on our thighs if we don't watch it. I think it is all a Romano plot or tradition, God knows that family has more traditions than you can shake a stick at," Becca informed Frankie while slicing into her manicotti.

"This food hasn't had any effect on Jack's mother. Did you get a good look at her? I don't think I was that thin when I was born. She's in unbelievable shape. I hope she never asks me to go for a jog with her, because I really don't think I could keep up with her!" Frankie sounded a bit frightened.

"Yeah, she is in great shape, and even his father and brother. It must be hereditary. I really hate that!" Becca revealed after she swallowed another large bite of manicotti. "Are you happy about your engagement?" Becca asked.

"Yes, very."

"Did you dream about it? Did you know?" Becca couldn't help herself.

"No, I didn't have any dream about him asking me to marry him. Not even the ring." Frankie held up her hand and wiggled her finger with the large diamond on it.

"Jeez, that thing freaks me out. Aren't you afraid you are going to lose it or that someone will steal it?"

"Scared to death of what my mother will do to me if I lose it. God help the person who might want to steal it from me. I think I would go totally crazy on that person. I could see the headlines now. 'Local vet knocks man unconscious then resuscitates him after he tried to steal her engagement ring!'" Frankie looked down at the enormous emerald-cut diamond that graced her finger, remembering how Jack slid it on. "I think I should tell him about my dreams. It's time. I don't want any secrets."

"Everyone has secrets, Frankie." Becca spoke into her manicotti, "Everyone!"

After they ate, they went into the living room, which was nearly empty except for a tall floor lamp in the corner, which barely lit the room. Frankie brought a bunch of pillows from her bed so that they could hang out on the living room carpet and talk while they ate their ice cream, an afterthought and a nice treat after their meal.

"What's that?" Frankie pointed with her spoon to a large, bulging, expandable folder resting near the door to the apartment.

"What?"

"That." Frankie dropped the spoon into the container of dark chocolate ice cream and physically turned Becca's face to see the folder.

"Yeah, I'm going to get to that," Becca looked back into her vanilla ice cream container hoping for inspiration as to how to begin.

"Spit it out," Frankie's intense blue eyes, sparkling like precious stones, insisted.

"More like get up." Becca put down her ice cream container, pulled Frankie to her feet, and walked over to the window that faced the front of Frankie's apartment building. She twirled the wand on the blinds and focused the view to the street. Just down the street sitting on a bench was a man reading a newspaper. His head was looking around constantly, and it was obvious he wasn't reading at all. Down at the opposite end of the street, a man stood speaking into his cell phone. He was leaning against a lamppost, not a chance he was having a conversation with anyone. "Come here, I want to show you something. Shut that light off, too." Becca pointed to the floor lamp.

Snapping off the light, Frankie walked next to Becca. She followed Becca's stare. "What is it?"

"That." Becca pointed to the man on the bench. "That one is yours, and the one over there on the cell phone, that one is mine. But there are others."

"Others? What are you talking about?" Frankie just stared at the men in the street then looked back with questioning eyes.

"I'm not sure—private investigators? I don't know. But that man," Becca pointed at the man she said was hers, "is impossible to shake. He's been following me for a week at night, maybe more. I'm not sure, but that is when I first noticed him. He follows me everywhere. I can't lose him. And believe you me, I have tried. He is always there every time I turn around."

Frankie's mouth hung open. "Do you think they want to hurt us?"

"Oh, no. They could have hurt us a hundred times over by now. It's something…else…" Just as Becca was about to finish her thought, her eyes snapped to the darkened lamppost directly across the street. In that instant, a large man, with his head bent, struck a match and as he raised the match to the tip of his cigar, the light from the flame illuminated his face.

Becca gasped. "Romano!" She quickly turned her back to the window spinning Frankie's shoulder in the same direction. Then without warning, Becca, after muttering a fistful of curses, drew up the blind and flung open the window letting in a cool blast of wintery air.

Anthony waved at her as if Becca was expecting him. A giggle escaped from Frankie. *What in the world is he doing outside her apartment*? She wondered.

"Romano!" Rebecca shouted.

"Please, call me Anthony." Anthony didn't shout at all, and the funny thing was they could hear him perfectly.

"Why you Italian chauvinistic pig!" Becca shouted, half hanging out the window.

Frankie's mouth flew open listening to Becca's obvious dislike for Anthony, which seemed odd because they had all spent the holidays together, and she never heard Becca speak to Anthony in this manner.

"Sicilian." Anthony corrected in a low deep tone. "Rebecca, such compliments will get you everywhere." His voice almost sounded amused as he crossed the street, looking up at them with the most enormous smile on his face.

Frankie shook with laughter at the sight of him, but Becca glared at her friend before turning her attention back to the man who crept to the forefront of her mind on a daily basis and without warning, which was really starting to piss her off.

"Does that mean you have changed your mind about marrying me?" Anthony asked with his hand over his heart, the other hand holding a cigar outstretched.

"Marry? Anthony? You didn't tell me that Anthony asked you to marry him!" Frankie questioned Becca, staring at Anthony. He looked absolutely adorable.

"Are you drunk?" Becca could only conclude.

Anthony shook his head negating her presumption.

"I am not going to marry you. I'm never getting married," Becca yelled down from the window.

"We shall see about that. We...shall...see." Anthony was speaking to the cigar held between his fingertips, as he tapped the ashes off the tip.

"Look, Romano. Tell your goons to go home and to stop following us!" Becca was turning red with her rising blood pressure.

A mere few minutes of conversation with this sexist oaf, and her blood boiled like lava.

"So sorry, but I cannot do that." Anthony stated emphatically. "Hello, Francesca. How is my favorite future sister-in-law?" Anthony ignored Becca, as she slapped her open palm on the limestone windowsill.

"Fine. And how is my favorite future brother-in-law?"

"Just wonderful," Anthony stuck his cigar in his mouth for a quick puff then held up his arms to heaven, "Just wonderful."

"Favorite? He's your only future brother-in-law." Becca glowered at the image outside the window. Anthony was so handsome with his hair shining and his smile gleaming white in the dark. His face was lifted upward, and with that enormous smile, even from this distance, Becca begrudgingly admitted to herself that he was hot. Damn it!

Anthony pointed to the man sitting on the bench. "That is Roberto. Francesca, he was hired by my father to make sure you are safe and sound."

"Anthony, please tell your father thank you. But I am safe and just fine, really." Frankie was leaning out the window resting on her elbows.

Roberto thought she was so beautiful and very easy to follow. She only went to three places: her apartment, work, or the farm. She was a piece of cake to guard.

Frankie waved. "Hello, Roberto. Nice to meet you," Frankie called to him, and Roberto waved back.

"Nice to meet you," Becca mimicked Frankie in a slightly high-pitched, sing-song voice, "For the love of God, Frankie, work with me here!"

"Becca," Frankie tried to sound stern.

"Don't Becca me! The Romanos are keeping tabs on our every move. Don't you get it Frankie?! Every move!"

"So what? I have nothing to hide. I kind of like knowing I have a guardian angel following me around." Frankie was still waving at Roberto.

"Stop that." Becca reached up and snatched Frankie's hand back to the sill.

"Rebecca," Anthony called, "this is Carlo." Anthony pointed to the man holding the cell phone, waving at her.

"Go to hell, Romano!"

"Becca!" Frankie admonished again.

In just the short time the guards were hired, Becca was already on her second team. They couldn't keep up with her nocturnal activities. It seemed the girl never slept. The newest member of the team, Carlo, was much younger and didn't seem to mind the energetic activities that Rebecca seemed to partake of late into the night. When Carlo described to Anthony some of her after hour's behavior, Anthony thought his head was going to shoot right off his shoulders into space. He was heated and now determined to curtail all of those activities, unless she wanted to do them with him. So every night from now on, he was just going to show up wherever she was and watch her, hoping that he would make her feel so uncomfortable that she would have to remain celibate for a little while anyway, until she realized that he was the man for her.

"Get lost, Romano." Becca hollered again.

"Sorry." Anthony shrugged.

"Anthony." Frankie called to him. "You can send Roberto home. I'm in for the night."

Anthony nodded, and Roberto blew Frankie a goodnight kiss. She pretended to catch it and blow it back. He pretended to catch it and put it in his pocket.

"Goodnight!" Frankie called out sweetly.

"Will you stop encouraging this? This is not funny. This is an invasion of our privacy!"

"You know, Becca, it is really very sweet of Nicholas to be so concerned for us. There are a lot of whackos in the city."

"And you think you're telling me something I DON'T know! Gosh Frankie, I counsel more than half the whackos in this city." Becca swept her hand to encompass the area.

"What about you, Rebecca?" Anthony called up to her to get her attention once again. "Are you in for the night?"

"Oh, I'm in for the night, Romano, and just to prove it, here why don't you just hold onto these for me." Becca removed her jeans and threw them out the window right at his head. Anthony caught them with one hand and slung them over his shoulder.

"And this," Becca shouted again, taking off her sweatshirt and sailing that out the window as well.

Now, standing in her underwear in front of the open window, Carlo looked on quite amused with the picture she made.

When Becca reached her hands behind her back and unsnapped her bra, Anthony could feel his blood pressure soar. Just as her ample bosoms were about to be revealed, Frankie reached for the blind and tugged it closed, but not before Rebecca tossed her black lace bra down into Anthony's open palm. Frankie quickly reached behind the blind and shut the window with a thud.

With her clothes swung over his left shoulder, the black lace bra lying in his open left hand, his cigar clenched between his teeth, Anthony raked his right hand through his hair. "Damn it, this woman is going to make me old before my time," he swore to the bra now dangling from his index finger. Removing his cigar he called out to Carlo, "Call me if she leaves, no matter what time," Anthony instructed Carlo.

"Yes, Mr. Romano." Carlo stifled his laughter and fought his tone not to sound amused.

Reaching for the afghan that laid on the floor near the pillows, Rebecca closed it around her.

"What the heck is going on? Why didn't you tell me about Anthony?" Frankie's head nodded towards the window.

"He is the single most chauvinistic man I have ever met in my life! He's so old-fashioned! I wouldn't be surprised if it was reported that he was at least two hundred years old, if a day, disguised as a thirty-year old." Becca was talking to herself, but Frankie heard it all. "Of all the nerve, having us followed around! To think! To think, that that man is going to know my each and every step!" Becca was still swearing as she made her way, clad in the afghan, to the file folder. "Frankie, I want you to take a look at this." Becca turned with the folder, while trying to manage the afghan.

"What is it?"

"Here—look." Becca pulled open the folder and started removing newspaper clippings and magazines. Within seconds, Frankie realized that she was looking at Jacqino. Jacqino when he became president of Romano Enterprises. A photo of Jacqino on his wedding day, with his bride looking more terrified than happy. Jacqino standing on The Rose described as the multimillionaire with a flair for shipbuilding. Jacqino in a tuxedo at a political fundraiser with his arm around the President's shoulder! Jacqino being described as one of America's most eligible widowers, after the death of his wife, Victoria. Jacqino resigning as President of Romano Enterprises and on and on it went. *Hadn't she seen that very photo?* Frankie thought back.

"What is this? Where did you get all of this?" Frankie questioned Becca.

"One night, when you said his name in your dreams, I put two and two together. After all, how many people are named Jacqino? Plus, I have a patient who is utterly obsessed with the family. I wasn't sure if you knew who he really was, what he was all about. This is the man you are marrying, Frankie."

"I didn't know." Frankie was stunned. "I almost don't recognize the faces in these articles. I know they're him, but they're almost not. Do you understand?"

"Yes, I think I do. He almost appears untouchable in these photos. But we both know that that isn't him." Becca adjusted the afghan. "Frankie, I know you have been busy with working at the animal hospital and with your illness, and I know you haven't had time to check out America's most eligible bachelor interviews in the hottest magazines, but this is the person you are marrying— probably one of the wealthiest men in America, and I just wanted you to know."

"He never said anything. How could I be so out of it?" Frankie still held the glossy magazine with the beautiful face of Jacqino staring back at her. His black hair was slicked back and his dark eyes were lit with the silver flecks she knew so well. "Is that why we are being followed, because they think we are going to hurt them?"

"No...no, I think when any Romano gets seriously involved with a woman, that woman needs to be protected from people like my patient who obsess over them. I think it is for our own protection, not so much theirs. No one can touch them or the ones they love. And I mean no one." Becca emphasized.

Frankie was staring at her ring. It was enormous. "My ring must be worth..."

"One hundred twenty-seven thousand dollars, according to the...ahh...here's the article," Becca held up a picture of Anthony and Jack leaving *Tiffany & Co.* Becca began to read the article aloud, "This reporter has been informed by a very reliable source that Jack Romano, 'THE' Jack Romano of Romano Enterprises, just purchased a seven-point-two carat emerald-cut diamond ring set in platinum for his future bride. The ring was sized at just under four. We can only presume that the little lady will have to hold it up with her other hand when she wears it."

Frankie thought that that was almost the truth. "What am I going to do? Anthony is going to tell Jack that I know about the bodyguards or whatever they are."

"You can bet on that. Those brothers are tight. They really are much closer than the press realizes. In fact, when Jack gave up his position with Romano Enterprises to start in a private venture, later discovered to be architect and historical designer, they had a full article about the bantering between them. It was kind of cute, actually." Becca leafed through the papers. "Here it is! Anthony, of course, is such a punk! This is on the day Anthony takes over as President after Jack stepped down. 'If my brother changes his mind about working for Romano Enterprises, we always need help in our warehouse facilities.' And then the article goes on to explain the start of the Romano empire blah, blah, blah." Becca held the article out for Frankie to take.

"Becca, this really changes nothing. I'm so hopelessly in love with Jacqino. I've been in love with him most of my life. I don't care what he has or what he doesn't have, as long as he wants to be with me and loves me."

"I thought you should know. I know you love him, and I can see that he loves you, too." Becca was beginning to doubt whether it was a good idea to show her best friend all of these articles.

"Becca, will you be my maid-of-honor?"

Becca beamed then realized who was most likely to be the best man. "Hmm, always a bridesmaid, never a bride," Becca grumbled.

"Please?"

"I suppose that idiot is going to be the best man." Becca jerked her thumb toward the picture of Anthony in the paper then scowled as Frankie nodded. "You owe me. I'm going to have to dance with him at the wedding and stuff, and I'm going to have to be nice to him. That bites," Becca hissed.

Frankie pleaded with her eyes.

"Yeah, yeah, I'll do it."

"You're the best!" Frankie squealed and swung her arms around Becca's neck.

Chapter Twenty-One
The next morning...

Becca left Frankie's apartment very early the next morning with the large expandable folder tucked neatly under her arm. She was wearing Frankie's jeans, which were too long and far too tight, and a borrowed sweatshirt. Forget about the bra! Becca knew that that would never fit. She still had to get home, shower, and dress before her first appointment, which was at eight. *I hate these early morning appointments*, Becca thought as she ducked down an alleyway to her own apartment. The alley was quiet and it was still dark, but she knew the way by heart and had used this cut-through hundreds of times. Just as she passed a large dumpster a large hand came out and grabbed her arm.

"Rebecca." Anthony stated clearly.

Startled, Rebecca screamed. "Romano! What are you doing here?" Becca stood still holding her hand over her heart, which was racing uncontrollably in her chest, the other hand clasping the folder to her side.

"What did you tell Francesca?" Anthony pressed her for an answer, grasping her upper arms.

"Let go of me."

"What did you tell her, Rebecca?" Anthony demanded. He seized the folder from her and started to scan what was inside.

"I told her who Jack Romano is, that's all. She would have found out sooner or later, I just sped up the process. She had a right to know. Now, give me back that folder, you overgrown brute." Becca pulled her file away, but Anthony was quicker and held her arm so that she would not move.

"You could have waited until *he* told her." Anthony lowered his voice.

"When? He had plenty of time," Becca countered right back. "Let go of me, Romano, or I'll..."

Anthony released her. Then leaning his head down until he was just an inch from her face, he defended his brother's actions. "Jack was going to explain things to her, but you had to stick your nose in where it doesn't belong."

"Shut up, Romano!" Becca took a step backwards. "Frankie has been my best friend forever, and no one, not even the high and mighty Romanos is ever going to change that. And another thing, you had better stay clean, Romano. Because one screw up, one little hint of Mafia, one little hint of any criminal activity, and I will go running to Frankie no matter what day, time, or place. You got that, big boy?" Becca mustered up her courage and started to poke at his chest.

Anthony smiled down at her. He silently admitted she was haunting his dreams and igniting his thoughts while wide awake. He reached behind her neck and drew her to him quickly, kissing her hard on her lips. At first Anthony could feel her stiffen, but then she relaxed in his embrace. His fingers circled her nape, and her soft shiny curls tickled his knuckles. He softened the kiss and let his tongue enter her mouth gently, searching, and discovering. She circled inside his mouth, and he thought his heart stopped beating in his chest. With his other hand, he began to gently stroke her back underneath the baggy sweatshirt, up and down, pressing her against him. She was missing her bra and the feel of her smooth skin against his fingertips caused him to forget why he was angry with her in the first place. He pulled away and waited for her eyes to flutter open.

"Stay out of the alleyways, hmm, darling. I want you safe, and besides that, it gives Carlo the creeps." Anthony smiled his all-American-smile, as he softly reprimanded her with his finger under her chin, tilting her face upward. And just as quickly, he disappeared, leaving without another word, to a waiting silver limousine parked at the end of the alleyway with the letter "R" scrawled on the side.

Becca stood in shock waiting to feel her feet, her legs, and her body again, waiting for her head to float down from the clouds. *Oh boy. I'm in trouble. I'm in big trouble*, she thought. Becca shook her head to clear her thoughts.

"Come on Carlo, I have to get my butt home, then to work." Becca handed him the file folder that suddenly became too heavy to carry since Anthony turned her muscles mush.

"*Si, Senorita.*" Carlo agreed and followed behind but without the usual distance, much closer and much wiser after the display between her and his boss.

⁀⁌

Francesca arrived at work clad in her seven-point-two carat

diamond engagement ring wondering whether or not she should call Jacqino. Frankie almost didn't make it into work. Her stomach felt uneasy. Probably too much pasta and ice cream, Frankie guessed, as she pressed her hand against her lower abdomen. But once she opened the doors to the hospital, all hell broke loose, and her stomachache became secondary. *Not again*, Frankie wanted to scream! The hospital was jammed, and the waiting area spilled over into the receptionist's space.

"Dr. Frankie, you're early, that's great!" Betty declared over the rim of her bifocals.

"What is happening? Why does it seem that everyone is seeking veterinarian services when I only have two days left? Don't these people need to return unwanted Christmas gifts?" Frankie questioned softly over the counter.

"Maybe their families don't exchange gifts, so they have nothing to return." Betty shrugged while stepping over something blocking her way toward the fax machine.

That is when Frankie noticed Snuggles lying on the receptionist's floor. "Don't tell me I have to examine Snuggles. You know snakes are not my expertise, besides I really don't like the way he tries to crush my windpipe," Frankie whispered.

"Stop it, Dr. Frankie. You know you just love Snuggles. Isn't that right?" Betty started talking baby talk to the very large python while she patted his head. As long as she kept moving, he never bothered her.

"They should've named him Strangles. Last time it took Robin and the New York City Fire Department nearly an hour to get him off me."

"Good thing for you we just have to dial three little numbers in case of an emergency."

"Very funny! Alright, I'll see him before my first appointment. I was kind of hoping I could catch up on my paperwork. I'm leaving in two days and I just want to make sure all my T's are crossed and my I's are dotted."

"Wishful thinking! You are going to have to come back at midnight to get that kind of paperwork done. I'll have Robin set Snuggles up in exam room two."

"Thanks Betty, a lot," Frankie curled her lip.

"You're quite welcome," Betty shot back.

Frankie stopped into her office, checked her voice mail, and leafed through some mail. Then she put on her white examination coat and made her way to Snuggles. The day never stopped after that. It seemed everyone was going on vacation at once. Pet after pet needed their kennel shots, before they were permitted to board. Someone actually brought in a black, panther cub. And of course, the animal hospital is required to report such incidences to the proper authorities which, in a nutshell, meant 'more paperwork' for Frankie. When she finally had a minute, she made her way back to her office, pulled out her cell phone and saw that she missed Jack's call. She quickly called him back before the next onslaught.

"Francesca?" Jack spoke slowly into the phone.

"Jacqino?" Frankie whispered back just as slowly.

"Francesca, I tried your cell then I called the hospital at about eight this morning and Betty said you were already all tied up. Did you get my message?"

"No, I haven't had a chance to collect my messages yet. I was examining a twenty-foot long python when you called, and believe me, that reptile had me pretty well tied up for a while."

"Do you mean like in SNAKE—python?" Jack raised his voice. He thought she only took care of dogs and cats. More like puppies and kittens. Whatever made him think that!

"Yes, of course, silly."

"Oh Francesca," Jack shuddered breathlessly, putting his hand over his heart in an effort to stop it from racing. He was really frightened for her. "I think I have a problem with that. Can't you just stick to dogs and cats?"

"Actually some of the dogs I care for could snap my arm in two with one bite, as opposed to the python who would just strangle me to death, then swallow me whole."

"I think you might have to find a new profession," Jack shivered openly.

"Cute."

"I heard about last night."

"Oh."

"So how mad are you about me not telling you who I really was. Kind of like *Superman* or *Batman*?"

"Can you leap tall buildings in a single bound?" Frankie teased.

"Forgive me. I just assumed you knew but didn't want to discuss it."

"Jacqino," Frankie whispered.

"I should have explained sooner but…No—No!" Jack began to shout at someone. "Don't lay those columns in the mud. They have a finished coat from the manufacturer on them. Francesca? Are you still there? Sorry, but we just got the delivery of the support columns for the front porch. Wait until you see the place. The men are hell-bent on getting this job done by the end of the week. And I think they just might pull it off. Listen, Francesca. We will talk about all of this when you come home. I know you are busy settling things at the animal hospital, so I was waiting for the right time to tell you, unless you want me to come down tonight?"

"Would you mind?" Frankie softly pleaded. She needed him.

"WHOO HOO!" Jack exclaimed causing Frankie had to pull the phone away from her ear. "Mind?! Are you kidding? I'll pick you up at seven. We'll have dinner, French or Italian, never mind, I'll pick and we will let the press have a good look at you, hmm. Better wear something special, we'll probably be on the front page of every entertainment section tomorrow morning. I really don't know how you've remained a secret for this long."

"Stop it. It's not going to be any different than any other couple going to dinner."

"You'll see. You have no idea what Anthony and I have gone through our entire lives."

"Would you mind very much if you picked me up at eight? I don't think I will be ready by seven."

"My pleasure angel and I think I'll call Paul, take him off of Anthony's hands for the night. He will be thrilled to chauffeur us around the city tonight. Really, though, anywhere you want to eat in particular?"

"I'll leave that up to you, Jacqino."

"All right, angel. Don't think about anything except how much I love you. I'll see you in…" he stopped to calculate the time on his watch, "…eight hours. I'll explain everything then."

"I can't wait."

"I love you, angel."

"I love you, Jacqino."

Chapter Twenty-Two
At five o'clock that evening…

Tonight was the early night at the animal hospital. The last appointments were scheduled no later than four, so by five the place was pretty much emptied out. There was always a crew on the second floor who took care of the overnight patients and any emergency patients. Frankie had one patient staying in the overnight facility. Crystal, the injured feline with no family, was spending the next few days overnight due to the serious injury to her paw. The infection would have killed the poor thing, but after cleaning the wound, stitching it up, and administering high doses of antibiotics, the cat was just starting to come around. Drinking a little, but still not eating. Of course, the partners were furious with the expense of an unwanted animal, but Frankie assured them that she would pay the bill and take the cat with her before she left. She just figured she would bring her to the farm.

After Frankie finished checking in on her, she worked her way back to her office. It was close to six when she finally sat down at her desk. *Maybe now I will be able to catch up on some of my paperwork*, Frankie thought. She figured that she could work on some of her files for the next half-hour, grab a cab that would have her at Becca's in minutes, so that she could borrow something since she had almost everything already at the farm, shower, and be ready for Jack by eight, no problem. With her head lowered she immediately dove into updating her files and scribbling notes for the next vet. Unexpectedly, she felt a chill, and when she looked up, Mr. Scarpelli was standing in her office.

"Mr. Scarpelli!" Frankie heard the surprise in her own voice.

"Dr. Frankie."

He looks nervous, Frankie thought. Dark circles under his eyes. His face looked drawn, very weathered, unshaven, yet glistening.

"I just saw you, yesterday. Is everything all right? Where's Nick?" Frankie asked looking down at the floor. Just then two men walked up behind Mr. Scarpelli looking equally nervous and… deadly. One had a cut lip that was bleeding, and the other looked to have two red eyes, already starting to discolor and swell over.

Frankie felt panic rise up within her, as her heart began to race wildly.

"Dr. Frankie, we have a problem. You will have to come with me so that I can explain. Do you understand?"

"Okay, Mr. Scarpelli," Frankie tried to appease him. "Whatever you want me to do. We can talk. No problem." Frankie reached down for her purse and before she could reach it something crashed down on the top of her head. Her eyes flashed open briefly as she tried to fight the sharp pain in her head. Later, she could feel herself being dragged. Again, she fought to open her eyes and there in the corner, near the dumpster, crumpled up in a ball of pain was Roberto. His head was bleeding, and his face was swollen, covering his eyes and mouth completely. *My God! Roberto!* Frankie's mind screamed, but no words escaped her mouth.

When Francesca finally woke it took some moments to realize that this was not a bad dream, but a real live nightmare. She was sitting in a chair, her eyes were covered, and a gag was tied over her mouth as well. Her hands were tied behind her to the chair. Her feet were tied, too, one to each leg of the chair. As her senses became sharper, she could feel the fierce thud of a pounding headache. She tried to breathe through her nose, slowly, in and out, in and out, in an effort to calm herself. *Why was this happening? How could this be real?* As she tried to concentrate, the last images in her mind that came into focus were that of Mr. Scarpelli, the sweet old man from her childhood neighborhood, looking nervous. Then sharper images of Roberto curled up behind the animal hospital, bleeding and laying still, very still. One minute she saw everything unfold as two men dragged her to a black car and then nothing, complete blackness. As she became aware of her senses, she realized she was not alone. Something or someone was leaning or slumped up against her. Maybe it was Roberto. She struggled with the rag tied over her eyes. She rubbed it against her shoulder and managed to get one eye free. She blinked back excruciating pain then blinked several times more to adjust her vision to the black space. Suddenly the image was clear—it was Mr. Scarpelli tied and bound!

Chapter Twenty-Three
Unbeknownst...

Jack was thrilled to be taking Frankie out on the town. It was their first real date. *That's horrible,* Jack thought silently. He had to admit that he hadn't courted her at all and before he knew it, he was proposing to her and, thankfully, she accepted.

As Jack stretched his long legs out in the back of the limo, he promised himself that that would change. He would start taking Francesca to Broadway shows, dinner, and dancing. He thought about holding her in his arms looking deeply into her deep, blue pools and waltzing her around the dance floor. When he looked up he saw Paul's face in the rearview mirror. Paul was actually tickled pink even while he maneuvered the limousine through the hated, snarling traffic. He picked Jack up an hour earlier than requested, but Jack didn't mind. He told Paul where they were to go to dinner and afterward, they would go to The Plaza for a special night.

Now on the drive down to the city, Paul couldn't stop saying enough about Francesca. She was the most beautiful woman he had ever seen, so caring, so special. It was obvious that Paul approved of his choice in his pending nuptial. Jack knew she was all that and more. She was a loving woman, and soon she would be his. He had every intention of telling her about his wealth. About the villa he owned in Florence. About the dilapidated castle he purchased in Ireland and how he was renovating it online with contractors abroad. He would tell her about his fleet of private jets and the latest ship he was building, which was twice the size of The Rose. He would tell her how much he was worth, right after she had her first drink. And by God, he had every intention of discussing with her, at length, about her choice of pet patients. *Pythons, I most definitely have to put a stop to that,* he thought. *My mother would faint dead away if she saw Francesca with a twenty-foot long snake and then when she came to, she would slap me for allowing Francesca to take care of such a thing.* Jack wondered how the heck she even examined a snake. Shaking his head, he realized he would find out soon enough when she started her practice at the farm.

Jack tried to talk her into moving up sooner, giving her

employer less notice, but she was dedicated to her patients, and she felt obligated to make sure that she wasn't leaving her patients or her employers without proper notice. He couldn't wait to smooth her hair away from her cheek as he studied his right hand, the hand that always caressed her cheek, the hand that kneaded her breast and explored her deepest inner secrets. He couldn't wait to kiss her lips and to make love to her again. The mere thought of her made his chest clench. He couldn't wait to see her.

When they arrived at her apartment building, Jack decided to take the stairs. Clad in a navy blue, pin-stripe suit, a crisp, white oxford shirt, and bright, blue silk tie, hair slicked back, he took the stairs two at a time until he reached her floor. He was never at her apartment before, which she said was just a place to sleep and shower. He knocked on the door and ordered his heart to settle down. He felt like he was in junior high on his first date.

Jack waited a few minutes then knocked again. "Francesca?" Jack called to the closed door. *She must still be at the animal hospital. Maybe she had an emergency.* Jack raced back down the stairs and out to the waiting limo.

"Paul, let's go to the animal hospital. She must have gotten tied up. Let's surprise her, alright?"

"Sure Mr. R."

Without much warning Paul stepped on the gas, slamming Jack into the back of the rear seat.

"Paul, slow down," Jack cautioned.

"Sorry, Mr. R. I just don't want us to miss her."

Jack called the animal hospital on his cell phone, but only heard the automatic recording, then her cell, but there was no answer. A few minutes later, Jack jumped out of the back of the limo and tugged on the front door of the animal hospital. It was locked. He turned to Paul and raised his hands in defeat. Paul motioned toward the building's rear entrance and Jack circled around behind the building.

Jack pulled on the rear door and it opened. No one seemed to be on the first floor, so he took the elevator up to the second floor toward the infirmary. Jack knocked on the locked wooden door, and knocked a second time, much harder.

"Jack?" Robin asked, pulling open the heavy wooden door.

"Robin, hey, how are you?" Jack gave her a quick hug.

"What's up?"

"I came to pick up Francesca for dinner."

"Oh, right. She told me you were coming to take her out tonight. That's so sweet. But I'm sure she left already."

"Are you sure?"

"Well, let's check out her office, okay?"

Jack nodded and together they made their way back to the elevator, taking it down to the first floor. Jack felt uneasy. Francesca was always on time, and whenever she was late coming up to the farm, she would always call even when she would be just a few minutes late. As the elevator doors opened, Paul stood, holding up a man who was bleeding and swollen.

"Robin, call an ambulance." Jack turned to her, but she was frozen. She looked like a deer caught in the headlights. Jack gently shook her. "Robin." Jack spoke in a firmer voice. "You need to call this man an ambulance."

"Yes, yes, of course, I'll be right back. Put him down in there." Robin pointed into an examining room. Paul maneuvered the man onto the table.

"Who is this?" Jack asked quietly.

"This is Roberto, the man who has been watching Francesca." Paul looked down at the lifeless form. "Last night, when your brother was having words with Francesca's friend, Rebecca, I waited just down the street with the limousine. Your brother introduced this man to Francesca as Roberto. He told her that your father had arranged for this man to watch over her. She was so sweet. She called hello to him and thanked him for looking out for her." Paul blinked with instant awareness, "Dear God, if he looks like this, what have they done to..."

"Don't speak it." Jack raised his hand as if to halt the onslaught of terrifying thoughts, but it was too late.

"Yes, Mr. R."

"I'm going to call Anthony. You stay right here and wait for Robin to get back." Jack clutched his chest.

"They have almost beaten this man to death." Paul was sickened.

Jack quickly exited the back door of the animal hospital and dialed Anthony's cell phone.

"Hello?" Anthony asked. Very few people had his cell number, so without looking at the number he knew it had to be a family member.

"Anthony, it is Jack."

"Jack, how are you?"

"Where are you?"

"Umm, I am just on my way to curtail my future wife's little nocturnal interests."

"What?"

"Never mind. It is a rather long story."

"Look, I have a little problem." Jack started to get serious.

"What kind of problem?" Anthony figured that Paul was acting up and, damn, he was just starting to enjoy driving himself tonight.

"Roberto..."

Fear hit Anthony like a blow from a bullet, because Jack didn't know anything about Roberto.

"What about Roberto?"

"He's practically DEAD!" Jack shouted into the cell phone, nearly losing control.

"WHAT!"

"Someone has Francesca. I know it. Something is wrong."

"Where are you?"

"We're at the animal hospital. Robin just called for an ambulance." In the distance the sound of sirens were breaching the cold December evening air.

"I'll be right over." Anthony tried to sound reassuring. "Francesca is fine. No one would hurt her. No one would do anything to her."

"I don't think so, Anthony. I feel sick to my stomach. Hurry, damn it, just hurry." Jack cut the call off.

"Mr. R, Roberto is awake," Paul called from the rear entrance.

Jack sprinted back to the examining room and lowered his face close to Roberto's blood-stained swollen face. Robin was trying to clean his wounds. She had packed his right hand in ice. It was severely swollen and appeared broken in many places.

"Roberto. I'm Jack Romano."

Roberto tried to nod his head, but the blackness kept calling to him. He wanted to close his eyes and forget the pain he felt all over his body.

"Francesca and I are engaged to be married. That is why my father asked you to look after her."

"I know. I'm sorry."

"I know you did your best. Who took her? Can you remember?" Jack spoke softly, resting his hand lightly on the man's barrel-shaped chest. Although he was massive, he looked as though he had been thrown around easily. For a brief second, he wondered how the hell Paul managed to carry this man in here. He had to be twice as large as Paul!

"Come on, Roberto. I know you got it in you," Paul coaxed.

"Paul, please." Jack held up his hand to stop him.

"It was...it was..." Roberto was squeezing his swollen eyes shut.

Robin couldn't understand why anyone would want to take Frankie and then it clicked. Jack in that suit, the way his hair was combed back off his forehead, the gold watch gleaming at his wrist, the large gold ring with a letter 'R' encrusted with diamonds on his left hand. It finally hit her. This was 'THE' Jack Romano, from the newspapers, from the glossy magazines in stands she passed on her way to the animal hospital.

Jack looked at her and could tell that she recognized him and that that recognition was sending her into shock. She was as white as a sheet. He could read her eyes and knew she was frightened about everything. Her lips grew white and her eyes stared into space. Just then, they could hear people shouting.

"Police! Police! Open up!"

Jack stood straight readying himself for the onslaught of questions and confusion.

Roberto whispered, "Scarpelli. It was John Scarpelli and two others. They took her. I couldn't stop them."

"You're a good man, Roberto."

Chapter Twenty-Four
Jealousy and revenge sail an uncharted course…

Anthony entered through the hospital's back door, as the police and ambulance were now pounding on the front door to the animal hospital. His eyes took in the situation and the beating Roberto suffered. He knew that this situation was much graver than he first thought.

"Jack." Anthony spoke quickly. "Listen, I spoke to Dad, but we have to leave before the police come in and bog this whole situation down."

"Paul, you know what to do." Jack directed his attention to Paul.

"Of course Mr. R no problem," Paul nodded.

"Take care of Robin, Paul." Jack was now looking at Robin. She was pale and trembling.

"Sure thing Mr. R., come here, Robin. Why don't you sit down right over here?" Paul was leading Robin to a chair next to the examination table talking to her in a quiet voice.

Jack leaned over Roberto whispering softly. "Stay strong, Roberto."

The brothers hurried out of the hospital, and just as Anthony and Jack pulled out of the parking lot in Anthony's white Mercedes coupe, the police and ambulance workers swarmed into the examination room. It was so crowded that Robin's eyes started to roll into the back of her head as the situation became too overwhelming and she completely collapsed against Paul. When the EMTs spotted Roberto, they began to cut away Roberto's clothing to inspect his injuries. Paul caught glimpses of bruises already starting to purple over. Another ambulance worker started to help Robin onto a gurney, and wheeled her from the room, trembling and mumbling incoherently.

"Who are you?" a deep voice commanded Paul for an immediate response.

Paul turned around. "Who me?" Paul started playing dumb.

"Yeah, you! I'm looking at you, aren't I?"

"Who are you?" Paul asked.

"Detective Matthew Mitchell, Thirty-fourth Precinct," Matthew flashed his badge for reinforcement.

The voice was unmistakable. This detective was the biggest pain in the ass in the entire city, including in his own precinct from what Paul heard about him. Paul had seen this man personally harass the Romanos for everything. This guy was hell bent on believing that the Romanos were Mafia. They weren't, but there was no telling this cop that, because he knew it all.

"Mitchell, I think I know you." Paul looked perplexed tapping his index finger to his temple.

"Great. But what I want to know is who the hell are you? You got it? Or do I have to drag you down to the station to help jog your memory?"

"Easy now no need to start threatening."

Jeez, this man is about to experience some serious violence in about two seconds, the detective thought. "Who the hell are you? I want to know your first and last name, address and why you were here? Do you know this man?" Mitchell was pointing to Roberto.

"Whoa, my memory isn't that good. Can you ask me these questions one at a time?" Paul was pointing to his temple again and shrugging.

"Last name," Detective Mitchell asked again. His annoyance level was starting to reach 'red alert' status.

"Who's last name, mine, hers, or his?" Paul pointed to all three.

"That's it. I've had enough of your antics. You're going down to the station." Matthew started to haul Paul from the room.

"Okay, whatever you say, detective." Paul accepted being dragged through the animal hospital and out to the waiting police car. He knew this interrogation would give Anthony and Jack the time they needed to find Francesca, especially since family was involved with her disappearance. That kind of news in the papers was just bad for everyone.

When Anthony and Jack got to Romano Enterprises, they entered through the underground parking facility. The only way into the underground parking facility was through security. It was simple—without proper identification, no one got in.

"Roberto is beaten so severely, I don't know if he is going to live." Jack sounded very far away.

"He's a good man, very loyal. He could have easily high-tailed it out of there when he saw trouble coming." Anthony remarked, running his hand through his blonde hair.

"He told us who did it." Jack looked down at his hands, studying them because they hadn't stopped shaking since he saw Roberto.

"Who would do this?"

"Uncle John. John Scarpelli did this." Jack stated in a low hate-filled tone.

Anthony hit the brakes, a clear reaction to that piece of information then looked over at Jack before accelerating again to his parking space. "Dad is going to lose it when we tell him."

"I know."

Nicholas was already waiting in Anthony's office, pacing in front of the large windows. When he saw his sons enter, he knew this was a serious situation.

"What has happened?" Nicholas asked, concern etching his face.

"Uncle John and two other goons took Francesca." Jack didn't waste any time and came right to the point.

"Roberto?" Nicholas asked, before dropping onto the couch.

"I'm surprised he was still alive when Paul found him." Jack continued to fill in the missing pieces. He told his father that he wanted to explain to Francesca in person about their wealth and that's why he came down from the farm.

"She didn't know?" Nicholas was shocked.

"No not until just last night. Rebecca had told her, but that's another long story." Anthony rolled his eyes.

Jack was pacing now. "I don't even understand why Uncle John is involved in this. I know her parents live down the street from him and Francesca takes care of his dog at the animal hospital. Other than that, I just can't figure it out," Jack wondered out loud.

"Your mother is going to be sick when we tell her it was her brother who took our Francesca." Nicholas rubbed his throbbing temple.

"We have to find her." Jack was starting to grow pale. "You don't think they would hurt her, do you?"

Nicholas felt his stomach turn over. The feeling reminded him of what it was like to be caught in high seas. "No, no, Jacqino. No one would harm a hair on her sweet, golden head." Nicholas wanted to sound reassuring, but wasn't sure if he pulled it off.

"We need to call Uncle Tony." Anthony was trying to think clearly. "He will know where to find Uncle John."

"Do it." Nicholas stated firmly.

But before Anthony made the call, Uncle Tony was walking through the doors of Anthony's office puffing away on his cigar. It was obvious that he knew.

"We have a problem," Uncle Tony started.

"No shit!" Anthony snapped.

"Watch your mouth," Uncle Tony scolded. "My brother has taken Francesca." Uncle Tony's voice was laced with concern.

"You know?" Nicholas was stunned.

"Of course, I know! I have had my brother watched for the past thirty-five years. I just always thought he would try to take Angelina away from you, Nicholas, or maybe try to hurt one of the boys. I know everything about him. Everything!" Uncle Tony rubbed his face. "He has no friends. No one in the family speaks to him. All he does is play numbers, go to the racetracks, eat fast food, go to the bank, and take his dog to the vet. I know everyplace he goes from the time he gets up until the time he goes to sleep. And tonight I got a phone call. Apparently John and two others took her from the animal hospital," Uncle Tony was tired of his brother. "He takes that damn dog of his there almost every week." Uncle Tony told everyone. "You know, Nick, his bulldog…"

"NICK?" Nicholas stood up placing his hands on his trim waist under his suit jacket.

"Yeah." Uncle Tony looked mildly amused that his brother would name his dog after Nicholas Romano. "Sorry. Well anyway that dog must be sickly, because he visits that damn animal hospital almost every week. I'm not sure whom he sees when he is in there, but we have to presume that it is Francesca."

"Yes, it is." Jack spoke succinctly while pacing.

Nicholas and Anthony stood by Jack, who was looking out the window. The park was dark but for the old-fashioned lampposts that lit the walkways. He could make out the bare, intricate tree limbs from what little light the lampposts offered. Jack just shook his head. He was going to make this night special and explain everything to her. He was going to suggest they honeymoon in Greece and then take a quick trip to see the renovations in Ireland. He was craving to see her, to touch her, to speak to her. He filled his head with everything except thoughts that included Uncle John hurting Francesca.

Francesca's head was pounding. She couldn't understand why Mr. Scarpelli would take her. What did she have that he wanted? It was obvious that the situation had turned on him, because now he was tied to the chair next to her. She could hear other voices and noises from above, as she fought to stay awake trying to rattle her brain for an answer. Whatever possessed Mr. Scarpelli to be a part of such a thing? Maybe he wasn't a part of it at all and poor Roberto. She kept hoping that someone had found him by now and was helping him, as she drifted back into unconsciousness.

Upstairs, the captors paced the floors and wondered what they were going to do with them? Kill him? Kill her? They were hoping the old man would wake up so that they could find out why he hired them to kidnap an animal doctor, her name and title clearly embroidered on her white coat which they ripped off of her before they took her into the basement.

"We didn't even get all the money from him yet," the larger captor said to the other one who was putting out a cigarette butt on the dark-stained floor.

"I told you not to hit him in the head, stupid!"

"I had to shut him up!"

"Forget about that now. We need to figure out how we are going to get paid or how we are going to kill 'em."

"Maybe we should just loot some of his stuff?" The shorter one said to his partner, pointing to an oil painting in the living room, but the larger kidnapper waived a hand at him in annoyance.

Back at Romano Enterprises, Uncle Tony repeated the conversation in graphic detail he had with the private eye. He was told that John and two men beat Roberto senselessly, mostly with their gun butts.

Jack swallowed down the bile that kept rising up in the back of his throat, as his Uncle Tony continued to tell them how the private eye watched as Roberto repeatedly got up again and again, only to get knocked down. The private eye thought the man must be dead.

Anthony finally broke Uncle Tony's litany of the beating. "Why the hell didn't he stop them?"

Uncle Tony explained the private eye believed the only thing that was going to stop those men from kidnapping Francesca would have been a bullet and he didn't want the girl hurt in the crossfire. He added how the private eye described how they took the blonde girl from the back of the animal hospital, and it appeared John had collapsed, because the thugs picked him up and dumped him in the back of John's Lincoln. They drove around for about an hour and then arrived at John's house, pulling the town car directly into the garage and closing the door behind them, cutting off all further surveillance.

"According to my private eye, who called in another man for back up, no one has come in or out of the house." Uncle Tony was perplexed. "Do you think he wants ransom money?"

"I don't care what he wants!" Jack barked to his uncle causing him to lean backwards. "Let's go!" Jack strode to the door.

"Wait!" Nicholas called to his son.

"No, I'm not waiting another second. I am going to kill him, Father." Then Jack looked at his uncle. "I am going to kill your brother with my bare hands. On second thought, I don't think **YOU** should come." Jack pointed to his uncle, shaking from the level of rage he felt at that moment.

Uncle Tony only nodded. His brother deserved everything he got from the boy and more. John was lucky Nicholas hadn't killed him 35 years ago when he had created so many lies between him and their sister, Angelina. Their arranged marriage had another layer of stress because of John's lies.

"Jack, please," Anthony pleaded.

"Jacqino, he is your mother's brother, too." Nicholas added.

"I don't want to hear it." Jack held up both hands to stop the logic. "Are you coming or not?" Jack looked from one to the other. They all stood very still in the room. In fact, they were far too still for his lack of patience, as he turned toward the door.

"Of course we are, son." Nicholas walked over to Jacqino.

All four men rode the elevator down to the parking garage

in complete, eerie silence, each one completely lost in their own thoughts.

Silently they all piled into Anthony's car and headed towards Uncle John's. Not a word was spoken on the drive, and after Anthony parked his Mercedes just down the street from his uncle's brownstone, the men exited the vehicle in a calm, determined manner and started to walk the distance to Uncle John's front door.

"Wait," Uncle Tony whispered, turning everyone's attention to him. "Let me go to the door first so that he won't be suspicious, then when he lets me in, you can push in behind me. If he sees us all standing on his front stoop, he won't answer the door. I know I wouldn't."

"Good thinking, Tony." Nicholas pressed a reassuring hand on Tony's shoulder.

Just then, it started to rain. Not cold enough for snow, but chilly enough to feel it from head to toe.

Inside, John Scarpelli started to stir. His brain registered pain, a pain so severe that it caused him to moan. Like a bolt it came to him. He had been double-crossed, and the kidnappers took Francesca for themselves. With his eyes covered and his hands and feet bound, he was leaning on something. Of course—Francesca! Who else could it be? John managed to manipulate his face enough to loosen the gag.

"Francesca?" John choked her name, but no answer. Those idiots had them both tied up! They had no idea that John was completely worthless to them. They should have dumped him somewhere on the road and kept going, but they didn't know that. Thank God. But it wasn't going take long for those two to beat it out of them. So as fate would have it, this was better that they were together. With pain shooting through his head like a repetitive shock wave, he could hear arguing from above. It sounded to him as though they didn't know what to do with them. *I have to think*, John tried to focus. *If we don't give them something, anything, they are going to kill us. If they kill me, that should be no problem. But if they kill Francesca, that is going to be a big problem; especially when the family finds out. They all love this girl and who wouldn't? She was perfect and a lucky charm all rolled up into one.* He took a deep breath and tried to settle himself. He started thinking rationally for probably the first time in his life. He couldn't steal people. He wasn't supposed to hurt people. He hurt plenty of people in his lifetime and that only caused him pain and loneliness. He used Francesca, and for what, for money? He had money! John felt like an outsider and what he saw made him sick to his stomach.

My God, I've been carrying my great-grandfather's grudge over one stupid immature comment for far too long. Because old, man Romano called my great great-grandfather a pig in front of the whole village in Sicily what seemed like a million years ago, and let him get away with it, why should that be my problem? Why should I continue the vendetta? Instead they taught us to harbor ill feelings towards an entire family, holding onto that hate and to pass it on, generation after generation, hoping someone down the line would achieve revenge. *What a coward his great great-grandfather was? He wanted others to fight his battles!*

The marriage between Nicholas and his sister was supposed to be a peace offering, almost like a new beginning, to bridge these two, strong, wealthy Italian families together. That caused John to laugh. Then just as suddenly he stopped.

Such madness! It's sick. I'm hurting my sister, my nephew, and so many others who have done absolutely nothing to me. Nothing! It stops now! It stops tonight! John turned to Francesca and whispered encouragement. "We gotta get outta here. They are going to kill me then they are going to torture and kill you. These guys are gonna want money and much more than I promised them."

The four men stood back and watched Uncle John's house looking for any sign of movement. Jack continued to look at Francesca's parents' home, hoping no one would notice him. He also kept looking at Aunt Rose's front door, also hoping the same. Uncle Tony left the group, climbed up the front stoop, and rang the doorbell. He waited. When no one answered the door, Uncle Tony called to his brother in a loud tone which would attract attention. "John, I know you're in there. You might as well let me in."

A flash of light spilled through the transom and onto the front stoop where Tony stood. It opened slightly and before anyone had a chance to blink; Tony was yanked into the brownstone.

Nicholas reacted first, almost instinctively. He grabbed the metal garbage can from the sidewalk and rushed the front door with such force that the entire frame of the door splintered into the house, nearly killing Uncle Tony. Anthony and Jack ran in behind.

The smaller kidnapper scrambled to get his gun which flew out of his hand. Anthony was all over him in a heartbeat, with Nicholas backing him up. Anthony grabbed the gun and knocked the man senseless with the gun butt.

Watching the larger kidnapper hold a gun to Uncle Tony's head, Jack slowed down his movements and held his hands up. "Listen, man, we don't want any trouble. We'll give you whatever you want."

Anthony and Nicholas got to their feet and moved slowly next to Jack. *At least we got one of the kidnappers—just had one more to deal with*, Anthony thought.

"Whatever I want?" The thug continued to dig the nose of the gun into the side of his uncle's temple, but Tony didn't flinch.

"Sure," Jack promised.

"I want to know why I just kidnapped that girl. And I want money, a lot of money."

"Of course you do," Jack agreed.

"The girl, I think she's worth a million bucks?"

From the open doorway behind the kidnapper, a figure appeared in the shadow and entered slowly. Jack, Anthony, and Nicholas made sure not to make eye contact with him or else Uncle Tony would most definitely be killed. This kidnapper had nothing to lose.

"Whatever you want, man!" Jack reiterated.

"Ya know what? We're all gonna go down the basement and talk about the payment you're gonna give me. Got it, everybody? Let's move, you first old man."

"I think he means you, Dad." Anthony waved his hand toward the basement door.

"But Tony is older than me." Nicholas tried to distract the kidnapper.

"Shut up!" The kidnapper pulled the gun away from Uncle Tony's temple long enough to allow the man in the shadows to whack a splintered piece of lumber right over the kidnapper's head. Carlo stood over the kidnapper and watched as he crumpled to the ground. The man fell to the floor, as Uncle Tony clutched his chest.

Jack ran to him, but Uncle Tony quickly directed his attention to Francesca. "I'm fine, I'm fine. Go get Francesca."

Jack stood up and slapped Carlo on the top of his shoulder. "Good work. I didn't know how we were going to get out of this." He followed his father, already through the doorway leading to the basement.

Carlo, a man of very few words, just nodded. He reached for a length of rope the kidnapper had in his back pocket and quickly got to work disabling them.

Downstairs, Nicholas' voice carried up to them. "You bastard! I have had all I am going to take from you, you little worm. I am going to finish what I started thirty-five years ago." Nicholas' face was but an inch from John's increasingly pale face, his expression contorted in a mixture of hate and fear. Anthony grabbed his father's arm desperately trying to hold him back. He almost lost his grip when Jack moved in. He knew that Anthony could not stop his father alone. Jack pushed everyone aside, as if they were as light as feathers. John's fear was visible, and he openly cowered against Francesca.

"Get away from her, you spineless..." Jack lowered his lips toward the man's face, his voice laced with rage and deep disgust. His hands were clenched in tight fists, ready to explode.

John looked at his nephew and hated himself. Hated everything. Hated the hate he felt for this family. Hated that he missed his nephews growing up. Hated that these boys, now young men, were taught to hate him. Hated his father when he arranged the marriage between his sister and Nick. He hated how he threatened Victoria's family because of the money her father owed him. He hated how he forced them to make their daughter pursue Jack and marry her as a form of payment. He knew Victoria paid for the sins of her father, but he still used her to satisfy his own hate. His hatred went so far as to prevent Jack from having children, from creating an heir to the Romano fortune. He hated himself for using Francesca, because he saw a way to punish them further. He remembered how she would sit outside his window on the bench he had placed next to his front stoop and eavesdrop on how she knew what was to happen long before it ever did. He hated that he kidnapped her to hurt his nephew. All of this flashed before his mind's eye in seconds and at that moment he realized just how much he hated himself. He began to sob. Then he cried openly and hysterically.

Jack's eyes were wide with shock. This is the man his father spoke about who had no scruples, no conscience, and no fear. "Notorious" was how his father referred to him. Yet, here this old man sat before him, so weak that he cried like a baby when confronted. Jack whirled on his father, "Get him out of my sight." Jack turned to help Anthony who was struggling to untie Francesca, still unconscious.

John began to sputter everything out before anyone realized what he was doing. Still tied up, he spoke volumes. "The hate started more than two hundred years ago. We were taught at such a young age to hate the Romanos. It was a hate that was carried down from my great great-grandfather. My father wanted to break that cycle and made my sister marry you." John gestured to Nicholas. "She didn't want to marry you at first, because we were taught to hate all Romanos. She was afraid, so afraid, when our father announced the arrangement. Afraid that you might abuse her or mistreat her," John nodded his head remembering how his sister cried and cried, so terrified to be alone with Nicholas Romano. "I was only trying to protect her and to live by the code I was taught to honor."

John took in a deep, shaky breath trying to understand the years wasted on a life with no meaning, no purpose. "When Jack became older, I knew I had to stop him from creating an heir. Victoria paid dearly for my hate."

Nicholas felt sick.

Jack felt as though he just received a blow to the head. Red with fury, blood pounding through his veins like a freight train, he scooped up Francesca's lifeless form into his arms, her breathing shallow.

"Her father owed me a fortune. He was a drunk and an unlucky gambling fool, so I used that debt to continue to feed my hate, but it could never be satisfied. That kind of hate is insatiable. She was forced to pursue you, Jack, and win you. She was forced to marry you and the only way the note would remain paid is if she never gave you children. She was to stay married to a man she never loved and never bear any children. That is how I had her father repay his debt to me."

Jack felt the room spin. He passed Francesca over to his father and held onto one of the columns in the basement. *Did he say to repay a debt? He used me. He used Victoria.* For three years, he was married to Victoria. All those years were a prison term for her and all because of her father's debts. He remembered how she tricked him at first into believing that she loved him. How after they were married she was cold and... frightened. He realized now that she must have been frightened to death when he pushed to start a family. It was a lifetime prison term with no chance of parole.

Without rational thought, he advanced on his uncle. His hands were around John's throat even though he was still tied to his chair. Anthony and Uncle Tony tried to pull him off. From far away, he could hear his father begging him to release his uncle's throat.

"Jacqino, Jacqino. Think of Francesca. Think of Francesca. We need to get her help. Do you hear me?"

With Carlo's help, Anthony and Uncle Tony pried Jack's hands from John's throat, as John began to cough violently. Jack was so full of life, full of a love John would never know.

"I am going to kill you, John. I swear, I am going to kill you with my bare hands when this is over," Jack threatened. "How dare you interfere in my life? Whatever made you think you had the right? They started it, you continued it, and I will finish it. I promise you."

"Please, let me finish, Jacqino."

"You'd better shut your mouth," Nicholas warned his brother-in-law.

But John pleaded and choked, trying to catch his breath, trying to remember all the years of hate. "Please, I have to finish. Francesca was never supposed to be a part of the hate I felt for all of you. She was separate until you asked her to marry you. She has that gift and I thought you wanted it for yourselves."

"What gift, you fool?" Nicholas spat.

"The gift to predict the future, you know, she sees things before they happen. She rattles off four digits for me and they come out in the Lottery the very next day. She knows what's going to happen before it happens." John was now studying the faces of each man in the room. They all looked bewildered.

"Are you delusional?" Anthony started to advance on him. "What are you talking about?"

"You don't know? How could you not know?" John saw their confusion. "I thought you all knew. I thought that is why you were taking her away from me." John lowered his head and shook it, trying to comprehend. *They didn't know—they really didn't know.* And then it dawned on him. She didn't know, either. Francesca didn't realize the extent of her abilities. She knew some, because he had heard her speaking about it outside his window. Why else would she have continued to work so hard at that animal hospital when all she had to do was win one big race or one whopping lottery?

Everything just changed in a blink of an eye.

John couldn't help but notice the strong Scarpelli resemblance in Anthony. He was fair like all the Scarpellis and not quite as physically large as the Romanos, but close. "What I am telling you is the truth! She also has dreams, dreams that come true. I have heard her describe dreams to her friend and then, within months, they come true, exactly the way she said they would."

"I am sick of your lies, old man," Anthony leaned toward him threateningly.

Francesca started to wake. She blinked several times and thought she was looking at Jacqino for a moment. Then she realized it was his father. He pressed a gentle kiss to her forehead. He whispered gently to her in Italian, *"Mi innamorata tesora, innamorata tesora. Tu se sicura, mi innamorata tesora."* He repeated the phrases over and over to her: my sweetheart, sweetheart, you are safe, my sweetheart.

She was resting her head against his strong chest, his calmness filling her with peace. "Roberto, Roberto?" Frankie cried out.

"He is safe, too. He is safe, little one. Just stay quiet." Nicholas didn't know what else to say. His heart clenched with the thought that she was only concerned with Roberto and not herself. It physically hurt him how loving she was and how this should never have happened to her.

When Nicholas looked up he did not understand the expression on Jack's face. Why wasn't he taking the girl he loved into his arms? Why wasn't he forcing him to release her to him? Instead he watched as Jack backed up, unwilling to come near her.

Francesca felt Nicholas tense up. She looked up to see Jack's wild-eyed expression. She whispered through tears that spilled from her eyes. "Jacqino." Unimaginably, through those tears, she watched as he turned away and darted up the stairs. She felt her heart break. She felt pain so real that she forced her eyes closed to stop the image of him turning away from her, before it became imbedded in her mind forever.

Jack couldn't breathe, he couldn't think. He had to get away from everyone. He darted up the steps and just as his right foot hit the very last step, Nicholas bellowed so loudly that his voice shook the rafters in the old brownstone. "No, Jacqino! Noooooo!" But it was too late.

Anthony stared in disbelief. Nicholas pressed Francesca closer to him, wanting to absorb the sobbing pain that was shaking her body.

Jack tore through the brownstone, past the two kidnappers tied in heaps on the floor.

Uncle Tony couldn't believe that Jack fled. John's head sunk in sheer exhaustion, his hate spent watching his nephew's lost expression. The overwhelming sadness, burning Jack's black eyes to jet, was something John would never forget, and it was all because of him.

Once outside, Jack ran down the stairs and down the block, not really heading in any particular direction as the icy rain pelted his face. He could hear his brother calling for him, but he didn't want reason—he wanted answers, and he wanted them now. Jack quickly ducked down an alleyway as his brother's car passed in a flash of white. Without realizing how he got there, he was standing in front of his old apartment building. The place he called home with Victoria for years. Home? It was hell for her, her prison.

The doorman opened the door immediately upon seeing Jack. "Good evening, Mr. Romano."

Jack only nodded, completely soaked as he strode to the bank of elevators. He punched a code into the elevator panel for the penthouse, feeling his heart pounding in his chest. The doors glided open soundlessly, and Jack stepped into the foyer. Silence is what greeted him. Everything was exactly the way he remembered it the night of the accident, except for the thick layer of dust now covering all the black and gray surfaces, making them appear white and ghostly. Even his shoes left prints in the once highly polished, black, marble surfaces. He looked around and wondered, *did he really live here for three years or had he just imagined it?*

The apartment reminded him of walking through a cemetery, eerie, and unsure where to place his next step. It was as though he sat at a gravestone asking questions, and was intent on finding the answers. He walked into the master bedroom suite, directly into her closet. There was no scent, nothing to remind him of her. He was careful not to brush against the black garments now covered in dust. He reached a cabinet in the center of her wardrobe and pulled open the door, behind which were concealed many drawers. He pulled the first one open and found black underwear—the next contained more black undergarments, stockings, the next black slips, and so on. Now he knew why she wore black. She was mourning her own life, because she knew her life was over.

At first he didn't disturb anything then he began to pull the drawers out and dump the contents onto the carpet one by one. Finally his eyes caught what he was looking for. A sign. A sign of what was the truth—birth control pills. It was a sign to him that Uncle John was telling the truth. He blinked several times unbelieving. He had to get out of here. He had to get away. He needed to think. He felt physically sickened. He couldn't breathe. He left the apartment and as he walked through the lobby he asked the doorman to hail him a cab.

As Jack waited for the cab to pull over, the frigid December wind now laced with sheer ice, lashed a harsh reminder that winter was here. He fell into the back of the cab and said one single word. *"Kennedy."*

Chapter Twenty-Five
A long night ahead…

Nicholas looked down at the sweet child he held in his arms. She was no longer frightened. She was resting her hand against his cheek soothingly speaking barely above a whisper. "He will come back, *Padre*. Don't be angry with him."

She called me Father, Nicholas thought silently, and his heart broke into so many pieces at that moment, he knew it would never be whole again.

Anthony was banging on the front door to the apartment.

"I'm coming! I'm coming! Hold your horses!" The voice called from the other side of the door. Rebecca peered out the peephole and saw Anthony, his hands braced on each side of the frame of her apartment door, his head down. She was just about to tell him to take a long walk off a short pier, until he lifted his hung head and she saw his expression. His perpetually calm façade and never-ruffled appearance was gone. He stood just outside her door upset. Very upset. His gray-blue eyes glistened as though he had been crying. *Crying? That can't be*, Rebecca thought. He repeatedly raked his hand through his hair, except this time it didn't settle into its proper place; instead, it fell over his eyes. She pulled the door open not listening, but questioning.

"What?" Rebecca asked as Anthony stepped into her apartment.

"It's Francesca." Anthony took a breath in and out in an effort to try and slow down his heart rate, which hadn't eased since he received that fateful call from Jack. He took another deep breath. "We can't take her to the hospital." Anthony looked at the wall and not at her, all the time his hand unsuccessfully tried to rake his white-blonde hair off his forehead.

Rebecca reached for his arm and pulled him around to face her, to get his attention. Rebecca could see that he was severely distressed, so she asked again in a gentler tone. "What happened?"

"I…" Anthony started to answer, turning away from her again. *How was he going to explain that his uncle was a low-life and that Jack seemed to have taken off? How was he going to explain to her that for years he thought that Victoria was making his brother's life miserable, when all along she was miserable and trapped? The thoughts made him almost sick to his stomach. To think, I wanted her dead! I was glad when Victoria died! God forgive me.*

"Is she hurt?" Rebecca started to approach his back.

"She has some swelling on the side of her face," Anthony pointed distractedly to his temple area. "I think what she needs is her friend. She needs her best friend."

"Are you alright?" Rebecca looked at his stunned expression when he turned back to face her. His gray-blue eyes looked older somehow.

"No. I may never be right again!" Anthony half shouted then started to pace her living room.

His size filled the room and his strong woody scent, mixed with the scent of rich cigars, quickly filled the air. Rebecca watched him pace like a caged animal just waiting for the right moment to make his escape. He turned around to face her again, his stormy eyes piercing her soft, golden-brown ones. "I'll get her and bring her here."

"Maybe I should go with you?"

"Good idea." Anthony started for her door.

Again she reached for his arm and pulled him to face her. "You know. You know about the dreams?" It was obvious, but Rebecca asked anyway.

"The dreams," Anthony's expression was lost, then explosive.

Rebecca knew there was no way out now. She would have to explain everything to him. His eyes bored straight through her, nearly pinning her to the wall behind, and she knew she wouldn't be able to skirt his questions. "Frankie dreams about things that are going to happen in the future. That's what this is all about, right?" Rebecca asked.

"Rebecca, I don't think you understand. Francesca can do more than just dream about the future. She can predict it. So many things were said tonight. I don't think I will ever be able to comprehend it all. I don't know how Jack can process everything he was told. His emotions must be on overload. He took off like a bat out of hell, and I'm not even sure where he is. The whole situation is a mess." Anthony took a deep breath then explained to her how his uncle had used Francesca almost as a prize.

He repeated the story about Jack's first wife and how she was used to pay a debt to his uncle. He got that sick feeling again just repeating the story to Rebecca, still not believing it himself, as Rebecca remained calm and silent, and yet reassuring with expressions and nods that helped him unload the angst of this despicable night.

When Anthony had expelled all that was weighing so heavily on his mind, Rebecca turned away. She was trying to understand how someone could harbor so much hate that they would use another person to achieve their goal of retribution. Rebecca visibly shuddered.

Anthony came up behind her and began to speak to her, much the way she heard his father speak to Francesca upon meeting her. He whispered something softly in his foreign tongue and encircled her from behind.

Rebecca leaned against Anthony, as he held her close. He felt so solid, so real, and so right. *Why the hell was she fighting it?*

Anthony wanted to tell her, right then, right there, that he loved her, that she was the only woman for him forever. He didn't know how he knew it, he just did. But she wasn't ready to hear that now. *Will she ever want to hear me tell her that I've fallen in love with her?* Anthony wondered, inhaling her fragrance. Pushing aside his hopeless thoughts, Anthony returned to the problem. "Let's go. She needs you."

Anthony returned to his uncle's home holding Rebecca's hand. Together they walked around Carlo who was guarding the kidnappers, still passed out in the foyer. And after prying Frankie free from Nicholas' embrace, Anthony drove them directly to the farm. Repeatedly he looked in the rearview mirror to see Rebecca holding Frankie to her shoulder, a bag of ice held to the side of her friend's head, which was quite swollen now. She wasn't crying anymore, but she was sad, so sad. Sadder than he ever believed anyone could be. His father sat next to him rigid and unmoving. It was well past midnight when Anthony and Nicholas escorted Rebecca and Francesca into the cottage.

Retta and Nelson were surprised at company arriving at that

late hour. But one look at Frankie's head told Retta that something was very wrong, as she silently braced herself.

Carefully, she put her arm around Frankie's shoulders and guided her into the farmhouse. She took Frankie upstairs, with Rebecca following in their wake. Anthony and Nicholas stood at the bottom of the stairs with Nelson.

"What happened to her?" Nelson inquired.

"She was kidnapped by my brother-in-law," Nicholas stated flatly, directing his response up the staircase, his hand squeezing the newel post with such force that his knuckles turned white.

Nelson didn't ask any more questions. He just watched as both men left the house hurrying to the car, leaving in a flurry of gravel and dust.

Father and son had but one thing on their mind—where was Jack? Anthony knew he was upset and needed to digest all that happened tonight, but...Anthony quickly derailed his current train of thought. *Who am I to judge my brother?* He questioned himself silently. He wasn't in Jack's shoes. He didn't know what he was experiencing. Silently he berated himself. *I don't know how he feels or what he is thinking. It seems that everything he knew from Victoria to Francesca was a lie. My God! Jack could have paid any debt her father owed his uncle a hundred times over! Paying for her father's wrongs was not Victoria's obligation. She didn't deserve that. It wasn't her fault her father was a loser. She was doing everything she could to spare him. And now she was dead.* His thoughts went back to Francesca and truly wondered whether she could really predict the future. *Did she know where Jack was at this very moment?* Anthony tried to shake the thoughts from his mind. He raked his fingers through his hair, still so confused and tired.

Retta gently removed Frankie's filthy clothes and slipped a nightgown over her head. She pulled back the comforter and carefully helped Frankie into bed. She smoothed her silky blonde hair away from her cheek and whispered sweet, caring things to her.

Retta cleaned Frankie's face with a warm washcloth. "You rest now, child," Retta whispered and kissed Frankie's cheek just before she clicked off the bedside table lamp.

Rebecca and Retta looked at each other then walked into the hall. "We'll have to wake her all night long just in case she has a concussion."

"Okay." Rebecca understood. "Maybe I'll call Robin to see if she can come."

"That's a good idea."

Anthony and Nicholas were at a loss. All the way back to the city, they were racking their brains trying to figure out where Jack would have gone.

"He can't be on his boat, because The Rose is still docked at the farm," Anthony thought out loud.

"Right," Nicholas confirmed.

"And he can't be with Paul in the limo, because the stretch is still parked exactly where it was when we just passed it."

"Maybe I should call the pilots and see if he asked for his private jet?"

"Good thinking, Dad." Anthony agreed and continued to drive not really paying attention to the direction he was headed. He listened to his father's call.

"Nothing, Jack hasn't called Tommy. He must be in the city, but where?"

"I have an idea." He drove the car to Jack's old apartment building, where he lived with Victoria. They pulled the car up to the front door and the doorman greeted Anthony and Nicholas.

"Good morning, gentlemen."

Nicholas stayed seated in the car. "Good morning? Of course, that's right. It's after midnight, isn't it? By any chance, was Jack here ahh…last night?"

"Yes, sir, he was. He was only here for a few minutes. When he came downstairs, he asked me to hail him a cab. I think he was headed for the airport."

"Yes, wonderful. You've been very helpful. Thank you."

Anthony stepped on the gas, hurtling toward the airport. "Do you think he took a flight to Italy?"

"I don't know, Anthony. I don't know where his head is at. Jack must be so confused and upset. This kind of deception is going to be felt for a very long time." Nicholas' concern clearly etched in his expression.

Chapter Twenty-Six
On the streets of New York...

Anthony's cell phone rang, causing both Anthony and Nicholas to jump. Nicholas grasped at his chest. "My nerves are shot."

"Hello?" Anthony picked up the phone.

"Anthony?"

"Jack!" Anthony swerved his car to the side of the road, screeching to a halt. "Where in God's name are you?"

Nicholas pulled the phone away from Anthony.

"Listen, it doesn't matter where I am, I just didn't want you and Dad to worry."

"Jacqino...son, come home. We will talk. Straighten this whole mess out. Please, Jacqino," Nicholas pleaded into the phone.

Jack's heart was clutched with an indescribable pain. The lump in his throat prevented him from speaking. What could he say? He didn't even understand how he was feeling. He felt lost, completely at the mercy of some intangible force.

"I can't." Jack choked through a throat thickened with emotions. "Not yet."

The phone went dead. Nicholas just stared at it.

At police headquarters, Paul finished the last round of interrogations. Thinking enough time had passed for the Romanos to find Frankie, he decided to exercise his rights.

"Listen, if you don't have any different questions, and since you've been holding me here for what, five, six hours, I think I have a right to a phone call! I think I might need a lawyer. I don't know what the hell I did, other than finding some beat up guy near an animal hospital dumpster and waiting around for the police to show up. I could have just taken off."

The detectives knew he was right and couldn't hold this man just because he was the Romanos' chauffeur. "Alright," Detective Mitchell didn't want to do it but he knew he had no choice, "You're free to leave. You can pick up your personal belongings at the front desk from Sergeant Reilly."

Paul opened the door and closed it behind him, walked purposefully to the front desk, signed a waiver, and collected his belongings. He was told that the limo was towed away and could be picked up at the impound lot after 9 a.m. *Great*, Paul thought, *just great!*

Chapter Twenty-Seven
Sun-up at the farm...

In the morning when the sun rose, Frankie curled herself around the pillow next to her. She pulled it in close and held onto it for dear life as realization set in. How was she going to face the day without Jacqino? What could she do to help him understand? She was afraid to tell him about her dreams, afraid of his reaction and, with obvious good cause, she thought. But when the time came to get herself out of the bed, Frankie could not, or would not, move.

It was as though some overwhelming force prevented her from rising. She was finding it harder and harder to breathe. Her mind started playing tricks that minds always play when one encounters an enormous unknown. She couldn't even imagine her life without Jack, and she certainly couldn't imagine her life with anyone else. That thought was so revolting to her that she vaulted from the bed and ran for the bathroom. She barely made it to the sink where she proceeded to vomit almost violently. She held on while the emotions within her took over, as wave after wave of nausea ripped through her body. She wretched and wretched until there was nothing left; collapsing to the floor, she curled up into a ball and cried until every tear was spent. *How am I going to fix this?* She wept until Retta caught her in her large brown circle and held her tightly, rocking her back and forth, as though quieting a small child.

As each day passed, Anthony hoped, beyond hope, that Jack would return. He and his father discovered that Jack took a flight to Ireland, but they knew that they would never be able to bring him home unless that was Jack's wish. *I would just like the opportunity to talk some damn sense into him*, Anthony's mind shouted. He paced the length of the windows in his office, fighting the urge to chase after his brother.

Nicholas was also finding it more than difficult to likewise restrain himself from flying overseas to speak face-to-face with his son. He wanted to embrace him and tell him that the worst was over, and that only the best was ahead with Francesca. Nicholas knew that, but Jack's youth prevented him from seeing that. Nicholas knew Jack was locked up in that dilapidated excuse for a castle, so he made the necessary telephone calls to make sure he knew exactly what his son was doing at all times.

Angelina was disgusted and disgraced by what her brother did to her son and told him exactly how she felt about his betrayal to her, her son, the family, and especially Francesca and how the same family blood they shared meant nothing to her anymore. Nothing! She told him she considered him dead, just as their brother, Tony, and their sister, Rose, did. They were all repulsed by him. It was over. They had all, one by one, washed their hands of this much-despised man. Now, Angelina just concentrated on praying for her son to find some kind of peace in his mind and return home where he belonged with Francesca.

When Frankie's parents were told that Jack was away, they left it at that. New Year's Day was the date of Frankie's official permanent move to the farm, and Thomas and Corrine wanted to express how happy they were that she had made the permanent move, so they stopped by for a surprise visit. What they found horrified them. Their daughter was so thin and gaunt. She had dark circles under her eyes and looked unkempt. Her hair was straggly, as though little attention, if at all, had been paid to it. Her mother noted that she was wearing a pair of jeans and Jack's oversized Irish cable knit sweater that was in need of washing. Her mother was worried the cancer might have resurfaced, and they began to pepper her with questions. That's when Frankie finally broke down and told her parents everything.

"I don't understand." Thomas stated again.

"I have to agree with your father, Francesca. Where is Jack? What is happening to you?" Corrine eyed her daughter from head to toe.

Frankie fumbled with the sweater poking her fingers in and out of the large holes between some of the beautiful, knitted work. "He found out," Frankie whispered to her hands.

"What darling? You can tell us." Thomas encouraged.

"He found out…that I can…well sort of…know what's going to happen before it actually does."

"You can WHAT?" Corrine shouted as she shot up out of her chair.

"She's second-sighted," Thomas looked at Corrine, who was

still very confused. "Clairvoyant, oh my grandmother was also gifted." Thomas looked lovingly at his daughter.

"Clairvoyant," Corrine questioned her husband.

"It means you have another sense the rest of us don't, that's all. You can see things that others can't. My grandmother drove my grandfather insane, because she knew what he was going to do and say long before he did it or said it. She could predict most anything. In fact, she told me I was going to marry you and that we were going to have a beautiful daughter."

Corrine fell back into her chair, dazed and confused, "Oh my."

Frankie looked at her father and studied him. "You knew," Frankie asserted, with a note of irritated annoyance in her voice.

"No daughter. I didn't know you had the gift, but I understand where it comes from. That's all. So that's why Jack left? He heard you were special and headed for the hills?"

"I guess." Frankie told them exactly what happened. She explained only what she knew about that night, which was only half the story.

As days grew into weeks, Frankie became less depressed and more on autopilot. At first, she just wandered around the old farmhouse and knew that Jack had redesigned this molding or that bookcase. She ran her fingertips along the mantles around the fireplaces and knew which ones Jack had reconstructed from heritage pictures. Bruno followed her around, never leaving her side. She would sit in the kitchen and polish the beautiful silver Anthony had purchased for them months before as an engagement gift. Its intricate pattern required many hours of physical motion, but in some odd way, it brought Frankie a sense of calm as she sat at the large farmhouse table and looked out at the river's bend. Occasionally she caught a glimpse of herself in the silver, gaunt with dark smudges under her eyes, but she quickly rubbed the image away with the polishing cloth.

Two weeks after Jack's disappearance, everyone became very nervous for Frankie. She was not working, nor was she eating, according to Retta. She refused to leave the farm, and refused to speak to anyone uttering no more than one- or two-word responses.

In Ireland, Jack was in a similar condition, as he wandered the cavernous castle. It was cold and damp, and he wondered why the hell he even bought the godforsaken place to begin with. Each day seemed like the day before, cold, raw, and raining. Winter in Ireland was a gray time, which certainly matched his mood. As he stood on the landing looking out over the rolling hills, he was still trying to understand why Victoria hadn't told him the truth. He could have paid off her father's debts, yet she remained his wife, having sex with a man she hated. He tried to shut the image out of his mind. When he had tried so intently to conceive a child with her, she must have been out of her mind with fear and hatred. He balled his fists and stood standing with his feet apart. Squeezing his eyes shut, he could feel his body shake from the rage that coursed through his body directed at his Uncle John. The man had no qualms about twisting up the lives of other people just to suit his distorted needs. But somewhere deep in his subconscious, visions of Francesca flashed, causing him to falter. His fists unclenched. He missed her completely, but she had kept secrets from him, too. He wasn't even sure he understood her secret, but his uncle had tainted his bond with her as well.

"He's lucky I'm a damn continent away from him," Jack said aloud.

"Beg your pardon?"

Jack whirled around to see a small man standing at the base of the large winding staircase.

"Who the hell are you?" Jack roared down to the man at the foot of the staircase.

The man openly shrank, quickly taking a step back. He removed his cap revealing a full head of silvery hair. "I'd be the glassmaker." Mr. Flaherty spoke with a deep Irish brogue.

"The what?"

"I'm here to be lookin' at the stained glass window you wanted repaired. That one…I believe…would be it." The man pointed to the boarded-up transom window, taking another step in retreat.

"Oh…right. I just wasn't expecting anyone today."

"Aye," The man took out a handkerchief and started to mop his brow. *Sweet Jesus, for a minute it looked as though the man knew I had just spoken to his father. It was as if he could see right through me with those black, piercing eyes. Straight into a man's very soul,* Mr. Flaherty deduced. Mr. Flaherty wondered if it was such a good idea, after all, to take Mr. Romano up on his offer to report back about his son's whereabouts. "You nearly scared the devil out of me."

"Sorry about that. My mind was somewhere else." Jack descended the stairs and shook the man's hand. "I'm Jack Romano."

"Aye, Mr. Romano. I'm James Flaherty."

"Please, just Jack."

"Aye, Jack. And you may call me Mr. Flaherty."

Jack cocked an eyebrow studying the older man's face, which showed no sign of emotion. "Okay, Mr. Flaherty. So how do you plan on tackling that heap of broken glass?" Jack pointed up to the stained glass window which was boarded up from the inside. The glass window had been boarded up for more years than anyone could remember and was enormous. The mural was approximately three stories tall and more than fifteen feet wide, reaching to the impossible ceiling height.

"Well, first off, I'm goin' to set up some scaffolding. Then I'll be needin' to remove all the boards. I'll repair and replace all the glass needin' repair and try to match the colors exactly. If something is missin', I'll just be asking the locals, who I'm sure will have a bit of knowledge about that window, if they can recall the colors. After all, it's been here for hundreds of years, so I'm sure I'll be able to restore it close to the original, if that's what you'd be wantin'?"

"Yes, that should work. I'm sure you know what you're doing, because you came highly recommended."

"Aye thank you Jack. Now if you'll excuse me, I'll be startin' straight away."

"You're going to set up scaffolding by yourself?" Jack sounded surprised.

"Aye."

"You want some help?"

"Well lad, let's see." James Flaherty studied the young man before him, *tall and strong, but his eyes showed a kind of sadness, or maybe it was a sign of being lost.* "Since my worker took with a nasty bug and will be laid up a bit, I'd appreciate a hand today."

Jack walked past the man and through the large entranceway. In the back of his truck were boards and steel piping. He started to construct the scaffolding rather methodically, disconnecting his mind from aching for Francesca.

Chapter Twenty-Eight
Penance...

"So this is what you will do." Nicholas began to pace his office, watching the smug form that was sitting in one of his high back chairs that faced his large cherry desk. "You will apologize to each and every person. Do you understand?"

The figure in the high back chair studied the ring on his finger with that detached 'fuck you' look smeared across his face.

"Why, you're a piece of shit, quite literally stuck to the bottom of my shoe!" Nicholas leapt at the figure before it had a chance to react. The man was hurled from the chair and thrown to the floor. Nicholas placed his highly polished leather shoe at the base of the man's throat, his eyes black with fury boring down from above. "Do you understand me?"

"Yes I understand," John squeezed those few words out while trying desperately to push Nicholas' shoe off his throat.

"You're sure?" Nicholas added yet a little more pressure to his brother-in-law's throat.

"Yes," John choked.

"Good. And you will start working at the farm." Nicholas relieved the pressure ever so slightly off his throat.

"Oh, no, I won't!"

"Yes, oh yes you will, John, or I'll go to the police and tell them all about the kidnapping and how your goons beat a man half to death. And your gambling business...do I need to go on?"

"Roberto is going to be fine, and I won that money fair and square."

"Shut up! When I am done with you, you will be respectful of other people's feelings. You will help, and you will be considerate. You will not offend people anymore. You will learn how to be a member of **this** family, even if I have to get Anthony and Paul to provide you with a slight attitude adjustment, as I deem necessary, until the day I bury you."

"You wouldn't dare," John tried to rise from the floor.

"Don't test me! I swear you will lose. I am not inclined to make idle threats." Nicholas pushed John back down onto the floor with the sole of his shoe. "Since your entire family has disowned you, you good-for-nothing piece of trash, I'm sure they would be only too happy to see Anthony and Paul lay a real thrashing on that fat, lazy ass of yours."

"Just disown me, too. Make it easier on us all."

"Make it easy for you? Well, I don't plan on making it easy." Nicholas lowered his head closer to his brother-in-law's face underscoring the point. "You didn't make it easy for me or my son, and so many others. I plan on reforming you, John."

John shook his head disbelievingly.

"Whether you are skeptical or not, we leave for the farm in a few hours. Have your bags packed and your business affairs in order, because you aren't coming back to the city until I damn well say you can. You will not be permitted to leave the farm for any reason, and if you do, I will report the entire kidnapping incident to the police. Roberto and Francesca will be only too happy to file charges against you."

John nodded his head again.

"You will show me respect. You will answer me with a clear and precise *Yes*. You got that?" Nicholas was advancing on John still sprawled on the floor.

"Yes." John held up his hand to stop the onslaught of Nicholas' wrath.

"And you will do the same with everyone you interact with, understood?"

"Yes." John knew Nicholas was dead serious. John mentally calculated that by the time he finished apologizing to everyone, he risked being pretty beaten when all was said and done.

An hour later, Paul was waiting at the curb for Mr. Romano, just outside the entrance of Romano Enterprises. When the front door opened, Nicholas Romano and John Scarpelli walked through the door, and Paul was on John without forethought.

"Why you piece of crap! You got a fuckin' nerve showing your ugly face at Romano Enterprises. But I'm gonna fix that face of yours real good."

"Paul, please." Nicholas cautioned in his usual understated tone while removing an invisible piece of lint from his right suit sleeve.

"Yes Mr. Romano?" Paul questioned angelically.

"Please let Mr. Scarpelli up."

"I don't think so, Mr. Romano. I think I'm gonna fuckin' attach his face to the sidewalk right here so that we can wipe our feet on it right now."

John was gasping for air, the lower half of his body twisting wildly.

Paul straddled John's body as his hands continued to increase pressure to his airway.

"Paul!" Nicholas again tried to reason with the chauffeur.

"Come on, Mr. Romano. He's scum. No, he's slime. After what he did to Francesca…" Paul's voice trailed off.

Paul increased the pressure around John's throat further and enjoyed watching the older man's eyes grow wide as his airway narrowed in Paul's grip.

"I can't…"

"Breathe." Paul was only too happy to finish his sentence. "That's right. Slime isn't allowed to breathe. Slime doesn't deserve to breathe."

"What is going on out here? Security just called me to find out if I wanted the police called." Anthony called out to his father as he walked through the doors of Romano Enterprises. "Scarpelli!" In one quick movement, Anthony flung Paul to one side, and Anthony was now choking his uncle with more strength than Paul. The force had a definite underlying layer of hate. "I see we have an unwanted visitor," Anthony spat directly at John's reddened face.

"Anthony, I do not think that your uncle can breathe." Nicholas stated softly, again brushing imaginary lint from the other sleeve of his suit jacket.

"And the problem with that would be?" Anthony scowled quizzically at his father.

"If you suffocate him, he will not be able to make his apologies. Isn't that right, John?"

John nodded his head the best he could with Anthony's hands wrapped around his throat.

"You don't say." Anthony looked at his uncle. "Well, I don't want your apology." Anthony spat out the words an inch from his uncle's face.

"Of course you do." Nicholas bent over, resting a hand on Anthony's shoulder, to better study his son's handiwork. In fact, no one can kill him until after he has apologized to each and every person that he has ever caused some kind of pain to, even inadvertently. Isn't that right, John?"

Again, John tried to nod his head.

Anthony jumped up and brushed his suit jacket flat. "Well then hurry it up Father; because once he's done with his penance I am going to kill him." Anthony stared directly into eyes that were so similar to his.

"Lucky for John it could take him years to apologize to all the people he has managed to upset, which will probably prolong his life." Nicholas again spoke softly.

"Well if he is going to start with anyone, I suppose that he should start with you, Father?" Anthony began to poke his uncle's chest. "Don't you think so, John?" Anthony was showing a clear sign of disrespect by not using 'Uncle' to address him, which was not lost on John.

John began to rub and clear his throat. "Nicholas, I apologize for anything I have ever done to hurt you."

Anthony stared at his uncle rubbing his chin. "I not sure, but I do not think that was sincere enough. Paul what did you think?"

"Lame-very lame apology," Paul nodded his head in agreement.

John straightened his shoulders and looked deep into his brother-in-law's dark eyes just before speaking very softly in his native tongue. "*Niko, sono molto spiacente.*"

Nicholas looked at his brother-in-law remembering the nickname they had all called him so long ago. He saw the deep lines around John's mouth and eyes. He could see the sincerity, could feel the honesty in his simple Italian words, *Nick I'm very sorry.* Nicholas reached out his hand and shook his brother-in-law's hand firmly. When John pulled him in for an embrace, Nicholas did not fight it. He held John tight and knew this was the right rebirth for his brother-in-law. He had many bridges to mend. "Don't stop now, *Cognato.*"

"I agree." John turned toward his nephew and watched an array of raw emotions dance along the young man's handsome face. But when he apologized to Anthony, he called him son in Italian, and Anthony had to fight to keep up the hate he felt for this man. He could feel his uncle's sadness and knew he was taking hard steps to right so many wrongs. When John asked Anthony for forgiveness, Anthony stared silently at his uncle.

"Maybe in time, *Zio*," Anthony spoke softly.

John continued his apology to Paul and Paul was astounded that this man was humbling himself to the family chauffeur!

With each apology came a new and different experience. His apology to his sister, Angelina, was done while she was getting her hair done at the salon. Women came to stand by her, as protection; her hair was set in rollers as she sat under the dryer. John yelled his apology over the machine so that she could hear him. Angelina looked at her husband in shock then accepted the apology with her eyes. She knew that Nicholas was devoted to family, and he would not stop until everyone accepted John's amends.

John knew the hardest apology would be to Dr. Frankie and her parents, which he certainly thought would most likely put him in the emergency room at the local hospital, especially after how he used their daughter's gift for his own gain, and then went on to kidnap her. *What was I thinking?* He questioned himself quietly. *Whatever possessed me to do that?* But he knew what the answer was—irrational hate, quite simply. Hate has a self-propelling power, which requires little sustenance to survive, but love—love takes work, time, and patience.

During the ride to the farm, everyone seemed to be lost in their own thoughts, but Nicholas was highly concerned how Jack was doing emotionally. He could tell that John was nervous beyond belief; as Nicholas watched his brother-in-law's hands tremble in his lap. John's bag was in the trunk of the limo and his dog was in the backseat. Little Nick, the English bulldog, was panting and slobbering on the leather interior, which caused Nicholas to wince. Anthony was going to have a fit when he saw the scratches this dog managed to carve into the leather upholstery. But Anthony needed a little mess in his life, Nicholas pondered.

A cold, gray, darkening evening greeted the men at the farm. The wind whipped off the river with relentless force and biting cold. John made his way to the cottage pulling his collar up around his reddened throat. After being introduced to Retta and Nelson, John began his explanations and apologies. Retta and Nelson had a hard time understanding why this man was brought to them. He caused them no harm.

"Oh, but I did," John protested.

Retta shrugged.

"Dr. Frankie is upset because of what I did to Jack, and you are upset that she is upset, I think." John had to sit down. "It's like dominos. When the first one falls, it leads all the others to fall, too. What I did to one caused a chain reaction of hurt to others."

Nelson stood behind Retta not saying a word.

"John will be working at the farm," Nicholas interjected.

"I see." Nelson acknowledged.

"Why?" Retta asked.

But Nelson was quick to stop that question's answer. Shaking his head and squeezing his wife's shoulders gently. "It's none of our business why you want him here, but, by God, if you do anything to upset Doc, no body, and I mean no body will find your body. You got that, Mr. Scarpelli? She's family, and we don't take kindly to her being hurt."

John nodded his head in understanding, knowing Nelson meant every word he said.

"She is in such a fragile frame of mind right now. I just hope she can handle this," Retta wondered out loud.

Nicholas agreed. He knew she was extremely distressed, but he was working on a plan.

Nelson voiced his simple opinion. "There is plenty of work to do with all the boarded horses we have taken in already. They all need to be exercised, fed, groomed, and the stalls need to be mucked out daily. If we could just get the doc to open her practice, we know it would help her feel better."

"Maybe I can help with that." John rose from the table tentatively, feeling much older than just that morning and still weighed down by burdens too heavy for one person to bear. *I put those burdens on myself one by one, didn't I?* John left through the rear of the cottage following Nicholas along the brick walkway to the back of the farmhouse, with Nelson and Little Nick trailing behind.

Through the back door he saw her sitting at the old large wooden farmhouse table. Her chin was resting on her folded arms that rested on the old wooden table. A plate filled with food sat before her, untouched. Bruno woke from his guard post beneath Frankie's feet and barked at the approaching form. Frankie shuddered when she saw Mr. Scarpelli. Startled, she jumped up from her chair, unintentionally knocking it to the floor, stepping as far away as she could, in fear. Bruno sensed Frankie's fright, and his bark deepened into a growl, baring large, white teeth. When the intruder didn't take that as a sign to back-off; Bruno lunged against the back door causing John to fall backwards.

"God almighty," John shouted from his fallen position looking up at Nicholas. "That dog's gonna tear my head off!"

"Funny, but he doesn't normally act that way toward anyone." Nicholas looked at Bruno's expression. "He does seem a bit... agitated."

"Agitated?!" John swallowed hard.

Francesca unlocked the door once she saw Jack's father.

"NO!" John shouted.

Like a shot, Bruno launched himself out the door, landing squarely on John's chest, knocking him to the ground, and barking just inches from his face. Huge gobs of drool spat onto John's face and coat. When Nicholas shouted, '*Cease,*' the sound of his voice reminded Frankie so much of Jack's that she started to sob uncontrollably.

"Shh. Don't cry sweetheart, please don't." Nicholas folded her up in an embrace. "I'm sorry. Did we scare you?" He held her tight, holding her trembling thin body until the shaking and tears slowed.

"No, you didn't scare me, *Padre*. It's just that your voice reminds me so much of Jacqino's. I miss him so very much." Frankie whispered through her throat, choked with emotions. She had been upset all day. Just that morning, The Rose's skipper removed the boat from the dock to bring it downriver for the harsh winter months. It needed to be moored to its own dock and winterized with lack of use, but Frankie took it as another sign that she was never going to see Jack again. She thought Jack had called his Skipper and not her, but the Skipper explained that he was just following the usual schedule. She looked around Nicholas to see John still sprawled out on the brick walkway just outside the back door. "Why is he here? Why would you bring him here?"

Nicholas loved this girl. He knew his son would come back for her, he just hoped he wouldn't wait too long. Francesca was sad now, Nicholas knew, but if his son didn't return soon, eventually that sadness would be replaced with other emotions, so that she could continue to function as a normal human being. "He is here for a few reasons, Francesca. Right, John?" Nicholas called over his shoulder.

John stood up, brushed off his backside and made his way into the kitchen, as the dogs walked alongside of him. John could not believe how thin and frail she looked. She actually looked worse now than she did when she had cancer, he noted. It seemed as though she no longer had any hope. Silently he made a vow to fix things. As God was his witness, he pledged he was going to fix everything.

Frankie trusted Nicholas, so when he asked her to sit and listen to what John had to say, she did. Nicholas stood behind her, his hands rested on her shoulders, a sign of support and love.

At first the words just wouldn't come, then little by little, John spoke about his past. He spoke about the hate that was passed down from generation to generation. So many years wasted on hate. He told Frankie how, after Nicholas and his sister married, he swore revenge, but that revenge was misguidedly released on his nephew, Jack. He went into great detail how he had used people over and over again to feed his hate.

When he spoke about Victoria, Frankie grew pale, to the point of looking faint. She didn't understand that kind of hate and manipulation. She didn't know what it was like to be taught by your own family to hate others. But as Frankie tried to comprehend this concept, she began to realize the depth of what Jack must be going through and realized why he hadn't returned to her. He must be confused beyond measure. He could not trust anyone or believe anything. When Frankie walked over to John, his head rose up with each step she took.

John thought she was going to slap him. In fact, he was silently hoping she would slap him. That would probably make him feel better. Instead he watched her open her arms to embrace him. In her frail embrace, John cried tears of great magnitude. And the tears he cried washed away years of hate and years of sins.

"Please, I beg of you, you must forgive me. I don't think I could stand it if you didn't."

"Mr. Scarpelli..." Frankie started, but was interrupted by John.

"Please, if you can find it in your heart, please call me John."

"Uncle John, I couldn't hate you. I have to admit I'm a little afraid of you, but I don't hate you. And Jacqino doesn't hate you either. He will forgive you, too. He just needs time. Isn't that right, *Padre*?"

"*Si angela*," Nicholas smiled down at the beautiful angel before him.

Francesca smiled back. "Well, Uncle John, *Padre*, I guess I better prepare for two overnight guests." Frankie started to turn to leave.

"Oh no, sweetheart I'm going back to the city tonight, and John will be staying in the barn." Nicholas spoke matter-of-factly.

"THE BARN!!" Frankie and John shouted in unison.

"Yes, the barn." Nicholas clarified softly in case each one hadn't heard him correctly the first time. "Little Nick can stay in the house with you if you'd like, Francesca, but John will be in the barn. John will be working up here at the farm, while you start up your veterinary practice. He will take care of any animals that board at the farm or in the hospital."

"But *Padre*, I haven't even opened my practice for business yet, and the farmhouse has several guest rooms. It would be..."

"Well, that is ALL going to change. I think you better rest up, because I believe the hospital is open for business in the morning." Nicholas stopped to look at his watch. "My, my... look at how the time has flown right by. Isn't that so, John?"

"Yes, time does pass quickly, too quickly."

"Goodnight, Francesca." John kissed her forehead.

"Goodnight, Uncle John. I'll take care of Little Nick."

"Okay." John agreed.

Nicholas studied his brother-in-law's retreating form. "The bastard named his dog after me," Nicholas muttered to no one in particular.

Frankie had to stifle a giggle.

Nicholas whirled around to see her smile. It was the first time he had seen her smile in weeks. Then they both began to laugh.

Chapter Twenty-Nine
A busy day ahead...

The next morning, Retta made a big breakfast in the old farmhouse's newly renovated kitchen. The smell of bacon and eggs woke Frankie up and, for the first time in quite a while, she was actually feeling much better and hungry. At least she didn't feel like vomiting this morning. She showered quickly and pulled on a pair of clean jeans. She considered Jack's Irish knit sweater, then tossed it into the hamper and opted for a denim shirt instead. She tucked it into her jeans and added a black leather belt and matching low-heeled boots. Funny, but her clothes felt a little snug. Shrugging, she made her way down the large, curved staircase, through the hallway, and into the kitchen. John and Nelson had already started eating breakfast.

"Good mornin', Dr. Frankie," Retta called from the stove where she was managing three cast-iron pans at the same time: eggs in one, bacon in a second, and cornbread browning in the third.

"Morning all!" she called back.

John grumbled something about his back and more mice in that barn than in the city, and Nelson muttered something about once Crystal the cat was well enough, she would probably solve most of that problem. John was apparently not a morning person.

Frankie took a huge, dark green mug, filled it with steaming coffee, and wrapping her hands around the mug, she inhaled the strong brew. Something was different. She could feel it, sense it.

At exactly 8:00 a.m., while everyone ate their breakfast, her former patients from the animal hospital arrived by the vanloads. Others came from the neighboring communities as the grand opening of the new facility was heavily advertised in the local papers. Anthony was driving one van and Paul, the other.

"I told you it would have been quicker to take the thruway," Paul complained.

"And I told you that Route Two-eighty-seven was the more scenic view and a much more pleasant ride," Anthony scowled at Paul.

"Thank you handsome," Mrs. Mastellon patted Anthony's shoulder.

"Go to hell!" shouted Max, the very outspoken macaw, from inside his carrying case. Anthony tried to hide his shock at the bird's profanity.

"Did that bird just tell you...," Paul started to laugh hysterically.

"Don't even ask." Anthony closed his eyes, and his ears, in an effort to try to forget how that bird cursed off everyone in the van, including his own owner.

"Here, let me help you. Please watch your step," Anthony smiled pleasantly to each of Frankie's clients.

Rebecca poked at Anthony's ribs.

Anthony whirled around to see Rebecca all-brown, glossy curls, in a denim skirt, and a thick midnight blue, turtleneck sweater. She looked like a blue hourglass perched on a pair of four-inch, high-heeled, deep maroon leather boots that disappeared under the denim skirt.

"Yeah, keep smiling blondie, because when this shipment goes back, there's another pick-up after lunch."

Anthony's smile faded. "No. Please tell me that isn't so."

"Oh it is so, big boy." Rebecca called over her shoulder, as she led the group of people with their pets to the hospital entrance.

Anthony walked up to the farmhouse and rang the bell, sounding off a long row of deep musical chimes.

Frankie opened the door looking refreshed and flushed. "Anthony! What a surprise! Come in. We were just having breakfast." Frankie opened the door wide.

"I always have time for some of Retta's excellent cooking." Anthony tapped his flat stomach. "But I am afraid **you** do not have time to dawdle. The waiting room at the hospital is filled to capacity!" Anthony pointed his finger at Frankie.

"Oh that's silly. I haven't even opened for business..." Frankie trailed off because in the distance, she spotted Mrs. Mastellon and the familiar red carrying case in which she carried Max in whenever she came for an appointment. "...Is that Mrs. Mastellon?"

"Yes, it is. Such a lovely macaw she has."

"Oh, I know. He is one of my best patients," Frankie added.

Anthony looked at her in shock. *Did she say best? Jeez, what was the worst one like?* "Why don't you head over to the hospital?" Anthony suggested as he made his way toward the stove.

"I think I better."

"I'll bring some coffee over for everyone in a few minutes."

"Okay," Frankie started to leave, "Hey Anthony!" Frankie ran back to him, threw her arms around him, and held him tightly. "Thank you," Frankie whispered.

Anthony kissed the top of her head and returned the embrace. She ran off and all he could do was thank God. Maybe this would take her mind off Jack. Maybe...

Frankie walked into the waiting room greeting both old and new patients, but there was no receptionist and no assistant. Becca stepped in and hugged Frankie.

"I'll play receptionist, okay?"

"Becca, you're the best. Thanks."

Since most of the patients came by the vans, they knew they would need to wait until their entire group had been seen by Dr. Frankie. So they worked one full van of patients, then the other. The locals who came for the opening were led around by Paul, who gave them a tour of facility. He handed out the new business cards and "Ten-Percent-Off Your First Vet Visit" coupons. Many were impressed and did schedule appointments as Becca frantically penciled in names and times. The phone started ringing and the foul-mouthed macaw was cursing off the lady with a baby sheep.

"You look a little bewildered, sweetie," Mrs. Mastellon called over the counter that separated the receptionist from the waiting area.

"I don't know the first thing about animals or how to be a receptionist. To be honest, I'm a psychologist." Becca shrugged.

"Well, would you like a little help? I used to be the receptionist for The Mandarin Spa in New York," Mrs. Mastellon offered.

"Really, oh my God, I love that place!" Becca broadcasted. She motioned for her to come around the counter and take the seat beside the phone.

"How about I turn on the computer and see if we can start imputing names and phone numbers into the appointment calendar. A little billing, perhaps?" Mrs. Mastellon suggested and settled the macaw on the counter. Max enjoyed being on stage and managed to call the woman with the sheep a stupid ass and the man with the vicious Doberman, a barrel ass. Becca and Mrs. Mastellon agreed "ass" was the word for the day.

People blushed and giggled as the colorful bird let loose a blue streak of the coarsest language and, curiously, no one seemed to be offended.

Frankie hurried out after her first patient and took note of Mrs. Mastellon in the receptionist's chair. She looked great there.

"Hey, that spot suits you," Frankie called to her.

"Hey, that white coat suits you," Mrs. Mastellon bantered back.

Frankie walked around the receptionist's desk, and giving Mrs. Mastellon a hug, whispered in her ear, "I have no idea what we are supposed to charge for these visits."

"Oh, don't worry about that," the older woman whispered back. "I know what some of the fees are, and I just called Robin to fax me a more detailed list—everything from nail trimming to all types of surgeries. Don't you worry about that! I will do the billing, too, if you'll have me. You just go be the...vet!"

"Alright then if you say so...."

"Well...I do." Mrs. Mastellon called the next patient into the examination room.

"Move it, fat ass." Max shouted, as he strutted back and forth.

Becca started to giggle and her curls bounced with each shake of mirth.

Anthony walked in holding a tray of coffee, cream, sugar, stirrers, and cups for all. He placed it to one side of the receptionist's counter, catching Becca's smiling eyes. *God, what a beauty*, he thought. "Coffee's here," he announced to everyone. Anthony served coffee to the waiting patients. It was certainly not his day job, but he was actually having fun. Being near Becca was reward in itself.

It was just as Max started to call Paul his favorite word of the day, when Uncle John walked in and heard someone cursing. "Hey, hey, who's got the foul mouth in here?"

"Uncle John, take it easy." Anthony placed a large hand on his uncle's shoulder. He couldn't believe he was actually touching the man he nearly choked the life from just a day before.

"What do you mean take it easy? Who is cursing like that

around all these lovely ladies?" Uncle John started to turn on the charm when he spotted Mrs. Mastellon.

"It was my bird, mister..."

"Please, call me John," Uncle John cooed.

"John it's nice to meet you. I'm Margaret...Margaret Mastellon." Mrs. Mastellon took his extended hand, which was a little rough. For such a smooth, un-weathered face, he didn't look like he would have calloused hands.

"Now Maggie," Uncle John instantly nicknamed her, "Don't tell me that a sweet lady like you is the owner of that foul-mouthed bird?" John asked.

"I'm afraid so. I think he picks it up from my neighborhood. I place him in the window over the kitchen sink in my apartment, and he must hear other people call out those unpleasant words all day long." Mrs. Mastellon peered at the bird. "I think we have all had enough of you." Maggie held her arm out for Max and guided him back into his cage. "I know exactly where you will be quiet." She carried the case into the examination room where Frankie was working.

"It seems the bird never curses in front of Frankie," Becca explained.

"Really, why is that?" Uncle John asked.

"I guess he knows she can skin him alive."

Frankie whispered something to Max who fluffed his feathers and settled himself in the far corner of the cage.

"He's such a show-off in front of Dr. Frankie," Mrs. Mastellon remarked on her way back to the receptionist's station.

The morning flew by in a whirl of dog fur, cat hair, and feathers. Anthony was really looking forward to the afternoon shift. When he spoke to Robin just a little over a week ago, they had conspired to make this day Frankie's grand opening at the farm. Robin had called some of Frankie's patients from Park East Animal Hospital even though she knew it was wrong to solicit business away from PEAH, but she wanted to help Frankie. With a few phone calls, the word spread fast and with a little advertising, the veterinarian farm was open for business.

Uncle John stopped in every hour on the hour to see if Mrs. Mastellon needed anything—anything at all. But she just blushed and told him she was just fine.

Becca left for the city. She had scheduled all of her appointments for the late afternoon and early evening, and Anthony made it a point to walk her to her car.

"This isn't necessary. I'm very capable of taking care of myself."

"Yes, I can see that," Anthony agreed. He lifted his right hand to finger a shiny brown curl that was calling to him all morning.

"Please, don't." Becca looked at his hand in her hair. She noticed that his touch was gentle, like a whisper.

Anthony dropped his hand by his side.

"Remember the only reason why we are seeing eye-to-eye is for Frankie's sake. I don't want her upset anymore than she's already been and if she sees us going at it, that will only make her feel bad again."

"I agree." Anthony reluctantly took a step back and jammed his fists deep into his pockets.

"It really isn't necessary for you to have Carlo follow me around either. I've been living on my own for some time now. I really don't see the need for a...umm...bodyguard, if that's what you call it, because I've been perfectly safe without one. See?" Becca held up her arms and twirled around in a circle.

"Sorry. You will have to take that up with my father." Anthony flashed her that beautiful, white smile. "My father can be rather forbidding, so choose your timing carefully."

"Humph, you are such a thick-headed Italian." Becca turned away and got into her little, white, Mustang convertible.

"Sicilian!" Anthony corrected again, as he watched her start the engine and drive her car along the driveway and out onto the dirt road. *I hope to be your thick-headed Sicilian very soon,* Anthony wished silently.

Frankie was absolutely exhausted when the final patient left. John drove Margaret Mastellon and Max back to the city. She promised to be back first thing in the morning. And Robin was starting tomorrow, as her full-time assistant.

"We have to discuss your salary," Frankie started.

"Please, there is plenty of time for that sweetie." Mrs. Mastellon patted Frankie's hand that held hers. She was so happy to be needed and useful. She didn't care if she ever got paid. Now she sat next to John and wondered where he had been all her life and John sat quietly behind the steering wheel wondering the same thing.

Frankie waved goodbye thinking if Margaret and Robin would relocate up here, I think I could make this work. *I think I'll call my father and tell him about my wonderful day, and see if he could find places for Margaret and Robin.* Frankie was overwhelmed by the caring efforts of her family, Jack's family and friends. She never would have been able to open her practice without their concerted efforts on her behalf.

After she showered and settled down in front of the fire that Nelson had built for her in the master bedroom, she sipped the mug of hot cocoa Retta made for her every night. All became quiet and, with the quiet, came thoughts of Jacqino. The stillness brought visions and memories, visions too real, memories too precious to not want to recall. She swallowed hard against the substantial lump in her throat and made her way to her bed. Pulling back the comforter, she slipped into the large bed and called for Bruno to join her. Little Nick struggled to get up onto the bed, so Francesca lifted him up. Petting the dogs, she quieted herself to sleep.

After January passed in a flurry of wind, snow and, fur-yes-fur by mid-February the animal hospital was in full swing. Robin had found an apartment in the middle of town over the pharmacy and was, thankfully, at Frankie's side every day. Margaret was interested in a small one bedroom cottage about ten miles from the farm near a babbling brook. She was in the process of selling her condo and was just thrilled with the prospect of relocating out of the city.

Frankie threw herself into her work each day. The sounds of animals bouncing off the walls in the hospital masked the sound of Jack calling her name, which she seemed to hear whenever it was quiet. At night she collapsed on the bed too exhausted to think, so she slept dreamlessly.

It was towards the end of February that she had her check-up to see if the cancer remained in remission and that no new growth was evident. When she arrived at the doctor's office she was nervous and unsteady. She hadn't been back to the city since the night John had kidnapped her, and she feared the unknown, the "what ifs" were nearly driving her mad. *What if I have cancer again*, she questioned herself. *I have to stop thinking like this. I just have too.*

"Frankie, you are looking well. Tell me how you feel," Dr. Rabinowitz began.

"Fine and I think I've gained some weight since the last time I was here. Retta, who helps at the farmhouse, is such a wonderful cook. And every night before I go to bed, she makes me a huge mug of hot chocolate. It probably sounds silly, but it is the best I've ever had."

"Well, I think that is very promising. A good appetite is always something we like to see. In fact, the weight looks very healthy on you, and you're glowing. I think starting up your own practice was the smartest thing you could have ever done. You look happy. It really shows."

Does it? Frankie questioned herself silently. *Can't anybody see that I miss Jacqino so much that it physically hurts? It hurts all over,* Frankie drifted off into her own thoughts, as her doctor took her blood pressure.

"Excellent. One-twenty over eighty. We'll draw some blood then I'll call you in a few days with the results. Good to see you again, Frankie."

"Thanks."

"I'll speak to you soon."

For the next three days, Frankie walked around in a fog. *What if the cancer has come back? Will I have to have surgery and chemo again?* She shook her head to shake the dark thoughts away.

"What is it sweetie?" Mrs. Mastellon asked as she watched Frankie tremble.

"Nothing—nothing," Frankie said quietly. "I had my check-up a few days ago." Frankie spoke to the patient's chart in her hands.

Then it clicked. Cancer! Margaret panicked. "What did the doctor say?" Margaret started to feel numb.

"Oh, he said I looked fine. But I still haven't heard back about the blood results." Frankie didn't want to go into too much detail.

"I see," Margaret replied, but she didn't see at all. Margaret knew that something happened to Frankie's fiancé, because all the way home after the first day she came to the farm, John had literally spilled his guts to her. Margaret knew that Frankie was under great strain wondering if her beau would ever come back, and now she had to add waiting for test results on top of that.

"It'll be alright, I'm sure. I feel healthy. I eat constantly, which I am going to have to put a stop to, soon." Frankie opened her crisp white doctor's coat to reveal her tummy. "Look, I can't even button these jeans today." Frankie giggled, and Margaret laughed too. Just then, Retta walked through the door of the animal hospital.

"I figured you were too busy to stop in for lunch, so I thought I'd bring lunch to you," Retta called over a small tray she was carrying. A large basket swung from her arm, laden with fresh baked rolls.

"Are those fresh-baked pumpernickel rolls?" Frankie asked, spying a roll that peeked out from beneath the checkered cloth.

Retta walked around behind the receptionist's counter and set the tray on the credenza behind the photocopy machine. The tray was lined with a bed of ice and nestled in the ice were a variety of whipped cream cheese spreads. She set the basket down and underneath the checkered cloth were a dozen fresh, baked rolls, including whole grain, poppy seed, rye, and pumpernickel. "Your favorite," Retta winked.

"Oh my, they're still warm. Thanks, Retta." She bit into the roll, thinking she had surely died and gone to heaven.

When her doctor called the following morning, Frankie asked Margaret to reschedule the afternoon appointments. She needed some time to think. She had to think. She replayed the conversation, still trying to adjust to the doctor's report.

"Frankie, you're in excellent health. Your blood work came back clean, and you are certainly much healthier to me when I saw you."

"Thanks. That's good news." Frankie was so relieved. She had been worried for days.

"There is one more bit of good news," he continued.

"Oh?" Frankie held the phone in her hand tipping her head forward, spilling a curtain of gold to shield her face.

"Umm, maybe you know already?"

"Know what?" Frankie asked.

"You're pregnant."

Pregnant! Did he say pregnant? "Pregnant," Frankie whispered in a shocked tone. Now everything made sense, the sickness in the mornings, the first loss of appetite, and now the increased appetite, the swelling around her mid-section, as she raised a hand slowly pressing it to her stomach. *Jacqino's baby! I'm going to have Jacqino's baby!*

"Yes, I'm holding the results right here. I could have you re-tested if you think…"

"No, no, that won't be necessary." Frankie managed.

"I recommend that you see an obstetrician as soon as possible. I wouldn't have recommended it, the pregnancy, that is, so close to just finishing your chemotherapy treatments. There may be…for a lack of a better word…consequences."

"Oh," Frankie murmured. A rush of emotions overcame her. She was pregnant with Jacqino's baby, but she might not be able to take it to term. What if they told her the baby was imperfect in some way? She tasted bile rising up in her throat. She would never abort Jacqino's baby, never.

"Frankie?"

"Yes, I'm still here." Frankie swallowed, forcing the bitterness back down.

"Remember you need to make an appointment immediately with an obstetrician."

"Yes, I'll call her today."

"Very good. Let my secretary know who you will be seeing so that I can forward her your file. It is important she have a complete picture. So our next appointment will be in six months. I'll connect you to the appointment desk so that you can schedule that now."

"Yes."

"You should be a mother by then."

"Yes, a mother," Frankie whispered. "Thank you."

"My pleasure. It's not everyday I tell someone that they are going to have a baby. In fact, I never have."

<hr />

Sitting on the dock, with Bruno and Little Nick by her side, she prayed for guidance. *Should I try to reach Jacqino? Should I tell Anthony or Nicholas? Should I tell my parents?* Eventually, everyone would know, especially after she started to show. Frankie figured she conceived after they went sailing. She inhaled to unbutton her jeans then exhaled with relief from loosening the restrictive fabric.

At the top of the hill, Uncle John watched Frankie sitting on the dock. Tears stung his eyes. He wondered how long she would wait for his nephew. When he asked Nicholas about Jack, he just shook his head. No one seemed to have an answer. Frankie was a lost soul without Jack, and he knew Jack must be feeling the same way. *It is all my fault,* John scolded himself, as he took a bandanna from his back pocket to wipe his eyes. It was so damn cold out there by the river. He wondered how long she was going to sit on the dock in this temperature. She didn't look like she was going to come in any time soon.

Nelson walked up behind John and rested his hand on the man's shoulder. Nelson liked John and enjoyed the company in the stables. John had a way with horses and worked hard, considering the man never labored a day before in his life. *Penance,* Nelson thought, *can change a man. Change a man's soul.*

"She'll be along."

"She must be freezing down there. The river's just about a block of ice." John was angry, but only at himself. He watched in real time what his actions did, how much pain he caused and was ashamed.

"She'll need to come up and check on her patients staying overnight in the hospital."

"Yes, you're right. It just gets to me. It's all my fault."

"None of my business, but let's not let her see us worrying about her. I think that upsets her the most."

John looked at Nelson. He found it amazing that Nelson knew so much about someone else's feelings after only being acquainted with them for a short time. "The last thing I want to do is upset her more."

"Come on, then. Let's get back to work."

Frankie still sat on the dock, sighed, and shivered.

Thousands of miles away, Jack was staring at another bleak, gray sky. The rain had stopped for today, but it was still quite raw and damp. Jack seemed to shiver all the time. He missed Francesca so much and that feeling of loss was painful.

Mr. Flaherty studied the boy from high above the scaffolding. He didn't know anything about Jack, except for one thing. He was sad. Sadder than he ever knew anyone could be. He hardly spoke, he never saw him eat, and all he did was work. He hauled new lumber into the castle and hauled the rotten lumber out. He addressed any problems quietly and resolved them without fanfare.

As time passed, the only thing that gave Jack rest was working until he dropped from sheer exhaustion. And if didn't push himself into an exhaustive sleep, he walked the halls of the old castle swearing he could hear Francesca call his name. He would shake his head trying to stop the sweet sound, but it never worked. He stood at the top of the staircase and stared at the stained glass mural. The glass looked unremarkable. Most of the sections were in need of repair and more than half the glass sections were still missing. Like the stained glass window with so many damaged and missing pieces, Jack felt the same, damaged with pieces missing.

Jack hadn't received a call from his family in months. He checked for voicemails, as well as emails, on his cell phone constantly, but there were none. He even checked the voicemail he set up for his architecture company, but no one called there, either. While he hauled the debris to the back of the castle where they were allowed to burn most of the old decayed wood timbers in a huge bonfire, he knew it wasn't right that he left, but he didn't know how to fix it. He could fix a castle and an old farmhouse, but he couldn't fix the mistrust, the hurt, and the pain.

Late that night, Jack was sitting in front of his laptop when an e-mail came in from Scott. It was simple-it just read "WTF!" Jack hit the 'Reply' button and sent Scott his response and explanation.

Son of a bitch, Scott cursed at the computer screen when he saw Jack's e-mail reply. He couldn't believe Jack's timing because he knew he was going to Frankie's the following night for dinner. The end of the email was short-it read:

> *"Scott please print out this*
> *e-mail and give it to Francesca:*
>
> *Dear Francesca,*
> *I want you to know that I still love you and will*
> *always love you. I guess I am just asking for time.*

Please give me some time, to settle this anger I am feeling for John. Please, Francesca, please forgive me for leaving like I did, but I am still struggling with the pain I put Victoria through.

Love, Jacqino

Chapter Thirty
Never hide from the truth…

On the farm, Frankie invited everyone for dinner tonight, and, as usual, Retta was thrilled to cook for such a large group. But when Frankie mentioned that she was craving baked ham, Retta's antenna went straight up.

"Would you mind?" Frankie asked.

"Of course I don't mind."

"Could you put a lot of those black things on the top?" Frankie scanned her brain for the name of the herb. She knew very little about cooking.

"Cloves," Retta asked.

"That's it." Frankie snapped her fingers. "And some sweet potatoes with maple syrup," Frankie licked her lips. She wore a baggy sweatshirt to cover her tiny swell in her belly and after more tests than Frankie cared to recall, with her bladder stretched to capacity on one occasion in particular, she was given the green light. She was loaded down with pamphlets, books, and enormous vitamins, which she cut into threes in order to swallow, but she felt wonderful and alive. She tried not to think of Jack, and only when Nicholas came by did her head swim with images of Jack, because they were practically identical in every way. Her business was finally drawing a profit, and she had to think about the future. She would raise her child with or without Jack. Her mind was completely made up.

"Anythin' else," Retta's question pulled Frankie back to the present.

"How about chocolate-anything for dessert…if it isn't too much trouble?"

"Why don't be silly. It's no trouble. No trouble at all, Doc." Retta continued to study Frankie. The blue of her eyes was clear and crisp, and her hair was long and flowing, so shiny and silky. She also noticed that her face was a little rounder and more serene than it had been in weeks.

"I better get back to the hospital."

"Alright then I'll have everything ready for dinner at eight?"

"Yes that'd be great. Thanks, Retta." Without warning, Frankie threw her arms around her and kissed her check. Then in a flurry of blonde, silky hair, she was gone just as quickly.

I'll be, Retta thought silently. *I think our little doc is going to have a little one herself. Has to be Jack's baby*, Retta was certain. *The girl did nothin' but work and then work some more. And she never let any man come sniffin' 'round her.* Retta wondered how everyone was going to take the news. It was obvious that she was going to make the announcement tonight. *Well, hopefully,* Retta thought while she pulled the ham to begin preparation, *everyone will be so full of food and wine that they won't get too upset.* She was sure that Nicholas would take it the hardest. *Lord, I wish that boy would come home*, Retta prayed, as she reached for the cloves from the spice rack.

At 7:45, Frankie was trying to find something, anything that fit. Her pants were all too snug and would definitely grow more uncomfortable as the meal wore on. She ran her fingers through her clothes and selected a tweed skirt from the closet. *Perfect,* she thought. *This one was a little loose on me before I started my treatments.* Once in the skirt, she pulled the zipper, but couldn't button the button around the waistband.

"Damn," Frankie muttered to no one. She chose a long, dark brown sweater to cover the unbuttoned skirt and pulled it over her head. She stepped back into the bathroom and brushed her hair until it shone. She applied a little mascara and a little lip color. Her mother would like the results. She looked down and spoke to her unborn child. "Well tonight is your big night. I'm going to tell your grandparents, family, and close friends that you are on your way." Frankie lovingly stroked her slightly protruding tummy. *This summer I'm going to be a mother,* she thought in amazement. She put away the things she had tried on earlier, which all failed the waistline-test. She couldn't even pull the zipper up on most of her clothes. *I better try to get in some shopping.* And then Frankie smiled. Her mother would be bombarding her with maternity clothes as soon as the news was told.

She went down the stairs and into the foyer. She could hear Retta doing some last minute preparations in the kitchen. The dining room table was clad in linens and candles, and a cheery fire crackled in the fireplace. Nelson always made sure the fires burned brightly in the house. It never went unnoticed, and Frankie made sure it never went unappreciated. She paced the black-and-white marble front hall waiting for the first guests to arrive. When she saw headlights, she took a deep breath and pulled the large front door open for her parents.

As the steady stream of usual guests arrived, plus Uncle John and Maggie, Nicholas, once again, became the bartender and made sure that all glasses remained full. After the appetizers were eaten and everyone settled down at the long dining room table, Frankie started to lose her nerve. Her parents always looked so happy together. *Maybe someday I will have that*, Frankie prayed quietly, *someday.*

Angelina could not get over how her brother, John, had changed. She had never seen him act this way before. How he helped Maggie take her seat, making sure she had enough to drink, if she was comfortable, if she wanted him to check on her bird. *Her bird!* Angelina repeated in her mind. *My God, what's gotten into the man?* Then it struck her all at once. He's in love.

Nicholas placed an arm around her thin shoulders, and she turned to face the man she loved for most of her life, even long before she knew it.

"My brother?" she asked her husband.

"*Si* he's in love." Nicholas answered the unspoken question.

As Retta placed the main course on the table, Frankie stood to make a toast. *Well, it's now or never,* she encouraged herself. She raised the wine glass she purposely filled with purple grape juice, "I would like to make a toast."

The murmuring stopped. "Brace yourselves," she warned. "I have some wonderful news, and I wanted to share it with all of you tonight. Mom, Dad, everyone, I'm pregnant."

Thomas and Corrine were up first. "Wonderful," Thomas shouted.

"Thomas, we're going to be grandparents," Corrine called out to him looking at her daughter through watery eyes.

Nicholas and Angelina were next. "Wow, Grandparents!" Nicholas held Frankie and his wife close in a circle, pressing a kiss to her soft golden crown.

Thomas and Nicholas shook hands and slapped each other's backs.

Anthony stepped forward and kissed Frankie on both cheeks.

"I want you to be the baby's godfather. I know Jacqino would have wanted to ask you as much as I do," Frankie whispered into Anthony's ear, pressing her cheek against his.

Anthony felt his emotions rise. "It would be my honor to be godfather to your child," he choked back.

Anthony released her, and Becca pulled her in tight. "It's a good thing I have a medical plan at my job," Rebecca whispered into Frankie's ear pulling her closer.

"Why's that?" Frankie asked, not quite following.

"You practically gave me a heart attack. We have got to work on that delivery of yours!" Rebecca shot back to her dearest friend, and Frankie laughed out loud, not missing the pun.

"Ya think?" Tears started to spill from Frankie's blue pools. "I want you to be the baby's godmother."

Rebecca could only nod in answer, too choked with emotions to speak, while her eyes filled up with sadness that Jack wasn't there to share in this special moment.

Each person said something wonderful and endearing, but Uncle John's response was the most moving. "I will guard your child with my life, with my soul...with my very soul," John whispered, kissing the top of her golden head.

"Thank you," Frankie whispered back.

Scott watched her stand proud and full of Jack's life, not his, making her announcement. And at that moment it was crystal clear to Scott that Frankie was in love with Jack, she would always be in love with Jack, and tonight he knew just how deep and profound that love was. He understood how hard it was on her these last few months when he watched the raw emotions race across her face, sadness yet joy, regret but contentment, just before her parents jumped to embrace her. That was love, unconditional.

"I have something for you," Scott hugged Frankie close. When he pulled back he handed her Jack's email. "He doesn't deserve you."

A note from Jack, Frankie's mind raced and she smiled, cupping Scott's cheek, as her eyes glistened turning the deep blue to crystals.

Scott kissed the tear that rolled down her cheek.

Frankie looked at the note in her trembling hand. She almost couldn't breathe and slipped it into her pocket.

At the end of the meal, and as everyone started to leave. John pulled Nicholas to the side. "You have to tell, Jack." John held his brother-in-law's shoulder.

"No, now more than ever, we cannot. If we bring him back now, Francesca will believe he only came back for the sake of the babe, and not her. We must let this be. We mustn't say a word, even if he should call. It is up to him to right his wrongs, as well."

"What wrongs? I caused all those wrongs." John snapped back.

"No John, you didn't. He left, and no one is holding him away now. He could come back anytime, but he chooses not to. That is not your fault." Nicholas' hand remained on his brother-in-law's shoulder.

"He doesn't know. I don't want him to miss this. She looks so beautiful and proud carrying his child. I never had that. I missed that opportunity so long ago, and I don't want him to miss it. Can you understand that?"

"*Si* I understand." Nicholas understood more now of John than ever. "But that doesn't change my answer. He has to come back of his own free will. That is something **you** must understand. When you have children, it is impossible not to tell them what to do all the time, because you have lived and made mistakes, and you don't want them to make the same mistakes you already made. But there comes a time when it must stop, when a father can't tell his son right from wrong. That is when you just pray that all the fathering you gave him throughout his life will guide him when he becomes a man. Just wait, brother-in-law, give it time and patience."

After all the guests left for the night, Frankie wandered around the farmhouse, too nervous to read the note, at first. She sat down in the Library and Bruno and Little Nick went to lie down by the fireplace. She curled up on the couch and pulled the afghan over her legs. When she pulled the note from the pocket, she saw that it was an email from Jack to Scott and read his words carefully. He was confused. He was still hurting. But he loved her. He was asking for her to give him time, and she would. She knew she would wait a lifetime for him.

When John got back to the barn after taking Maggie home, so thankful that she had moved into the small cottage by the brook just ten miles from the farm instead of back in the city, he pulled out his cell phone. He hated the damn device, but one needed to keep pace with the times, because the times might just run you over.

"John?" Tony Scarpelli was still getting used to his brother calling him. It was well past midnight and the timing of the call was a little unsettling.

"*Si,*" John spoke softly. "I need a favor. I need you to get a message to Jacqino."

"But John, you know how Nicholas feels about us contacting him."

"I don't care. Blame it on me." John paced his small bedroom at the rear of the barn.

"But…" Tony did not want to upset his brother-in-law or sister.

"Francesca is having Jacqino's baby." John heard nothing on the other end and he knew he had his brother's attention. "He can't miss this. He needs to know. It is his baby, too." John listened at the silence and waited for his brother's response. Finally, Tony spoke.

"What do you want the message to say?" Tony got up out of bed and went to his home office to turn on his computer. He would send his private investigator an e-mail. He would stress that he urgently needed to get in touch with his nephew in Ireland.

Chapter Thirty-One
Open your eyes...

Weeks later, Jack did what he did every morning. He checked for messages or e-mails. After a double-take, Jack immediately opened an email that was forwarded from his Uncle Tony marked *Urgent*. It was short and read, "You need to come home." Jack didn't know what was wrong, but he knew he had to get back. His uncle's simple note carried more weight than a detailed explanation. Something has happened.

Dressing quickly, Jack would need to tell Mr. Flaherty that he was going back to the States. With the first rays of sunlight in months, Jack descended the grand staircase of the old castle and was awestruck. The sunlight was streaming in through the stained glass to reveal the most amazing picture. Mr. Flaherty stood on the scaffolding just to the bottom right of the towering stained glass picture. Jack's gasp of breath was so loud that it caused Mr. Flaherty to stop and look at him.

"What might you be thinkin', Jack?"

"I can't believe my eyes."

"Aye, these are the ghosts who still walk the halls of this mighty castle." Mr. Flaherty pointed to the figures in the stained glass.

Jack's eyes glowed in the jeweled-color reflection of the light dancing about the room.

"The glass reveals the young couple who lived here in these very rooms and descended those very steps you'd be standing on."

The amazing collage of colored light displayed a large man with black hair clad in armor. The letters "R. E." scrolled on the front breast plate, green vines twisting through the letters, and beside him stood a petite woman with flowing, golden hair. Animals were everywhere in the glasswork. Birds flew overhead and squirrels ran up tree trunks in the distance. A snake lay beneath the woman's feet and a large dog stood by her side. Both of them had their hands pressed to her stomach, obviously swollen with child.

"Tell me about them," Jack asked, dropping onto the step,

unable to take his eyes off the stunning, stained glass portrait before him.

"Well legend has it," Mr. Flaherty began, "that the man in the glass was a Roman soldier, a great warrior, strong and mighty. The R.E. here on his breast plate stands for the Roman Empire. After he won many a battle for his emperor, he was granted his freedom from the binds of the military. Joseph, the man shown here," Mr. Flaherty pointed to the male figure in the portrait, "decided to travel. He happened upon this town right here in Ireland and immediately fell in love with the land, the people, and their way of life. When he settled on a spot, the King, himself, deeded this very land to him. Of course, the land was conveyed under strong persuasion from the Emperor of Rome. The castle was designed and built by Joseph with the help of many fine craftsmen from the area." Mr. Flaherty replaced a sharp tool in his tool belt switching it for another.

"The story is simple and has been told and retold over centuries. Joseph walked through the small village that lay just below the very spot this castle rests upon," Mr. Flaherty reached down for the putty and pinched it in between the glass and the frame, cleaning the edge with a sharp blade, "when he spotted Francine. Legend has it that this doesn't do her even the wee bit o' justice." Mr. Flaherty waved to the stained glass that portrayed the woman. "She was breathtakin' and full of life. She had a way with animals, too, that is why you see so many in the glass." Mr. Flaherty pointed out other small creatures, like the colorful bird that Jack missed when he first took in the portrait of glass.

"They fell in love instantaneously and deeply. So when the Roman Emperor called Joseph back to Rome because of civil unrest, Joseph left her behind, heartbroken, because duty is bred in only the finest soldiers. They were not married as yet, but when it was discovered that she carried his child, the King was greatly distressed by the pressure her family and clan placed upon him to rectify the matter. After all, these people opened their arms to this Roman soldier, and he took their beloved Francine and defiled her. Such a scandal, it was!"

"Hmm, I could imagine." Jack rubbed the stubble on his chin which was a few days old.

"No, Jack. You could not begin to imagine what it was like so long ago. A man, not from her own clan, bedded her, and he wasn't her husband! A disgrace is what it was, yet she felt no shame and carried her head high every day. Unfortunately, Joseph's head was obviously not on the battle, because he nearly lost his life. It took him many months before he recovered enough to return home where he belonged. When he did return, this stained glass mural was commissioned. The artist captured the way they looked at each other, at that moment, as they pledged their love to one another for all eternity."

Mr. Flaherty drew a camel's hair brush from his work table, dipped it in black ink, and inscribed their initials in a heart at the bottom of the stained glass that time had worn away. JVR & FCO.

Those were the same initials as Jack and Francesca's. Jack was momentarily stunned. He was already prepared to leave after the urgent message from his uncle, but somewhere deep within his subconscious he thought he heard his father's voice reverberating softly through the cavernous castle. "Jacqino, come home."

Jack clamored down the stairs. He reached up and grasped Mr. Flaherty's hand, pumping it vigorously. "I'm going home, Mr. Flaherty. Thank you."

"You're quite welcome, lad." Mr. Flaherty looked down into those dark, piercing eyes, and saw something different. Something came to life. It was like a light went on behind them for the first time, showing intelligence, love, and hope. *That's it, for sure— hope*, Mr. Flaherty thought quietly, as he watched Jack run back up the stairs, taking three steps at a time. Mr. Flaherty descended the scaffolding, took out his cellular phone, and placed a call to the States.

Chapter Thirty-Two
The promise of spring…

As Frankie studied the fabric choices for the bedding and windows in the nursery, she glanced out the window and noticed car after car pulling into her drive. With Reflections and the other horses neighing, Nelson and John came out of the barn to see what all the commotion was this bright, early Saturday morning. Francesca had a strict policy for taking no appointments on the weekends, so she couldn't imagine what was going on.

Nicholas, Angelina, and Anthony were the first ones out of the limo, followed by a truck full of wood and lattice. Frankie even thought she saw a priest? Was she seeing things clearly, as she blinked her eyes to re-focus? *Maybe I should have slept a little longer this morning, instead of jumping up at sunrise*, she muttered to herself as she left the nursery and headed downstairs to see what prompted this visit.

In the short trip to the front door, Frankie's mother and father arrived, also Rebecca, Scott, Robin, and other people Frankie had never met before in her life. Some of the people looked vaguely familiar, like some distant cousins she only saw at weddings and funerals on her side of the family.

Tents were being set up and tables were being placed under them at Nicholas' direction.

"Morning, love," Nicholas called waving to Frankie, as he held the cell phone to his ear.

"Morning," Frankie waved back, unsure what in the world was going on. Was there some party she had totally forgotten about? Oh maybe it was a baby shower, and they just decided to have it here at the farm. *What a wonderful idea*, she thought as she crossed the drive to kiss her parents.

"Good morning, dear." Corrine kissed her daughter's full cheek.

"Mom? Dad? What a nice surprise!" She kissed her parents hello.

"That sundress looks so lovely on you." Thomas noticed how healthy she looked and couldn't be more pleased. The dress was the exact one Frankie had dreamed she wore when Jack returned. She wore it many times, but he did not return. She gave up on that idea now. It had been too long, and her dreams were no longer clear. And the once clear, bright vision of him was disappearing. "Thanks, Dad."

Thomas looked around recalling his phone call with Nicholas late last night. He told him there might be a wedding, and that they would all be going up to the farm as early as possible Saturday morning. "Yes, I'm making preparations for a wedding, but I'm not quite sure who's yet."

"Very well then we'll make it our business to get to the farm first thing then."

And that was about the extent of the conversation had between the two fathers, but much more passed in what was not said. It meant Jack was back, but that Nicholas could make no promises.

Chapter Thirty-Three
Outside looking in…

Late Saturday afternoon, as the jet flew over Kennedy on its final approach against a brilliant blue background, Jack straightened his tie, closed his jacket and started to fumble with his watch again. He wound it and reset the time so that it was correct. Then he rewound the watch again. Took it off and snapped it back on, then took it off yet again. *My God, I'm a nervous wreck.* Jack looked heavenward, his heart pounding in his chest. *What if my family doesn't want to speak to me? What if Francesca tells me to take a long walk off her short dock? I can't believe what a mess I've made. Why didn't I just stay and talk things out? Why didn't I listen to my father?* Jack rubbed a hand over his jaw. He never listened to his father and that was probably his biggest mistake. *It's been months! Months!* He placed the watch back on his wrist. *So much time wasted,* Jack thought. *What a fool I've been!*

Jack walked through the airport and pulled his cell phone from his breast pocket. While holding his carry-on bag in his other hand, Jack scrolled down the contacts until he got to his father's number and pressed the call button. "Dad?"

"Anthony?" Nicholas knew exactly who it was, but why make it easy?

"No, it's Jack."

"Jacqino! Wonderful to hear from you!" Nicholas sounded busy.

Wonderful to hear from you? I haven't spoken to him in months! Jack stared at the cell phone for a moment.

"Jacqino, I have to hang up now. I'll call you tomorrow." Nicholas sounded distracted as though he was speaking to many people at the same time.

"Tomorrow? Dad, maybe you don't understand. I'm home!" Jack clarified.

"Isn't that nice." Nicholas sounded unaffected.

"Isn't that nice?" Jack nearly croaked into the phone.

"Jacqino, I'm sorry. I'm a little busy right now."

"Is everything okay? Is everyone alright?" Jack felt so immature at that moment. The message from his uncle had him picturing his entire family in the hospital, as well as Francesca, and her half-crazed dog-okay, entirely crazy dog. For months all he did was sit and sulk.

"Yes, son, but I'll be honest with you. I hope you don't take this the wrong way, but I'm helping Francesca with her wedding, which is to take place tomorrow. So I am very busy." Nicholas tried to sound apologetic, but wasn't quite sure if he was pulling it off.

Shock ripped through Jack's entire frame. "FRANCESCA'S WHAT?" Jack stopped short in the middle of the airport; something was clearly wrong with his cell phone as he looked at the device menacingly.

Nicholas was forced to remove the phone from his ear. *Now I've got the boy's attention,* Nicholas grinned. Wiping the smile off his face and trying to sound concerned, Nicholas continued to bait him. "Things have changed. So much time has passed. Maybe you should talk to Anthony. Your brother didn't want Francesca to marry Scott."

"ANTHONY? SCOTT?" Jack half screamed into the phone.

"I'll speak to you later, son." Nicholas spoke so softly just before he hung up the phone before Jack could respond or ask any more questions.

Jack stood in the middle of the terminal just staring at his phone. His bag slipped from his hand and dropped to the ground. "What the hell does that mean?" Jack spoke out loud to no one, as people continued to walk past him. Most of the passersby shot him a "what a whacko" look. *Maybe I should talk to Anthony? Anthony didn't want her to marry Scott? Scott? I should have known! Scott was never the same after I asked Francesca to marry me and she accepted. He probably didn't even give Francesca my note!* "Anthony wouldn't," Jack continued to speak to himself. "I'll kill him! I'll kill him!" Jack started to chant. He headed to the exit and had the skycap call for a cab. Jack threw his bag into the back seat, fell in behind it, and blurted out the address for the farm. The cabby arched an eyebrow.

"That's gonna cost ya..." The cabby started to speak, but Jack quickly cut him off.

"I don't give a damn what it costs. If you make it in under an hour, I'll tip you a hundred bucks." Jack held the bill up to make sure the driver knew he was serious.

"You got it, mister. Hold on!" The cabby shouted and hit the accelerator.

On the front lawn of the farm, Nicholas slid his cell phone into his breast pocket, as Angelina, Aunt Rose, Uncle Tony, Uncle John, and Scott all started to chuckle. Anthony wasn't finding the situation so funny.

John wondered if his brother's message brought Jack home and what the consequences would be when Nicholas found out.

"He's a little upset with you, Anthony," Nicholas advised his son.

"I can't imagine why." Anthony started to rake his hand through his hair as his father noted his son's nervous reaction.

"He's going to beat you first and ask questions after," Uncle Tony predicted.

"Thanks for the play-by-play." Anthony cocked his head to look at his godfather. "I don't understand why Paul couldn't be the scapegoat."

Paul overheard the comment from where he was standing by the limo and started to laugh.

"He wouldn't have believed that for a second," Nicholas waved his hand. "And adding Scott to the cocktail made it more real. But now I'm thinking that you better watch his right hook," Nicholas looked warningly at Scott.

"I can handle his right hook…and his left hook, for that matter." Scott just nodded confidently.

"He is going to be unreasonably Scarpelli by the time he gets to the farm." Anthony braced himself.

"Watch it son, we're outnumbered here." Nicholas looked at his wife, her sister and brothers-in law. "Let's start going over the plan. I figure he will be here in less than an hour."

As Nicholas watched the arbor take form, he couldn't help but reminisce on the long-standing Romano tradition to erect a new arbor and gazebo for each new bride. Many of his Sicilian relatives had made winding flowerbeds among the many arbors to the gazebos in Sicily. One man had seven daughters and seven arbors all intertwined with the most amazing paths and flowering beds that led to one large gazebo. Nicholas liked this spot right next to the rose garden Francesca planted the week before with Uncle John. Perfect. Now all they needed was the groom. He smiled heavenward and thought, *Life is good, life is very good.*

Nicholas had The Rose brought to the farm today in preparation of the wedding plans. If Jack thought to come by boat he was going to be out of luck, since it was already on its way upriver to the farm.

Nicholas, Anthony, Uncle John, and Paul were waiting just a few miles down the road from the farm, the limo stretched across the road acting as a blockade.

As the cabby came to a gritty halt, Jack gave the cabby the promised tip and slammed the passenger door shut with such force, it caused everyone to flinch. With his bag in his hand, Jack made his way to the limo coming toe-to-toe with his Uncle John, but not before he shot Scott a killer stare, because he was next!

"Get out of my way," Jack growled baring his teeth, as he stared down at his much-shorter uncle, dropping his bag to the ground with a thud.

"Jack, is that any way to say hello?" Uncle John baited him further.

"Oh, I can think of another way, you bastard." Just as he drew back his right fist, Anthony leapt forward pushing his uncle out of the way, taking the blow directly on the corner of his left eye.

Anthony sailed across the hood of the limo and collapsed into a heap at Paul's feet. Nicholas ran to Anthony and held his head in the curve of his arm. Jack's rage was so fierce and blinding that it took him a moment before he realized whom he struck. On bended knee Nicholas looked down at his half-unconscious son and then up to Jack's sorrow-filled face. "Welcome home, son."

Jack took Anthony from his father just as his little brother started to come around. As Jack studied his brother's puffy eye he knew that it must hurt. "Sorry, little brother."

"It was worth it," Anthony replied, tentatively touching the side of his eye.

"Whaaat? It was worth taking a hit meant for him?" Jack shot his uncle a sizzling look. His hand still itched to rearrange the man's face.

"Yeah," Anthony whispered. "He has changed since you have been away. A lot. He's not a slime-bag anymore. He has been working at the farm." Anthony shot his thumb up in the direction of the farm.

"Farm," Jack asked as he winced at his brother's quickly purpling eye. Then images of the white farm danced before his mind, "Working?"

"Mucking out the stalls, feeding the horses, and taking care of the animal hospital, stuff like that." Anthony reached for the bruise with light fingertips and winced out loud. *Man, this is going to hurt for a long while.*

"Mucking? Hospital?" Jack was stunned and disoriented.

"The hospital is a hit. Robin and Mrs. Mastellon moved up here just a month ago. Uncle John and Nelson help with the bigger animals. You know, like the horses and stuff."

"Mrs. Mastellon?" Jack was confused. "So Francesca? Dad said I should talk to you." Jack started to press for answers.

"More beautiful than ever. Listen, brother. Now is as good a time as any. I have asked her to marry me, seeing as you left her here for such a long time without a word. And with Scott in hot pursuit," Anthony shot his thumb toward Scott.

Again Jack whipped his head around to glare at the man he thought was his friend.

"I was hoping you would give us your blessing...ouch!"

Jack dropped Anthony in a heap on the gravel road. "I've not even started with you yet." Jack pointed his index finger in Scott's direction.

Scott nodded as he watched Jack leave the group of men. "Anytime, anyplace Romano!"

"Get me into the limousine," Anthony shouted at his father and uncle. Each man took one of Anthony's arms, wrapped it around their shoulders, and walked him to the rear of the limo. Paul pulled ice from the bar in the back of the limo and wrapped it into a napkin, which Anthony held to his eye. Paul retrieved Jack's forgotten bag and popped it into the trunk. They all waited in the limo until Jack reached the farm.

Jack figured his blood pressure must be off the charts, because a whooshing sound was crashing through his brain. Off in the distance he could see the white tents and people moving about. Pieces to a band were being unloaded, and with a double take, he stopped for just a second as he spotted The Rose sailing upriver towards the farm. "They're using **my ship** for the honeymoon? MY SHIP!" Jack was incensed and repulsed.

As Jack reached the end of the drive with his jacket slung over his shoulder, a warm breeze with the promise of summer swept off the river causing his tie to dance about. He began to loosen his tie as it continued to toss about in the wind. Horses danced in the corral, a woman with a colorful parrot was talking quietly to Robin. From the corner of his eye he spotted Bruno. He charged Jack and skidded to a halt directly in front of him.

"Have you been a beast while I was away?" He spoke softly, the dog's ears twitched back and forth to the sound of his voice. Jack softly rubbed the fur on the dog's large head. Tongue hanging out, caked with dirt and grass as usual, his ears perked up. "Where's Francesca?" But he didn't need Bruno to guide him to her. Jack could feel her eyes on him as he rose to stand up straight. Her hair was long and tossing about in the wind. The sun was performing a light show with the help of her golden locks and the image it portrayed made Jack's chest squeeze tightly. *My God, how I've missed just looking at her. Just to see her standing in the sunlight…*

As the wind tugged at her dress, Jack noticed the swollen belly, which caused his heart to crash into his ribs almost violently. He couldn't catch his breath. The image from the portrait of glass in Ireland flashed through his mind. *What am I going to say to her? Why didn't anyone tell me? Is that why my uncle sent me the message? How could she ever forgive me for running away when she needed me?* It had to be his baby; he just knew it had to be. He felt puerile and insignificant as he approached her. He wouldn't blame her if she slapped him and told him to go to hell. He didn't even deserve that!

Again the wind tugged the long sundress against her stomach, as Jack watched Francesca's hand spring protectively against her belly. He noticed she no longer wore his engagement ring and why would she? When she lowered her head her hair curtained her face concealing her expression from him. Even though there were many people there, Jack heard only silence, not even the wind.

This is just like my dream, Francesca thought, her body started to tremble. But what will happen next? She knew some of what was to be said, but the end of the dream was unclear. The fear of that unknown had their unborn child kicking vigorously due to her pounding heart.

Two shiny, black shoes came into view. Frankie inched her eyes up his long legs to his belt, past his expansive chest, to his piercing black eyes that looked like stormy thunderheads, revealing an emotion she was unfamiliar with. Was it shame?

Slowly she tilted her head to one side, studying. She missed him. His hand rose up slowly to gently stroke her hair away from her face, but she stepped back away from him.

Jack felt his heart shatter into countless pieces at that moment, dropping his hand to his side in defeat. He looked deeply into her eyes, trying to convey his love. Then he saw it! Her blue eyes grew to midnight, and, in that moment, so much was revealed to him. He knew that in that split second she still loved him, but she might not ever forgive him. What could he say? How could he explain?

"Francesca, I didn't know," Jack began, but this time when he reached out to stroke her hair away from her face with an unsteady hand, she didn't back away. He was finding it not only difficult to find the right words, but virtually impossible to speak past the enormous lump that formed in his throat. "I love you, Francesca. Forgive me. I beg of you, please forgive me. I don't think I could love you more than I do right now. Tell me what I should say to make everything right between us." She looked so beautiful, full of life carrying his baby. Placing his hand on her protruding belly was the only gesture she waited for. An array of emotions crossed over her lovely features. *Was it forgiveness?* "Please say that you will still be my wife. Please."

"Jacq..." Francesca started to speak, but she stopped when he lowered his head to kiss her.

Jack cupped her cheek, closing the distance between them. His hand still rested on his child; safe within the woman he loved. He lowered his head and pressed his parted lips to hers encouraging her to open for him and when she did, relief washed over him, tasting her as if for the first time.

Nicholas tapped his son's shoulder. "Jacqino, you will come with me."

"Dad. Please. I need to beg Francesca for her forgiveness."

"Yes. There will be plenty of time for that later. Now you will go with your mother, Francesca, and get ready." Nicholas mumbled something about why his son had to take after his wife, *typical Scarpelli temperament, so difficult—such a damn difficult group of people to deal with!*

"Ready?" Francesca questioned.

"Your mother will explain it to you. Jacqino, you will come with me." Nicholas took hold of Jack's arm and led him through the crowd of relatives and people he had never met before. He quickly scanned the group and noticed Anthony leaning against a tree. His eyes reached out for his brother to help, but Anthony just gave him a mock salute with the glass of red wine he was starting to enjoy. Nicholas swung open the large barn door and continued to direct Jack into the large tack room. Uncle John, Thomas, and Nelson followed behind.

"Dad, why are you dragging me away from Francesca? Can't you see that I'm here to apologize? Hell, to beg her to forgive me. I've been so stupid. She's having my baby!"

Nicholas started to wave his hand, so much like Retta's hand waving, as if he didn't know that Francesca was having his baby.

Jack winced slightly while studying his father's expression. It was certainly not humorous. A scowl creased his forehead.

"You will marry her. You WILL marry her tomorrow morning, if I have to hold a gun to your head. I have all the relatives here, and if I need them to help me drag you to the altar physically, you know they will. *Capisce*?"

"*Padre...*" Jack started to plead lifting his hands upward.

"*ABBASTANZA!*" Nicholas bellowed, and the unfamiliar sound of his father's voice ringing to the rafters made Jack stand stock still. "YOU WILL MARRY HER! SHE IS CARRYING MY GRANDCHILD, AND YOU WILL NOT DISGRACE THIS FAMILY NOR FRANCESCA AND HER FAMILY." Nicholas continued to shout as the beams shuddered from his volume, causing dust to filter down, visibly cascading through the sunlight that streamed in through the windows.

Just then, Anthony came into the barn removing his sunglasses.

Jack reached up, holding his father's flushed face in between his hands. He could feel his father's hot temper against his fingertips, which was very unusual. "*Padre*...you are not listening to me. I am here to beg her to marry me, but you hardly gave me a chance to speak to her."

"You will not get another chance to speak to her until the wedding. I may not even let you look at her." Nicholas started to pace. "You will sleep on The Rose and be guarded until morning, at which time you will be escorted to the side lawn to where we are erecting the gazebo."

"The gazebo…" Jack had almost forgotten. All the Romanos built a new gazebo for each wedding. It was tradition.

"Where do you think you are going?" Nicholas pulled his son back around to face him.

"To help build my wedding gazebo, that is, if it isn't too late…" Jack looked back at his father. "You can hold a gun to my head while I build it, if you want. I intend to stand under its roof, freely, and marry the woman who means more to me than I could have ever hoped for, if she'll still have me."

"She'll have ya," Thomas called to Jack.

Jack walked over to his future father-in-law and embraced him. "I'm so sorry for the pain I've caused. Please forgive me," Jack whispered, but Thomas was too overcome with emotion to respond, so he just patted his future son-in-law's back. He knew that his daughter was still very much in love with him. He could sense it as soon as their eyes met. It made Corrine cry quietly.

Jack stopped before Anthony, pressing his hand to his brother's shoulder. "Sorry about the mouse."

"MOUSE! You call this a mouse! I might need surgery!" Anthony pointed to his still-purpling eye that was now nearly swollen shut and throbbing. Anthony and Jack hugged fiercely.

As Anthony and Nelson started to leave the tack room with Jack following behind, he stopped to stand before his uncle. Uncle John braced himself. He feared that this apology might actually break his heart forever. He felt an unspeakable pain for what he did to his nephew, Victoria, and so many others. These were sins he would pay for dearly, he knew. An emotion so deep it clenched his soul. "I'm so sorry for all…" John started, but was quickly stopped by Jack's fierce, strong hug.

"I need help building my gazebo, Uncle." Jack held his uncle in a strong embrace speaking softly, as he rested his cheek on the top of his silvery, white hair.

"I'd be honored to help." John squeezed the words from his tightened throat as he held his nephew close, thanking God for the opportunity to be part of the family he rejected for so many years.

Nicholas was so relieved to see that his eldest son found his way home and right back into the arms of the woman he knew loved him so deeply.

Inside Francesca was led up the stairs by her mother and an entourage including Retta, Angelina, and countless aunts from both sides. Two of the aunts were carrying a large box which they set on the bed.

Her Aunt Mary pulled a lovely, white gown from the large box. It was formal, yet at the same time not, accented by a dark, blue ribbon woven through the skirt that tied in the back. It had short cap sleeves with a wide boat neckline that bared the shoulders. They helped her out of her sundress and into the gown. It fit perfectly as Frankie studied her reflection in the mirror.

"You look lovely." Aunt Mary studied her niece. "Your mama bought it."

Frankie turned and embraced her mother. Her mother's eyes were damp from the tears that didn't seem to want to stop.

"Now you will rest." One of Jack's aunts helped remove the gown as another placed the sundress back over her head.

As Frankie's head poked through the top of her dress she cried, "But, I'm not tired." Frankie's defiance fell on deaf ears as the white quilt was turned back on the bed. Sitting on the edge of the bed, her sandals were removed so that she could lie on the cool sheets.

"You will rest, or we will tie you to the bed," Aunt Cecelia spoke, as though they had done that very thing before, while wagging her finger. "Remember the time we tied Angelina in her room before she was to marry Nicholas? Those were the good old days."

"Alright everyone she's settled down now. You can all go back to the preparations." Angelina waved everyone out.

"Preparations," Frankie asked.

"Your wedding sweet girl," Angelina patted her hand that rested softly on her swollen belly.

Corrine bent over to kiss her daughter softly on her cheek. She whispered quietly in her daughter's ear, "Do you still love him?"

"With all my heart," Frankie blinked slowly.

"Then, I have a lot of work to do." Corrine turned to face Jack's mother. "Angelina, I'll meet you downstairs in the kitchen." Corrine spoke softly as she pulled the sheers at the windows just before leaving the room quietly, gently closing the door behind her.

"I'll be down in just a minute," Angelina called out. She turned to face Francesca propped up on lots of white pillows her hair spilled over them in a golden waterfall. "We need to talk."

"Have I done something to upset you?" Frankie started to sit up.

"No, no, darling—lay back. You are wonderful. In fact, you are too wonderful, too perfect for my son, but that has all got to change."

"Change," Frankie questioned, having a hard time understanding.

"Yes. Yes. You see my son is an ass!"

"Oh."

"Yes! I'm his mother, so I would know. And since he is an ass, as most men are, you need to teach him some rules, especially when it comes to a man that is built like a Romano, but emotional like a Scarpelli."

"I see."

"No. No, you don't. But you will, because I am going to teach you how to control that arrogant male I gave birth to." Angelina paced and waved her hands in the air at the same time. "It infuriates me that he is just as stubborn as anyone on my side of the family. Why he couldn't be more like the Romanos, like Anthony, is beyond me?"

Frankie raised an eyebrow wondering how she was going to keep up with this conversation, because Jack's mother was having a conversation with herself as well.

"Yes. Well, back to Jacqino. He is a man that is built like a Romano, but thick and stubborn like the Scarpelli. On your honeymoon when you take The Rose up the coast, at least I think you will be heading up the coast," Angelina tapped the long, pink fingernail of her index finger against her lip, "not that it matters because you won't be spending a lot of time looking at the coastline…"

"We won't?"

"No silly." Angelina waved her hand like Retta's. "That is when you're going to make your demands." Angelina punched her fist into the palm of her other hand.

"Demands," Frankie wanted to clarify.

"That's right! You tell him that he is never to leave you again. No matter what! *Capisce!*" Angelina pointed the same pink, clad fingernail but inches from Frankie's nose then proceeded to kiss it. "You will tell him that you will shoot him if he even, so much as, thinks about leaving you again."

"Shoot him!?" Frankie swallowed.

"Right! Good. You're such a fast learner! You make it clear to him that you know what his thoughts are all the time and that he had better be thinking of one thing and one thing only—you. Are you following me?"

"I can't read minds."

"Whatever! Work with me!" Angelina raised her hands heavenward. "Think about the big picture! You tell him he had better walk a straight, tight, and narrow line or it's *ciao.*"

"*Ciao,*" Frankie repeated.

"Right! Good girl! I knew you had it in you. Now rest up, because tonight we are going to have a big dinner, and then tomorrow is going to be the wedding." Angelina pulled the sheet over Frankie's swollen belly. "I love you daughter-in-law."

"I love you, *Madre.*"

"Rest, Francesca. Just rest quietly. We will bring you something to eat soon."

"Rest, that sounds really good right now. I'm suddenly feeling a little tired."

Frankie slept and was awakened by the family women some time later to run her bath. After she soaked her bones in the warm, rose-scented water, she massaged rose-scented cream into her moist, warmed skin. It felt wonderful to indulge in this simple pleasure, something she hadn't done in a while. When she came out in her thick, terry cloth robe, a wonderful feast was set in front of the blossom-dressed fireplace. Retta had filled all the fireplace openings with such wonderful blooming baskets of flowers, because she didn't much care for the empty, black fireboxes in all the rooms.

Frankie ate most of the Italian food that was laid out before her; spaghetti and meatballs, sausage and peppers, and Retta's home-baked Italian bread. Francesca's Aunt Mary, her father's sister, made the traditional Guinness-battered fish and chips, but Frankie just picked at that. She craved Italian cuisine at the moment.

Outside in the rose garden Frankie studied the almost-finished gazebo. It was beautiful with lattice and scrollwork on the side that Frankie couldn't quite make out.

"You're not supposed to peek," Aunt Cecelia jokingly scolded Frankie.

"I didn't know," Frankie pulled away from the sheers and giggled—guilty as charged!

Aunt Cecelia waved and pulled back open the sheers. "But everyone always does."

"Oh!" Together, they watched as the men continued to work. The roof seemed to be the most intricate part of the whole project. Jack stood at the top of a ladder, shirtless, holding a measuring tape, shouting down numbers so each cedar shake could be cut perfectly. He glanced up and saw Francesca watching him and smiled broadly, then winked, causing her to blush.

"I think Jacqino has lost some weight." Frankie spoke aloud without thinking, watching him work in the bright sunshine, sweat glistening on his toned torso.

"You will find out soon enough," Aunt Rose added, causing the women to giggle.

As the evening drew near, little lights illuminated the areas around the tents. Candles that were set in hurricane holders flickered from the river's breeze. The men and women all ate together, but Frankie and Jack were purposely separated, seated at the same table, but at opposite ends. The conversation flowed, as did the wine, and Jack hadn't realized how the tradition of the Romanos' restraint and abstinence of the bride for several days before the wedding could drive a man to the brink of insanity. He was only being forced to stay away from her for less than twenty-four hours, when typically the minimum was three days.

"Having difficulty focusing?" Nicholas asked smiling.

"What?" Jack murmured, staring at Francesca who seemed so relaxed, laughing at something his brother was telling her. While building the arbor and gazebo, it was explained to Jack that they only made up the story of Francesca marrying Anthony because of Scott, in order to get him to the farm as quickly as possible. *It worked*, Jack thought and had already apologized to his friend.

"Having difficulty focusing?" Nicholas asked again.

Jack turned to see his father smiling from ear to ear. "We have had to tie some men down before the wedding. I hope we don't have to do that to you. Uncle John might actually get a kick out of that."

"That won't be necessary," Jack stated firmly in a low deep tone. "I can control myself..." Jack trailed off because Francesca was standing up saying goodnight to everyone at the table. Jack quickly jumped to his feet. His father held him in place. "I want to walk her to the farmhouse," Jack pleaded.

"Not tonight. Her mother will do that."

When Frankie made her way around the table, she felt almost shy near Jack.

As for Jack, that simple forced separation was creating a far greater force drawing him to her.

"Goodnight," Frankie called from the distance her mother created between her and her bridegroom.

"Goodnight," Jack and Nicholas called in unison. Nicholas could feel Jack tug on the arm he was holding.

"You will not be allowed to go to her. If you get past me, there are many more who will stop you," Nicholas whispered. "You will never forget the way she was withheld from you tonight. You purposely stayed away from her, but now you know what it feels like to have someone take her away from **you**. It is something I never quite got over myself, and I still yearn for my wife to this very day. It is always in the back of your mind. It seems like such a simple tradition, but it is probably the most powerful because it provides a lesson for a lifetime. It taught me—to want and need." Nicholas loosened the grip around his son's arm.

"I think you'd better get those ropes. Better yet. You might want to make it chains," Jack confessed not taking his eyes off Francesca watching her kiss everyone goodnight on her way back to the farmhouse. Bruno walked close to her side, and Little Nick just behind Bruno, trying hard to keep up with his short, stubby legs.

Chapter Thirty-Four
The wedding day...

Very early the next morning, with the bright, spring light filling her bedroom, Francesca awoke slowly. Was this all a dream? Her mind seemed foggy. Did Jack really come back? Then a noise outside her window had her up, and she pulled back the sheers to see. Jack, Anthony, and Nicholas were putting some finishing touches on the gazebo. Anthony was draping garland, with big yellow roses in full bloom, all around the gazebo. Nicholas was following from behind handing it up to him with instructions to lower it or raise it to match the curve of the swag before. Jack was filling two half-pillars with yellow roses which flanked each side to the entrance of the gazebo.

Off in the distance, Frankie could see workers in a flurry of hands and feet straightening the tables and chairs and setting them with fresh linens. Food stations were already being set up.

Just then, someone knocked, and her bedroom door flew open. "We don't have much time," Angelina called to the women following in her wake. "The wedding is to take place at eleven. The reception will follow, and then they will be off on The Rose."

"Good morning," Frankie called.

"Good morning," answered the chorus of female voices.

The bath was drawn and Frankie was shooed inside with a slice of fresh-baked cinnamon raisin toast slathered with fresh raspberry jam, her favorite. The mug of decaf coffee filled her senses with rich aroma as she took her first sip. She had had another lesson from her mother-in-law late last night, received cooking tips from Jack's Aunt Rose, laundry tips from her own Aunt Mary, and an analysis of both families from Becca. Yes, all of this attention could break a weaker woman, but not Frankie. Her nerves felt like reinforced concrete.

She bathed and spoke softly to her unborn child. "Today is our big day." Standing sidewise, Frankie looked at her naked reflection in the mirror. Would he find her unattractive because she was pregnant? Would he be afraid to touch her? The aunts had solved the first half of the problem as her mother and a few others went out and purchased a full-length lace nightgown, pure white and delicate, with a matching lace robe. It was provocative, yet concealing. She continued to brush her hair and then she slipped the diamond engagement ring back onto her finger, which she hadn't worn for months. She pulled on her robe and opened the bathroom door. Aunt Mary handed her all of her undergarments and pushed her back into the bathroom. Frankie dressed in the same white lace as the nightgown: white panty and bra with lacy, white thigh-highs and a full-length slip, all to match. She opened the door again and the gown was slipped over her head.

"We're running a little late," Aunt Cecelia spoke while she buttoned the back of the dress. The white satin buttons were tricky to close because of the delicate lace loops. *Jack is probably going to tear these buttons clean off this dress* she winced, wondering how they would ever be able to repair the fine lace around each buttonhole.

"You make sure he unbuttons this dress," Aunt Cecelia warned.

"Unbutton...right." Frankie confirmed.

"Who cares if he rips the dress right off of her?" Aunt Rose questioned.

"We won't be able to repair this intricate lacework," Aunt Cecelia complained, waving to the back of the dress.

"A wedding dress is only meant to be worn once." Aunt Rose patted Frankie's shoulder. "You just go where he leads."

"Go where he leads," Frankie repeated while nodding.

She sat still as a local hairdresser came in and a manicurist started filing her nails. The hair stylist applied only the faintest of makeup then started to design her hair by pulling the top half back away from her face. She curled the entire mass of hair into intricate curls and pulled wisps from her temples. Fragrant tiny tea roses, in white, were nestled inside the curls. The effect was dramatic. She stood perfectly still while the aunts oohed and aahed. The dark, blue satin ribbon was looped at the small of her back. Tiny rosebuds were intertwined in the lace ribbons cascading from the bouquet of bright yellow and white tea roses. She was ready.

Frankie stood in front of the full-length, cheval mirror still disbelieving this day had finally arrived. For the first time in her life, she couldn't believe how beautiful she looked. "Thank you, everyone," Frankie whispered. Tears started to well up in her eyes and threatened to spill over.

"NO, NO! Don't ruin your makeup. Please don't cry!" Corrine embraced her daughter tightly. "If you start, I will start too. You look beautiful."

Frankie was hurried from the room, with Becca following just behind. Becca's dress was of similar lace, off the shoulders, but cut high above the knee in the front and cascading to the floor in the back. Her hair was smoothed back with a few shiny, brown curls pulled loose, creating a sexy, tousled look; three tiny tea roses clustered together and clipped behind her right ear.

"You look gorgeous." Frankie held her best friend's hands tightly. Then she whispered in Becca's ear, "Anthony is going to be blown away."

Together, the women descended the stairs. Thomas, decked out in a stunning classic, black tuxedo, waited for his daughter at the foot of the staircase.

"Francesca, you are going to steal Jack's breath away."

"Daddy, I love you." Frankie pressed a kiss to his clean-shaven face, holding him tightly for a moment.

Someone flashed a camera, but Frankie didn't really pay attention. Frankie and her father exited the front door and walked around the brick path to the side yard. A harpist and violinist began to play the wedding march, and Becca strolled down the pathway scattering white and yellow rose petals before her.

Frankie caught Jack's eye. He was standing in the gazebo with Anthony at his side. Jack had been ready for hours it seemed, pacing the deck of The Rose threatening to wear the finish right off the teak. It just didn't seem that eleven o'clock would ever strike. But it did and here she was walking to him, smiling, carrying his life within her, making him whole again, as his heart squeezed with the joy she gave him just by her presence.

Out of the corner of his eye he caught a glimpse of Mr. Flaherty from Ireland with a cat settled comfortably in his lap. *How the heck*...Jack wondered, and then smiled at the man in the third row as he winked back! In the second row sat Scott and Robin, Roberto and Carlo, and in the front row were his parents, Uncle John and a woman with a colorful bird perched on her lap. Uncle Tony, his aunts, and Retta and Nelson sat next to them with Bruno guarding the end of the row with Little Nick panting by Bruno's side. The feeling was indescribable to see the many friends and family together as one, celebrating their marriage and their love, their moment.

When Francesca reached Jack, her father shook Jack's hand, gave his daughter that precious kiss, and placed her hand in Jack's. It felt wonderful, beyond words, to finally touch her, to protect her small, delicate hand in his larger one again. The pressure to keep them apart, being watched around the clock last night on The Rose, was a serious head game he never wanted to repeat. His father even threatened to take the ship out to sea in order to keep him away from her for the evening and to give everyone a chance to sleep. Jack learned the lesson meant to be learned. Cherish the time you are with her. Cherish her because one day you may not have her, just like last night. Jack watched her glorious smile brighten and her blue eyes watery with tears, threatening to spill. *I love you*, he whispered, and she whispered the same words back.

Father Michael began the wedding by introducing himself as one of Jack's cousins. Francesca met him only briefly last night, but instantly fell in love with him. He was genuine with an unbeatable sense of humor. He mentioned how Jack would pummel him and most of the other cousins' at most major holidays. Jack cringed at this reminiscence, pulling at his collar in an effort to relieve the pressure of guilt, as a concerted laugh rose from family and friends.

"I usually prayed the same prayer again and again." Father Michael looked down and read from the Bible, "*Put on then, as God's chosen ones, holy and beloved, heartfelt compassion, kindness, humility, gentleness and patience, bearing with one another and forgiving one another if one has a grievance against another, as the Lord has forgiven you, so must you also do.* "

Jack looked at Francesca silently drawing from the message that forgiveness is vital to be at peace with everyone.

Father Michael continued. "So we are all gathered here today in this wonderful gazebo, which is a long-standing tradition in the Romano family, on a day that only God could create, to join this woman and this man in the Holy Sacrament of Matrimony, and not a minute too soon." Father Michael glanced down at Francesca's bump causing everyone to giggle again.

The breeze from the river blew the fragrance of roses all about them. Jack stood next to Frankie, his arm brushing against hers, his hand holding her hand while his thumb rubbed a quiet reminder at her wrist that he was here and here to stay. When he slipped the diamond wedding band on her hand, he was so pleased to see that she was wearing her engagement ring again.

"I now pronounce you husband and wife!" Father Michael declared. "You may kiss your bride, cousin."

Jack turned and smiled. He cradled her face, capturing his precious wife gently, lifting her face slightly as he lowered his head. He kissed her sweetly, cherishingly, as she encircled her arms around his waist. He could feel the swell of her abdomen against him and placed one hand there to embrace their unborn child as well. He was complete, and he mentally thanked God, as the photographer captured the moment.

"Come on now. There will be plenty of time for that later," Anthony teased, causing the crowd to cheer which turned into laughter. Each well-wisher came into the gazebo to kiss the bride and groom.

As the crowd made their way to the tents, Jack pulled Francesca's hand to his lips. "You are so beautiful. More beautiful than any other time I can ever remember in my mind. Let's enjoy our wedding day together." The photographer's camera flashed, as Jack's lips kissed his bride's palm.

"Jacqino, you look so handsome today, too. I love you so much." Again a camera flashed as Jack lowered his head to kiss her cheek so softly, tenderly.

The afternoon passed in a flurry of laughter, good food, drink, and photos. Frankie and Jack danced, as friends and family broke in to hug and congratulate the happy couple. Anthony managed to steal Frankie away for a dance.

"He's such a show-off." Becca sipped her iced water, as the wine was starting to make her feel woozy.

"Tell me about it," Jack shot back, flashing Becca an enormous, white smile. "Wait until he falls in love. He's going to make a bigger jackass of himself than I have."

Becca laughed out loud.

"Come on. Let's show them we know how to show off, too!" As Jack twirled Becca around the dance floor, he was continually interrupted by so many of his aunts who insisted on pinching his cheeks much like when he was a little boy. He would bow his head and take it like a man. Some berated him for staying away, but most just shared in the love and tenderness that infused the day.

After the cake was served, Jack leaned over to Frankie taking her small hand in his. "It's time we set sail."

"Okay, I guess we should start saying goodnight to everyone." Frankie felt little butterflies take flight in her stomach. She hadn't been with Jack in months, and the unfamiliarity of the merest contact with him was starting to play tricks on her insides.

More than an hour later, after the goodbyes were delivered to each and every guest, Frankie and Jack started to walk back to the farmhouse.

"No." A large hand came down on Jack's shoulder and when he turned around, it was his father stopping him.

"*Che*?" Jack questioned in Italian.

"You will wait for Francesca on The Rose. She will need a few minutes with her mother."

Jack looked at Frankie with a look that said it all. *I can't wait to be alone with you.* "Alright, *Padre*," Jack acquiesced.

Frankie left in a swirl of white lace with her arm looped through her mother's. Inside Corrine spoke to Francesca softly. "Remember that your father and I have taught you to never hold grudges. People make mistakes, and it is best to forgive and forget. Especially the ones we love most."

"Mom, I wouldn't have married Jack if I didn't love him unconditionally and couldn't look beyond these past months alone. It taught me a great lesson."

"And that is?" Corrine questioned.

"Months, years, it doesn't matter. He is the only man I will ever love. I forgave him long before he came back to me."

Corrine's eyes swam with tears threatening to spill onto her lovely silk dress. That is what she wanted for her daughter, a love so profound and deep—a love that would last and weather any storm. The tears spilled freely from her eyes down her cheeks, as Frankie rushed over with a tissue to dab at her mother's tear-stained face.

"Mama," Francesca softly whispered. She hadn't called her mother that since she was a small child. That term of endearment only made Corrine weep more.

Jack paced the length of the dock while his father and father-in-law stood at the end of the dock closest to the shoreline watching for her.

Nicholas decided that this was the perfect time to go into great detail how one of his cousins changed her mind and decided that she did not want to be married right after the wedding ceremony. As he retold the story, Jack stood gaping in shock at him. When Nicholas shrugged thinking *stranger things have* happened, he swore his son stopped breathing. But when they saw Francesca descending the steps, one arm laced through her mother's and the other through her mother-in-law's, Jack released the over held breath he had been holding during this excruciating wait.

Jack walked to the end of the dock, past his father and father-in-law, taking her hand in his. He bent and kissed his mother-in-law's cheek whispering softly, "I love your daughter and will never hurt her again."

Corrine just nodded. She was finding it very difficult to speak without tears. Jack shook Thomas' hand as Thomas reached over to kiss his daughter sweetly on the forehead.

They walked the few steps to Nicholas and Angelina.

"Have a safe voyage, son." Nicholas grasped his son's strong hand holding it firmly. He was a good son, and now he would be a strong husband and an excellent father. He knew it. He kissed Francesca softly on the cheek whispering softly to her in Italian, "*Angela mi di bellezza.*" Jack and Francesca kissed Angelina, as she dabbed a tiny, white hanky at the corner of her eyes. Angelina quietly whispered something in Jack's ear.

Jack escorted Francesca carefully along the dock up to The Rose. He swept her into his arms and carried her carefully up the steps onto the deck of The Rose. As the ship was untied and slowly shoved off, most of the guests waved *bon voyage* with their white napkins, like birds soaring in flight.

Together they stood at the railing of The Rose and waved back. Jack pulled Francesca close to him. He was never going to let her go again, never. He almost let her slip through his fingers once, but he would never tempt fate again. He was given a second chance and would hold onto that chance for an eternity.

As The Rose glided up the coast, Jack turned Francesca in his arms. "Francesca, let's get out of these things. Then we can sit and talk. I know we need to talk. Then I am going to make love to you." Jack's eyes grew black, as a curl blew onto his forehead. Frankie reached her fingers up to brush the thick strand back. Jack took her hand, turned it over and gently pressed a kiss to the inside of her wrist.

Hand-in-hand, they walked through the boat to the master stateroom. Jack held the door open letting her pass, pulling it softly closed behind him.

Frankie entered into the bedroom area and spoke softly with her back turned to him, unable to look into his dark, passionate eyes, her head lowered. "Jacqino, I feel...shy. I know that sounds so silly when I'm carrying your child, but..." Frankie couldn't find the words.

"Francesca, I am going to fix that." He came up behind her passing his hands lovingly up and down her arms. "It was wrong of me to leave you. That night still haunts me." His hands dropped from her arms as he began to pace, so much like his mother, Frankie noted. "It was disgraceful what I did. I just couldn't seem to process it, digest it, or comprehend it. Victoria didn't have to be a prisoner. I could have paid her father's debts hundreds of times over." Jack stopped abruptly. "I couldn't fix what Victoria and I had because there was nothing there, but this, this I can fix. Do you know why?" Jack asked brushing the back of his hand over her flushed cheek realizing how much he missed the feel of her sweet cheek. "I'm going to answer that—because I love you. I've never loved anyone until you, Francesca."

"Jacqino, I..." Francesca already knew the entire twisted story from Uncle John. She struggled to understand that level of despise and then struggled with the Romano family's ability to forgive. "Why did you come back?" She needed to know.

"I came back because I realized that I almost threw away what people have only dreamed of. Love so right, love so strong, love so real; that it lives forever." Jack held her shoulders in his hands and pulled her close. "Wait, I need to say this. I need to finish." Jack took a deep breath in and out. "You make my heart skip a beat every time I look at you."

Frankie smiled up at him, but he could sense that she had some doubts.

"You do! Here give me your hand." Jack slid her hand in

between the studs of his crisp white tuxedo shirt under his black jacket.

Frankie could feel his curly hair brush against her palm, his warm flesh coupled with the strong beating of his heart. It thudded under her palm quickly.

"You and I, we were meant to be together, together for an eternity. I know this. I know this to be true."

Frankie stepped closer and with her other hand captured his face, cupping it, memorizing it, touching it, while her other hand felt the pounding of his heart increase, as his skin grew hotter.

Jack lowered his head, brushing his lips over hers softly, tasting each corner. My God, how he missed her.

Frankie could feel his heartbeat accelerate. She stood on tiptoes opening her mouth beneath his, as his tongue began to dip, to taste, to savor. She missed this man. She missed being held by him. She missed kissing him, missed his scent, his warmth—in a word **him**.

Frankie tugged the corner of the black necktie until it came undone. Sliding her hands along his shirtfront, she released the studs from their buttonholes, while she felt his hand reach into her tresses, tugging on the hairpins as tiny tea roses fell; dropping to the carpet silently. Slowly her golden hair began to slip from the twists that had been so carefully arranged, spilling onto her shoulders.

Jack studied her tresses and the effect made her appear as though she were glowing.

Frankie pushed his jacket from his shoulders, then his shirt. Bare from the waist up, she pressed her lips over his heart. She heard Jack moan as he pulled her into his strong embrace. She felt his fingers on the back of her gown. Her head felt light and drifted back as he pressed soft kisses on her throat and across her collarbone to her bare shoulder.

Jack started to unbutton the gown. He painstakingly, carefully, unbuttoned the first few then passion overcame his patience, causing Francesca to panic as she heard the lace tear.

"Jacqino, Aunt Cecilia made me promise."

"Promise?" Jack asked still kissing her throat, drinking in the rose scent that he missed so dearly.

"Yes, promise that you wouldn't tear the dress. The lace is very intricate..." But before Frankie could finish, Jack's head flew up and a devilish smile danced across his face. In one pull the dress was in ribbons at her feet.

"Jacqino!" Frankie shouted.

"Let Aunt Cecilia talk about that until the next wedding," Jack pointed to the heap of lace piled all around Frankie's feet. She started to giggle which caused him to laugh, as he lifted her right out of her shoes spinning her around. He stopped just as abruptly. "The baby?" he whispered.

"Fine, we're fine." Frankie confirmed as she rested a hand on the swell over her lace slip.

Holding her, Jack lowered her softly to the bed. Her hair falling over the sage comforter created an image of spun gold. He toed off his shoes and rested next to her holding her face remembering the words his father had spoken to him while he waited for her on The Rose. "Be gentle. You must be very gentle when your wife is with child."

Carefully, he pulled the slip gently off, rising up on his knees so that he did all the work. Tossing it aside, he studied her. She wore a white lace, strapless bra and panties. Her breasts were full and rose and fell with each breath she took. The swell of her belly rose up and down as well—his life safe within her. She was still incredibly thin, and her long, tapered legs were clad in thigh-high lace stockings. "You're beautiful. I might just sit right here and stare at you all night." He smiled then admitted quietly. "I'm afraid I'll hurt you...the baby."

"You won't. Please don't stop." Frankie sat up as she looked deeply into his dark eyes. "Don't ever stop touching me. It's been so long. Please love me."

Jack groaned softly as he rested her back down onto the comforter. Lying beside her, he began to kiss her mouth, softly. Then using his tongue he began to flick his tongue against her lips arousing them open. Her tongue greeted his urgently. He skimmed his hand over her skin and the parts covered in lace. The lace tickled his palm tempting him to remove it. As his hand cruised over the swell he could feel the baby move, and his lips parted in a smile on top of hers.

Sliding his hand up he reached for the snap between her breasts and released the lace that held her fast. With the back of his hand he brushed the white lace away, revealing the perfect, creamy breasts before him. He lowered his head kissing her breasts, then the sides. He heard her moan and sway urging him to take her breast. He did so, but so softly and gently, licking and sucking in soft tugs. His reward was her whispering his name over and over.

Francesca was lost. Her head felt light. The things Jack was doing to her were making her fall into an abyss of passion, love, and tenderness. She reached up running her fingers through his hair. He came back up pressing gentle kisses along the column of her throat, rubbing his open palm over her breast in gentle, circular movements.

"Francesca, open your eyes," Jack whispered watching her lids flutter open. "You're so beautiful. Watch me touch you. Watch me love you."

She kissed his jaw, and then pressed kisses along the side of his throat, gently nipping him down to his shoulder. She helped him off with the rest of his clothes touching wherever she could reach as more and more of his skin was exposed. She lied back down as she felt his hands caress her. As he slid his hand over the swell of the baby he whispered, "Thank you for this gift," and kissed his unborn child.

"Jacqino," Francesca breathed.

Again his hand moved and slid over the lace panties and along the top of the hose. Frankie had to fight to keep her eyes open. For Jack, he was so undone by her reaction to his touch he wondered how long he could hold off, if at all. He tugged her panties down slowly and guided his hand to her center, brushing the back of his hand over the soft, light-colored triangle. Slowly, not taking his eyes from her, he traced his finger along each curve and fold, but not penetrating. He lowered his head to kiss her softly on her lips. "Stay with me," he encouraged. Her eyes had already grown darker, but he knew there would be a deeper passionate level, and he wanted it for her and with her.

Francesca began to writhe. Her hand was over his, pressing and arching her hips up to let him slide into her deep mysteries.

Jack fingers found her wet and wonderfully warm. Her breathing came in short puffs of air against his face. "I love you," he whispered as he studied her eyes. "My whole being is in love with you."

"Jacqino, I've loved you my whole life. My whole life..." She was finding it hard to breathe as the intensity of his touch increased. "I wanted to tell you. I wanted to tell you that I had dreams, so many dreams of you." She cupped his face trying to read his expression.

"Did you dream of this?" He removed his hand positioning himself over her. Opening her legs wider, kneeling down before her, he gently pressed his stiffness slowly into her, as he watched her eyes grow yet darker, deeper blue. Clasping her lacey-clad legs, he guided them up and around his hips. Neither could speak. The process of speech at that precise moment was impossible.

Frankie watched in wonder. Here he was loving her, holding her, and entering her with such tenderness; it was stealing her breath away. She watched as he fought to keep his eyes on her, witnessing his attempt to hold his own need at bay.

Together they moved, but the swell of her belly made him turn them over so that she rose up over him. His hands were free to explore, to glide, and touch. She moved slowly at first, as he held her thighs encouraging the slower pace. Each one whispered the other's name. Sweet endearments tumbled out from one to the other, while the room grew dark, holding two lovers center stage.

As each reached the peak of release, Francesca fell forward resting her lips against his throat where she could feel his pulse throb rapidly. Its rhythm wild, his skin felt hot to the touch. She could feel his powerful hands skim up and down her sides, over the sides of her breasts.

As he rolled her to her side, her head resting on his shoulder with his hand caressing her back, the other hand brushing soft sweeps over the swell from the baby, The Rose gently swayed, inducing peace.

"I'm so in love you, Francesca," Jack whispered before placing a quiet kiss to her forehead.

"I love you, too."

"I'll never leave you again. I'll never hurt you like that again."

"I know."

"Sleep my love." Jack whispered.

"I don't think I can sleep," Frankie confessed. "I want to talk, to tell you everything so that nothing will ever separate us again."

Jack was tentative at first, then nodded. "Tell me," Jack whispered, lying back, continuing his caresses.

Timidly at first, Francesca started to replay when she first started to remember her dreams and about when they started to come true. How alone and afraid she felt until she shared her dreams with Rebecca. Once she revealed her secret to her best friend, she explained, it became easier. She told Jack that Rebecca helped her to deal with the dreams when they came true. "Although Becca knew about most of the dreams I remembered, I never told her of my dreams about you."

"Why?" Jack asked quickly.

"I'm not sure." She studied his features, still missing him somehow, running her fingertip along his jaw. "And I never told my parents about any of it."

"Really," Jack sounded surprised.

"I didn't want them upset, thinking their daughter was a freak."

"You're not a freak." Jack calmed, as he ran his hand along her smooth cheek. "Uncle John said you could predict things. Is that true?"

Francesca shrugged. "Your brother told me that Uncle John asked me for lottery numbers and that whenever I gave him a set of numbers, they always won. I had no idea I could do that. But apparently I underestimated my curse."

"Gift," Jack corrected. "It only makes sense that someone as pure as you would be rewarded with such a special gift because you would never abuse it."

"Well…that's not exactly accurate. After I found out about the lottery numbers…" Francesca trailed off and bowed her head, as her face blushed to the perfect shade of pink.

"What? Uh oh, what have you done?"

"Well, you remember Mrs. Mastellon, Maggie? You met her at the wedding."

Jack nodded remembering how his uncle never left the woman's side.

Well, both Robin and Maggie are working at the animal hospital, and they needed a place to live. So I played some numbers, nothing too big, and gave them the money to help them with, let's call it…relocation costs!"

Jack just rolled his eyes and shook his head.

"And I couldn't possibly leave out Roberto, because he really needed a four wheel-drive vehicle if he was going to watch over me and the baby at the farm.

Jack laughed. "You don't have to worry about money, ever. We have so much money it will make your head spin, and the fact that we never signed a pre-nuptial made the corporate attorneys' heads spin. In fact, with the shares we own in Romano Enterprises, you never have to work another day in your life, even if you divorced me tomorrow. You would be a very wealthy woman. Correction…you are a very wealthy woman."

"I want to work. I love what I do and besides that, Robin is finishing up her schooling, so soon I will have a partner. "

"Alright," Jack understood.

"And, I'm not going to divorce you, because I have a secret weapon, just in case." Frankie looked up at her husband.

"Secret weapon," Jack questioned.

"Your mother," Frankie just nodded, and Jack laughed.

"Do you know what my mother said to me just before we boarded The Rose?"

"No."

"She said that when I get back from our honeymoon, she is going to slap me, but that she didn't want to do it now, because it might ruin the wedding pictures."

Frankie was giggled, "I love my mother-in-law."

There was a moment of quiet, when each touched the other reverently, just staring into the other's eyes. "I'm sorry I didn't tell you about my dreams. That was a mistake. I was afraid that you would be petrified of me. And I certainly couldn't tell my parents I didn't want to date, because I was waiting for a dream. They would have had my head examined." Frankie stopped to take a breath, touching his face warmly. "It seemed in some of the dreams, you were so real, that I could feel you and others not. I just wasn't sure. You're so beautiful and handsome. I use to say to myself he can't be real, 'only in my dreams'." Frankie touched the black, glossy hair close to his temple.

Jack lifted his hand to cup her cheek. "I'm real and I'm here." Grazing his thumb softly over it, he smiled down at her. "You are a dream…so lovely, all golden and warm. You're like holding springtime in my hands." He lowered his head kissing her deeply. Pulling her as close to his chest as he could, he whispered, "I will make all your dreams come true."

Epilogue
A little more than a year later…

Frankie and Jack watched their one-year old daughter, Antoinette Rebecca Romano, grab at a clump of fur at Bruno's neck. They had just returned from their trip to Jack's castle in Ireland, where Francesca stood in wide-eyed astonishment before the stained glass mural. An exact miniature of that same stained glass was brought by Anthony when the farm was first being renovated, and was just installed in the wall over their headboard in the master bedroom at the farm.

Now as she stood on the front porch holding her husband tightly, she watched as her daughter used Bruno for support as she tottered unsteadily on chubby legs toward her parents. Saliva dribbled down her chin as she grinned, a huge, happy gaping hole of a smile up toward her Mama and Papa.

Frankie and Jack laughed as they held each other close.

"Who would have thought that a one-year old would be the one to tame that beast?" Jack teased as he held his wife close in his arms, watching his beautiful daughter, his eyes filled with love and pride.

"I think she could pull out his entire coat and still he would stay right by her side," Frankie defended her once-crazed boxer. He had calmed down dramatically since the birth of their daughter. The dog constantly followed Toni wherever she went. "Do you think she will be as tall as you?" Frankie asked her husband.

Jack turned his face to look into his wife's ever-changing blue eyes. *His wife*, he thought silently. *How wonderful that still sounds!* Jack silently gave thanks. *Thank you for my golden wife. Thank you for my beautiful daughter, her jet-black hair, her dancing diamond, blue eyes, and her drumstick-sized wobbly legs.* Jack smiled before he spoke to his wife's upturned questioning face. "You never complained about my height before?"

"It's just that if she is as tall as you…I mean who will want to marry a giant of a woman?"

"We will send her godfather around the world until he finds a seven-foot tall husband for her. He can find anything anyone asks. But, we will have to have her godmother analyze him first."

Frankie looked up at her husband and let out a small laugh.

Honor and cherish. Honor and cherish. It is as simple as breathing when you are completely in love.

The End

Here Is A

Sneak Peak At

The Next Romance

Novel by

Debra A. Daly

"The Marriage Proposal"

"You can ask me anything." Anthony took her lovely hand in his to reassure her. "We are family now."

Rebecca took a deep breath just before she popped the question. "Will you marry me?"

Anthony shook his head knowing for certain that he must have misunderstood her. "I'm sorry?" Anthony leaned in closer in the hopes that she would repeat her last question.

"It will only be temporarily," Rebecca assured him.

"Temporarily, married?!" Anthony reiterated.

"Yes," Rebecca nodded her head to affirm.

"Temporarily," Anthony asked again, not quite believing.

"Yes." Rebecca nodded again to verify.

"Is this some kind of a joke?" Anthony instantly dropped her hand.

"No. No joke. I'm serious."

Anthony nodded while looking around wondering who was behind this prank. She couldn't be serious? "Why do you want to 'temporarily' marry me?"

"Because I want to adopt a child," Rebecca looked away quickly, because her eyes started to well up. Anytime she spoke about Trevor, a large lump formed in her throat and tears stung the back of her eyes making it impossible for her to speak and see clearly.

It was obviously heart wrenching, and Anthony could see the anguish on her face just before she turned away. "Come here." Anthony pulled her close and held her while she cried softly. "There, there." He circled his arm around her lovely shoulders and walked her over to a bench so that he could understand exactly what she needed from him. "Here take this and dry your eyes, darling." Anthony handed her a clean, white handkerchief.

"Thank you." Rebecca said as she sniffed and dabbed at each eye. "My face must be a mess."

"No." Anthony thought she was stunning. With mahogany eyes that appeared golden in the bright light of day. Her complexion was flawless and reminded him of fine porcelain. Her hair was swept up with tendrils of deep, shiny chestnut-colored curls gracing her face and neck causing her to appear dreamy. *No darling,* Anthony thought silently, *your face takes my breath away.*

"The Marriage Proposal"
Is the next Romance Novel by
Debra A. Daly.
Visit our Website at
www.dalyromance.com
for the Release Date